Blood of the Wolf

by

Steven A. McKay

Also by Steven A. McKay:

THE FOREST LORD SERIES

Wolf's Head

The Wolf and the Raven

Rise of the Wolf

Knight of the Cross

Friar Tuck and the Christmas Devil

For my Grandma, who always wanted to see a book of mine in the library.

I hope I made you proud.

Acknowledgements

First and foremost I'd like to thank all my readers. Your incredible support has been the greatest encouragement any writer could ask for.

Thanks must go, as usual, to all my beta readers, particularly Robin Carter who actually sowed the seed that grew into the plot of this book, and Nicky Galliers who helped me hone the early drafts with her fantastic knowledge. Similar thanks go to Bernadette McDade, Blair Hodgkinson and William Moore for flagging up early errors and great moral support. My editor Richenda deserves huge praise for helping me take my books to a higher level.

My son inspired me every day with his wonderful, wild nature, and my daughter is always a big help, even taking some great PR photos of me in my study. Not bad for an eight year-old!

Since this is the final book in this series I'll also thank my cover designers More Visual, for creating such great art and helping me find a wider audience than I could have imagined, and Nick Ellsworth for bringing the audio versions of my books to life so entertainingly.

I've been blessed to have you all around. Thank you.

CHAPTER ONE

Dewsbury, England.

1326AD, Summer

Little John didn't expect the attack on his leader. It came as a shock and, cursing inwardly, he knew he should have learned by now not to judge someone on how they looked.

Still, the little landlord's punch was weak and, although it hit Robert Hood – commonly known as Robin – flush on the side of the face, the lawman barely seemed to register the blow. He instinctively lashed out, ramming the flat of his palm into the landlord's cheek, sending him flying sideways into a table, drinks flying and patrons roaring in anger at their spilled ale.

"Watch what you're doing there man, for fuck sake!" one shouted, but closed his mouth and looked the other way when he noticed Little John's glare fixing on him.

"Up, you."

Robin leaned down and hauled the landlord to his feet effortlessly, the muscles in his huge archer's arms bulging. "Since you won't discuss this reasonably we'll have to go somewhere more private." He practically lifted the man off the floor and headed towards the room behind the bar, John following at the back. The half dozen men drinking in the Boar's Head grumbled to one another, watching the lawmen with distaste.

"Fucking arseholes. Weren't so happy to treat us like this when they were outlaws themsel –"

"What's that?" Little John spun, leaning down to meet the seated drinker's eyes. "Did I hear you saying

1

something?"

The man who'd spoken shook his head nervously and John nodded in satisfaction just before a stool shattered into his back. He dropped to the ground as splinters flew all about him and the sodden rushes he landed on.

"Get the bastards!"

The landlord grinned when he saw the altercation but his enjoyment didn't last for very long, as Robin punched him right on the bridge of the nose, hurling him into the wall. He slid down, legs gone, and sat on the floor holding his face.

Little John had three men on top of him, all raining punches down on his head and body, while another three tried to aim kicks between their comrades, thankfully without much success. The fallen giant struggled to throw the attackers off, shaking the rafters with his frustrated roar.

The villagers' senses were dulled by alcohol so their blows were mostly ineffectual but John knew the ale, and force of numbers, would also make the men more likely to try and use deadly force. He strained his great body, teeth gritted, face scarlet as he attempted to stand up, but a foot caught him in the ear and he collapsed with a cry, trying to raise his arms over his head.

Abruptly, one man's weight disappeared, then another, and the giant bellowed like an enraged bull, throwing the final assailant off as he shoved his way back to his feet and looked about the room, ready to destroy the next person that came near him.

Robin stood, panting, watching the villagers who could still move stumble out the front door. He held a cudgel in his hand and two of John's attackers lay on the vomit-encrusted alehouse floor. One groaned, rubbing the back of his head, while the other was unconscious.

The three who had been standing aiming kicks at John backed away, palms held out in apology as the huge man threw his shoulders back, his head almost touching the ceiling. He stared balefully at them.

The landlord tried to follow as they turned and sprinted for the open door, jostling one another in their haste, but Robin was too fast and grabbed the man by the collar, dragging him back and throwing him onto the ground where he lay, panting and wide-eyed.

"You're a damn crook, Hood," he gasped. "You're supposed to be one of us."

Robin shook his head and spat. "You haven't paid your rent, Martin. I'm just doing my job. Now – pay up or I'll throw you out on the street and find a new landlord."

"You can't do that," the man shrieked. "What about my family? This is our home!"

"Pay your rent then," Robin said. "Like everyone else in the town. I've already given you extra time but you're messing me about and it ends here."

The landlord looked across at John pleadingly. "How can you just stand there and let him do this?"

"Your mates just about broke my back there," the huge bear of a man replied, although he looked at his leader uncomfortably. He hadn't expected to be collecting money from poor folk when Robin accepted the position as Sheriff Henry de Faucumberg's enforcer and then asked John to be his second-in-command. "We all have to pay our rent," he finished lamely.

For a few moments the landlord just lay there propped up on his arms, glaring, as though he would murder them with his eyes.

"Come on," John said, not unkindly, as he reached down and grasped the man under the armpit, raising him to his feet just as Robin had done a short time ago. "If you don't have it all just pay whatever you can. That's all right, eh?" He looked at Robin who shook his head.

"He's had enough time to gather the money, John." He looked back to the landlord. "Do you have it or not?"

"No." The reply was barely a whisper.

Robin strode forward and dragged Martin away from Little John who watched in bemusement while his friend opened the inn door and shoved the landlord out into the street.

"I'm evicting you then. I'll place your belongings in the barn, there, at the side of the building. Think yourself lucky I'm not arresting you."

He slammed the door in the shocked man's face and turned back to John.

"Come on, we have to gather his stuff and secure the place before it's too dark to travel. I want to get home to Matilda and Arthur!" He grinned at the thought of his family waiting on him back home in Wakefield.

Little John eyed Robin as he strode past towards the stairs to the upper level with a determined look on his handsome face. Didn't he care about the fact he'd just made another family homeless for the sake of a few coins?

He knew the bailiff was simply doing his job and they were following the letter of the law but…

In the name of Christ, it didn't seem right somehow.

When they'd been pardoned by Sir Henry de Faucumberg three years ago, Robin was given command of a few of the sheriff's soldiers but guard duty didn't suit the former outlaw at all. So, after a few months of that he'd been made captain of de Faucumberg's guard but, again, there was too much standing around Nottingham castle – away from his family – for Robin's liking. After that he was made temporary bailiff of one of the towns near Wakefield, which was fine, but then the regular officer returned from illness. For the past year Robin, with John who'd been at his side for all those years, was employed as a sort of roving bailiff. He retained the title, and salary, but instead of being tied to one place he went all around Nottingham and Yorkshire, collecting unpaid rents and fines and generally bringing low-level law to the people.

"Hurry up!"

Robin's shout broke his lieutenant's reverie and, with a heavy sigh, John climbed the stairs to help shift all the evicted landlord's possessions outside.

Thankfully, there wasn't much to collect. The landlord was married but there were no children – thank God, John thought – so it didn't take very long to gather the few items of clothing, bedding, a tired-looking old sword hidden under the sleeping pallet, and various other small items.

"Good work," Robin nodded, tossing an armful of his own into the blanket before John pulled the corners together and hefted the lot over a shoulder. "Let's go."

They clumped down the stairs and the young bailiff glanced back over his shoulder as they neared the bottom. "I'll give the man a coin so he can find somewhere for him and his wife to stay for a night or two. They won't be out on the streets."

John raised an eyebrow but only grunted in reply. It was better than nothing, he supposed, but the whole thing still seemed wrong. The fact he himself was the one carrying all the landlord's belongings outside meant he couldn't really upbraid Robin; he was just as much at fault as his friend. And they *were* merely doing their job.

If they didn't do it, someone else would, he knew, and they'd probably be even bigger bastards than he or Hood.

"Here's your stuff," the massive lawman rumbled as they made their way outside to face the sullen evictee. "Check it's all there if you like." He looked away uncomfortably, just glad the man's wife wasn't around. This was bad enough without another furious woman screaming at him in the street. "Nice sword," he added, somehow hoping the compliment would make up for what was happening to the man, but the words were hollow. It was a shit sword and they both knew it.

"Sorry, Martin," Robin said, standing and looking down

directly into the landlord's eyes. "I'll need the keys from you too." The bailiff appeared quite at ease with the situation and John wished he had the same composure and sense of self-belief as the younger man. Robin always seemed to believe what he was doing was right and did it with total conviction.

The inn-keeper put hand inside his tunic and drew out a small bunch of keys which he tossed to Robin with bad grace.

"Here," Hood said, catching the keys in one hand and offering some coins to Martin with his other. "Take this and find a room and a meal for you and your woman." He pressed the money into Martin's hand and then spread his arms wide. "If you can find the rent money within the next couple of days and get it to Earl Warenne's steward, he might let you move back in."

"Doubt it," the evicted landlord spat. "He's probably got a new tenant already lined up."

"Don't mention it," Robin retorted sarcastically and John wondered if his friend really expected the man to thank him for the small monetary gift when he'd just been made homeless.

Maybe he did – the bailiff had changed quite a bit in the past three years.

"Right. I'm away home," Robin said, walking across to the stable at the side of the inn and climbing into his horse's saddle. "You coming with me? I'm sure Arthur and Matilda would be glad to see you."

John shook his head. "Tell them I said 'hello', but I want to see my own wife and son so I'm off to Holderness. I'll meet you in Wakefield in a couple of days and we'll see what Sir Henry has lined up for us next, eh?"

"All right. Take care on the road!"

They waved to one another and rode off eagerly towards their homes.

Martin stood forlornly outside his old inn, wondering

how he'd explain this to his wife and wishing he had the balls to burn the damn place to the ground.

CHAPTER TWO

As promised, John rode into Wakefield two days later, the summer sun shining high overhead as he reached Robin's house.

The bailiff was in the garden with his infant son, Arthur. They didn't seem to be playing any structured game as such, just running around on the well-tended grass whooping and shouting but the little boy was loving every second of it. The huge grin on Robin's face suggested he was having fun too.

John watched somewhat wistfully. His own son, also named John, was thirteen now and almost a man. The big lawman missed the days when he could play such innocent, nonsensical games with his own boy. Still, his visit to Holderness had been enjoyable. His wife, Amber, was always glad to welcome him home with a fine meal before they went out to the alehouse together and danced to the music played regularly by a couple of farmers who fancied themselves as minstrels.

Amber was the perfect companion, John thought. She rarely complained about anything and, after John's long years living in the greenwood as a wolf's head, she'd been overjoyed to finally have him back living in their home when the sheriff granted Robin's men pardons.

"Uncle John!"

Arthur spotted the bearded figure on horseback watching their game and sprinted for the gate, his little arms and legs working furiously as his father watched with a fond smile.

The massive lawman slid somewhat clumsily from his horse and grabbed the boy under the arms, tossing him high into the air. Arthur squealed in delight and terror, laughing as John caught him and hugged him close.

"Hello, you little rascal!"

Matilda appeared at the door to the house and waved.

"I'll pour you some ale," she said, and disappeared back inside as John came through the open gate, placed the excited child back onto the grass and grasped forearms with his captain.

"Well met," Robin smiled. "Come on inside and have a drink. I haven't heard from the sheriff about our next job so we've got some time to relax and do nothing."

The interior of the Hoods' house was cool after the blazing sun that had been John's companion on the road that morning and the ale that Matilda poured for them was most refreshing.

Robin's wife joined them at the table as they chatted idly and drank and ate gooseberries which Matilda grew in the garden, knowing her husband liked their sweet sourness.

"Come on outside, John," Robin finally said with an appreciative nod to his wife for their repast, pushing his stool back from the table. "I better check on Arthur – he's gone quiet and that's often a sign he's up to mischief."

The two men went outside, squinting in the sunlight and Robin was happy to see Arthur sitting quite innocently on the grass watching a line of ants hard at work.

Just then the sound of thundering hooves came to them and the lawmen instinctively grasped their sword hilts, eyes searching along the road in the direction of the noise.

The rider soon came in sight – a man in the familiar blue livery of the sheriff's guards.

"Well met, Thomas," John boomed, as the rider reached them and brought his mount to a noisy halt.

"God give you good day, big man." The soldier grinned in return before turning his attention to Robin. "Sir Henry requests your presence, bailiff."

"What, now? I was just telling John that we'd earned a few days rest."

"Now I'm afraid, aye," Thomas confirmed. "Well, I say

now, but I'm sure I have time for a drink or two, and my horse to have a rest before we set off."

Matilda peered out at them, shaking her head.

"What is this? Am I to feed all of Barnsdale today? Those gooseberry bushes only yield a small harvest you know." She smiled at Thomas and beckoned the men inside again. "Come on, I'll see what's left. You can tie your horse to the fence there. Arthur!"

The little boy glanced across, covering his eyes with a small hand to try and stop the sun getting in his eyes. "What?"

"Come and get some oats. You can feed Thomas's horse."

When they were seated and the messenger had slaked his thirst with a long drink of ale he leaned back on the stool and looked at Robin and John seriously. "There's trouble in Holmfirth and de Faucumberg wants the pair of you to deal with it."

"What sort of trouble?" Robin wondered, lifting another plump fruit from the trencher in front of them.

"Whole place has been bewitched!" Thomas replied, eyes wide. He made the sign of the cross and nodded emphatically. "It's true. Satan himself's taken control of the village."

Robin turned to meet John's gaze but his friend simply frowned in puzzlement. Stranger things had happened; demons and devils were real weren't they? There was no reason to doubt the story although the idea of facing a village full of evil spirits sent a shiver down the bailiff's back and he felt for the reassuring hilt of his sword.

At least it would be a change from evicting poor people...

"All right then," Robin said decisively. "Your horse looks rested enough to me Thomas – my boy's fed him most of our oats from the looks of it. Come on, John – mount up."

"Hang on a minute," the giant replied, shaking his head fearfully as his captain walked back out into the sunshine. "Are you sure about this? We're lawmen, not priests."

"That's exactly why we'll head for the church first," Robin nodded grimly. "Come on."

"The church? Hold on –" Thomas shouted, trailing in the bailiff's wake as they left the house and Robin went to fetch his mount from the small stable that abutted his dwelling.

"If Holmfirth has been taken over by the Devil we're going to need someone qualified to fight him off, aren't we? That means we go to St Mary's before making our way down to Nottingham for Sir Henry's orders. Don't worry, I'm sure you'll get another ale or two when we're there."

"But why the church?" Thomas asked as he hopped nimbly back onto his horse. "Who's going to help us there?"

Robin kicked his own mount into a walk and rode past the sheriff's messenger with a grin, Little John following at his back.

"Who do you think? Friar Tuck of course!"

When Robin had first been pardoned three years ago he found it hard to adjust to life as a normal man on the right side of the law again. He and his friends had spent so long as outlaws that he'd begun to wonder if he'd ever be free, so, when the sheriff granted him a pardon it was like a gift from God.

It was true, a huge number of people in England were declared outlaws at one time or another in their lives, only to be allowed back into society later, and some of those were criminals of the very worst kind. And yet men like Will Scaflock and John Little had been wolf's heads for years without any sign of redemption and, although Robin was gifted with a great sense of self-belief, it had, at times, seemed as though he was doomed to live in the greenwood until some forester or bounty hunter finally put an end to him.

The sheriff's pardon gave him a new life though, and he knew he should show his gratitude for such good fortune in some tangible way.

He was a wealthy man, having stolen huge sums of money from many noblemen during his time as a wolf's head, and the old parish church of St Mary's in Wakefield had seen better days. It was an easy decision for Robin to pay for, and oversee, the renovation of the place, while also extending it with a section dedicated to that other redeemed sinner, his patron, Mary Magdalene.

Not only had Robin worked with a mason from Nottingham – an acquaintance of the clerk, Piers, one of the later recruits to his gang – to come up with the simple design of that new section, but he'd helped the labourers and stonemasons in any way he could to rebuild the modest, yet attractive, place of worship for his fellow villagers.

Built close to the waters of Ings Beck, which had always seemed a friend to Robin, the renovated church looked much the same as Father Myrc's original church, with its long, low section and a tower at the western end. The new extension made it all a little bigger though, and the fresh new stone transported from the quarry at Sheffield for that part looked wonderful; clean and unspoiled, perfectly symbolising Robin's new start in life.

It brought the former wolf's head a deep satisfaction when the building was completed and Father Myrc said his first ever mass there on Christmas Day two winters ago.

Robin was sure the new church would be a wonderful place for the people of Wakefield to celebrate their weddings, baptisms and the passing of loved ones. And, when Tuck needed a home, Father Myrc had gladly agreed to take the jovial friar in.

St Mary's was where Robin, John and Thomas found their old friend now and recruited him into their band of exorcists bound for Holmfirth on the sheriff's errand. It didn't take much to persuade the portly friar, who – although he enjoyed living in Wakefield, assisting Father Myrc and ministering to the villagers – rather missed the excitement of his time in Hood's notorious outlaw band.

"I've heard of this happening before," the tonsured clergyman mused after he'd ushered them into the manse and, to Thomas's delight, produced ale and bread. "Bad business for everyone – the folk that are possessed can't be reasoned with, while those who manage to avoid Satan's black touch find they're outcast in their own insane village."

The burly friar set his mug down and wiped his mouth with a grey sleeve. "We should do something about this as soon as possible, Robin."

The bailiff met Tuck's eyes and nodded agreement. "We're leaving right now, my friend. You'll come then?"

"Of course! Unless you plan on taking your blade to everyone in Holmfirth – and I know you better than that – you're going to need God's help. I'll ask Father Myrc to accompany us as well. There's bound to be a ringleader. Hopefully we can bring him – or her – to their senses and everyone else will fall into line." He shrugged, having no prior, personal, experience of exorcising an entire village. "Who knows? I'd suggest we carry quarterstaffs with us just in case the villagers *can't* be reasoned with."

Little John grunted and patted his own massive staff which lay propped against the table they were sitting at. "Any of those demon-spawn come near me and they'll be getting this in the damn teeth."

Thomas laughed and Robin shook his head with a weary smile, but Friar Tuck glared at the giant lawman.

"Defend yourselves, of course. But remember, these people are bewitched – they're not in their right mind.

They need help, not violence."

John's head bowed and he hid behind his mug which he emptied slowly, mollified by the friar's scolding. He always felt like a naughty boy when Tuck gave him that look.

Thomas leaned back in his chair and made to spit a glob of phlegm onto the floor before he remembered where he was and swallowed it again with a grimace.

"Do you think you'll be able to cast out the devil or...whatever it is that's taken over the place?" He jerked a thumb over his shoulder. "Back in Nottingham I remember dealing with a man that'd been possessed by some demon. The priests couldn't do anything – in fact, he killed one of them and tore another's face open with his bare teeth. We had to kill him in the end – it was the only way to stop him." He sipped his ale thoughtfully. "I don't fancy dealing with a whole village as mad as that."

The four men sat in silence, nursing their drinks and imagining how things might go when they reached Holmfirth.

Hopefully the tales of the villagers' possession had been greatly exaggerated and all would be well...but Robin fingered his sword-hilt, knowing a quarterstaff might not be enough to deal with whatever they came up against.

"All right, lads, we better get on the road. We have to go south to Nottingham first for the sheriff's orders and, I assume, collect some of his men to back us up. Let's move!"

* * *

"In the name of the Holy Spirit, I command thee –"

"For fuck sake, Tuck, move!"

Little John's staff snaked out and the butt caught the man on the side of the head, toppling him to the ground in a daze before his grasping, dirt-encrusted hands could reach the friar's throat.

"I don't think there was any need for that," Tuck muttered, dismounting and kneeling to place his bible onto the fallen villager's chest, glaring balefully up at his huge saviour.

"You're welcome." John grinned in reply, kicking his horse into a walk beside Robin and Thomas, the rest of the sheriff's soldiers following at their backs nervously while Tuck and Father Myrc attempted to exorcise the would-be attacker.

The five travellers had made their way south from Wakefield and met with the sheriff in Nottingham where he'd given Robin his orders over a fine meal and tried to explain the situation in Holmfirth a little. After a night's sleep Sir Henry sent twenty of his guards off with them before dawn broke and promised to pray for the success of their mission.

"Try not to break too many heads," he shouted to John with a raised eyebrow as the horses clattered from the castle courtyard. "Those villagers are all taxpayers and the king needs every penny he can get right now, what with Queen Isabella and her troublemakers."

They had reached Holmfirth the next morning. It was, to Robin's eye, an inhospitable place with its rolling hills and steep roads. A heavy mist collected in the lower parts of land and, as they approached the place each one of them grasped their staffs – or their bible in Father Myrc's case – nervously.

A village in the middle of the week – even before the sun climbed above the horizon – should greet travellers with certain sounds and smells: a blacksmith's hammer striking the anvil, children's playful shouts, dogs barking, or the welcoming scent of a baker's fresh loaves rising in his oven. But there was none of that.

The only sounds they heard as they neared Holmfirth was the cawing of crows and the occasional scream or laugh, totally incongruous and infinitely sinister in the heavy, oppressive fog.

There were no smells of cooking; even the stink of piss was mostly absent as they passed the tanner's on the outskirts of the place which lay silent and seemingly unoccupied.

Father Myrc started to pray loudly but his voice only seemed to make things even more otherworldly, swallowed in the mist as it was, and Robin was glad to finally ride into the village which was surrounded by hills.

His relief faded when half-a-dozen men and women streamed out of the first two houses flanking the dirt road that ran the full length of the place.

Robin had never seen anyone behaving like those people. Each of them wore a crazed look – wide-eyed and wild-haired, their mouths ringed red with sores, apparently from licking their lips repeatedly which they did as they capered out into the street to greet the five riders and the accompanying soldiers.

"In the name of the Holy Spirit –" Tuck began again, but one of the older village women turned her back, lifted her skirts and showed her bare backside to him.

"Fuck off!" she cackled, gleefully.

The riders winced at the unpleasant sight, although Little John gave a snigger and Tuck glared at him reproachfully.

"In the name of the Holy Spirit, I command thee to leave these people and return whence thou came!"

Father Myrc's strong voice was swallowed by the fog as he pointed a large crucifix at the dancing lunatics who shrank back, apparently in fear at the sight of the cross, and ran off into the village, screaming and crying like scolded toddlers.

"In the name of God," Robin breathed, eyes scanning every section of the street, "these people truly are possessed by demons. I'd thought it would all turn out to be a storm in an ale mug; didn't expect to see – or hear –

that."

"What are we going to do about it?" John muttered, hefting his staff. "We can't just go through the place cracking heads, can we?"

His leader shrugged and spurred his mount forward, guiding it towards the centre of the village. "If that's what it comes to," he said. "Come on, let's try and find the headman, or whoever's in charge around here. They may have lost their sanity, but even madmen follow some of the rules of society – there's bound to be a leader who can help us put a stop to this insanity."

As they trotted along the main street faces appeared in doorways and from behind shuttered windows. There were more strange noises – screams and laughter and shouted, blasphemous profanities accompanied by thuds and thumps as of axes chopping into wood.

No-one else came out to challenge them, though. Not until they reached the village green.

"Looks like we've found our leader," Little John said, gazing through the fog at the shocking scene before them, while the two clergymen came up behind and gasped in horror.

The grass in front of them – site of so many Mayday, midsummer and St Crispin's Day celebrations over the years – now played host to a gallows. It was a crude structure but that, and the blanket of chill mist, only added to its loathsomeness. The corpse hanging by the neck from it didn't help either. Not just any man, this was a clergyman; the local parish priest no doubt.

Father Myrc crossed himself and visibly shrank back in his saddle while Tuck muttered an un-Christian oath. Before Robin could tell him to wait, he'd dismounted and was walking towards the grim construction and the people that occupied the platform.

"Let's move." Robin climbed down from his own palfrey and John followed although he grumbled as he did so, not being quite as lithe as his friend. "You men," he waved an arm at the blue-liveried soldiers. "Fan out behind us. Be prepared for attacks from any side but use your staffs unless it's absolutely necessary to kill."

As he hurried to catch up with the irate friar, Robin took in the strange sight before them.

Standing on the filthy boards of the gallows were two men and a bent old woman, while directly behind the hanged priest sat a stocky middle-aged man with short, dirty blonde hair. His seat appeared to be a poor representation of a throne – it had a high back, and was topped off by gargoyles that were probably torn from the nearby church. Robin wondered inanely what stopped the gurning stone monsters from falling off the pitiful throne since they looked far too heavy and precarious to balance as well as they appeared to.

"In the name of Christ our Lord and Saviour –" Tuck shouted, hefting his quarterstaff menacingly, but the man seated on the gallows chopped his hand down angrily.

"Speak not that name here, cleric, or suffer the fate of your brother there." Without moving his head he rolled his eyes up to look at the hanged man and grinned.

Robin hesitated for a moment, something – some memory – flaring in the back of his mind at the sight of the apparently possessed villager's expression. It seemed strangely familiar…

"Pah!" Tuck reached the gallows and started to pull himself up, his face a mask of outraged fury.

"Hold, Tuck," Robin called, hurrying to catch him as Little John and Thomas stopped, feet spread wide and staffs held out defensively, ready for whatever might transpire next.

Without warning the withered old woman on the platform screamed in laughter and fell to her knees, pressing her face close to Tuck's. Never before had Robin seen anyone that looked as much like a witch as this apparition with her blackened teeth – stumps mostly – and numerous warts on her skin.

Yet the friar stood his ground and met her gaze as she shouted at him.

"Your Christ has been banished from Holmfirth. Now, my lord Satan rules in his stead!"

Robin heard the soldiers behind him draw shocked breaths and knew more than one grasped their sword hilts, despite his order for there to be no bloodshed.

Tuck was made of stern stuff, though. "Get out of my way, woman," he grunted, reaching out to grasp the kneeling woman by the hair and dragging her bodily from the raised platform onto the sodden grass at his feet. She tried to fight him off, scratching and clawing and biting, but he held her down and Father Myrc ran forward to help.

Robin turned his gaze back to the villager on the ridiculous throne, taking in the thinning, straight blonde hair and the disdainful curled lip before the man got to his feet with a bellow.

"Get them! I command you, in the name of our dark lord and master – kill them all!"

The lawman's heart sank as the sound of crazed screaming filled the air on all sides – coming not only from the throats of men and women, but children's voices also seemed to join in with the hellish chorus. He whirled, staring into the fog, knuckles white on his staff, desperately trying to see where the first attackers would hit them.

"Should I go after him?" Little John shouted, nodding at the man on the gallows who, with his remaining two companions was climbing down from the other side of the platform to make his escape.

Robin shook his head, his eyes widening as the villagers' army of the damned appeared through the fog, racing towards his small force of men.

"Leave them! I think you're going to be needed here for

now..."

CHAPTER THREE

Gasping in desperation, Robin dropped his left shoulder, narrowly avoiding the meat cleaver that was about to carve his shoulder wide open. At the same time he rammed his staff into another assailant's midriff then swung the weapon back around to catch the first attacker's legs, sweeping them out from under him. The man dropped his cleaver with a roar before he was silenced by a brutal blow to the forehead. Without stopping, Robin twisted and cracked his quarterstaff into the second, winded man's temple, felling him like a rotten tree.

The young bailiff blew out a long breath and spread his legs in a defensive stance, looking around, searching for another threat in the pitiful army that faced them.

His soldiers were targeting the fit young men first, and, once they were beaten down, it was a simple enough matter to hold off the women and children who – despite their Satanic madness – were cowed by the sight of Little John's massive bulk tearing through their ranks like a righteous whirlwind. Some of the villagers, however, wielded daggers or chipped axes normally used for chopping firewood, and more than one of the sheriff's men were hurt before they could take down their attackers.

The sound of running footsteps approached to his rear and Robin turned to see a woman with a dull but deadly knife coming for him, a murderous look in her eyes. He raised his left hand as she lunged and grasped her fist, twisting hard so her whole body snapped back as if struck by lightning. The knife dropped to the ground, as did the woman and, loathe to assault her, he shouted on Father Myrc. The priest hurried over and sat on her chest, loudly intoning a passage from the bible as Robin stood.

He saw a tall, thin man with a wispy beard charge at

Tuck, and winced as the Friar lifted his arm straight up and hammered it right into his attacker's neck, slamming the unfortunate man to the ground, dazed and choking.

The battle, inevitably, didn't last long, though. The villagers – enraged and insane as they were – had no chance against the staffs and superior training of Robin, John and the sheriff's soldiers.

There were many injuries. Some of the locals were unlucky and didn't recover from the blows they received, while half-a-dozen of the possessed men were so lost in their madness that there was no reasoning with them. They bit and clawed, howling like wolves as they did their best to murder the lawmen who retaliated with brutal yet restrained efficiency. Finally the fog had burned away in the afternoon sun and, at last, the village green lay strewn with unconscious or dead villagers.

Friar Tuck and Father Myrc moved amongst the survivors, offering blessings – or exorcisms in the more severe cases – in the name of Christ, and it was enough to restore sanity to Holmfirth. The madness seemed to have lifted now that their ringleader had vacated his 'throne' and those who could walk made their way sheepishly back to their homes to reflect on the whole bizarre experience, Father Myrc exhorting them loudly to be at mass the following morning to seek forgiveness from God.

Robin ordered Thomas to stay behind with the rest of the soldiers so they could restore order to the village while he, Little John and Tuck would report back to Sir Henry. The village headman – an old fellow with skin like parchment – was arrested and bound. The bailiff attempted to question him over the madness, in particular the priest's murder, but it was a waste of time, since the man, like the rest of his fellow villagers, was in a state of shock. So they decided to take him with them to Nottingham and the sheriff.

Father Myrc offered to stay on in place of the hanged

clergyman for a while, until he was sure the devil had truly been cast out, and Tuck promised to look after the church in Wakefield until the priest returned home. Father Myrc would also see to his murdered brother's funeral and he moved off now, shouting for someone, anyone, to cut the pitiful body down.

None of the sheriff's guardsmen had been killed, although a few were quite badly injured.

The mission was a success, and Robin should have been pleased. Little John certainly was – the grin on his bearded face looked wide enough to swallow a wheel of cheese – but Robin couldn't get the man on the throne, the ringleader, out of his head. There was something unpleasantly familiar about him, but, for now, the young lawman was unable to put his finger on it.

Ah well, he was sure it would come to him eventually, he mused, as they rode out of Holmfirth along the road back to Nottingham. They'd have to hunt the man down and arrest him after all, before the maniac could cause any more trouble.

* * *

"Wine?"

Robin nodded and Sheriff de Faucumberg filled a mug himself before handing it over to the young man who'd become something of a friend these past few months. He told people Robin was his "mastiff", who he could let off the leash whenever anyone around his jurisdiction was being troublesome, and the former wolf's head would dutifully deal with the issue quickly, effectively and sometimes brutally.

"So you managed to restore the people of Holmfirth to sanity," de Faucumberg said, sipping his own wine, a fragrant red which had just been delivered to his bottler that morning. "Without too much bloodshed I trust?"

He raised an eyebrow and Robin, who'd waved John and Tuck off at an inn in the city an hour earlier, nodded. "Aye, have no fears on that score. I know you don't like the people to be treated unfairly so I made sure the men were as gentle as possible. All is well again, although, unfortunately the ringleader managed to escape, along with two others. We caught one of them – a local – but the others got away. The leader looked strangely familiar to me; came to Holmfirth from out of town apparently, not long ago and somehow managed to get the superstitious villagers to do his bidding. Shame he escaped." He raised his cup and sipped the liquid, grimacing; he didn't have a taste for the expensive stuff the way the sheriff did. "I'll catch the bastard one day, though. I'll not forget that face, you can count on it."

"Strange business all around," de Faucumberg sighed. "A whole village possessed. How can that happen?"

Robin shrugged and lifted a small piece of cheese from the trencher in the middle of the table which was piled with fresh foods. "According to the headman their parish priest probably caused the whole thing," he said, popping the food into his mouth with relish. "Apparently the clergyman – a newcomer to the place – was forever warning against demons and devils and seeing witchcraft in the most innocent of situations. The whole place was on edge as a result and...you know how it is: any emotion can be contagious. One person thinks the devil's taken control of them and it frightens someone else who starts to see bad omens in the blood that was in the shit they did that morning, or the fact their cow gave them a funny look when they milked it, or anything else that seems out of the ordinary. Before you know it some poor bastard – the priest in this case – becomes a scapegoat for all the pent up fear and, once they've given in to the madness the people feel free to do whatever they please."

De Faucumberg gazed at his young charge thoughtfully.

"Very perceptive," he grunted at last. "You're not just good with a longbow are you?"

"That's why you like having me about," Robin grinned, draining the last of his wine. "Five years ago, Sir Henry, if you'd told me we'd be sitting here – drinking mates – chatting about the ills of the world, I'd have laughed and thought *you* possessed by a devil."

They sat in companionable silence for a time, eating and drinking their fill, before the sheriff stood up and called for a servant to take away the cups and plates.

"Where to next?" he asked, as his man quickly and efficiently cleared the table, head bowed the whole time as he left the room almost like a ghost.

"Back up the road to Mirfield," Robin replied, also getting to his feet and pulling on his green cloak. "A baker there has an unpaid fine which the local bailiff has been unable to extract from the man so..."

The sheriff looked at him seriously.

"Do you enjoy this job?"

Robin shrugged. "Aye, I suppose I do. It's interesting travelling around the county, even if it can be unpleasant putting people out their homes and the like. Someone has to uphold the law though, eh?"

"Indeed." De Faucumberg waved the big lawman farewell but he stood, lost in thought, for a long time after Robin had gone.

* * *

His relationship with the Sheriff of Nottingham and Yorkshire may have blossomed surprisingly over the years he'd spent in the man's service, but right now, it was the situation with his own wife that worried Robin.

"I'm sick of this," Matilda stated, flatly, her voice barely betraying any emotion. As if she really meant what she said; she'd truly had enough.

"Sick of what?" Robin demanded, feeling his temper rise as it always did when these discussions started. "Sick of our nice house? Sick of the fine clothes you and our son wear? Sick of me being at home rather than being stuck in the damn forest living the life of an outlaw?"

"You're never here any more," the girl said. Some of the anger went out of her face, which was still unlined and, Robin thought, as pretty as ever. "Keep the money and the clothes and you might as well still be a wolf's head. You're out doing Sir Henry's bidding all the time. I miss you. Arthur misses you."

She glanced over at the little bed next to theirs, where the four year-old boy was sleeping and smiled. The lad had a room of his own but Matilda liked him near her all the time, especially when Robin was away working in other towns and villages.

"We don't need money; we've got plenty from your days as the fabled outlaw the minstrels all sing tales about. You could do anything you want, here, in Wakefield, with your friends and family."

"Like what?" he demanded. "Be a blacksmith? Or a farmer? Or a baker? That's not any life for me." His voice trailed off. "I wish it was, but..."

"Where are you going now?" Matilda growled, as he turned his back and pulled his green cloak around his shoulders. "It's late."

"I'm going to the alehouse to see Tuck and John. I'll not be out too long – I've got an early start in the morning –"

"So you're going out drinking with your mates as if you were still a daft boy? Then pissing off to some other town as soon as it's light, leaving me and Arthur behind as usual?" She stepped in close and glared up into his eyes. "I'm not living like this, Robin. In the name of God I deserve better."

He shook his head and pulled away from her, stepping out into the cool night and slamming the door closed, shaking his head, a lump in his throat born of sadness and confusion as he gazed out at the village wondering what to do.

All of a sudden the door was thrown open behind him and he braced himself.

"Did you have to be so loud you selfish bastard?" Matilda hissed out into the gloom. "No thought for your sleeping child, it's always about you and what you want."

Robin waved a hand angrily, dismissively, and muttered an oath before he made his way along the street towards the local alehouse. He could feel his wife's stare burning into him every step of the way until he turned a corner and his shoulders slumped visibly as he walked.

It had been like this for a few months now. They'd been trying to have another baby for a long time but for some reason Matilda had never, thus far, managed to conceive again. They'd prayed and made offerings at St Mary's, and Tuck had even performed a blessing on them but all to no avail. Arthur remained an only child.

In truth, Robin was quite content with the situation – he loved his son so much and they had so much fun together, despite Matilda's harsh words, that he wasn't desperate for another crying babe in the house just now.

But Matilda took it hard, he knew. She never said much about it, so he wasn't sure whether she blamed herself, or Robin, or even God for her barrenness, but he'd noticed her mood becoming darker and darker until it seemed he could do nothing right these days.

No wonder he was happy travelling so much.

Aye, Matilda was right. He *did* enjoy his job and it was extremely important to him. For long enough he'd been a wolf's head – an outcast, and a man anyone, even the lowest beggar, could strike down with impunity. But the sheriff had given him a position that held real power – he didn't mind admitting to himself that he enjoyed the respect he saw in people's eyes when they knew he was a lawman. Yes, respect and even fear.

Of course, he'd had that when he'd been an outlaw too – the people loved him and his men after all. But now he had all that *and* he was a free man, dealing out justice to those who deserved it and able to enjoy the money and status his position afforded him.

He couldn't do that when he'd been living rough under a fucking tree in the pissing rain in Barnsdale, could he?

The alehouse door gave way to his gentle push and the sounds of men laughing filled the air. He sighed heavily and made his way inside to join his friends.

Things would work out he thought – they always did.

CHAPTER FOUR

"What are we going to do now then?" Eoin asked, his low voice betraying the hint of an Irish accent.

Philip was a big man at a shade under six feet tall, and powerfully-built too, but he was dwarfed by his companion, who looked at him now, ready to follow wherever his friend said they should go.

"Dunno," Philip shrugged in reply. "Shame those lawmen turned up in Holmfirth and put an end to our fun. We were living like kings there." He laughed and slapped Eoin on the arm good-naturedly, resuming their walk towards the village of Flockton where they hoped to buy some supplies. "I suppose now we're outlaws we should find some more of our kind to join up with. My brother was in a gang around here, or so I heard a few years ago. We could try and find him."

"How?"

Philip shrugged again. "Ask in the villages hereabouts."

Eoin nodded. He was happy to go along with whatever his friend suggested.

He'd met Philip in a tavern one night, a little over three years ago. Eoin's great size had, as it so often did, drawn attention and he'd been attacked for no good reason by three drunken idiots. They were unskilled but armed with knives and things would have gone badly for the big man had Philip not taken it upon himself to take Eoin's side.

Three corpses later the fight was done and witnesses were quick to tell the bailiff the three drunks had been killed lawfully, in self-defence.

Ever since then the two men had been friends, although Eoin was sometimes disturbed by Philip's tendency to violence at the slightest provocation. Especially since the older man was so good at it.

But Eoin was loyal and felt he owed Philip for saving his life so the pair remained close no matter what.

They hadn't planned on making the people of Holmfirth go mad. It all started when they'd tried to find work labouring for the blacksmith who they were told had just been awarded a big contract to craft weapons for the local lord. The man had been happy to hire them at first, but after a few days began to grow frightened of Philip's somewhat unhinged nature. He soon came to believe his new worker was possessed by the devil and Philip had played along, for fun, ordering the blacksmith first to pay them double the agreed wages, then to allow him to sleep with the terrified man's wife.

Somehow, the blacksmith's fear was transmitted throughout the village and Philip, revelling in his satanic role, milked the whole insane situation for all he could. The women slept with him, the men paid him homage in food and coin and it was all harmless enough until the priest tried to step in and put an end to things.

Hanging the man had been the villagers' idea, so far were they gone in their madness. Eoin wanted no part of the brutal business, but Philip encouraged it, knowing the priest's murder would only make the peoples' bond to him even stronger.

If the sheriff's men hadn't turned up they'd still be living as nobles in Holmfirth right now, rather than hiding like animals in the forest, hoping to find someone they could steal a crust of bread and a jug of ale from.

"Hold!"

The cry was high-pitched but filled with aggression.

With the promise of violence.

Philip stopped dead in his tracks, eyes scanning the foliage all around them.

"Who said that?" Eoin rumbled. "Show yourself."

A small man stepped out from behind the massive trunk of an old yew tree, longsword in hand. He was clean shaven with dark eyes, and appeared to be quite filthy. And yet, when he grimaced at them, Philip was surprised by the fellow's full set of almost white teeth.

"You two look like you can handle yourself," the small man noted. "So I won't get any closer." He laughed unpleasantly. "Take my word for it though, if you don't do as I say my mates will fill you with arrows so quick you'll die looking like a pair of giant fucking hedgehogs. Drop your weapons and throw your purses over here. Quick now. Those hares strung around your neck too."

Eoin glanced down at Philip, who simply nodded and slipped his coin-purse – which was as good as empty – from his belt and tossed it onto the ground in front of the robber. Eoin followed suit, although his purse really *was* empty, and so light it flopped sadly to the ground only a short distance away from him.

"Oh for fuck sake," the little robber spat in disgust. "Is that it? You two were hardly worth it." He held up a hand and, with an air of bored resignation, spoke to the trees.

"Shoot the big one first. I'll deal with the other one myself."

Philip dropped instantly, and swung his leg around, tripping Eoin just as an arrow tore through the air where they'd been standing.

He pushed himself back up onto one knee and drew his dagger.

"Get that ugly bastard," he growled.

The thief brought his sword back, ready to charge, but Philip swept up a short, stout branch from the forest floor and threw it at his face. The man parried it just in time but the manoeuvre left him off balance, and the huge weight of Eoin barrelled viciously into him. They fell onto the ground with a thud that Philip imagined he could feel as well as hear.

"Hold him down," he shouted to Eoin. "By the neck!"

He turned and addressed the trees and bushes all around

them, a grin splitting his face as if this was a great game.

"You out there – you can shoot us, but my big friend there will snap your leader's neck before he dies. Or, you can come out and we can talk."

Eoin wasn't just holding the downed robber; outraged at the attack, his hands were squeezing inexorably on the man's throat.

"All right, all right!"

A man no older than forty, longbow in hand but with – in stark contrast to his downed friend – no front teeth at all, slipped out from his hiding place to their rear. "Leave him be, let him up. We didn't plan on killing you, I was aiming for the big man's leg –"

"Then you'd have taken our money and left us as good as dead in the middle of the forest?" Philip finished the sentence sarcastically. "Well, as you can see..." he retrieved the coin-purses he and Eoin had dropped and emptied them into his hand. "We haven't got any fucking money. Did have, but we left it behind in Holmfirth when the law chased us out."

Eoin had let the small robber up by now and they stood glaring at one another now: the giant and the purple-faced, breathless thief.

Philip gazed across at the little man, sizing him up, and came to the conclusion he'd rather go toe-to-toe with Eoin.

The dark-eyed robber had a maniacal gleam in his eye that was deeply disturbing; reminded him of himself, truth be told. They'd need to be careful around this one although...if they could get him on their side...

"Come," he smiled, walking forward and grasping the little robber's hand. "We're all outlaws together aren't we? You must be as hungry as we are."

He reached up and pulled the hares on the string around his shoulders over his head with a grin. "Let's eat."

It was a cool night but the fire brought a comforting warmth and light to the otherwise pitch-black forest.

The hares had been finished earlier – skinned, gutted and spitted they'd made a fine, if small, stew for four hungry men, and the smell of their bodies roasting still seemed to permeate the air.

"What's your story then?" the small robber asked, picking at a stubborn piece of gristle in his fine teeth. "You wolf's heads like us?"

Philip snorted humourlessly. "Aye, I reckon we are now. Had some trouble in the last village we were in and a clergyman found himself on his way to meet God sooner than he'd expected."

He upended his wineskin and took a short draught of the strong liquid.

"What about you boys? Just the two of you eh? I expected more when you ambushed us." He jerked his chin at the little man who was so clearly the leader of the outlaws. "What's your name? I'm Philip and my big mate here is Eoin."

The man eyed him for a moment, apparently wondering if he could be trusted. Finally, eyes locked on Philip's, he replied. "Mark of Horbury. I've been living in and around Barnsdale for the best part of seven years. The law have probably forgotten all about me but I like it out here, where I don't have to work like some beast of the field. Out here I just take what I need from anyone that comes along the road."

Philip whistled softly. "Seven years eh? That's a long time to evade the foresters."

Mark smiled, still staring disconcertingly at Philip who looked back unperturbed. "Not just foresters. After the Lancastrian revolt the king's men were all over the forest like flies on a tasty turd. And, since Robin Hood was living around here at the time, the man known as the Raven – Sir Guy of Gisbourne – was always a threat." He laughed shortly. "Until Hood tore him a new one, that is. Things have been a bit quieter around here since then."

Philip and Eoin had both spent the last decade or more down south, around London, until recently so, although the tales of Hood and the Raven had reached them, they'd not placed much stock in the fanciful stories.

"Last I heard my younger brother was an outlaw somewhere around here. You know of him?"

Mark shook his head when Philip named his brother. "Never heard of him, friend. There's a lot of us around here."

Philip smiled. "No matter, I've not seen him in years anyway, probably wouldn't even recognise him if I met him. If there's so many of you," he went on, "why don't you all band together? Surely it'd be safer than roaming around in pairs."

Mark looked into the crackling fire they'd roasted the hares over, his eyes shining orange in the glow. "Who'd be the leader in a big group like that?" he wondered, before returning his stare to Philip. "I don't like taking orders. I like *giving* orders. But so do lots of men, especially wolf's heads. Nah," he grinned and stood to leave the firelight to relieve himself. "We're happy as we are, ain't we Ivo?"

His toothless companion grunted assent over the sound of his leader's piss splashing onto the forest floor but Philip thought Ivo's response lacked enthusiasm and the acorn of an idea began to grow in his head.

Still, it would be better if they didn't need to kill Mark...the little lunatic would be a good man to have on their side. Assuming he could be controlled.

Philip would have to take things slowly; win these men over, before they could move onto bigger things.

If he was to live as an outlaw, he may as well do it in style.

"You being hunted?" Mark asked, settling back onto his log by the camp-fire. "From that village, where was it?

Holmfirth, aye. The law searching for you, d'you think? Should me and Ivo be on our way in the morning in case your trail leads them right to us?"

Eoin shook his great head. "Nah. They had their hands full when we left, didn't they?" He grinned over at his friend and Philip returned the look with twinkling eyes.

"Aye. The villagers attacked them just as we decided to run for it. Although," the mirth left his eyes and he turned thoughtful. "I doubt those fools lasted long against the two lawmen. Big lads they were – one was a fucking giant, biggest man I've ever seen. He was even bigger than Eoin."

Mark was gazing into the fire again, apparently lost in its hypnotic flickering, but his eyes snapped up now and he spat an oath. "Little John. And, no doubt, his captain: Robin Hood himself."

Philip shrugged. "Aye, could have been. I never thought about it until now but, aye, all the stories I heard about them said Little John was bigger than any other man. I assumed it was a joke; a play on his name. And he was taking orders from another hard-looking man with the broad shoulders of a longbowman so...aye, you could be right."

"Fucking traitors." Mark growled, his hand falling to his dagger apparently of its own accord, instinctively, as if the little man wished he could take it then and there to the lawmen. "They were wolf's heads like us. Just like us. Worse if some of the stories I've heard about them are true. Hood sliced the fingers off a nobleman in his own manor house, you know? Aye, and they murdered countless churchmen too before they killed the king's bounty hunter. Yet what do they get?"

He glared at Philip and Eoin, who shuffled his feet nervously under the smaller man's crazed stare.

"A pardon and places on the sheriff's own staff, that's what. And now they ride around northern England dispensing justice."

"They hunt outlaws?"

Mark shook his head. "Not like us. They just collect taxes and stuff like that. It's only a matter of time though." He picked up a small twig and broke it into pieces before tossing the fragments absent-mindedly into the fire. "Like I said, there's a lot of thieves and cut-throats hiding in the forest and, since Gisbourne's death, there's been no-one leading any real effort to hunt us down. It won't last forever and who better to send after a forest full of outlaws than the most famous wolf's head of all?"

All the more reason to bring the gangs together into one large, powerful group then, Philip thought, but kept the idea to himself.

"How would you like a couple of extra members of your band, Mark? We know how to fight, you've seen that for yourself."

The outlaw sized them up before nodding and smiling. "Fair enough. Just make sure you do as I say and we'll all get along fine."

Philip grinned his thanks and raised his wineskin to Eoin in salute. "Looks like we've got a new home for a while, big man."

It wasn't much, but it was a start.

* * *

There was a storm during the night and Robin slept fitfully. The ale he'd shared with his friends didn't help, but the sound of the wind battering their home always made him fretful; he knew there'd be things needing repaired in the morning.

Matilda hadn't said a word to him when he returned from the tavern. She'd pretended to be asleep and Robin had been glad at that. No more arguing.

Arthur was fast asleep beside her but the little boy shifted around in the bed a lot during the night and every movement brought Robin awake again – he'd always be a light sleeper after his time living as an outlaw in the forest.

As a result of all this he woke in the morning with a dry mouth and an aching head, wishing he didn't need to travel to Mirfield that day on a job.

Matilda got up and made a small breakfast of black bread softened in ale for Arthur, who fed himself the sodden chunks greedily before growing bored and sending the remainder flying around the floor and mashing it into the table with a determined grin.

Matilda scolded the boy but said not a word to her husband, who dressed himself and gratefully downed the cup of water that she'd left out on the table for him.

"I have to go to a job in Mirfield."

No reply.

"It shouldn't take me too long; might be back by early afternoon. Maybe we could ask my ma and da to watch Arthur and we could go for a walk with some cheese and ale? We haven't done that in a while."

"Didn't you get enough ale last night?" The words were spat through gritted teeth and Robin shook his head in anger, lifting his weapons and throwing his light cloak around his shoulders. He kissed Arthur on the cheek and bid him a loving farewell but Matilda's voice harried him out the door as he left, barely listening to her words.

Sometimes he wondered if he'd be better off living in the forest again.

The common room in the alehouse was empty that early in the morning, but Alexander Gilbert, the landlord, appeared when he heard Robin coming in the front door.

"I'll have an ale, please, Alex," the big lawman grunted, somewhat embarrassed to be drinking at that time but knowing the stuff would cure the hangover that threatened to ruin his morning. "Where's John? I'd expected him to be

37

up and ready and emptying your wife's kitchen of its contents."

The landlord shook his head as he handed the mug over and pocketed the proffered coin. "Haven't seen him, lad. Must still be asleep."

Robin quickly quaffed the ale. It wasn't like the giant to oversleep. All the men who'd been outlaws with him were in the habit of waking early, ready for whatever – or whoever – the day brought to them.

"I'll check on him."

Alexander waved him towards the hallway. "He's in the second room along there."

Robin drew his dagger as he walked silently along the gloomy corridor which was short and had no windows. He stopped at the door and placed his head against it, listening intently.

A groan came from the other side and Robin quickly wiped the sweat from his palm before gripping the dagger again. He softly pressed down on the latch, then rammed his shoulder into the wood, rolling onto the ground and coming up on one knee inside the little room with his blade held out before him.

"What the fuck are you doing you madman?"

The guest room had a window which was un-shuttered to let in fresh air and the early morning sun. John's face looked green in the pale light and Robin got to his feet with a crooked smile.

"Hangover eh? I was worried someone was in here killing you."

The huge man's beard was damp and flecked with bits of regurgitated food and he retched over the chamber pot pitifully, although nothing came up, which was just as well as it was already close to overflowing.

"Not a hangover," John muttered, rolling back onto the pallet and holding a hand over his eyes. "Had plenty of them in my time – this is something else. I've not stopped shitting and puking for hours."

Robin's smile dropped away and, without even thinking, he lifted the stinking pot from the floor, emptying the contents out the window into the grass outside. "You want me to fetch the barber from Pontefract?"

"Nah, I think the worst of it's over. It's all out now. I hope." He lifted a hand away from one eye and peered up at his friend. "Thanks for emptying that, you're a true friend. I've shit my breeches too – you fancy taking them to the Calder and rinsing them out for me? Or asking Matilda to –"

"Fuck off," Robin broke in with a horrified glare. "My friendship has limits. You can wash them out yourself when you get up. You won't be coming with me to Mirfield today in that state, eh? Oh well, can't be helped, I suppose." He placed the chamber pot back onto the floor beside John's recumbent figure and patted him on the arm. "I'll tell Alex to send you some bread and ale."

John looked queasy at the idea but grunted his thanks nonetheless. "Tell him no more of that stew he fed me last night, though. That's probably what's given me the shits." He retched again, but only a wet, awful smelling, belch came out and Robin shuddered.

"Aye, all right, I'll tell him. See you when I return."

He passed the message to the landlord and made his way back to his house where he stood for a moment, wondering if he should go inside to bid farewell to his family again, but decided against it. He mounted his horse and trotted along the main road towards Mirfield.

His job that day was to collect monies owed to the sheriff from a baker. The man had been fined – the second time that year – for selling underweight bread, and had made a couple of payments in good time, but there had been no word and no money from him in three weeks. Sir Henry had told Robin to find out what the problem was, and to add an extra ten shillings onto the fine as a penalty for late payment.

It wasn't a job that Robin expected he'd need Little John's quarterstaff to back him up on, but the big man's company made these journeys more pleasurable. And there was always the threat of robbery or worse from the ubiquitous gangs of wolf's heads that dotted Barnsdale and the rest of the surrounding forests.

The idea of making the trip on his own also meant he'd have time to dwell on his problems with Matilda., which wasn't a pleasant thought.

He sighed as he reached the outskirts of the village and resolved to push his mount hard so he could complete the job as soon as possible.

"Where's John?"

Robin glanced to the right at the voice, the smile returning to his face as he saw Tuck outside St Mary's, collecting broken roof tiles which must have been dislodged in the night by the storm. Indeed, the whole of the small churchyard was a mess of debris and one of the young trees that had been planted when Robin was a child lay on its side, roots completely torn from the earth. Father Myrc, who had just that day returned from Holmfirth, was visible at the far corner of the building, a brush in his hand as he tried to clear shards of slate and other detritus from the pathway.

"He's not well – dose of the shits from the looks of it." Robin waved a hand at the look of concern that creased Tuck's usually jovial features. "Don't fret, I think he's over the worst of it but he's not up to travelling with me to Mirfield so I'm on the way there by myself."

For a moment, the friar's eyes scanned the devastation the wind had wreaked and Robin could almost see the thoughts flitting through his head. Tuck was a great friend, a great warrior, and a great man to share a few ales with but...he wasn't the greatest worker in the world.

"Why don't I come with you, then? Yes, I'd better come

along – can't have you travelling that road by yourself. There's outlaws all over the place and they'd like nothing better than to claim a lawman's head. Especially the fabled Robin Hood. Give me a minute!"

Robin grinned and nodded as the burly friar hurried into the church, reappearing moments later with his staff and a pack filled, no doubt, with food and drink to keep them going on their ride. He spoke to Father Mryc for a time before he disappeared again, this time to the rear of the church where the stables were located.

"Right then." Tuck was a fine horseman and he expertly guided his rouncy past the windblown debris in the churchyard and onto the road beside Robin. "Let's be off."

Father Myrc watched them go, arm in the air in farewell, a weary but fond smile on his face before he returned to his sweeping.

CHAPTER FIVE

"Afternoon, Harry." Robin lifted one of the meat pies from the counter in the baker's shop and bit into it, nodding appreciatively as the juices filled his mouth. "Freshly baked, eh? Very nice."

The baker, a bald man with a grizzled beard and thin lips, glared at him as Tuck hung back near the door, watching with interest. He'd never really spoken to Robin in any detail about his new line of employment, and this was the first time he'd ever seen his former captain doing a job for the sheriff.

"That'll be a penny," Harry muttered, holding his hand out, his stare never leaving the young bailiff's face.

Robin reached into his pocket and tossed the coin over to the man, who fished it from the air expertly.

"Your turn now." Robin pulled some papers from his pocket and stared at them for a moment. He wasn't a great reader but, eventually, he went on. "You haven't paid off your fine, Harry, as you know. I'm here to collect it."

A customer walked into the little shop then, seeing Robin, backed out and hurried off to find sustenance elsewhere.

"How am I supposed to get the money together when you're chasing away my customers?" the baker demanded, voice rising an octave in frustration. "No, I don't have the cash. I only have half." His voice dropped again but his eyebrows went up and he spread his hands wide. "Give me another week, eh? I'll have it by then, I swear it. Those loaves might have been a little underweight but they were best quality! I'd rather make a good small loaf than a worthless heavy one."

Robin continued chewing the pie and then wiped the grease from his lips with a sleeve. "I don't think I can give you any more time, Harry. The sheriff was pretty insistent and you've had weeks already..."

He trailed off but looked expectantly at the baker who returned his stare for a moment, clearly wondering what he should do next and Tuck felt a wave of pity wash over him for the man. Harry didn't have the look of a sot or waster – he simply looked like a villager who was struggling to make ends meet. His merchandise was tasty and of a high quality, judging by Robin's reaction to the meat pie, and the price asked for it. The man was clearly a fine baker but not much of a businessman. Perhaps if he used cheaper ingredients and charged a little less for his wares he'd not need to resort to making underweight loaves and would, as a result, make a better living in these hard times.

Some craftsmen took their art too seriously to do it in what they saw as a half-arsed way though and now Harry, who made pies and savouries fit for noblemen, was suffering because his only customers were the poor peasants and yeomen of Mirfield.

"Like I say, I only have half the remaining fine," the baker mumbled, shoulders slumped. "What if I give you ten shillings for yourself, and you give me another week to collect the full amount?"

Robin nodded, lowering his voice conspiratorially.

"I'll take that for now then, just between you and me. I'll fob the sheriff off for another week, all right? Don't tell anyone, though – I don't want people to know I'm a soft touch."

Tuck felt a coldness sweep through him at what he was witnessing. He watched as the baker disappeared into a tiny room in the rear of the shop and returned moments later with a handful of coins. He held them out to Robin who took them with a smile.

"Thanks Harry," the sheriff's man muttered, tucking the money into his purse. "I'll tell the Sir Henry you're doing your best and deserve a little extra time. How does that sound?"

The baker's eyes flicked from Robin to Tuck, back in the shadows, and Tuck felt the man's despair almost like a kick in the stomach. But Harry simple lowered his head and, in a voice that was barely audible replied, "That sounds fine, my lord. Thank you, I'm very grateful for your kindness."

"Excellent!" Robin slapped his big hand on the counter and grinned. "I'm glad we sorted this, Harry. I'll be back next week to collect the full amount, I'm sure you'll have it all by then. I hate throwing men out of their businesses." He turned and nodded to Tuck who eyed the baker sadly then walked out into the street.

"That pie was tasty," Robin said over his shoulder as he followed the friar outside. "You should really charge more for them – maybe you'd not be in debt if you did!"

Tuck made his way over to his mount and untied it from the tethering post before dragging himself into the saddle with some difficulty. Robin looked up at him in surprise.

"What's your hurry?" he demanded. "Don't you want to stop awhile in the tavern for a couple of drinks and some food? The *Wayfarer's Arms* has some great ale, I've been there a few times recently. Prices are fair too."

Tuck grunted and kicked his horse into a walk without waiting for his companion to follow. "I need to get back to Wakefield and help Father Myrc tidy up after the storm. You head off to the *Wayfarer's,* and I'll see you later."

Robin stood, open-mouthed, for a moment. Since when did Tuck refuse a meal?

"Wait," he shouted, freeing his own palfrey from its tether and vaulting nimbly into the saddle. "Wait," he repeated, urging the horse into a canter. "What the hell's the matter with you?"

There was no reply and Tuck simply stared at the road ahead as his young friend caught up with him and grabbed hold of the friar's reins.

"What's going on? You've never been in a hurry to sweep leaves in your life, especially not when there's freshly-brewed ale on offer. What's the problem here?"

Tuck turned, at last, to glare at Robin, who let go of the other man's reins.

"What's the problem? You took a bribe from that poor baker."

Robin smiled in disbelief. "So? I did him a favour. If I hadn't given him extra time to gather his rent I'd have had to throw him out onto the street. He'd have lost his livelihood." He raised his arms in supplication. "Isn't this better? You're a man of the world; I assumed you'd understand or I'd never have brought you along."

Tuck pointed a meaty finger at him angrily. "Man of the world? Pah. Will he have your rent next week, when you return?"

Robin shrugged. "I hope –"

"No, he won't. You know it as well as I. He'd done his best to gather half the money and you took ten shillings of that for your own pocket? He had little enough chance of paying his debt off as it was but you've made it impossible. Why, Robin?"

The anger had left Tuck, to be replaced now with disappointment.

"You were a wolf's head yourself. You used to talk about society's injustice and how you wished you could make things fairer – better – for men like Harry. And now, here you are..."

Robin kicked his mount into a walk and muttered something about just upholding the law and trying to be fair. Tuck followed, pulling his horse away from what seemed to be a particularly tasty piece of grass.

"No wonder Little John felt sick at the prospect of coming here with you today. I feel like going for a bath in the Calder myself after seeing you in action –"

Robin rounded on him, face scarlet, horse's head dragged

rudely back as he brought it to a halt.

"I uphold the law, Tuck. That's my job. I'm not a wolf's head any more." He seemed to wilt under Tuck's stony gaze though, and urged his mount forward again, its heavy hooves thudding gently on the soft earth as they left Mirfield and joined the main road again.

"How many men have you thrown out of their homes or businesses?" Tuck asked softly.

Robin shrugged before replying moments later. "A dozen? Two dozen? I don't keep count." His eyes swivelled to look at Tuck. "I never put anyone out without the law on my side. It's not my fault they didn't pay their debts."

Tuck couldn't believe his friend – the fabled Wolf's Head of so many ballads – was talking like this. "When you took up with de Faucumberg I assumed you'd become a bounty hunter for him. Hunting down rapists and murderers. Not throwing honest bakers out onto the street!"

"The man sold underweight loaves," Robin countered. "He's as much a criminal in the eyes of the law as any rapist."

"Listen to yourself," Tuck muttered, shaking his head. "That man making his tasty meat pies is as bad as a rapist or a murderer?"

"In the eyes of the law," Robin said. "They're all lawbreakers –"

"Peace." Tuck turned back to the road and his horse gathered speed again. Robin didn't bother trying to catch up this time and the friar was glad of it.

Truth be told, Robin had acted just as everyone would have expected when he was first tasked with collecting fines and overdue taxes. He'd gone easy on people and even, in some cases, felt so sorry for them that he'd quietly paid off their debts using his own money. But word had soon got around that he was a soft touch and folk started to take advantage. It took him a while to realise it and it had hurt when he did – were people really so selfish that they'd exploit any opportunity to line their own pockets at the expense of someone trying to do right by them?

So he'd had to grow a thick skin and deal with everyone the same way. Aye, he took the occasional bribe, but so what? Every other bailiff he knew would take much more in bribes than he ever did and leave the people with no chance of ever making up their debts.

Robin wasn't heartless, but he liked to believe he'd grown wise and if folk owed money, they'd have to pay, it was as simple as that. He didn't enjoy that part of the job though, it was true and now, seeing the look of disappointment on the friar's face, it irritated and even, deep down, shamed him.

The journey back to Wakefield seemed to take forever but, at last, the trees parted and St Mary's steeple came into sight. As he dismounted, Tuck stood and watched Robin's mount carry him towards the village.

"Ask yourself if your work is worth it, Robin," Tuck called. "Is it worth giving up all your former principles? Is it worth losing your family?"

Robin had told them about the recent, growing, troubles with his wife when the companions had been in the alehouse the previous evening and now Tuck thought he understood why Matilda felt as she did.

The friar raised his eyes to heaven and prayed his young friend would find his way, before it was too late.

* * *

The next few days were not really memorable for Robin. Matilda was polite if distant towards him, but Arthur continued to grow and develop although the lad was something of a firebrand and often got into trouble with the other local children, adding even more stress to his parents' relationship.

Tuck avoided him which was hurtful, but the young man was too stubborn to try to talk the friar round and Little John stayed by his side so he never felt too lonely while he continued to travel around the villages of Nottingham and Yorkshire dispensing the sheriff's justice.

Tuck's words in Mirfield played on his mind, though. Maybe the money and power had gone to his head, for he *had* become basically a tax collector. Yes, the people he evicted had been given fair time to repay their debts but...the friar was right – this wasn't what Robin wanted to do with his life. If he was going to be a lawman he wanted to take down truly wicked men, not humble villagers fallen on hard times.

He knew John didn't enjoy their work either, but the giant was too loyal to his best friend to make much of a fuss. Robin had no doubt he would eventually get fed up with it though, and then what? Would he lose John's friendship as he seemed to have lost Tuck's?

And Matilda...

She'd given up haranguing him over his work, but she'd also given up sharing his bed. They'd talk about Arthur, or other family matters whenever Robin was home, but that was the extent of their relationship and it shocked him to realise he was glad.

Not glad that they'd drifted apart, just relieved not to have her complaining all the time.

Their son had fallen asleep early that night – his eyes rolling in his head as Matilda tried to get him to eat the vegetable soup she'd made for dinner and Robin decided to go out to the alehouse again. He didn't like being alone with his wife any more – it was awkward, as she tutted or huffed to herself whenever he did anything – so he'd taken himself off without a word.

Tuck was there but he simply nodded a half-hearted greeting to his one-time captain and Robin scanned the room, hoping John would be there. He wasn't, of course, so he joined a couple of other locals he'd grown up with. Good men who had a lot of respect for Robin, but, as he nursed his second ale he found himself completely outside their good-natured conversation.

The men spoke of their wives, their work, the mildness of the summer that year and any number of other mundane topics which the former wolf's head felt bored and even mildly irritated by, and he found himself drifting off into his own thoughts as he gazed into his ale mug.

Times when Matilda had spoken harshly to him filled his memory. Things she'd said during their many arguments about him being a terrible husband and father...

He hated her, he thought. He'd be better off without her.

A sigh escaped his lips and he sipped his ale, oblivious to the roars of ribald laughter from the men beside him sharing some inane joke.

No, he didn't hate his wife – he loved her as much as he ever had. He just wanted things to go back to normal between them, so they could enjoy their life with Arthur as they'd always wanted.

He'd been too stubborn – too selfish, he admitted – to see it before, and it had taken wise old Friar Tuck to finally get through to him, but now he knew what he should do.

In the morning he'd ride to Nottingham and ask Sir Henry to find him a different job. Even if it was simply as one of the sergeants in his guard.

Matilda would be pleased and all Robin's troubles would be over.

With a grin on his handsome face the big lawman drained the last of his and ale stood up, smiling a farewell to his companions. He even managed to catch Tuck's eye and smiled broadly at his erstwhile friend as he paid one last visit to the landlord before heading home to bed.

The friar would appreciate the free ale Robin had paid for, there was no doubt about that. It was the least he could do since the portly clergyman had doubtless saved his marriage.

As he strode towards the door with a glad heart a small man bustled up to him, an angry look on his round, weather-beaten face.

"Hood! Hood, here!"

The little man waved angrily at him as he approached through the crowd of drinkers and Robin recognised him as one of the village carpenters, although for the life of him he couldn't remember the fellow's name.

"Well met, my friend," the bailiff smiled, nodding a greeting, but the carpenter glared at him in return and stood before him, blocking his way to the door.

"Don't give me that bollocks. Do you know who I am?"

"Aye. You're..." he trailed off into an embarrassing silence, as everyone in the place noticed the confrontation and stopped their own conversations to watch the excitement.

"I'm a cousin of Martin Black, you know? The landlord of the Boar's Head in Dewsbury."

Robin felt the eyes of everyone in the place on him as he remembered the man he'd evicted not that long ago.

"Aye, I remember him. What about it?"

Without even being conscious of it he'd straightened up and let his hand fall to the sword that he wore at his waist but the angry man before him was unimpressed.

"I thought you'd like to know," the carpenter's voice rang out over the expectant silence, "that Martin's wife just died of fever. They'd been forced to sleep outdoors after you evicted them and that heavy rain we had last week got into her body and killed her."

Robin didn't say anything and neither did anyone else for a time. At last the furious carpenter stepped in even closer to the bailiff and pointed a finger up at his face.

"I hope you're fucking proud of yourself."

For a while Robin simply stood looking at the man.

What could he say? Eventually he muttered an apology and pushed past the carpenter as half the village watched, to make his way out into the night and home, walking as if there was a heavy weight on his shoulders.

* * *

"I'd like to speak to you about the work you've got me and John doing," Robin started but Sir Henry broke in distractedly as he watched the cloudless sky.

"I'm glad you visited me today, because I wanted to speak to you too. I have a new job for you and the giant to undertake, if you think you're able." He adjusted the leather gauntlet on his right arm and shouted some encouragement to an older member of the hunting party before turning back to Robin. "I think it will be perfect for you. Come."

It was a fine day – the sky was sunny but not cloudless and a cool breeze stopped it from being oppressive. A perfect day for the sheriff to indulge in one of his favourite hobbies with some friends and a few retainers: falconry.

Robin followed, gazing at Sir Henry as they followed the bird in the sky overhead, hoping his superior wasn't going to send him to collect more rents from some merchant. He hadn't told Matilda what he planned before he travelled down here but his mind was made up, no matter what the sheriff said.

"Have you heard of the outlaws in Barnsdale recently?" De Faucumberg asked, surprising Robin completely.

"Not in particular. I mean, aye, I've heard of them, there's always outlaws about the place. Any traveller knows to be wary when using the roads around here."

"You haven't heard of – or noticed – any increase in their activities in recent weeks then?"

Robin thought a moment then shook his head. "No. Should I have?"

The sheriff made a fist with his left, ungloved hand, gleeful as he noticed a pair of wood pigeons that his falcon was lining itself up to attack.

"Your gang was something of a rarity," he said over his shoulder, eyes still on the sky. "Around two dozen men united under one leader. Go on, my beauty. Watch this Robin – it's incredible. In a dive, the falcon is the fastest bird in the world you know?"

The party stopped as the bird of prey dropped out of the sky like a stone, aiming for one of the two pigeons. It hammered into the target and a handful of feathers exploded as the falcon carried its prize away, pecking downwards once with its powerful beak and killing the unfortunate pigeon before carrying it down to the ground.

"Yes! That's another one for the pot."

De Faucumberg glanced at the servants but they were already heading towards the falcon's landing site.

"I hope they hurry up. There's been times I've had birds take their kill away up into the trees, gorge themselves, then fall asleep high up in the branches. You can't get them down for hours!"

He laughed as if he'd just told a hysterical joke then, noticing Robin's bemused expression, forced himself to carry on with the previous line of conversation.

"Most gangs of cut-throats and robbers are small in number and tend not to cause too much trouble before they try to steal from the wrong person and find themselves dead in a ditch somewhere. Apart from you – and your predecessor Adam Bell before you of course – there's been no-one I can think of who's managed to unite any significant number of lawless men into one cohesive whole."

"Fulk Fitzwarine?" Robin suggested.

"That was a hundred years ago," de Faucumberg waved his gloved hand dismissively. "I'm talking about recently."

The sheriff's huntsman had reached the falcon by now

and managed to coax it away from its kill with a morsel of raw meat. Sir Henry whistled and the falcon swooped towards them, making Robin flinch involuntarily but the graceful, majestic bird landed perfectly on the sheriff's hand and accepted another bloody titbit in reward for its obedience.

"It seems we have a new Robin Hood," de Faucumberg said as he expertly hooded the falcon to keep it calm, the grin on his face at his pet's success belying the dread import of his words. "Someone is uniting the outlaws of Barnsdale again, and he doesn't have the morals you – or even Adam Bell – had."

"What do you mean?"

"Reports from villages nearby suggest at least three smaller outlaw gangs have joined forces. This larger group have robbed half-a-dozen parties making their way through the forest. Only one person survived – a young girl who must have been extremely fit, for she was able to outrun her pursuers and make it to safety. Which is just as well...God knows what the wolf's heads might have done to her."

"I can guess," Robin growled. "What about the other people they robbed?"

The sheriff handed his falcon over to the head huntsman and waved the man away before turning and making his way across the field towards the city gates as he undid the laces on the bulky glove.

"Merchants and clergymen but also a couple of simple folk going from one village to another on errands. As I say, the outlaws killed them all. The girl who escaped was sure one man was in charge."

"Description?"

De Faucumberg shrugged. "She was terrified and looking to make her escape before they had their way with her so she wasn't the most observant witness. All she could say was the fellow was big – about your size I suppose, with straw coloured hair. He smiled the whole time too, which she found unnerving, given the situation."

Robin's mind filled with the image of the man who'd orchestrated the madness in Holmfirth. The description fitted but...well, it could also describe a thousand men dotted around the north of England.

"So what do we do?"

The sheriff stopped in his tracks and spread his arms wide. "What in God's name do you think I brought you here for? You and your giant friend will need to find these outlaws and bring them in. It should be more interesting than collecting rents from folk, eh? If a tad more dangerous...But you're used to that. You and John are the best men for this with your knowledge of the forest and how to survive out there."

Robin nodded and followed de Faucumberg who'd moved off again, his stride long as he headed for some cool wine and fresh bread.

"I'll need more men," he said. "The two of us can't take on a whole force of outlaws by ourselves."

"Yes, yes, I know that. You know my garrison by now. Select a dozen of them – clear it with their captain first mind you – then get after these bastards." He glared over his shoulder at the young lawman. "I thought all this nonsense was behind me once I'd dealt with your lot. I can't be doing with it all over again, so destroy these scum as fast as possible."

Robin's face broke into a small smile as he trailed after the sheriff. This was ideal. He was finally going to do a job that was worthwhile. Matilda would be happy!

CHAPTER SIX

Mark had been surprised to find their new companions were even more uncompromising than he was himself. Well, the leader, Philip, was at least. The giant, Eoin, simply did as he was told, even when you could see in his eyes that he didn't really want to.

He followed orders though, no matter what, and that told Mark that Philip was a man to keep an eye on. A man not to turn your back on…

When they'd first joined forces, just the four of them, they robbed a young couple who'd been unfortunate enough to walk too close to the new gang's camp.

The pair looked no more than fifteen years old, and carried little of value which irritated Mark, who hated wasting his time for nothing. He punched the young lad a few times, broke his nose and knocked out a couple of teeth, then told Ivo and the other three to let the couple go on their way.

But his new companion, Philip, had surprised him.

Pulling his dagger from its sheath the newcomer to Barnsdale had slammed it into the youngster's back half-a-dozen times, his face bland in its murderous concentration.

Even Eoin looked stunned, while Mark and Ivo exchanged shocked glances. They had no problems with killing the folk they robbed, but only if their targets fought back. Murder was a sure way to bring the full force of the law down on you.

The girl was too stunned, and terrified, to attempt any escape then. She simply crumpled onto the soft grass beside her dead young friend, a high keening escaping her lips.

"Go and see if you can catch us a hare or two for dinner," Philip said to Eoin, who looked up from the bloody corpse, eyes wide in surprise and confusion.

"Off you go, big man," Philip smiled. "My belly's rumbling and I'm sure our new mates are hungry too. Aren't you?"

Eoin didn't reply but his mouth worked soundlessly, as if he wanted to say something but couldn't find a way to articulate it.

The girl's howls had dropped to a low sobbing by now, her face hidden against the neck of her dead friend and, when Eoin's eyes fixed upon her again Philip repeated, harshly, "Go and catch us something for dinner. Now."

Mark watched the giant outlaw as he struggled within himself, but, eventually, the big man nodded and lumbered off into the trees.

The crying girl was oblivious to what was going on, and Philip waited a few moments until the sounds of undergrowth being brushed aside faded away, then he grinned at Mark and undid the laces of his hose.

"Hold her down. I'm not going after you two dirty bastards have had a turn."

The girl wasn't Mark's type. She was too young, too skinny, and her face was covered in tears and snot. But he hadn't emptied his balls in weeks so, once Philip was finished, he'd taken his own turn. By the time Ivo had spilt his seed inside her her anguished cries had dropped to no more than a whimper.

And then Philip had told him to shut her up.

"She's no threat," Mark shrugged, leaving go of her wrists as Ivo stood up, a satisfied smile filling his toothless mouth. "We can let her be on her way."

Philip's ever-present smile disappeared just as the sun started to dip beneath the horizon, the shadows giving his face an ethereal, unpleasant look as he stared directly at the smaller man.

"She knows what we look like. Kill her."

Ivo glanced over at Mark, a worried expression on his

seamed face.

"I'm not killing her," the little outlaw shook his head. "We've had her way with her, you've stabbed her young man to death, and she's not a threat to us." He placed a hand on the hilt of his dagger and spread his legs. "Men are one thing, but I won't kill a young lass."

The girl's tear-streaked face was expressionless as she watched the exchange. Her spirit had been broken by her ordeal but her eyes widened as she saw Philip shrug, draw his sword and step forward to slide the point deep into her belly.

Mark knew better than to react to the agonized scream that tore through the forest then. He had no wish to show any sign of weakness to this man he'd chosen to join up with. Ivo, too, remained silent but his jaw clenched as he watched the girl's blood spill from the gaping wound onto the rich green grass of the forest floor.

"I don't know how you managed to survive this long," Philip growled, the smile slowly returning to his face as he withdrew the blade and wiped the bloodied tip clean on the girl's clothing before pointing it in their direction. "You're soft." He spoke to both of them but his eyes stayed fixed on Mark who bristled at the insult but didn't know how to reply.

"I'm away back to the camp; it's getting cold and Eoin will be along with something for the pot soon, no doubt. At least I know I can count on him."

He spat that final barb then made his way through the foliage to their camp-site as if he hadn't a care in the world, leaving Mark and Ivo to stand in his wake, wondering what the hell they'd got themselves into.

The girl was in obvious agony although she seemed unable to make a sound by now, and Mark knew she'd die a long, lingering death. He wondered if that had been Philip's intent and the thought made him shudder.

And yet her eyes seemed to accuse *him*, as if it had been

he, Mark, who'd run her through with his blade!

He couldn't stand her agonized glare any longer so he followed Philip into the bushes, back to camp, Ivo trailing at his heels as the young girl's gasps faded into the forest behind them.

Mark was silent as they walked, stunned by the brutality of their new companion. No good would come of this he was sure – the law would hear of it and come looking for them.

He sighed as the darkness drew in, battering foliage aside as he walked. Why did bad things always happen to *him*?

That had all taken place a few weeks ago, and since then their gang had grown, as Philip welcomed anyone they found living in the forest into their ranks without question.

The hierarchy, to Mark's fury, had slowly become clear: Philip was the leader now, at the top of the pile, with the lumbering form of Eoin to back him up, while everyone else – including Mark and Ivo – were simply there to do as they were told.

The little wolf's head would have left and gone back to his old haunts around Horbury, but he had a strange sense that staying with Philip would lead to interesting opportunities to make money. If nothing came of it, he thought, he'd simply knife the smirking bastard in the back and usurp his position.

"What are you thinking about?"

The familiar voice broke in on his reverie and Mark glanced up guiltily, wondering how the hell Philip had managed to creep up on him so quietly.

"Nothing," he muttered, and knew Philip could see through the lie.

But his new leader simply smiled down at him. "Well then, since you're not busy, why don't you and Ivo go and see if you can catch us something for dinner? I'm sick of bread and mouldy cheese." He gestured to a tree nearby, against which two fishing poles were resting. "Trout would make a nice change for everyone, don't you think?"

Mark bristled, enraged at the fact this strange newcomer to the area was giving him orders, but the smile never left Philip's face and Mark knew instinctively it would be a terrible mistake to challenge him now. Too many of the recent recruits to their group supported him, for some unfathomable reason. And there was still the threat of Eoin, who sat close-by, smiling stupidly as a couple of men – southerners from their accent – sang a ribald rhyme.

"Aye, good idea," Mark returned Philip's smile and rose nimbly to his feet. "I'm sick of bread and cheese myself. I'll take Ivo – and a skin of ale! – with me."

"Excellent. Just be careful you don't fall in."

With a humourless laugh, Philip moved away and joined in with the southerner's rhyme, leaving Mark to glare at him, wondering how he knew the words to their song.

"Ivo! Come on, we're going fishing."

For now he'd take orders, and see how things turned out.

* * *

Matilda groaned in pleasure.

"Shh, you'll wake Arthur," Robin whispered, and she returned his smile contentedly.

He'd returned from Nottingham that afternoon in a good mood, and his manner reminded her so much of the young man she'd fallen in love with that she'd found herself thawing towards him.

They'd shared a meal of fish with bread and ale before Robin brought out a toy he'd bought in the big city for Arthur. It was a carved wooden knight, complete with horse and lance. The little figurines had fired the lad's imagination and he'd spent the evening chasing his laughing father about the house.

When the little boy had finally fallen asleep they

finished the last of the recent batch of ale Matilda had brewed then Robin asked how her day had been. When she complained, mostly in jest, about how hard it was to help her father fletch arrows while Arthur was being wild Robin surprised her by offering to massage her back.

Now she lay on their bed – which was a fine one since they were no peasants – on her stomach, while Robin straddled her legs and used his strong hands to knead the knots and tension from her shoulder blades.

She turned her head to the side and looked up at him from one eye. "That's nice. You should do this more often."

His hands moved down to the small of her back, still gently squeezing and her legs jerked at the almost ticklish sensation that shot wonderfully through her body.

"Oh, yes, that feels good..."

He continued for a while, just kneading the flesh and muscles of his wife's back before he moved down to her thighs and, inevitably, her buttocks, which were firm and lean like the rest of her. She knew there would be an ever increasing bulge in his hose and it made her grin like a naughty teenager.

"What's come over you anyway?" she asked in a low, contented voice. "You've barely spoken to me for days and now this?"

For a time he didn't reply, just continued to massage her body, every so often surreptitiously squeezing her backside before moving back to her thighs or shoulders.

"I'm fed up with us arguing all the time," he said, at last. "I dread coming home to you every day. I know –" he stopped her harsh reply before she could open her mouth "– it's as much my fault as it is yours. Maybe mostly mine," he finished, somewhat sheepishly, no doubt in response to the fact she hadn't raised her lowered eyebrows yet.

"So this is your solution?" Matilda rolled onto her back

beneath him and met his gaze. "Ply me with drink and give me a rub-down?"

Her smock had fallen open when she turned over and Robin's hands, seemingly of their own volition, moved up to grasp her breasts softly. His fingers squeezed lovingly and, again, she felt a tingle course through her body.

It had been so long since they'd made love.

"You'll be glad to hear I've got a new job," he mumbled, bending to kiss her neck. "I won't be going from village to village collecting taxes any more."

"That's good," she smiled, putting her feet around him and pressing them down on his backside so she could feel him against her. "I'm glad."

He pressed his mouth against hers, kissing her again, and she forced her tongue into his mouth, now as desperate as he was to end their recent chastity.

"There's a new gang of outlaws in Barnsdale," he whispered, finally squeezing himself between Matilda's legs. "John and I are going to hunt them down."

Matilda felt as if someone had walked into the room and thrown a bucket of ice water into her face.

She stiffened but, for a few moments Robin didn't notice, as he continued thrusting into her unresponsive body.

"You're what?"

He spasmed and went limp, then, finally raised his head and, in the flickering orange glow from the fire in the hearth, looked at her in surprise.

"We're going after these outlaws," he said, his hand still caressing Matilda's nipple, but he sensed the change in the mood and his already softening manhood slipped out of her as he leaned back on one arm and watched her, his face a mask of confusion. "They're robbing people and raping women. They're scum," he finished, his words trailing off.

"So you've gone from harassing poor men and women to chasing after supposed murderers and rapists? And you think I'll be glad to hear it?" She sat up but kept her voice low – controlled – so she'd not wake their sleeping son who lay in the bed beside them.

Robin simply stared at her. The puzzlement evident in his eyes might, at one time, have elicited pity in her – a loving sympathy at his manly stupidity.

Now it just made her angry.

"Do you not remember where you were a few short years ago? Where we both were?"

"But –"

"But nothing," she hissed, slapping a hand onto her naked thigh. "Why would you accept this job? I assume it was Sir Henry's idea?"

He nodded, but the softness had started to leave his expression as his own anger bubbled to the surface.

"Why wouldn't I go after a gang of rapists for fuck sake? Who better to hunt them down than me and John, who know the forest so well? Or do you think we should just let them go around killing people? What's the problem here? Why do you have to complain about everything I do?"

"Keep your voice down," Matilda growled, glancing over at the sleeping Arthur who snuffled and rolled slightly at his father's enraged tone. "We were both outlaws not that long ago. Didn't de Faucumberg and Sir Guy of Gisbourne and all the other nobles around here spread rumours about us being brutal murderers? Didn't they say Will was a rapist? That you yourself had defiled a clergyman in an ungodly way?"

Robin waved his hand dismissively but Matilda carried on, shaking her head as if her husband was an imbecile. "That's what they do: they *lie*. So people like you won't help the outlaws."

"I know Sir Henry well now," Robin retorted, shaking his head. "He's not making this story up. Those men are committing crimes against normal people. Crimes none of my men would ever have contemplated. Well, maybe Matt

Groves," he ended, doubtfully, and Matilda jumped on the admission.

"So maybe these new outlaws have some sick bastard like Matt in their group. Are you going to punish them all for his crimes? Would that have been fair if Gisbourne had cut *your* face apart because Matt had raped some woman or young Gareth had stabbed some merchant? Are you going to destroy these men when you don't know a thing about them? When chances are they're just normal men fallen on hard times, *like you were?*"

They'd moved as far apart from each other as they could, and Matilda wrapped the bedclothes around herself while Robin sat, still naked, muscles taut, the low firelight glinting in his brown eyes.

"They're *not* like us," he said, finally, softly. "You know what we were like. We were good men."

"Who robbed priests and bishops and killed boys and ate children." She shook her head at his naivety. "Who knows where the reality ends and the stories begin? Yes, *we* do," she stopped his reply with a curt gesture, "but the people of Nottingham don't. The people of Hathersage don't. Or the folk in Penyston. All they know is what they hear from the minstrels, and most of the time those bastards are singing songs in order to please the nobles, so they'll toss them a coin or two." She lifted her legs around off the bed and placed her feet onto the rushes on the floor.

Robin, in contrast to his wife's movement, lay down and pulled the blanket over himself roughly, almost sending Matilda flying. He turned his back on her.

"So John and I will hunt them down and find out the truth," he said, his voice low, harsh and distant. He blew out the candle that flickered softly on the shelf next to him, sending angry, racing shadows across the still dimly fire-lit room. "Good night."

For a short while Matilda simply sat, deep in thought, before she lay back down and tried to get some sleep. The fire burned itself out and the room around her became dim, but, beside her, a low, contented snoring escaped Robin's lips.

She gritted her teeth and vowed never to speak to him again, as tears spilled from her eyes.

She didn't even know why she was crying.

CHAPTER SEVEN

"You lot ready?" Robin shouted irritably at the sheriff's men who'd accompanied him back to Wakefield and spent an uncomfortable night on the floor of the alehouse while he'd gone home to Matilda.

They looked tired and sore from their night's rest, but even so Robin wished he'd stayed with them instead of with his wife.

"Aye, we're ready, sir," one of the soldiers replied, hauling himself onto his mount's back with a grunt. "Lead the way."

Robin nodded and turned to Little John. "We still agreed Ossete is the best place to start looking for the outlaws?"

The two men had discussed a plan of action when they'd left the sheriff and journeyed home, and it seemed sensible to begin their investigation in the last place the outlaws had been reported.

"As good a place as any," John said. "Although you know as well as I do, they've probably moved their camp since that last report. It was over a week ago after all; they'd have to be mad to hang around there since the girl escaped to tell what they'd done."

"All right then, let's go."

He kicked his heels and led the way east, grim-faced, as John and the rest of the men followed.

They rode in silence for a time, pushing their mounts hard along the road which was well-maintained and allowed them to make good time. As the sun reached its zenith, though, John moved alongside his captain and shouted over the wind rushing past them.

"What's wrong?"

Robin jerked in surprise, not noticing John beside him until the big man spoke, then he turned his attention back to the road.

"Just some things Matilda said last night." He rode on for a while and John remained silent.

"We were outlaws ourselves not so long ago," he continued, at last. "Just like these men. Are we going to ride into their camp and cut them down without even hearing their side of the story? What if they're all innocent – or at least good – men fallen on hard times? Just as we were."

They'd slowed their horses' pace to make conversing easier but, even so, the countryside seemed to whip past as they neared the little village of Ossete which was by now visible on the horizon.

"I don't remember ever raping anyone," John said.

"Maybe these men didn't either. Maybe the stories have been exaggerated – just as they were when people told tales about us."

For a while John didn't reply, but they were almost at their destination and he was clearly confused.

"So what are you saying? We just let them go about their business? Why are we even here then?"

"I'm just saying we should give these outlaws time to state their case." He raised himself in his stirrups and turned to look at the soldiers following close behind. "You hear that? No-one looses an arrow until I say so. I want to find out what the leader of these men has to say."

"Assuming we even find them," John growled, not expecting his words to be heard.

"We'll find them," Robin vowed. "I'll make sure of it."

They rode into Ossete, villagers scattering at their approach as they spotted the blue livery worn by the sheriff's soldiers, although both John and Robin wore their own brown cloaks as they always did.

A visit from Sir Henry de Faucumberg's men could only mean trouble.

Robin dismounted and told his men to wait on the

outskirts of the place. So many horses riding through the cramped confines of Ossete wasn't a good idea.

"Come on," he waved to John. "The alehouse will be the best place to start, I'll wager. Men living rough in the forest need arrows and food but the most important thing is their drink."

Both lawmen knew the layout of the village well enough; they'd been there a number of times over the years, both as outlaws and, in more recent months on the sheriff's business. The alehouse was, as its name suggested, no more than a single-storey dwelling, although slightly larger than most of the others in the area.

One old man sat outside on a rickety bench, mug in hand and a contented smile on his face as the warm breeze blew through his thinning grey hair.

Robin looked at John and shrugged. Might as well start their search right here.

"Well met, friend," he smiled down at the seated villager. "Enjoying the sunshine, eh? Can't beat a warm day and a mug of ale."

The elderly man raised his mug and grinned, revealing a mouth completely devoid of teeth. "You got that right, lad," he gurned. "Get yourselves a drink and join me."

Robin shook his head. "We can't stay long, but I'll stand you an ale if you can help us. You heard of the gang of outlaws hiding out around here?"

The man might have been old but his eyes were still bright and clear and he met Robin's gaze with a shake of his head. "Seen them about, aye, but I don't know anything about them."

"Who did you see?" Robin asked. "Can you describe them for us? These men are extremely dangerous – rapists and murderers. Not the type you'd welcome into the village if you knew what they were about."

The man shrugged and took a long pull of his ale. "I care nothing for the business of outlaws. I might have stood up to them when I was younger and had a family but they're all dead now. The world passes me by as I sit here with my drink and that's the way I like it." He looked back up at Robin. "If these men are as dangerous as you say they are, they'd kill me if I told you anything about them. But I don't know anything anyway lads, sorry."

Robin sighed, knowing this was going to be the story they heard from the vast majority of people they questioned here. Without bribing or torturing people there wasn't much he could do to squeeze information from the nervous locals.

Without another word Robin pulled open the door to the alehouse and led John inside, where the landlord looked up and forced a smile onto his face at the sight of his two huge, dangerous-looking customers.

"Ale?" the man asked. "Freshly brewed yesterday."

"Aye," John rumbled. "My throat's as dry as the soles of a Saracen's shoes."

The landlord thought about that for a moment, trying to work out the apparent joke, then, giving up, poured two mugs for them.

"I'll cut straight to the point," Robin said, after he'd taken a drink. "We need to find the outlaws that were last reported around here. You must have seen them. I know how it works since I was a wolf's head myself for long enough; they'll have been in here looking to buy a large quantity of ale."

He watched the landlord for any reaction to his words and, from the man's darting eyes it was obvious the outlaws *had* visited him.

"If you know how it works," the man finally said, softly, "you'll know they threatened to come back and burn my place down if I spoke to the law about them."

Robin nodded. Threats had been a tactic he'd never really had to use as a wolf's head, because he'd joined an established and well-respected – feared – gang. Everyone around the north of the country knew them. But these newcomers had to protect themselves somehow, and violence was their most obvious, and effective, tool.

"Hopefully they won't be around much longer to burn anyone's place down," Robin said. "Can you give us anything? Descriptions? Any idea of where they might be based? Or is there anyone else in the village who might be able to offer us more information? Your headman maybe?"

The landlord shrugged. "I can't tell you anything other than they left the village by the south road, so their camp is probably in that general direction."

"Narrows it down a bit," Robin nodded, ignoring the sarcastic grunt from John who held out his mug to the landlord, hoping for a refill.

"Thanks for your time then." Robin reached out and grabbed the refilled mug before John could take it from the landlord. "I want you with a clear head, in case we do stumble across those outlaws," he smiled, and without another word walked out through the door, back into the blazing sunshine.

"Here, old one."

The man on the bench grinned and took the mug from Robin's hand, nodding his thanks as the two lawmen started off, heading along the road to see the headman.

"Be careful, lads."

They stopped, turning back to look at the elderly villager who was wiping froth from his seamed mouth and chin.

"One of those outlaws is almost as big as you." He gestured with the mug towards John and turned away to stare at the scene in front of him, as children played and women walked past carrying soaking wet clothes they'd been washing in the stream.

A man almost as big as Little John. It had to be the second man who'd escaped from them at Holmfirth; they were on the right track then. Robin waved his thanks for the little crumb of information, and resumed the walk to the headman's house.

The headman proved no more helpful than the landlord, offering provisions for their search but no useful information. Robin couldn't tell if the man was too scared to tell what he knew, or if he really didn't have anything to tell them. Yes, he said, a large force of men had visited their village two or three times recently but they'd behaved themselves and spent money which the locals were happy enough to take. Where their camp might be he had no idea, but they always rode to the south, just as the landlord at the alehouse had attested.

The sun was still high in the sky as they made their way back to their mounts and the rest of the men so Robin decided they might as well head along the main road in the direction of Netherton. Perhaps the outlaws would have left some trace of their presence along the way.

"Or maybe they'll just cut us down as we ride," John groused, his usual good humour sorely tested by their dangerous hunt.

"Maybe," Robin agreed. "But with fourteen well armed and armoured soldiers in our party it'll be a foolhardy outlaw leader that orders an attack on us."

"You would have."

Robin had to smile at that. "Aye, perhaps I would. But I wasn't followed by a rabble, was I? I was blessed with men like you, Will and Stephen to back me up. I'm hoping these outlaws we're after have no such men in their ranks."

John grunted thoughtfully. "Let's hope so." Then, lowering his voice and shaking his big bearded head, "I wish we had Will and the Hospitaller with us now. These lads are all right but I'd be happier with our friends beside us."

Robin shrugged. Will Scarlet was living in Wakefield as a simple farmer with his daughter Beth, while Stephen, the Hospitaller sergeant, had, the last they'd heard, taken a job as a bodyguard to a wealthy merchant in Leeds. Ever since his own Order made him outcast he'd been unable to settle for long and, chances were, he'd moved on from that town already.

They rode in contemplative silence for a time, eyes scanning the foliage that skirted the mostly well-maintained road, thinking back to their adventures as outlaws themselves.

"Maybe we should have brought fewer men with us." John muttered, eyes casting about the dense foliage that fringed the old road. "This group of wolf's heads can't be much more than a dozen men – you really think they'll attack us?"

The question didn't need an answer and Robin remained silent. John was probably right but until they had a better idea of the size and organisation of the outlaw gang he didn't want to take any chances. Aye, just the two of them riding through the forest would probably guarantee the outlaws would show themselves but it could also be suicidal.

He wanted to stop these men but not die in the process.

* * *

"I know those two."

Mark followed Philip's nod, gently shifting a branch to the side to get a better view of the travellers. He shook his head and allowed the thick leaves to hide him again.

"So do I. Robin Hood and John Little."

"That's the bastards that chased us out of Holmfirth," Philip said.

"And now they've come to chase us out of Barnsdale."

"I don't think so. Not this time. Come on, let's get the rest of the men."

It had only been a couple of weeks since Mark and Ivo joined forces with Philip and Eoin, but even in that short

71

space of time they'd managed to recruit more than half-a-dozen other outlaws to their cause. Men that were living in the greenwood around Horbury and shared the same suppliers as Mark heard the call and answered it. Word spread fast when it was known there was a new gang looking for members. Of course, any newcomers had to believe they were joining a group that could make their lot better than it was – make them richer in other words. And Philip's strange charisma, combined with Mark's well-known ferocity, convinced those new recruits.

So far, they'd only robbed a handful of poor, basically defenceless travellers. Now, Philip apparently saw a chance to put their gang members to good use and hurried off back towards their nearby camp-site.

Mark followed as fast as he could without making any noise that would alert the lawmen to their presence. Surely Philip didn't plan on ambushing Robin Hood? Even Philip wasn't that mad.

Was he?

CHAPTER EIGHT

Robin spotted the man in the road ahead before anyone else, and he instinctively pulled his hunting bow from its place on his horse's saddle and took the string from its little pouch.

"Hold," he muttered, bringing his mount to a stop and raising a hand. "There's someone on the road. Might be nothing but we better be prepared." He turned and gestured to Thomas. "You and those three – dismount and flank me and John. Have an arrow nocked." He slipped out of his own saddle, straddling his bow to string it, and John followed his lead.

"The rest of you stay on your horses but keep twenty paces back from us. And draw your swords and shields. Watch the trees as well as the road behind and in front – if the outlaws have an ambuscade prepared they'll hit us from every side."

He turned to John with a small smile. "Ready, big man?"

"Aye, let's go and see what this prick wants."

One of the sheriff's men took their mounts, along with the other archers', and tethered them to trees nearby.

"Glad I wore my helmet and this," Robin said, pulling back his cloak and patting the chain mail he'd donned that morning in place of his usual, battered old gambeson.

John laughed. "That won't stop an arrow if it hits properly. You'd be as well bollock naked."

"Thanks for that insight," Robin growled, raising an eyebrow irritably. "I feel much better about meeting this fellow now."

John's words certainly had an element of truth to them but Robin knew his giant friend had also chosen to wear a coat of mail under his brown tunic that day. They'd need any advantage they could get when it came to facing these outlaws, of that he was certain.

"Christ above, it's him right enough – that bastard from Holmfirth. The one that hanged the priest."

John squinted – his eyesight wasn't as good as his younger leader's – before nodding agreement. "Aye, looks like it. On his own too. I think it's safe to say we're about to be attacked."

Robin was stunned at the outlaw's confidence. Surely he hadn't managed to rally much more than a dozen men, and those surely just the usual untrained rabble that lived rough in the forest. Yet there the man stood, blocking their way, a little smile on his seamed face and again Robin felt a pang of familiarity.

"Are we just going to walk into his trap?" John hissed. "There's probably longbowmen hiding in the trees ready to pick us off."

Robin took in the terrain and mentally kicked himself. The outlaw had chosen his spot well.

Ahead, where the man stood, the road narrowed, and a massive fallen log provided cover should the outlaw find himself attacked by Robin's archers. To the sides the foliage was thick and John was undoubtedly correct in suggesting bowmen were concealed there.

Robin again lifted a hand and brought his party to a halt, wondering how best to proceed. The sensible thing to do would be turn around and avoid the outlaw altogether until they could meet the man in a better position. But Robin didn't feel like running away – he wanted to talk to this man and find out his story, although, knowing it was the murdering scum from Holmfirth told him pretty much everything he needed to know.

Still, he couldn't lead John and the sheriff's men into such an obvious trap.

"Dismount, all of you." He was glad to see the soldiers instantly follow his order. They were a formidable-looking bunch in their armour and blue surcoats, weapons at the ready, and he nodded in satisfaction. "You three," he swept his hand around to encompass the men on the right. "Head into the trees and clear out whoever you find there. Keep your shields up, don't be complacent and stop moving forward when I do." He gestured again, this time to the men on the far left. "You three take the other side and clear that." If there *were* bowmen hidden in the foliage they'd find it much harder hitting Robin's men if they came through the trees rather than out in the open road. "The rest of you, form a line in front of me and John. Hold your shields up, aye, like that. Good."

Only Thomas and his archers were left now and they took up positions flanking Robin and John as the whole party again started forward, towards the solitary outlaw who watched the whole thing with that strange smile on his lips.

"Very impressive." The wolf's head nodded and waved a greeting at Robin. "We meet again. Only this time I have the upper hand."

"Is that right?" Robin replied, listening intently for any signs of conflict in the trees either side of the road. "I don't think so. Your little band of rapists is outnumbered. Who are you?"

The man placed a foot on the fallen log and spread his arms wide. "Depends who you ask. The people of Holmfirth would probably tell you I'm Satan himself, or maybe one of his demons. But most people call me Philip."

Robin nodded grimly. "Well, Philip, we've heard reports of you and your mates raping and murdering travellers. Is that true?"

The outlaw shrugged expansively, his every move apparently calculated to be as infuriating a possible for the lawmen who couldn't believe the man's confidence.

"Bastard reminds me of you," John grunted. "Full of himself."

"He's a fucking arsehole," Thomas broke in. "Why don't we just fill him with iron? Me and the lads could hit him from here, easy."

Robin ignored their comments, the nagging feeling that he knew this man from somewhere else playing on his mind as he wondered what to do next.

"I know who you are," Philip said. "The famous Robin Hood. You're my inspiration." He cackled at that but it was a deeply unpleasant sound; not at all contagious. "I'm going to lead my merry men all around Yorkshire taking what I want and there's not a fucking thing the law – that's you – can do about it. My gang is growing every day and pretty soon I'll have an army."

Robin shook his head and returned Philip's smile. "An army of scum. The dregs of society." The smile fell from his face to be replaced by a furious glare. "You and your gang are *nothing* like me. My men were hard, trained soldiers. Mercenaries who'd fought in the Holy Land. Hospitaller sergeants-at-arms that had fought side-by-side with Templar knights. Warriors! We were able to evade capture because we knew how to hide in the forest but also how to fight better than the men that came after us. You and your rabble are a pathetic collection of criminals, and I'll not rest until every last one of you is swinging from the gallows outside the gates of Nottingham."

Philip simply stared at him, the smile undiminished. Eventually, Robin looked away, breaking the man's gaze and cursing himself for it, but it seemed like the crazed outlaw was in some trance.

"Damn it, I'm sure I know him from somewhere," he muttered to John, who nodded slowly.

"Aye, I get the same feeling." He stared at the wolf's head for a moment then shrugged. "Kind of looks like Matt Groves doesn't he?"

A chill flowed through Robin as he realised John was right. The thinning dirty-blonde hair, the eyes, the timbre of his voice...He thought back, searching his memory for times he'd actually shared a conversation with Groves, but the two men had never got on. After leaving their gang Matt had killed Robin's childhood friend Much and then become Sir Guy of Gisbourne's lieutenant. He'd finally murdered their minstrel friend Allan-a-Dale before being captured by the sheriff.

It had been a satisfying day when Robin watched the bastard hang.

"Matt had a brother," John continued, oblivious to his friend's musings. "I remember him telling a tale about his childhood once. His da beat them bloody one day and his big brother fought back then disappeared or something. I don't remember the whole story – Tuck would know better than me – but maybe that's him."

"Philip," Robin shouted. "You have a brother? Matt?"

For the first time the outlaw's smile faded and his face became hard, but only for a moment before he regained control and the smirk returned. "I don't think so," he replied. "Why d'you ask?"

"Matt Groves was a member of my gang."

Philip's expression was frozen, immobile.

"He was a sour-faced prick." Little John growled and was rewarded by a momentary scowl from the outlaw leader.

"Aye, he was a prick alright," Robin agreed with a grim nod. "Until I killed him. He died, shitting and pissing in his breeches on the gallows, as I stood and watched with a smile on my face."

There was almost-complete silence for a short while, as everyone held their breath waiting to see what would happen next.

"You talk of warriors," Philip shouted, eventually, as if the last few moments of conversation had never happened. "Is that what you've got with you today? I don't think so." He made a gesture and from the trees on each side of the road came the unmistakable snap of longbows being released, followed by thuds and screams and howls of pain.

"Kill him!" Robin brought his own bow up and loosed his arrow at the outlaw leader. John and the others beside him also let fly but Philip had already ducked beneath the great fallen tree trunk and was gone.

"What now?" Thomas shouted, as the sounds of men fighting amongst the trees fell away and was replaced by an eerie, foreboding silence.

"Fall back," Robin grunted, watching the foliage warily. "Get back to our horses."

"What about the rest of the men?" Thomas demanded, shooting an arrow blindly into the trees where Philip had disappeared and pulling another from his belt, ready to loose again.

"If they manage to defeat the outlaws they'll show themselves and all will be well. But if they've been beaten…I don't want to be standing here in the open, do you?"

Thomas shook his head as they retreated, obviously torn at the thought of leaving his companions behind in the forest. "Shouldn't we try and help them?"

"If we go into those trees we're dead men," John roared. "Now shut the fuck up and fall back like you've been ordered!"

They had just reached their tethered mounts, who watched their return skittishly, spooked by the sounds of dying and stench of sweat and fear that came from their riders, when the cry came from the foliage to their left.

"Loose!"

"Shields up!" Robin cried, dropping his longbow on the ground and wrenching the heater shield from his mount's saddle, raising it over his head and trying to make his great muscular body as small as possible.

Arrows hammered into their shields and the ground

around them, some striking the horses, some striking men. Screams of pain and fear filled the air, equine and human, Robin couldn't tell which was more horrific.

"Retreat! Fall back into the trees!"

The remaining men untied the surviving horses and hurriedly led them into the trees. Robin and Thomas helped a soldier whose foot had been pinned to the forest floor by a broadhead, pulling the arrow free from the earth and lifting him bodily into the foliage, whimpering in agony. John helped another injured man to the relative safety of the trees just as another volley of arrows filled the air.

Again, the lawmen raised their shields desperately, hopefully, over their heads but this time they had the forest around them and most of the missiles thudded into the bark of the beech and oak trees that ringed them. Another two horses, still in the open road, were hit, and their pitiful screams worked on the soldiers' nerves like a blunt knife sawing at a piece of gristle.

"We can't stay here like this," John gasped, his eyes wide. "Waiting to be skewered. We should attack."

Robin nodded agreement and opened his mouth to give the order but, before he could, Philip's voice – high-pitched and near-hysterical – came to them.

"You'll regret crossing me, Hood. Matt was my little brother and I *will* avenge him! You and your friends – all of them – will pay. I swear it! Already men flock to our banner. Men that hate you! Isn't that right Martin?"

"Aye."

From the trees to the right a shout rang out and Robin shared a look with John, both men recognising the evicted landlord's voice instantly.

"You took my livelihood and sentenced my wife to death, Hood, you bastard. I'll see you suffer for it though – our gang grows by the day!"

"These men aren't like you, Martin," Robin returned,

79

shaking his head sadly as he looked uselessly into the thick trees. "They're rapists, murderers...Men with no honour who'll stab you in the back as soon as look at you. Give it up now, all of you, or I swear, everyone of you will die: By the sword; with an arrow in you; or by hanging in front of a baying mob that laughs as you shit your fucking breeches!"

His voice had risen in power and fury as he went on but the pronouncement was met with silence.

For a long time, there wasn't a sound other than the occasional whimper of pain from an injured man or horse – it was as if even the forest animals and insects held their breath and waited to see what would happen next.

"I think they've gone." Thomas mumbled. "We should get the fuck away from here quick in case they come back to finish us."

"What about the men that went into the trees?" someone asked.

"They're dead," Robin sighed. "We can't go looking for them, it'd be suicide with our depleted numbers. We have to move."

They hurriedly helped the injured men to mount while Thomas, a man with great experience of horses, put the injured animals out of their misery.

It seemed to take an age before they were finally ready but, at last, the surviving members of the sheriff's party – eight men, including Robin and John – kicked their heels into their mounts and galloped back to the safety of Ossete.

CHAPTER NINE

"Oh, Christ above." Sir Henry de Faucumberg groaned and hid his face in his hands as Robin and Little John watched him, embarrassed. "You lost all those men to a bunch of outlaws?" He groaned once more. "It's happening again." He glared at Robin who met his eyes but felt the sheriff's anguish and looked away, abashed. "Another bunch of maniacs running riot in my forest and, apparently, there's little I can do about it."

He had half stood up when Robin told him of their losses but now he slumped back into his chair and laid his hands on the table. He stared at nothing for a while, apparently marshalling his thoughts, then, at last, straightened and spread his hands wide, palms up, almost begging.

"What in God's name are we going to do about these bastards?"

As they journeyed back to Nottingham with the remainder of their force Robin and John had discussed this problem. Clearly the sheriff's men weren't up to the job of hunting down such a ruthless, and ever-growing, gang of outlaws. Maybe, given time to train, time to learn the ways of the forest, the guardsmen would be adequate, but they didn't have time. The longer this went on the bigger Philip's group would get and, as their numbers swelled, so would their confidence. And their brutality.

Robin also had other things on his mind: they'd taken a detour to Wakefield on the way here and, when he'd gone home to gather fresh clothing and supplies, he'd discovered his wife and son were gone. Matilda had left and taken Arthur with her, to live with her parents, Henry and Mary, at the fletcher's workshop. She'd finally suffered enough.

He hadn't been in the mood for another argument and,

deep down, he was hurt and even frightened by Matilda's actions, so he'd gathered John and the men and hurried to Nottingham without even visiting the fletcher's.

Robin cleared his throat, now, not at all sure how Sir Henry would view the plan he and John had devised on the road south.

"We would like your permission to recruit some of our old friends."

The sheriff looked at them thoughtfully. "What's wrong with my men?"

"Nothing," John said quickly, glancing at his young leader, who nodded agreement, not wanting to cause any offence by casting aspersions on Sir Henry's soldiers.

"They're good lads. Hardy fighters."

"But?"

"They haven't a damn clue how to move silently in the forest." Robin stated, bluntly. "They don't understand how to read the signs in the foliage when a man's hidden there. Or to pick up on the little changes in the atmosphere when danger approaches through the undergrowth."

"They're city boys," John finished. "No offence to them, but they don't have the experience we need to catch this lot."

"So take the foresters instead of my own guards."

Robin shook his head while John snorted, trying to stifle a laugh.

"The foresters have more wood craft, aye, but they don't have the fighting skills we need. These outlaws are ruthless, as we've already seen. And the man leading them is, in my opinion, a lunatic. Trust me," he leaned down and looked at the sheriff steadily. "We need men that know the forest and can also fight like Templars."

"Our friends," John nodded.

"I'm sure they'll do it for a modest wage," Robin finished and the sheriff looked at him thoughtfully for a few moments.

"Fine, you've convinced me," de Faucumberg eventually sighed. "But even if you can persuade them to join you in this, there won't be enough of you will there?"

"No, but we can make up the numbers from your garrison. We'll pick out the best of your men – the ones that grew up in the villages hereabouts rather than within Nottingham's walls. With the likes of Will Scarlet and the Hospitaller, Stephen, we'll have enough to stop the outlaws before they can grow too powerful to contain."

De Faucumberg shuddered at the thought. "Pray to God you're right," he grunted. "For the king won't be best pleased to hear about another band of cut-throats roaming the greenwood. This could spell the end for me as sheriff. And," he pointed at them in turn, "that means the end of your employment too."

Robin doubted that prospect was particularly worrying for Little John; he wasn't even sure how he felt about it himself but...whatever happened, he knew they must stop Philip and his men.

The sheriff stood up and pulled the laces of his tunic in around his neck as though he was cold despite the summer sun streaming in through the window.

"I have other business to attend to today," he told them. "Take yourselves off to the barracks and choose more men. Take twenty. Along with your friends that should be enough, no?"

Robin looked at John, who shrugged. "Aye, that'll do, although we won't take them with us just now, they'd just get in the way. We still have to find the outlaws' camp first. Once we do, and are in a position to make an assault on it – I'll send word for your soldiers to join us. All right, my lord?"

"Good enough. Keep me informed. We must not let this get out of hand. Even if I have to" – he shook his head with a sigh – "petition King Edward for more men. That would be better than the outlaws growing to an unstoppable size. And that's possible," he warned. "We must stop this *now*."

The former wolf's heads bowed as the sheriff showed them out into the corridor, promising to let him know how things progressed in their hunt, then they headed towards the barracks which was located near the centre of the western wall.

"He's not a bad sort, is he?" John asked, quietly, the stone walls and high ceilings of the castle interior making him feel almost as if he was in a church.

"No," Robin replied. "He's as honourable a man as any, as I've come to learn over the past couple of years. But he'll do whatever it takes to win, in the end. He was an outlaw himself once, after all."

John stopped in his tracks, the clatter of his weapons echoing along the stone hallway. "Eh?"

"Aye, he was a wolf's head too, he told me the story a few days ago, didn't I tell you? No? Listen then, I'll tell you as we walk."

* * *

Henry de Faucumberg was born in Sheffield, earlier than the midwife had expected and, as a result, was a tiny babe. His loving parents had prayed to God that their second son – they'd already been favoured with a beautiful toddler, John, two years earlier – would survive.

God apparently heard their prayers, as little Henry was blessed with a hearty appetite; his mother's milk and, later, the fine meat, fish and vegetables that the de Faucumbergs' were able to afford, had seen him grow into a sturdy child.

He and his older brother were full of mischief, enjoying practical jokes which were often dangerous, like the time they balanced a metal bucket half-filled with iron nails on top of a door. Their French tutor, Jacques, had been knocked out cold when he'd sprung the trap and the heavy container with its sharp contents landed on the crown of his bald head.

Their father, Richard, had punished them with a severe beating for that trick, but they'd laughed about the joke for years afterwards, counting their thrashings worth it.

In general though, Henry, was a smart, intelligent boy who behaved himself and enjoyed learning about the world around him. John, on the other hand, only seemed to become more mischievous and wild as he grew into adolescence, until one afternoon he'd 'borrowed' a horse from one of their neighbour's stables and been thrown from the saddle, splitting his forehead open on a rock as he landed.

The lad had never been the same after the accident. Henry tried his best to remain close to his older brother but eventually grew frustrated at the change in John who seemed to have turned back into a four-year-old again, even if he had the body of someone ten years older.

Henry's mother, Diana, spent most of her time with John after the accident but his father, realising his first-born would never be the powerful magnate he'd always hoped, turned his full attention on young Henry.

While his brother was allowed to play with the old toys of their childhood, Henry was forced to study languages, history and philosophy, along with martial arts like sword-fighting although he was never as good at the physical side, excelling instead at his book learning, which he mostly enjoyed.

"When I was fifteen," he'd said to Robin, as the pair sat with drinks in the sheriff's study one evening after the bailiff had completed another job, "my father found me a position as steward to a hugely wealthy old merchant. The man was an importer of fancy goods from all around the world and I began to truly learn my trade: how to keep accounts, skimming just enough so the king's tax collector wouldn't notice; how to organise a workforce; how to foresee and prepare for problems in advance. In short, I learned how to be a successful businessman."

De Faucumberg shook his head, a small nostalgic smile on his lips. "That merchant made me work for my pay but those were good times. I owe much to that man, even if I did curse him as a slave-driver at the time."

His face fell and he raised his goblet to his lips, staring out the glazed window at the gently swaying trees outside.

For a long time he said nothing and Robin cleared his throat, breaking the man's reverie. "Then you became sheriff?"

"Oh, goodness me, no," de Faucumberg shook his head, replacing the goblet on the table and leaning back in his chair almost defensively. "Not for a long time after that. I was arrested first –"

Robin almost choked on his wine. "Arrested? You?"

"Indeed," the sheriff affirmed. "I too was a wolf's head for a time." He smiled again, but sadly this time. "As I say, my employer was a very hard task-master, pushing me mercilessly to earn ever more money for his coffers. It got too much one day and, when my shift was finished, I followed some of the labourers to a nearby tavern on the way home. They liked me well enough, as I was always fair with them and even managed to pay them a bonus once, without the old man knowing, so they were happy enough to invite me into their company."

"Were you a drinker?" Robin wondered. The sheriff often seemed to have a cup of wine in his hand since Robin had been in his employ, but he found it hard to imagine a teenage de Faucumberg joining a group of low-class labourers in some seedy tavern for a night's debauchery.

"Oh no. I'd been drunk once before that but the experience was so unpleasant that I'd decided never to make a habit of it. But that day, well, I was exhausted and it felt like my head would explode with one of the contracts my employer was asking me to negotiate with a Spanish fellow. Looking back on it now I realise the old man was taking advantage of me – I was much too young and inexperienced to have that sort of weight on my shoulders. But the old bastard was shrewd; getting an apprentice like me to run so much of his business was cheaper than hiring someone else."

He waved a hand good-naturedly. "I'm glad for it now anyway – it was a truly valuable period in my life but...well, it didn't feel like it that particular day. So I went to the tavern and, in my youthful bravado, tried to match the labourers drink-for-drink."

Robin grinned. "Ouch."

"Quite," de Faucumberg grunted. "By the time I staggered out the door I could barely remember my own name. It was a longer walk home than it was back to the merchant's premises so I, foolishly, decided to return to the shop. It was a cold night and, even in my inebriated state, I knew I'd want a fire to heat my office, where I planned to sleep on the floor. I also knew there was precious little fuel left for the hearth so...I decided to just take some from a store beside a house I was passing."

He shrugged. "I would have paid for the wood but...it didn't seem like a good idea to go knocking on the householder's door at that time of the night, pissed out of my mind, offering to buy some fuel. So I just grabbed some logs and made off along the street, giggling like a mischievous child no doubt. Unfortunately for me," he heaved a gusty sigh and met Robin's eyes, "I was spotted and, in the morning the bailiff came and arrested me."

Robin shook his head in disbelief; he'd never suspected this side of the sheriff's past. Still, he thought, sipping his drink, a skinful of wine could make *any* man act like an arsehole. He'd learned that more times than he could count while living as an outlaw with his friends in the greenwood.

87

"What happened to you then?"

"They fined me," de Faucumberg replied. "Not a lot. I didn't mind losing the money at all. But my employer saw the whole thing as a scandal – sent me packing, back to my father who wasn't too pleased I can tell you."

"At least you didn't end up in jail, or in the forest," Robin muttered. "As a peasant, with no way of paying the fine, would have."

The sheriff nodded agreement. "You're right of course. That's one reason why I try to treat people of all classes the same."

That was mostly true, Robin conceded. De Faucumberg was as fair a nobleman as he'd ever come across which was why he accepted a place in the sheriff's service when he and his men were pardoned.

"How the hell did you end up in such a high office then, with that crime on your record?"

"Money," the sheriff said, simply. "My father knew I'd been good at running the merchant's business empire so he took me on himself. I continued to learn the ways of business – of politics if you like – and I also began to meet powerful, important people. I built up a network of contacts – of noblemen who liked and trusted me, who valued my judgement on matters of importance. That all came in very useful but, ultimately, as I say, it was money that greased the wheels."

He stood, stretching his arms above his head and rolling his head slowly from side to side, grunting as he did so. "Been sitting too long," he murmured to himself, then continued, louder again. "When my parents died their estate should have passed to the eldest son: my brother, John. But my father had changed his will and, apart from some monies set aside for John's care, everything came to me."

He smirked. "Strangely enough, once I was a wealthy man in my own right, lots of those powerful men I'd become acquainted with wanted to ingratiate themselves with me. My star was in the ascendancy. Word reached the king of my astute business mind and he offered me the position as Sheriff of Yorkshire which I gladly accepted."

Robin stood himself and joined de Faucumberg at the window. "And you proved yourself capable so he gave you Nottingham too."

"Yes. I'm one of only two men to have ever been sheriff of both counties you know." His eyes sparkled with pride and Robin smiled, thinking again how ridiculous this whole situation would have seemed to him four or five years earlier when he was an outlaw.

Now he actually thought of Sir Henry as a friend.

"I'd started to fear Edward might have stripped me of my position here after the Despenser's rebellion," the sheriff said, his eyes following a tabby cat as it stalked across the grass beneath the window. "When you and your bloody friends were causing so much trouble and that mad bastard Sir Guy of Gisbourne couldn't catch you."

"It turned out well enough for us all in the end," Robin shrugged.

"Not for Gisbourne it didn't," the sheriff grunted with a snort of laughter, hand reaching up subconsciously to touch the faded scar beneath his tunic. The bounty hunter had, in a fit of insanity brought on by his total failure to bring Robin and his friends to justice, tried to kill de Faucumberg. He would have succeeded too, if Robin, aided by Matilda and his sister Marjorie, hadn't stopped him.

The two men stood in companionable silence for a time, sipping their drinks, lost in their own memories.

Eventually the sheriff belched and wiped his mouth with a hand. "We've both seen what it's like on the other side of the law. We can sympathise with how hard the system can be. But I can't allow this new outlaw gang to become as powerful as yours did, Robert."

There was steel in his voice and Robin took his meaning. It was up to him to stop Philip and his men, and he had to do it fast.

Before Barnsdale became a bloodbath.

CHAPTER TEN

Eoin bent his great frame and looked at Philip sympathetically. "You all right?" His friend had been in a strange, silent mood for days; ever since they'd attacked Robin Hood and his soldiers now that he came to think of it.

It wasn't that unusual for Philip to withdraw into himself – it happened every so often and Eoin had grown used to it. But normally he'd come out of it after a few hours, so this time was different and the big outlaw was genuinely worried for his leader's welfare.

"Aye." The word was ground out between clenched teeth, but Eoin heaved a sigh of relief to finally hear his friend's voice.

The rest of the outlaws – already wary of their new leader – had given him a wide berth once he'd retreated into his fugue state and Eoin didn't blame them. Clearly something was gnawing at the man's mind and Eoin knew better than anyone how that could lead to trouble. Brutal, bloody trouble, for anyone that annoyed Philip.

Eoin wasn't afraid of his friend though – he was much bigger and stronger than him after all. Aye, Philip was vicious and would stick a dagger in a man's back as soon as his guts but Eoin knew his mate wouldn't do that to him. They'd been through too much; they respected and even liked one another.

So while Philip was brooding in their camp Eoin brought him food and drink and even spoke to him, not the least bit put off when his conversational attempts met with blank silence.

He smiled now, happy that his perseverance had paid off.

"I'm all right. But that bastard Hood won't be. Did you

91

hear what he said?"

Eoin nodded and sighed softly although he knew better than to lay a sympathetic hand on his friend's shoulder as he instinctively wanted to do. "I did. I'm sorry."

"He killed my brother. D'you know when I last saw Matt?" He stopped, counting on his fingers before giving up. "I haven't seen him since I was just grown into a man. My da tried to beat me but I was too fast for him and I ended up kicking the shit out of him, while Matt watched and cried. He was only a little boy. But I had to leave – I couldn't stay there after that and I hated my da anyway." He slammed his clenched fist onto the ground before drawing his knees up against his chest again, the anger apparently gone. "I always planned on going back to take care of Matt – make sure my da didn't hurt him or anything but...I never got around to it for years. When I eventually did go back our house had a new family living in it. They didn't know anything about Matt or my da."

Tears rolled down his face and Eoin, without thinking, edged back a pace. This was a side of his friend that he'd never seen before.

"Years went past and word eventually reached me that my brother was part of an outlaw gang in Barnsdale Forest. I really thought we'd finally meet again when you and I turned up here."

The tears in his eyes had dried by now, to be replaced by a fire that made Eoin even more nervous.

"Those arseholes killed Matt. Robin Hood, Little John...All of them." He sat for a moment longer then pushed himself to his feet, hand resting on the pommel of his longsword. "Well my brother will have his revenge – we're going to make his killers pay."

"What about the rest of our men?" Eoin asked, waving a huge hand to encompass their camp and the more than a dozen outlaws gathered there.

Philip's smile returned to his face at last. "They'll help.

No-one will be able to stop us."

* * *

Will Scaflock was busy. He was busy and he was angry.

"Fucking storm," he growled to himself as he lifted a plank of wood and battered a nail into it, the muscles on his big arms cording, as he fixed it to the new fence post he'd been forced to sink following the previous night's gale force winds.

It was a mild morning, with a few grey clouds that covered the sun every so often, but the fence that penned his few sheep in was blown over and he was out repairing it now. He furiously hammered in the iron nails as if he they'd kicked him in the bollocks. He had better things to be doing that morning than mending a fence he'd put up not six months earlier.

"Bastard storm," he reiterated, thumping home the final nail and stepping back to check his work was sound. The fence wasn't the neatest, with posts at different heights and spars sloping this way and that, but it would hold a few sheep. Until the next storm at least, he thought ruefully.

"You Will Scarlet?"

He'd been aware of the three men approaching for a while. They made no attempt to hide in the foliage or mask their heavy footfalls, and their confident bearing – coupled with the swords each one carried at their side – alerted Will to the possibility that they weren't here simply to ask for directions to the nearest alehouse. He was glad his thirteen year-old daughter, Beth, was away that morning collecting supplies from Wakefield and visiting her friends there.

"No."

His reply threw the man, who was tall but incredibly thin. He glanced sideways at his two companions.

"You're not Will Scarlet?"

Will turned his back and walked along his mended fence towards them, shaking the posts to make sure they were sturdy enough.

"No."

The questioner looked confused, but one of his companions, an older fellow – probably in his mid-fifties Will guessed, but still brawny looking – drew his sword and pointed it at him.

"Aye you are. The villagers told us where to find you, and there can't be anyone else around here that fits your description."

Will turned and smiled sardonically at the man. "What description would that be?"

"Average height, stocky build, green eyes and an angry, *ugly* fucking face."

Will stepped forward, close to the older fellow, still smiling, the weight of the hammer reassuring in his hand which had started to sweat as the excitement of impending battle began to course through his veins.

"Do I look angry to you?" he whispered.

"You're going to look dead in a bit," the first, tall, newcomer muttered, drawing his own sword and moving in as the third man followed his lead.

Will was almost forty years old now, and his body was beginning to show it. Gone was the rock-hard, flat stomach and slim waist he'd had when he was a wolf's head, to be replaced by a burgeoning beer-belly and a slightly receding hairline. But, underneath the new layer of fat, his muscles were still hard – kept in shape by the work he did on his farm, like mending fences and shearing sheep, which was always a horrendous task for him, although probably insanely comical for anyone watching his clumsy efforts.

Before the older man knew what was happening, Will brought the head of his hammer straight up and into his jaw. The whole force of his brawny arm was behind the strike and Will was pleased to hear the crack of bone breaking as the grey-haired man's jaw snapped and he fell back onto the ground, making a pitiful whining noise and glaring up at the former outlaw from pain-filled eyes.

"My name," Will growled, turning to face the two remaining men, "is Will *Scaflock*."

He launched himself at the tall, thin man who'd drawn back his sword and swung it now in a low arc, but Will was too fast. He barrelled into his opponent, shoulder hitting him in the chest and sending the man flying back onto his back on the grass.

Will ducked, just in time as the final assailant's sword swung around, through the space his head had just occupied, then he battered the head of the hammer into the side of the man's knee.

He was rewarded with a scream and, again, the crunch of bone shattering. Just to make sure, Scaflock jumped across the grass like a spider and brought his hammer down once more, this time right in the middle of the fallen man's forehead.

The screaming stopped instantly and Will stood up.

The smile was gone from his face.

"*Now* I'm angry," he said, glaring at the two still-conscious but downed attackers.

The men glanced at each other, and then the taller one shouted, "Get him!"

Before he could even stand up Will's hammer came down on the top of his head, so hard it sent pain lancing through Scaflock's arm, but he couldn't waste time rubbing the jarred limb, as the final, older assailant lunged, broken jaw making his mouth hang open obscenely, but the edge of his sword sliced across Will's side, slicing his tunic and drawing a line of blood on his white flesh.

Dropping flat onto the grass, Will kicked out as hard as he could, his foot dragging the grey-haired man's legs out from beneath him and, as he fell with a tortured cry,

Scaflock dropped his hammer and threw himself forward, hands grasping the man's throat and squeezing, squeezing, until the would-be assassin passed out.

Will collapsed onto the wet grass, breathing heavily, his arms aching and the blood that oozed from the wound in his side now beginning to congeal uncomfortably on the top of his breeches.

Still, it was over and he'd won.

"Oh, fuck off." He pushed himself onto his elbows as the sound of horses approaching came to him, the thought of having to fight again almost too much to take and he smiled, in spite of the situation, knowing he'd have enjoyed this much more ten years ago.

Roaring in determination he lunged across the ground and picked up his dropped hammer, then pushed himself back to a standing position to face the riders who he knew he'd never be able to fight off. Not with just a hammer and not in the state he was in.

But he'd have a fucking good go.

"Looks like we're just in time."

"Aye, and the outlaws picked the wrong man to target first."

Will stared, trying to focus on the riders but he must have lost more blood than he realised as his head swam and he found it impossible to fix his gaze on the mounted men. Still, he raised the hammer, ready to go out fighting.

Then, at last, his brain caught up and, as he recognised the voices he sagged, sobbing in glad relief.

It was his old friends, Robin Hood and Little John.

"You're a bit late," he growled, then collapsed onto the grass.

CHAPTER ELEVEN

Will's wound was a minor one and John soon had it cleaned and wrapped in a fresh piece of linen he'd found in his friend's nearby cottage. He suspected Will's collapse was due to exhaustion rather than blood loss – the ex-mercenary was so driven, so determined to make a go of his farm, that he put every drop of effort he could into it. The excitement of the fight had been too much John thought.

Certainly, there wasn't a great deal of blood on the torn tunic.

But he knew it would do no good to tell his old companion he'd collapsed from simple tiredness, so when Will came to and complained about his wound the giant lawman grunted agreement and tried to sound sympathetic.

While John tended to their downed friend, Robin knelt by the surviving assassin whose lower face had already started to swell alarmingly.

"Wake up. Wake up you arsehole."

Slapping and kicking the unconscious man didn't have much effect but a bucket filled with rainwater soon had him gasping and mewling like a sodden cat.

"Who are you?"

The man grunted an obscenity at Robin and it sounded more terrible thanks to the smashed jaw, but the young lawman was in no mood to waste time.

"I asked who you are," he shouted, slapping the fallen man in the face, and was rewarded with a loud groan of agony. He brought his hand back for another blow but the man, eyes wide in rage and fear, recoiled in the mud and raised his hand.

He grunted his name but Robin couldn't make it out.

"Why are you here, trying to kill my friend?"

Again, the man grunted something and it took a few moments for Robin to make sense of the sounds.

He was a member of Philip's gang. An outlaw. As Robin had known all along, but he needed the confession. As a member of the sheriff's staff, and a lawman, he needed to be able to prove the man's guilt.

He pushed himself up to a standing position as he heard John and Will approach.

"He's one of the outlaws right enough, John. Looks like the bastards failed with their first attack on our old friends, thanks be to the Magdalene. We got here in time."

Will snorted at that, but Robin just grinned.

"What's that? What are you mumbling dickhead?" Little John bent his great frame and glared into the outlaw's eyes as the man tried to say something. "You're not the only ones?"

The words were repeated and, as before, it took Robin a short while to figure out the grunts and make words out of them.

"They're not the only ones sent to kill our old gang," he finally spat, glancing at Will and John worriedly. "Another group of them went after someone else nearby."

The outlaw sagged back, glad he'd manage to impart his final, barbed message. He tried to smile at them but winced in pain as his mouth opened, and, whining pitifully, his head fell onto the grass.

Robin stared at the man, mind whirling.

"What do we do?" John asked, looking to his leader for guidance. The giant was a formidable fighter and a loyal companion but he always bowed to his younger friend when it came to their next move.

Robin nodded towards the downed outlaw who was breathing heavily and making even more noise as the shock wore off and the real agony of his horrendous injury began to take hold.

"You said the rest of your mates had gone after a man."

The outlaw watched Robin but didn't reply.

"Was it a clergyman?"

The injured outlaw's blank look told Robin all he needed to know.

"It's not Tuck they've gone after then." He moved the point of his sword up to the man's eye and rested it on his cheek. "I'm done fucking about with you. Where have they gone?"

"I don't know his name," the outlaw gurned, his voice rising in pitch as he felt the blade press against the soft tissue of his eyeball. "A tanner. In Kirk'ees!"

"Edmond," John and Will said in unison. It had to be.

When Robin's gang were pardoned by the sheriff Edmond had gone back to his home village of Kirklees and used some of his share of their stolen money to rebuild his old tannery. He'd even, despite his strange fish-lipped face and bulky body, found himself a wife and, as far as Robin could tell when he'd last been in the village, the couple were happy enough.

Edmond was a decent fighter who could take care of himself well enough, but he was no mercenary – no professional soldier like Scarlet had been.

"Come on then," Will shouted, striding towards the door of his cottage to collect his weapons and light armour. "Maybe we can still be in time to stop the bastards."

"What about this one," John said to Robin as Will disappeared inside his dwelling. "We can't just leave him here. You want me to tie him up?"

The outlaw glared at them malevolently and tried to spit in Robin's direction but his injury meant the spittle simply trickled down his own chin and he grunted a curse instead.

"Aye, we better do that. Can't just kill him now we're lawmen ourselves. Grab that rope there – we'll leave him here for the headman, Patrick, to deal with."

They finished binding the man's arms and legs together and Robin glared at him, tugging hard on a knot which drew a squeal of agony.

"You and your mad leader should have listened to the songs people sing about me and my friends. No one crosses us. No one."

Will appeared in his doorway then, armed and armoured and already heading for the horse that stood, watching them balefully from the small stable attached to the house.

"Why didn't you just kill the bastard?" Scarlet wondered.

"I'm a bailiff now," Robin replied, climbing into his saddle with a last backwards glance at the bloodied and bound prisoner. "I have to follow the law."

Will smirked and shook his head. "You've gone soft you mean."

Robin shrugged and smiled.

"We'll see. To Kirklees!"

* * *

Matilda had been happy when Robin announced his plan to pay for an extension to St Mary's to her. They weren't short of money – far from it, actually – thanks to the riches he and his friends had stolen as outlaws. Much of those spoils originally belonged to wealthy clergymen like Abott Ness and Prior de Monte Martini, so it only seemed fair for the bailiff to spend some of it on good works for the church.

There was no harm in supporting the clergy whenever possible, Matilda believed – surely it could only be good for one's soul?

The young woman regularly visited the newly built section of the church to pray. Mostly for one thing.

Tonight was no different, as, once Arthur had fallen asleep she'd asked her parents if they would keep an eye on their grandson for a short while. They were always happy to oblige and now Matilda knelt in the gloom of St

Mary's, the only light a few candles and the last vestiges of sunset. It was a dry evening and the cool interior of the church helped her relax so she soon lost herself in her prayers.

"Lord," she mouthed, her head bowed. "I know You have reasons for everything you do and I'm grateful for our beautiful son, but why have You never granted me a second child? A brother or sister for Arthur to play with. So many of the other women have had four, five, six children, yet Robin and I just the one."

She sighed softly, thinking of those other mothers, knowing that, although they may have given birth to lots of children, many of them didn't survive past the first year. Like poor Agnes Reeve, who'd had three babies before she was eighteen, all of which had died within a week of their births, leaving the girl utterly bereft, a sad shell of her former self.

At least Matilda hadn't suffered such agony but she still felt as if something was wrong with her since she'd never even been able to conceive again after Arthur was born. Had she done something to make God angry with her? She couldn't think of any reason He might have to punish her in such a way but what other explanation could there be?

Her eyes became wet as she thought of Robin, who'd never berated her for not bearing him more children. He'd never blamed her for it – quite the opposite in fact, as he regularly thanked her for giving him Arthur, who he doted on.

And yet she'd made his life miserable for months now, because of the way she felt inside herself. Well, perhaps not entirely that – her husband was far from perfect but...

The tears spilled down her face but she wiped them hurriedly away and drew herself up, refusing to give into the gloom. She knew from experience that it did no good and would only make her feel even worse.

"Please, God," she closed her eyes and pictured her

blonde-haired smiling son and felt her spirits rise again. "Grant us another child."

She remained kneeling for a few moments longer, reciting the *Pater Noster* then got to her feet, wiped away the last of her tears so her parents wouldn't know she'd been weeping, then walked slowly back to their house, wishing Robin might be there and everything between them back to normal.

How could she ever become pregnant, after all, if her husband was never there to share her bed?

* * *

The smoke – black, greasy smoke, of things other than wood burning – told them they were probably too late.

They'd pushed their horses hard and made the journey to Kirklees by early afternoon, even with a hasty stop in Wakefield to make sure Beth didn't return to the farm before Patrick Prudhomme could send men to clear the two corpses and arrest the surviving, bound outlaw.

Now, they approached Kirklees from the east, so had to pass through the main village to reach the tannery, yet the locals didn't seem too concerned about the fire. Edmond, although he'd been a decent companion Robin thought, had never been popular in his home town. Growing up he'd been bullied, as had his brother, simply because they were a little bit different to everyone else, in looks and in how they'd been brought up.

It surprised Robin when he found out Edmond had gone back there after their pardon, but perhaps the tanner just couldn't see anywhere else as home.

Still, the locals' inherent dislike and mistrust of him – made even worse when he'd almost killed the inn-keeper in a fight – clearly hadn't lessened in the years since he'd returned from life as an outlaw. If anyone else's property had been on fire the whole place would be rushing to fetch buckets of water.

But the tannery, with its stinking vats of urine, was located a short distance away from the main body of the village and there was little chance of the fire spreading before it burned itself out.

"Are you people blind?" Robin roared as they whipped along the main street. "The tannery is burning – fetch water and help in the name of God!"

The people gave him sullen looks but they knew who he was and they respected – even feared – him. They moved to gather buckets but without any urgency. As far as they were concerned, Robin knew, the village would be better off without the stench of piss and the brooding, fish-lipped tanner.

"Maybe we should go in carefully," John shouted to his companions. "In case the outlaws are still there."

Robin thought about it but, before he could give the order one way or the other, Scarlet shouted, "I hope the bastards *are* still there!"

With a war-cry he pulled his sword free from its simple scabbard as his horse led the way to the tannery.

There seemed to be no-one around; no-one was outside the buildings at least, so Will slid from his mount and waited the few moments it took the others to catch up.

"Stay alert," Robin growled as he and John slipped from their saddles and the three of them headed towards the door of the workshop.

The roof at the rear of the building collapsed suddenly and a welter of flame and sparks and blackened embers roared up into the air, halting Robin in his tracks. He turned, eyes scouring the area.

"There's not going to be anyone in there," he said. "No-one still alive anyway – the place is about to cave in on itself." He nodded towards the house which was also on fire, but it hadn't quite taken hold yet. "You two check the house. The outlaws have gone, I think we can be sure of that, but Edmond or his wife might be in there."

John and Will moved unquestioningly over to the house, the bearded giant battering his shoulder against the door which came right off its hinges as he stumbled inside, Scarlet close at his heels as they disappeared from view.

Taking a deep breath, Robin pulled his tunic up, then he kicked open the workshop door, peering inside through the flames and the smoke which was almost unbearable already.

Edmond lay on the floor.

"Bastards. Bastards!"

Robin reeled back, away from the awful, searing heat and bent his head. They hadn't just killed the tanner, they'd tortured him too. Why, the lawman couldn't say; maybe just because Philip Groves was even more sadistic and hateful than his brother. The blood caking Edmond's battered face, and the stumps where his fingers used to be told their own story though.

Their old friend had not died well. Again, Robin vowed to bring Groves and his men to justice. Brutal, terrible justice.

The sounds of coughing came from the house and he turned to watch Will stumbling out of the house, followed by John who carried a female figure in his great arms.

They all moved away from the burning tannery, back, far enough that the heat and smoke didn't reach them. At last some of the villagers appeared with buckets filled with water and fought to control the blaze without much success.

Not that it mattered much now.

"Edmond?" Will asked, still hacking from the smoke he'd inhaled inside the house. "You find him?"

"He's dead. The scum tortured him then left his body to burn." His voice was hard but he had tears of rage and sorrow in his brown eyes. "What about her?"

Little John had placed Edmond's wife on the grass and

he looked up sadly. The woman was breathing but for how long…?

Robin came over and knelt beside her. She was a small thing although she seemed to share some of the facial characteristics of Edmond and the lawman felt a lump in his throat at the demise of the perfectly-suited young couple who had been just embarking on their life together.

"You're safe now," he said to her, softly, reassuringly. "We're old friends of your man's."

"You're too late," she mumbled through bruised lips. "Five of them. Their leader raped me then..." she sobbed, "he made his men rape me too. All of them!"

"What the fuck is wrong with this brother of Matt's?" John hissed. "He's a worse enemy than Gisbourne or Adam Gurdon ever were."

The girl spoke again, her words almost too soft for Robin to hear and he bent his ear to her lips, gesturing irritably for John to be silent.

"They made Edmond tell them all the names of his – your – old gang members, and where he thought they lived." She stopped and more tears streaked her soot-blackened face. "He wouldn't tell them but that bastard with the filthy blonde hair started hitting him and cutting him."

With a soft sigh she finished and her whole body went limp as the smoke she'd breathed in finally killed her.

For long moments the three friends remained silent, oblivious to the flames and smoke and shouts of the fire-fighters.

They were all hard men; they'd all seen and done things that would live with them for the rest of their lives but...the violence and sheer wickedness here shocked them. To have such ruthless outlaws operating in their own home county was a sobering, fearful thought.

"What now?"

Robin shook himself from his reverie and shrugged

without looking up at John. "We'd better find the rest of our friends before Groves and his men do or," he stared down at Edmond's dead, brutalised wife, "we'll have to deal with more of this."

One of the great vats filled with urine burst as the flames weakened the sides and the resultant flood ran handily downhill across some of the burning buildings. After that it didn't take long for the villagers to get the conflagration under control.

As Robin, John and Will walked back to their horses they discussed where they should head next.

"The nearest person I can think of is Stephen," Robin mused once he'd hauled himself up into the saddle. "He's working as a bodyguard for a merchant in Leeds, I believe, still hoping to be taken back in by the Hospitallers, which isn't likely to happen until the Grand Prior dies. You two make your way there and tell him what's going on. Persuade him to join us. The sheriff will pay a decent wage, don't worry about that." He hadn't even mentioned this to Will until now, just assuming his old lieutenant would return to their gang without any fuss; even if it was on the right side of the law this time.

"Where are you going?" Scarlet asked, accepting his position as one of de Faucumberg's – one of Robin's – men readily enough. He'd missed all this! Mending fences and collecting shit from cattle wasn't much of a life for a man like him.

"I'll head back to Wakefield and get Tuck," Robin replied. "He's likely to be high on Groves's list of targets. We know he doesn't think much of clergymen after all..."

Little John pulled on his reins and turned his horse in the direction of Leeds with a nod. "Matilda?"

"Aye," Robin replied. "I'll make sure she's safe. I'll pay some of the harder local men to guard them." He looked at Will. "I'll make sure Beth stays with them too, have no fears."

Scarlet grunted his thanks then he and John waved a salute and kicked their heels into their mounts' sides, cantering off to find Stephen, while Robin took the eastern road, back home to Wakefield, wondering what in God's name they'd have to do to stop this new outlaw leader and his twisted vengeance.

He shuddered.

It seemed as if Matt Groves was laughing at him from hell itself.

Would Friar Tuck be the next to die at the hands of Matt's insane brother, Philip?

Robin kicked his heels in, hard, and urged his palfrey along the road with little care for his own safety.

Not Tuck.

Please God, not Tuck!

CHAPTER TWELVE

"What now?" Eoin wondered, tearing a chunk of pork from the bone in his hand, the greasy juices spilling down his chin but the expression on his big face was that of a contented child, as the taste filled his mouth.

"Now we rest," Philip replied loudly, so the rest of the men could hear. "And enjoy the fruits of our labours." He raised his own plate of food in one hand, a pot of ale in the other and his followers cheered loudly, grins on their faces. The tannery in Kirklees had boasted a surprisingly well-stocked larder which they'd plundered eagerly.

After they murdered the tanner and raped his wife they ran off and waited a couple of miles to the south-west, to meet up with their three comrades who'd gone to Wakefield to deal with the farmer known as Will Scarlet. When the trio failed to appear the outlaws continued on their way south, across the River Calder and into the thick trees at Brackenhall, a tiny village not far from Huddersfield. They'd set up camp and were now relaxing, their missing companions forgotten already. It was a clear, moonless night, and a multitude of stars gazed back at Philip as he enjoyed his meat and stared into the dark.

"But what about the rest of Robin Hood's friends?" Eoin continued. "Are we not going after them now?"

Philip chewed thoughtfully for a while, gazing into the camp fire which was sending greasy black cooking smoke into the air. They should probably be more careful about giving away their position he mused, then discarded the idea. They were a dozen hard men – killers – and it was dark in Barnsdale. No-one would be sneaking up on them just now, so they could relax, eat and drink and, as he'd said, enjoy themselves.

"We're still going to kill all of Hood's old gang," he

nodded, eyeing his plate then selecting a tasty piece which he popped into his mouth with that ever-present smile. "But there's no rush. We've sent a message to him; he'll be shitting his breeches now, wondering who we'll go after next. And, in the meantime, we'll look to recruit more wolf's heads to our cause, until we become truly unstoppable."

"Or too much of a nuisance," Eoin grunted, "and the king sends an army after us."

Philip raised an eyebrow, surprised at his friend's perceptive observation, then shrugged and washed down a piece of gristle with some of his ale. "We won't let it get that far. We'll grow until we're big enough to defend ourselves against the foresters and the sheriff's men, and we'll take whatever we want from the villages hereabouts before moving on to another county and starting all over again. In the meantime," he tossed the last of his meal – mostly bones and fat he'd spat back onto the wooden platter – into the bushes behind him and got to his feet, "we'll pick off Robin Hood's friends one by one."

Mark had been listening to their conversation and he stood up now to follow Philip, who took himself a short way into the trees to empty his bladder. His new leader glanced at him as he undid his breeches and released a warm stream of piss with a sigh of relief.

"All right, Mark?" the outlaw captain smirked. "Did you just follow me into the bushes to see my cock?"

The smaller man's eyes blazed but he held his peace, as Philip knew he would.

"Nah, I needed a piss myself. And I have a suggestion for who we could go after next."

"Really?"

"Aye," Mark replied, pulling up his own breeches and facing his mad leader. "An old friend of mine, name of James. He used to be one of my men. I have a score to settle with the bastard, and you'll be interested to know that he's the reason Hood and his friends are still alive today. He took word that Sir Guy of Gisbourne was about to ambush them and that allowed Hood to turn the tables on the bounty hunter. If it wasn't for James your brother would still be alive and that fat Friar Tuck would be dead. I ordered James to shoot the clergyman and the prick turned on me. He struts around Horbury like he owns the place now, telling anyone that'll listen what a fucking hero he is."

Philip stared at him, for just a moment too long, until he could see Mark's hand nervously reaching down towards the dagger in his belt, then he smiled broadly.

"Horbury, eh? He sounds like the perfect target for us. Good idea. We'll let things die down for a bit then go after this friend of yours."

Philip moved past, heading back to the camp-fire, and wiped his piss-dribbled hands on Mark's arms with a grin that was stark in the flickering light.

He knew the short man with the perfect teeth hated him, and would have liked nothing better than to murder and supplant him, but he also knew Mark feared him and his giant friend Eoin. He'd intimidate the intense little fool and make a mockery of him until he either snapped or, more likely, fell under Philip's sway.

Either way, the outlaw leader knew Mark would have to be dealt with eventually.

Until that day came, though, his brutal nature and skill with a blade would come in handy. Especially when they went after this fellow James.

* * *

When Robin returned to his home village he urged his mount along the main street, oblivious to the angry cries of pedestrians sent spilling sideways as they avoided his charge. At last he came to the church, heaving a sigh of relief when he spotted Tuck outside, comfortably seated on a bench, enjoying a mug of ale and the wonderful orange sunset.

The friar looked up at the thunder of approaching hooves, his hand falling instinctively to his waist, where Robin knew he still carried his trusty club.

"What brings you here?" Tuck asked, bushy eyebrows raised. The two men hadn't spoken since their disagreement weeks ago, although the friar still wondered why his former leader had paid for a drink in the alehouse that last time they'd both been in there.

"Trouble," Robin half-shouted, reining in the horse and sliding almost-expertly to the ground, although his foot slipped just a little as he landed and he cursed inwardly. He'd never be a natural rider, even if he wasn't as bad as Little John.

Tuck pursed his lips and made a "pfft" sound. "When is it ever anything else?" He got to his feet though, ready to face whatever it was that Robin was fleeing. Or chasing.

"Real trouble this time, my friend. Edmond's dead. His wife too."

Tuck's mouth formed a silent, horrified "O", then his eyebrows drew down and he glared at Robin.

"Is this your fault?"

"What? No! Well, I suppose, in a way —"

"You and your extortion," Tuck broke in, face red with fury. "I knew it would bring trouble – knew you'd pick on the wrong person to blackmail – but Edmond? What did he have to do with it? Did you get him involved? Or was it him you were trying to fleece?"

Robin shook his head in confusion, lost in the friar's relentless stream of recriminations before he finally understood what was happening.

"No, it's nothing to do with any of that, Tuck. Enough!" He raised his palms and shouted almost directly in his portly friend's face. "Enough. Sit back down and let me

111

explain, for fuck sake."

"Watch your language," Tuck warned. "This is holy ground." But he did sit down, much to Robin's relief.

For long moments they sat in silence, absorbing the terrible fact of their companion's death. Poor Edmond – his life had been a hard one but he'd found a place with Robin's gang. He'd been a valued member of their fellowship and things looked bright when he returned to his tannery and found himself a wife, but fate had never been good to the fish-lipped man and now…

The image of his mutilated corpse, blackened and blistered obscenely, filled Robin's memory and the lawman wondered if he'd ever be able to forget it.

Tears sprang to his eyes and Tuck, finally calming down after the initial shock of the bleak news, laid a hand on his wrist and gripped it tightly, reassuringly.

"Tell me, lad."

"It was Groves." He saw the baffled look on Tuck's face and nodded. "Aye, you heard me right. Matt's come back to haunt us – his brother is leading a new gang of outlaws hiding out in Barnsdale."

The clergyman leaned back on the old bench and let his head sag backwards, stretching the muscles in his neck. His eyes closed, then, finally, he turned his gaze back on Robin. "I remember Matt talking about a brother, but he hadn't seen him since childhood. How in God's name does he come to be around these parts all these years later and what does he have to do with Edmond's death?"

The sun had by now dipped beneath the eastern horizon and without its rays the evening air turned chilly.

"Come inside and tell me," Tuck grunted, standing up and heading for the church door. "I need a drink, and so do you from the looks of it."

Robin smiled gratefully then, spotting a couple of young boys passing the church grounds he whistled and gestured them over. "Take my horse home for me, will you lads?

Make sure he's rubbed down and fed, if you can. Here." He tossed them a small coin each, which they took with wide eyes and toothy grins and then headed over to the palfrey, which was grazing on the grass over an ancient grave.

Then he followed the friar inside and told him the whole story.

"What will you do?"

Robin stared into the small fire in the manse's hearth, lips pressed tightly shut, the fingertips on his right hand incessantly rubbing against each other. He'd been asking himself the same question ever since he'd left the blackened tannery but he still wasn't sure of the answer.

He shrugged, almost spilling the watered-down ale he'd asked for. He was too weary to drink much that night, he needed a clear head.

"The sheriff had already given me permission to gather the men together again so the fact this bastard Groves plans on killing us all just means it's even more urgent. I wasn't sure if they'd all want to come back to a life of prowling the forests of Yorkshire but, well, I don't see that there's much of a choice for them now. And that includes you."

Tuck snorted and leaned back, away from him, a look of surprise on his round, jowly face.

"Are you joking? I can't rejoin you."

"Why not? You can still handle yourself. And it's too dangerous to stay here – Groves and his lackeys will come for you soon enough and even you won't be able to withstand their numbers."

The friar shook his tonsured head almost sadly. "I was too old and worn-out to be a member of your gang three years ago – remember, I returned to Lewes Priory for that very reason – and I've been in the wars since then too. I was badly injured that Christmas I spent in Brandesburton, you recall I told you about it?"

113

Robin grunted; Tuck had regaled him with that tale on at least a dozen occasions when they'd shared a drink in the past couple of years. The churchman had shown him the fleshy pink scars on his side and leg though, and he understood the truth of the situation: approaching his fiftieth year on God's Earth, Friar Tuck's time as a bounty hunter was long past.

Yet he could still be useful, Robin was sure of that...

They finished their drinks and embraced, their shared grief for Edmond and the threat of danger drawing them together again.

"Look, I know you're struggling with things just now. Your work, and family troubles and probably all the bad memories you've gathered over the years are weighing you down too. But you've come through harder times before. Stay true to yourself and remember: *hope*."

Robin nodded and a smile appeared on his tired face. He'd almost forgotten that word.

The two friends said farewell and then the young lawman, feeling six inches taller now, made his way to the fletcher's house. Matilda might not love him any more, but he had to make certain she and Arthur would be safe, whatever happened in the coming weeks.

He had to make sure *everyone* in Wakefield was aware of the situation. They'd need to arrange a local militia, ready to defend the village at a moment's notice should the wolf's heads decide to attack the place everyone knew Robin called home.

At least he had the ideal man to lead that defence. He just hoped the rest of the villagers would be up to the task.

At last, eyes drooping from sheer exhaustion – both mental and physical – he tapped on the fletcher's great, stout door and, smiling gratefully, was welcomed inside by the stern faced Henry.

"It's good to see you," Matilda's father said, his voice, and expression, neutral. "Bit late to be visiting though, isn't it?"

Robin could see his wife sleeping on the old pallet that had been hers as she'd grown up in this house, little Arthur snuggled under the thin blanket beside her, and he felt a pang of loneliness, wishing he was lying there next to them.

"It's a long story, Henry," he sighed. "And I'm too tired to tell it all again this night. Please, though, bar the door and have your axe next to you as you sleep. If it's all right with you, I'll sleep on the floor." He raised a hand to cut the worried fletcher off before the big man could begin questioning him. "There's no immediate danger, I'm certain, and I'll explain all in the morning, but...better to be prepared, just in case."

He could feel his eyelids drooping as he spoke and knew his father-in-law must have noticed it as well as he, thankfully, gave in and bade Robin find a place on the floor to sleep. He even threw an old blanket out from the chest in the small room he and Matilda's mother slept in.

As soon as he lay down on the hard floor next to his sleeping son – blanket pulled up, head resting on his bundled cloak – a contented smile touched his lips and he fell asleep.

CHAPTER THIRTEEN

"Who are you two ugly whoresons?"

Little John roared with laughter at the insult, but Will's brows, predictably, lowered into a menacing frown and a low growl rose in his throat.

"Your worst fucking nightmare, son," Scarlet retorted, facing up to the man who was about the same build but slightly taller and slightly uglier, with a nose that had obviously been broken more than once and a head shaved right in, leaving only stubble. "Now get out of the way or my big friend here will bite your bollocks off."

The grin left John's face, to be replaced by a look of surprise.

"I'm not eating anyone's balls, Scarlet. If you want to start a fight with this lad that's your business." He spat, then grinned mischievously. "You've got sharper teeth than me anyway."

The hired thug looked confused. Normally when he insulted people they lowered their heads and tried not to annoy him; he had no idea how to react to the banter between these two travellers who'd suddenly arrived, unannounced in his master's tavern.

"Is that the ritual insults done? Can we move on now and act like men instead of children?"

A new voice came to John and Will and a figure appeared from a side door, an irritated look on his face at their intrusion. He was an unremarkable man of average height and build, close-cropped brown hair and beard that were starting to show flecks of grey, and fine clothing. But his eyes were keen and intelligent and showed no signs of anxiety. This was a man of ruthless efficiency – Scarlet knew the type, having dealt with similar men many times over the years when he was employed as a mercenary or a bodyguard. There was no need to antagonise him, that wasn't what they were here for at all.

"What do you want in my establishment? From the looks of you" – the man curled his lip very slightly, conveying his distaste but not too overtly – "you aren't just here for a drink and some female company."

"We're just looking for a friend of ours," Little John said. "Man called Stephen. About this big," he raised a hand and held it level against his chest. "Pock-marked skin. We heard he was working for you, here – assuming you're Godwin Laweles."

John and Will had reached Leeds not long ago and asked some of the locals if they knew where Stephen was working. They'd known it was *somewhere* in this town but where, and for whom, they had to find out.

Thankfully, the former Hospitaller sergeant-at-arms stood out, thanks to his bearing and general air of competence. The men he shared bodyguard duties with were nothing like him the locals said, pointing them in the direction of *The Pewter Pot* – a tavern-cum-brothel owned by Godwin Laweles, the wealthiest, and most ruthless, merchant in Leeds – with warnings not to cause any trouble.

Laweles didn't take kindly to it apparently.

"And who are you?" he asked, not confirming or denying his identity. Three other men followed him through the side-door and they slowly moved to circle John and Will, with the first, shaven-headed guard directly behind them. Will could almost feel the violence emanating from that one in particular.

"We're friends of his," Will said, the hairs on the back of his neck tingling – it was a real effort not to throw his head back into the face of the thug behind him. "Can you just let Stephen know Will Scarlet and Little John are here to talk to him? It's important."

Clearly the man's bodyguards had heard of the former

outlaws, as their eyes moved warily to their leader to see how he'd react to this revelation. Everyone in England had heard of these two. And everyone knew they weren't men to get into a fight with.

Godwin Laweles wasn't a man to show any nervousness though, and Will was impressed with his calm, confident bearing even when his own guards were unconsciously moving ever so slightly backwards, away from him and John.

"I don't give a fuck who you are, I'll –" the shaven-headed man behind them began but his employer glared at him, waving a hand to silence him.

The tension in the room was palpable. Will did his best to look bored, and a glance to his left told him Little John was doing the same. John probably *was* genuinely bored, Scarlet thought, envying the big man his relaxed temperament.

"Stephen!" Laweles raised his voice, which was surprisingly powerful, slicing through the air like an arrow although his eyes never moved from Will. He'd clearly marked the smaller of his visitors as the most dangerous which might have been true and it might not, but Will knew his giant friend would have noticed the same thing and be ready to take advantage of it should the need arise. "You have visitors."

There was silence for a while and Laweles showed signs of impatience, leaning his weight from his left to his right foot and letting out a soft sigh, before he opened his mouth to call on the Hospitaller again.

Muffled shouts reached them, filling the gloomy interior of the tavern, and Will's hand fell to his sword hilt instinctively, even though, if it came to a fight, he'd use the long knife hidden inside his tunic rather than the unwieldy longsword which would be useless in such cramped confines.

Laweles's guards didn't appear at all perturbed by the

shouting though, and Will looked up at John who shrugged. Apparently this was a regular occurrence.

The voice grew louder, coming towards them from a corridor on the right of the main room, and a second, answering voice – high pitched and angry – could be heard now.

Suddenly the door from that hallway burst open and a man stumbled through, red-faced, furious, and still trying to tie the laces on his breeches back up.

A strong hand grabbed the scruff of the man's neck again and Stephen appeared with an expression of disgust.

"I don't want to see you in here again you arsehole," he shouted, pressing his pock-marked face up to the frightened man's ear. "I told you before – you don't get violent with the girls. Now get the fuck out of here." He slapped the man a ringing blow across the back of his head and watched as he stumbled out of the front door, clutching his skull and whining in pain.

An irritated sigh escaped Stephen's lips before he turned at last to his employer and, none too respectfully, shrugged. "I was busy when you called on me." He hadn't yet noticed his two old friends standing in the shadows.

"So I see," Laweles retorted, his lips a thin, furious line. "I already told you more than once that the punters can do what they want to the girls, as long as they pay and as long as they don't permanently mark them. Yet there you are throwing another wealthy man out into –"

"John! Will!" Stephen finally spotted the two men in his peripheral vision and turned to greet them, completely ignoring his employer's angry rebuke. "It's good to see you, my friends. What are you doing here in Leeds?"

"Come for you," John replied, a smile on his own bearded face, although it dropped away as he went on. "There's trouble brewing, Stephen. We're all in danger, including you."

"Aye," Will agreed. "You need to come with us. Back to

the greenwood once again."

Stephen shook his head but before he could say another word, to demand the whole story, Laweles broke in.

"You're not going anywhere. I didn't become a rich man by letting my employees leave whenever they felt like it." He strode across and pointed a finger at Stephen. "You signed a contract. You're *my* man now. If you want to leave my employ you'll have to buy out your contract. And that won't be cheap."

Will raised an eyebrow and looked at John who laughed out loud. Stephen shook his head.

"I didn't sign any contract – I told you I couldn't write, remember? All I did was make an illegible mark on your piece of paper."

"That's still legally binding," Laweles retorted, then softened his tone a little. "Look, to be perfectly honest, you're a shit employee. Your strict moral code is bad for business in a place like this so...I'll be glad to let you go with the two wolf's heads."

"I'm no wolf's head," John growled. "I'm a lawman, one of the sheriff's own men."

"Yes, yes, so you are." Laweles waved a hand over his shoulder irritably, watching Stephen for his response.

"I'll tell you what," the Hospitaller smiled. "I'm leaving, now, and you can keep the wages you owe me."

Laweles's eyes narrowed. "I don't owe you any money – you were all paid this morning."

Stephen shrugged. "Oh well, then. Let's go boys, it'll be good to get back to the open forest after being stuck here for so long."

"Stop them!"

Godwin Laweles wasn't the type to let his assets walk out on him without a fight, but Will was shocked when the man's fist hit him a glancing strike on the side of the face. Scarlet had seen the blow coming and moved just in time, thankfully, or he might have suffered a broken nose. The foppish little business owner appeared gaunt but he must have had strong, wiry muscles hidden under his fine clothing, as his punch had been quite a powerful one.

Will turned, following Laweles as his momentum made him overbalance, and slammed his elbow into the back of the businessman's skull, dropping him like a stone to the floor.

Thankfully, John expected the shaven-headed man behind them to react quickly at the order to fight. The giant lawman brought his hand up just as the bodyguard made to charge at Will, grabbing his testicles in a vice-like grip and squeezing. When the guard had begun falling to his knees John rammed his left fist into his nose then, with the other hand still squeezing brutally, flipped the tortured man up and onto a table, where he rolled onto his side and curled into a ball, whimpering like a kicked dog.

The remaining three guards hadn't moved and, as he straightened up, Will could see why. Stephen held a dagger in his hand and was staring at them, almost daring them to attack. None did. They'd worked with him for only a short time, but every one of them – hard as they were – feared him.

Without another word, the three friends made their way out the front door.

The old gang was coming together again.

Stephen grinned as the warm sunlight hit his face. It was good to be free again!

CHAPTER FOURTEEN

Wakefield was in uproar. Or, more accurately, the people gathered in St Mary's were in uproar.

Robin stood at the altar, flanked by Friar Tuck on his right and the flustered village headman, Patrick Prudhomme on his left.

"Calm yourselves," Patrick was shouting, arms raised, flapping his hands up and down in what might have been a comical way if the situation hadn't been so serious. "Let Hood speak."

"You're the sheriff's man now," one local – a large, middle-aged man Robin recognised as a labourer – shouted, slightly louder than the rest of the folk, drawing most of the attention his way as a result. "If this band of rapists and killers is coming to pillage Wakefield why isn't de Faucumberg sending soldiers to protect us?"

"Aye," a portly, ruddy cheeked woman agreed in a shrill voice. "He has a standing army – he can afford to send a few of his men here to make sure this gang don't murder us in our beds."

The voices were raised again, unanimously in agreement with their two compatriots and Patrick shook his head in defeat, stepping back to take a seat beside Father Myrc who smiled in sympathetic understanding.

"Settle down you people. Now!"

Robin flinched as Tuck's powerful orator's voice boomed in his ear and he gave the friar a withering glance.

It worked though; the people, gathered in the house of God after all, took in the sight of the impatient clergyman and the shouting dropped to a mutter which, eventually, as Tuck's gaze sought out the offenders, faded into a nervy silence.

"That's better. Robin?" The friar gestured with his palms

towards the lectern, a simple, undecorated wooden construction, and his younger friend nodded in gratitude, stepping forward to take up the proffered position.

"Thank you." He looked around, nodding at those he knew well, and noting with pride the respect he saw reflected in all the villagers' eyes. "As Patrick says, we have reason to believe this gang of outlaws may come here. In fact, some of them already visited" – he held up his hands before the nervous muttering at that revelation could turn into a rabble again – "but, unfortunately for them, they chose to attack Will Scaflock."

He grinned and the people laughed and cheered as they guessed the outcome of that meeting.

"So they are three men less thanks to Will, but they are growing all the time as more landless men come out of the woodwork and join up with them. From what we can gather their leader is...charismatic. He has a way of getting people to do his bidding."

"Sounds like a certain other wolf's head I remember," Alexander Gilbert, landlord of the tavern, shouted, but Robin didn't smile at the intended compliment.

"Make no mistake," he replied, his eyes sweeping the room, "this man is nothing – *nothing* – like me. He's already caused havoc in Holmfirth, even murdering their priest, and now he's spreading fear around the countryside."

"So where's the sheriff's men to guard us then, until the wolf's head can be brought down?" The portly woman repeated her question to a chorus of "aye"s.

"Sir Henry doesn't have enough men to send to every village and town the outlaws have threatened. It's as simple as that." Robin hadn't told the people the real reason for the threat to their village – he knew the people would resent Matilda and the rest of his family if they knew the outlaws were targeting them to get revenge on Robin. "We don't know when they'll come, or even if they

123

will for certain. We're just working from rumours. The simple fact is: you will have to defend the village yourselves."

There were some nervous grumbles at that, but not many wanted to show themselves up as cowards, especially the men.

"You can all shoot a longbow," Robin stated, encouragingly. "We all started practising as children didn't we? So set up lookout posts on the roads approaching the village and arm the guards with longbows and hunting horns. Then there's others of you, like John Cobble," he pointed to a brawny middle-aged man with a flat nose, "who fought against the Scots when they raided a few years back. You can use a sword can't you John? Aye, and you've seen action so you won't run like a girl if you're under attack."

"Hey!"

The lawman's eyes flicked to the corner of the room and his face melted in a smile. "Of course, some of the women can fight just as well as the men, eh Marjorie?"

"Good lass," someone cheered, and there was scattered applause as the villagers, growing in confidence, remembered Robin's sister taking on Sir Guy of Gisbourne three years earlier and surviving. The sleek black crossbow she could often be seen practising with on the village green was testament to that, since she'd taken it from the Raven's corpse after her brother had finished the madman off.

"What about you, Henry?" Robin addressed his father-in-law. "You're not going to stand by and watch if some piece of filth comes here looking for trouble are you?" The fletcher's face flushed scarlet as dozens of pairs of eyes fixed on him, but Robin carried on, drawing the looks back his way. "Of course you won't – the last time someone came here threatening your daughter it was Matt Groves, Gisbourne's captain. And you belted him so hard in the

124

face you almost broke his jaw from what I heard!"

Henry grinned and brandished his fist in the air as cheering broke out again. Matilda stood next to her father, little Arthur beside her, and she smiled proudly.

She'd barely spoken to Robin when she woke that morning to find him sleeping next to them. Robin had broken his fast with the Fletcher's, telling them what was happening and why he'd turned up at their door so late.

The lawman enjoyed sharing a meal with Arthur, helping the little boy eat slices of buttered bread and fresh cow's milk, and he'd found a new sense of determination to bring Philip Groves to justice as the family had filled their bellies before another day earning an honest living.

Wakefield wouldn't be an easy target for the bastards Robin vowed, while also mouthing silent prayers to God and the Magdalene to protect the village.

As he stood there, moving out now from behind the lectern to take up a position in the centre of the altar, Matilda still wouldn't meet his eyes but he didn't feel too downcast. His speech was working – the villagers had forgotten their initial, panicked reaction to the threatening news Patrick had delivered, to be replaced with a grim, and even somewhat excited, determination to meet violence with violence.

Still, though, many of the people looked nervous and unsure. They knew Robin would be leaving soon to lead his men in the hunt for the outlaws, leaving them leaderless. With the best will in the world, an army, even one as enthusiastic as the likes of the cobbler and the fletcher, needed someone to guide it.

And Robin knew the perfect man for the job.

"Friar Tuck here will be in charge of organising the defences." He gestured at his old friend whose head snapped around in surprise, mouth dropping open to protest, but Robin continued, giving the clergyman no time to protest.

"Tuck might be a man of God, but he's one of the hardest men I've ever met. And I've met a few," he grinned, glad to see the expression mirrored on many of the locals' faces as they shared his little joke. "You all remember Adam Gurdon, right?" Everyone did. A former knight who pretended to be the celebrated folk hero Adam Bell, he'd been the leader of Little John and Will Scarlet's outlaw gang when Robin first joined them. Eventually Gurdon had shown his true colours, betraying the gang to the sheriff in return for a pardon and being rewarded with the position of bailiff.

Adam Gurdon had been a Templar – a tough man and as skilled in combat as they came.

"Well," Robin went on, "I remember the first day I ever met Tuck. He stood toe to toe with Adam Gurdon and battered the man senseless with nothing more than a club." He allowed the audience time to look at the friar before finishing his endorsement. "Battered Gurdon in the guts before the bastard – sorry Father Myrc," a sheepish grin towards the stern-faced priest – "before he could react, then knocked him out cold with a blow to the back of the skull. Like that," he mimicked Tuck's moves, "it was over in a heartbeat. Never seen anything like it in my life."

Of course, the good people of Wakefield knew Tuck, and they knew he was no fool. Most of them hadn't really heard about this side of him though, and there was a new-found respect in their eyes as they contemplated the clergyman Robin Hood was nominating as the man to lead the defence of their village.

Father Myrc shook his head disapprovingly and Tuck had the grace to look somewhat sheepish, even if his eyes were dancing mischievously.

He hadn't always been a man of the cloth – as a young man he'd been an extremely accomplished wrestler, and even fought as a sell-sword for a time, before God sent him to rescue the Bishop of Norwich from robbers, twenty-five years or so earlier.

He'd become a friar after that but the church had used his considerable martial skills to guard their property and money as it moved around from county to county and even country to country.

Aye, Hood had chosen their captain well. A fearless fighter with God on his side – all he needed was someone to support Tuck in the task and help organize things since it would be too much for one man.

He wasn't sure who to ask though, despite going over options in his head for much of that morning.

"You'll need help Tuck," a voice piped up, and all eyes turned to gaze at the speaker who pushed through the crowd towards the front of the room. "Someone that knows how to train and how to fight and has experience of combat."

The hushed room became a babble of noise as everyone tried to talk at once but Robin was too surprised to call for order as the volunteer reached the lectern and stared at him defiantly.

"Marjorie's not the only woman in the village that knows how to fight," Matilda said to him then stepped up to stand before the people as she went on. "I stuck Gisbourne with a couple of arrows myself that day and I lived in the greenwood with Robin and Tuck and John and Will Scarlet and the rest of them, learning their ways."

The villagers watched her uncertainly and then her father broke the silence.

"You can't do this, lass," he rumbled, holding little Arthur in his arms where Matilda had placed him before moving through the crowd. "We'll need lots of arrows for our longbowmen so you'll be needed to fletch them with me."

Matilda shook her head irritably and chopped her hand through the air. "There won't be any need for arrows if we don't organise the defences properly, da. Tuck can't do it all by himself," she reiterated, "and I defy any of you – *any of you* – to stand here and tell me to my face that you can do a better job than me. My husband and I didn't just talk about making babies and what I was going to make him for his dinner of an evening over the years. I know how to fight and I know how to organise."

A couple of men near the back of the gathering raised their voice – more against the suggestion a woman should tell them how to defend the village rather than any opposition against Matilda personally – and Robin expected their dissension to spread rapidly and put an end to his wife's claim.

When he thought about it, her idea actually seemed a good one. She *was* a strong woman and more than a match for the majority of men in Wakefield with a short sword. If Queen Isabella could lead men, why couldn't Matilda?

Before he could lend his support to her plan, Friar Tuck's powerful voice rolled out over the room and, again, attention focused on the clergyman.

"I see nothing to argue about here," he said. "No-one else offered their services and, as Matilda Hood says, she's more than up to the job. I can vouch for her myself."

"As can I," Robin broke in, feeling his wife's eyes upon him but not wanting to return the look, fearing what he might see there.

Their influence was enough to silence any more arguments. None there wanted to stand up against the dangerous friar and unpredictable bailiff. Besides, what more could Wakefield ask for? Most of the villages around Yorkshire would be hard pressed to find such a strong war-leader and quick-witted lieutenant.

The heads in the crowd slowly began to nod in acceptance and that was that.

His job was done, Robin knew. To say any more would be over-egging the pudding. The people were confident enough now; they'd follow Tuck and Matilda's advice by setting up lookout points and patrols day and night. It would be enough, he was sure. Certainly he felt better about leaving his family behind to try and bring down Groves and his disciples...Still, he felt a tightness in his throat and wished...

His heart lifted as Matilda met his gaze and there was pride and gratitude in her eyes. He'd rallied her fellow villagers – not to mention her da, whom she doted on – and voiced his support for her. And he was her husband still.

That one look brought him hope that things would all turn out well, eventually, and he slipped out the side door of the nave unnoticed to make his own preparations for the coming fight.

Fight?

No.

This was going to be a war!

* * *

Will suggested it might be a good idea for the three reunited companions not to spend the night in Leeds, what with the slighted brothel-owner and his men probably looking to teach them a lesson or two.

"I don't want to wake up with some hired thug's dagger in my guts," Scarlet opined, climbing atop his courser, as John did the same. "But it'll be dark soon so we'd best get a ways along the road and find somewhere to camp for the night, before it's too treacherous for the horses." He glanced at Stephen who looked back up at him. "Where's your mount?"

"Haven't got one," the Hospitaller replied, spreading his hands out defensively. "I never go anywhere these days. What the fuck would I keep a horse for?"

Behind them, the brothel's doors opened and Godwin

Laweles walked out, his men at his back, nursing their wounds and glaring murderously at them.

"Aye, you'd better ride out of here, you whoresons," Laweles called. "You might think you're big men with big reputations but nobody comes into my place and beats up my men."

"Come on," Little John growled, eyeing the businessman and his thugs warily. "They'll grow a pair of balls between them soon enough and then we'll really have to fight. Let's get out of here. Where's the nearest stables?"

"There's one attached to the inn, about half a mile down the street there," Stephen replied as they moved off in the direction he indicated with a flick of his head. "Not sure if there'll be anyone around at this time of the day though."

"The stable boy will be about," Will said, his eyes never once leaving Laweles, who hadn't moved from his position outside the brothel. "We'll find you a mount, never fear. Even if we have to steal it. As John says, those pricks with your former employer will grow in confidence once we're out of sight and that's when the swords and the longbows come out. Let's move."

They rounded the corner, out of sight of *The Pewter Pot*, and Will kicked his heels into the courser's sides. "You two stay together and catch me up. I'll go on ahead and find Stephen something to ride."

"Aren't we going in the wrong direction for that?" John grinned, winking at the Hospitaller. "The brothel's back that way."

Will ignored the giant's poor joke and cantered off along the road on his errand.

Stephen had slightly misjudged the distance to the stables, or else Will had passed the one his friend was talking about, as it was more like a mile along the road before he spotted the big tavern with its attendant stable.

Light was spilling from the open windows into the red of the sunset that was beginning to bathe the town, and the sounds of drunken revelry filled the street. Will was glad he didn't have to live next to the place, the neighbours would never get much sleep.

Ignoring the main building he rode straight to the stable and reined in his horse, hopping out of the saddle and tying the reins round the tethering post before hurrying into the low building with its stench of animal breath and dung.

"Ho!" he shouted, eyes scanning the gloomy interior. "Anyone about?"

A young boy about eleven years-old appeared like a ghost from one of the stalls where he'd presumably been grooming the beast – a tired looking old packhorse – within. Wide-eyed and somewhat nervous, the lad peered at Scarlet but didn't come too close.

"I need a horse, boy. Your master got any for sale?"

"N-no, my lord," the youngster stammered and Will stifled a laugh at the idea he was a nobleman. The boy's master must tell him to talk to customers like that to try and please them; make them more open to being fleeced. "All these belong to travellers staying at the inn."

Will, grim-faced, walked along the row of stalls, eyeing each of the animals stabled there. There were   four, including the old nag the boy had been grooming, and only one, a chestnut-brown palfrey, looked up to much.

Sighing theatrically, he reached into his pouch and drew out two coins. He nodded to the sleek palfrey and told the boy to saddle it.

"But, my lord, that's Strawberry, it's –"

The lad began to back away, probably ready to make a run for it out the back door and in to the landlord but Will had anticipated the movement and grasped his arm, not painfully but with enough iron in the grip to let the boy know trying to escape wasn't a wise move.

"Here." Scarlet handed the smallest of the coins in his hand to the boy, whose already wide eyes almost popped

131

out of their sockets. It wasn't a huge amount but, to the stable-hand it probably amounted to a month's wages.

"Saddle the horse," he repeated to the boy. "This one," the second coin was held in the air and the sun's dying red light glinted off it, "is for its owner. This is probably double what the thing is worth so I don't think the owner will have a problem with the trade, am I right?"

The lad gulped and tore his eyes from the coin to meet Will's gaze. "Yes, my lord, you are. That's..."

"A lot of money, I know. And you better make fucking sure the money gets to Strawberry's owner, boy or I'll come back and tie your arms to the pillar here" – he slapped the post that held up the roof – "and your legs to the horse" – he pointed at the palfrey, whose long face seemed to take on a malevolent cast in the rosy light – "then I'll ride off. You understand me?"

The boy looked frightened at the mental image of his body being torn apart, but also affronted at the suggestion he'd shave some of the coin off for himself. He could tell this was a man who wasn't to be fooled with though, so he nodded and, when Will released his arm, hurried to saddle the horse that had been picked out.

"Good lad," Will smiled when the reins were handed to him. "God grant you a good evening."

"And to you, my lord," the stable-hand muttered, the small coin he'd been given for his services in his hand and a cheery smile on his face.

Will liked the look of the brown palfrey so much that he decided to keep her for himself. He tied the reins of the two horses together before hauling himself up into Strawberry's saddle.

"Go and pay the horse's owner that coin, boy," he shouted over his shoulder and, without a backward glance, cantered back along the surprisingly quiet road in the direction he'd come from.

He spotted the figures of his friends in the distance,

unmistakable given John's great size and grinned as he rode up to them.

"In the name of God, Stephen, you've let yourself go working in that whorehouse," he laughed, taking in the ruddy cheeks and breathlessness of the Hospitaller. "A gentle half-mile run and you look fit to drop."

"Fuck off," Stephen retorted, untying his new mount's reins from Strawberry's harness and, with an effort, dragged himself up into the saddle, teeth bared as he sucked in air. "That was more than half a mile."

Laughing, Will led them out of the town onto the main road, eyeing the horizon.

"We should have just enough to time to cover a couple of miles back towards Wakefield," he judged. "Then we'll find somewhere amongst the trees to camp. I doubt Laweles's lads will follow us but...better safe than sorry."

"Pfft," Stephen pursed his lips and made a disgusted sound as they urged the horses into a fast walk, single file. "I'm not the only one that's changed, Scarlet. A few years ago you'd have wanted to set up an ambush for that lot. Now you're talking about hiding from them. You probably won't even let us light a fire in case they sneak up and kick your arse."

John laughed loudly, watching Will for the expected sour reaction, but it seemed Scarlet really had mellowed, as he simply smiled and ignored the taunt which was, after all, tongue-in-cheek.

"What you got for my supper anyway?" the Hospitaller asked, eyeing John and Will's saddlebags. "Something nice I hope."

"Oh aye," John replied airily. "We've got a pottage of stewed pheasant, followed by roast kid and plums in wine."

Will burst out laughing but Stephen scowled.

"Bit rich for my taste, thanks all the same. I'll be glad with a bit of black bread and a skin of ale."

"Plenty of those too," John grinned as they rode on, mouths watering at the thought of even such a frugal meal.

A short time later, and with occasional glances over their shoulders for signs of pursuit which never materialised, John pointed to a spot off to the right. His experienced woodsman's eyes had noticed an overgrown trail leading into what was deceptively sparse foliage at that point.

"That must lead to something," the giant lawman mused, nodding towards the hidden track. "Maybe a clearing."

Will shrugged. "It's as good a place to stop as any we've seen so far, and the light's almost gone."

They dismounted and led their mounts through the bushes into the trees which grew thicker a dozen paces away from the main road. They didn't have to walk much further before John's guess proved correct and they came to a clearing.

Someone had camped here in the past, as stones formed a fire-pit, although the lack of embers or half-consumed firewood suggested it hadn't seen a flame in months or more.

"Perfect," Will smiled, tethering Strawberry to a nearby tree. "Get the ale out lads!"

"Are we lighting a fire?" John wondered, peering into the darkness to see if there was much kindling on the ground. "Or do you think there's a real possibility those arseholes will come looking for us? It doesn't seem very likely to me."

They both eyed Stephen who, ever the soldier, was pacing the perimeter of their camp-site, picking at the skin on his fingers, searching for places any possible attack might come from, and trying to gauge how hidden their position really was from the main road.

"What d'you think?" Will asked the Hospitaller. "They were your workmates. Are they stupid – or vengeful – enough to come after us?" It didn't seem probable but Will had no intention of dying in the forest at the hands of some louts who spent their days throwing drunks out of a whorehouse. Not after he'd survived for so long in the greenwood even when the likes of Sir Guy of Gisbourne sought to kill him.

Stephen shook his head. "I doubt it. They were hard enough, and some of them were vicious with it but...they kept their distance from me and I suspect they'll be even more wary of tackling you two." He threw them a withering look. "Right pair of bastards you two, everyone in England knows that."

"That's us," John agreed, opening his breeches and emptying his bladder noisily into the bushes on the edge of the camp. "Complete bastards."

"Nah, they'll have forgotten all about us by now," Stephen smiled. "But if we're going to be getting back to living rough in the forest like this, I'd say it'd not be a bad idea to set a watch. Just in case."

Will groaned at the thought but nodded agreement, brightening as he did so. "Aye, fair enough. It's early yet though, and getting chilly now the sun's gone down – let's build that fire and get comfy with some meat and ale!"

"Good idea," John said, moving to find some kindling. "And while we rest for the evening, maybe Stephen can tell me how he came to be a Hospitaller in the first place. I don't think we ever did find out. You can take first watch, Will. Better get some sleep so you're fresh for it..."

"Aye, fair enough," Scarlet agreed and disappeared into the gloom outside the camp-fire's radiance. "I'll have a nap. Keep the noise down, and wake me when you two want to turn in."

CHAPTER FIFTEEN

After a few ales and a frugal supper of bread and dried meat Stephen and Little John settled down for the night and the Hospitaller began his tale. Much to the John's surprise, Stephen said he'd spent his childhood learning to be a stonemason in the nearby town of Halifax.

"Aye, my father was a great artisan," the sergeant-at-arms nodded, supping a small mug of ale, eyes sparkling at the looks on the others' face as he started his tale, "and he took me under his wing."

"I can't see you having the patience to carve stone," Little John said. "You'd be a much better labourer. No offence."

Stephen almost managed a smile at that. "None taken. As it turns out you were right – I usually ended up just carting the blocks around and helping the labourers, much to my da's irritation, but..." He gave a shrug as if that explained everything.

"Some men like to spend time making things pretty, while others just like to get the job done and go home without any messing about," John mused, and the Hospitaller seemed to like that description of his qualities.

"Aye, that's about right. So I didn't learn much about the finer arts of stone masonry, but my body grew hard and strong from the work. One day some Hospitallers came to the town – we were working on the church, replacing a wall and fitting some new windows, I remember it as if it were only yesterday – and they were after some recruits to go to Rhodes where they were trying to set up a new base. I joined them."

"Didn't your da try to stop you?" John wondered, picking a piece of gristle from between his teeth.

Stephen shook his head. "We were never very close, as

his work took him away from home a lot. Not much work for a stonemason unless he was able to travel to the towns and cities roundabout so I never saw him all that much growing up. I was closer to my ma but her and my father both agreed I'd be better off learning my trade with the knights, since I'd never be a mason. And they were both God-fearing people who saw this as my chance to earn passage into Heaven."

"God help us all," John snorted. "Your cheery face in Heaven? Sounds more like Hell."

Stephen made a gesture with his hand that was so rude it might preclude his entry to paradise after all, then continued.

"I spent a few years in Rhodes, learning how to fight like a soldier. How to be a killer," he growled, looking pointedly at the giant who raised his hands in a mock defensive motion.

"We had to clear the Turks – Saracens – off the island before we could colonise it properly, and there were pirates controlling the waters all around. So I was taught how to fight on land and from the deck of a ship."

"And that's where you met Sir Richard?"

"Aye," Stephen agreed. "I was sergeant to another knight. A Frenchman named Sir Jean de Pagnac. He was killed though, in a tunnel beneath a little village..." His voice trailed off and he stared thoughtfully into the flickering firelight before shuddering and shaking his head as if to clear away some frightful vision. "Sir Richard's sergeant was killed in action that night too, so the Grand Master decided to put us together and pack us back home to Kirklees."

"A tunnel?" John demanded. "What the hell were you doing in a tunnel under a village?"

Stephen simply shook his head and refused to be drawn on the subject, his expression dark enough that John didn't push the issue.

"Where's Rhodes anyway?" the big man asked instead, changing the subject.

The strange atmosphere that had settled on their gloomy camp-site lifted as Stephen burst into laughter at his friend's lack of geographical knowledge.

"What? What the fuck's so funny about that?" John demanded, face flushing in the darkness, but that just made the other man laugh even harder.

"Keep your voice down," Stephen whispered gleefully, gesturing at the shadowy bundle on the forest floor. "You'll wake Scarlet."

Stephen finally replied to the original question when his mirth had lessened.

"Rhodes takes weeks of travel by a fast ship, and it's worth it, for it's always summer there. But Sir Richard and I came back to England and lived at the Hospitaller Preceptory in Kirklees for a few years. Good years." His voice trailed away, a wistful note creeping in as it became lost in the night and he idly picked at the dry skin on his thumb. "And then we met you boys and everything turned to shit."

"That's a lovely story, Stephen." An unseen man hissed at them from the darkness and the Hospitaller jumped to his feet, drawing his sword free from its sheath and moving back-to-back with Little John who'd grabbed his quarterstaff and stood now, face grim in the soft orange glow from the firelight, searching for the hidden speaker.

"I recognise that voice," Stephen growled, teeth pulled back like a wolf. "Edwin Baker. One of Laweles's men. Come on then, and let my sword taste your blood you ugly bastard!"

"Enough of the talk." A second voice spoke from the other side of their camp-site, and then a third grunted agreement from another direction, confirming what Stephen had suspected all along: they were surrounded. Probably by at least five or six of his erstwhile colleagues.

138

Odds of two to one didn't look good.

The man who'd spoken first stepped from the shadows into the light, a smile on his face, as if he knew the odds were stacked in their favour and he was going to enjoy repaying the fabled former-outlaws for the beating they'd handed out back in the *The Pewter Pot*.

"Why don't you just lay down your weapons there, lads," he said, with a smirk, "and we'll let you live. We'll take all your coin, weapons and clothes but you'll be free to return to your homes. Even if you will be naked." He barked a small laugh then nodded in disgust at Will Scarlet's bedroll. "Look at that – your mate's so ale-soaked he hasn't even realised you're under attack. I expected more from an ex-Hospitaller sergeant like you Stephen. You need to teach your friends some military discipline."

John looked down at the bedroll and filling his great lungs with air, roared, "Will!"

As Laweles's guards moved in to begin their one-sided assault there was a scream of pain from the deep shadows to the left. The air reverberated with the sound, which told of sheer agony, before it was cut off by the thud of metal striking bone. It was followed, eerily, by a grunt of sadistic laughter.

The attackers reeled in confusion and the leader's eyes narrowed, as he finally understood what was happening. He opened his mouth to urge his men on.

"It's a trick! The other one isn't lying on the ground drunk, he's –"

His words were cut-off as the end of Little John's staff - almost the trunk of a young oak tree – smashed into his mouth, sending him crashing back onto the ground where he lay, mewling and clutching at his ruined teeth.

"Fucking come on then, you arseholes!" John roared into the night, his shaggy brown hair and beard, and the feral, battle-fevered look on his face making him appear like some terrifying beast of the fields.

The thugs from Leeds, knowing there was an assassin hiding somewhere within the trees next to them, decided to move into the light and engage John and their former colleague, Stephen. At least they presented a target the men could actually *see*.

There was another outraged roar of pain from a different section of the encircling trees and Stephen knew that was one more assailant they needn't worry about. He had to concentrate now though, as two of Laweles's men came at him. One was armed with a sword, but the other, a small, black bearded man, only carried a long, heavy club.

Targeting that one first, Stephen swung his sword in a shallow arc towards him, and the man reacted as expected, blocking the attack with his club. The weight of the wooden weapon dropped his arm though, and, as he tried to recover, too slowly, the Hospitaller plunged the tip of his longsword into the bearded assailant's guts.

Tearing the blade free in a smooth, practised motion, he desperately raised it and deflected the second attacker's sword thrust, which would surely have torn his neck and throat wide open.

He dropped onto his haunches and plunged his sword upwards, deep into the man's belly, unfolding his knees as it went in and sawing it back and forward as he rose again to his full height. He paused for an instant to watch the light flee from the man's eyes but then, remembering they were still in a fight, turned to scan the camp.

John's sleeve was ripped apart and he sported a long gash which oozed blood as he traded blows with the final thug that remained in the fight. Another attacker lay unmoving at the giant's feet but the wound in his forearm was clearly hampering his use of the quarterstaff. Left to finish itself naturally, the fight wouldn't go well for the big man but, with a deafening war-cry, Will burst out of the darkness.

Stephen watched in relief as the tip of Scarlet's sword

exploded out of Laweles's man's gambeson in a spray of blood.

The blade was slowly pulled back and, huffing to catch his breath, Will bent and wiped off the blood on the fallen man's tunic.

The three friends looked at each other, all breathing hard but still alive, and they grinned like children that had just won a game of Hoodman's Blind.

"That was good," Scarlet grunted, replacing his sword in its leather and wood sheath.

"Just like old times," John agreed.

"Aye," Stephen finished. "But we still have to deal with that one."

He pointed his still bloody longsword at the thugs' leader, who yet lived, although with much fewer teeth than when the fight started. The man pulled himself onto his hands and knees but his head remained bowed towards the grass. He was obviously still reeling from the force of John's quarterstaff.

The fight was done and the battle-joy had left the three victors, who moved now to stand over of their final would-be killer.

"What do we do with him?" Stephen asked, before he kicked the man in the ribs just to make sure he didn't try anything.

"We could send him back to *The Pewter Pot* with a warning to Laweles not to fuck with us again?" John suggested, eyeing the man as he retched from the force of the Hospitaller's boot.

Will thought for a moment then shook his head. "Nah, I think we've already sent that message by killing all his men. But I'm bloody exhausted and I don't fancy sleeping with that prick still around, waiting for a chance to gut me."

The man turned his head, a look of hatred which quickly turned to disbelief as Scarlet's sword took him in the back.

"I'd just cleaned that too," Will muttered irritably as he dragged the blade along the dead man's breeches, which simply smeared the blood. Too tired to care, he sheathed the weapon and, with a shrug, moved back to his bedroll.

Removing the rolled up cloaks they'd stuffed in it to make it appear occupied, he lay down – for real this time – and closed his eyes with a yawn.

"It's your watch Stephen. Wake me when it's my turn."

CHAPTER SIXTEEN

Their next step, Robin decided, was to warn their former friends about Philip Groves's murderous intentions while offering advice to the towns and villages all around Nottingham and Yorkshire about defending themselves against the outlaws.

Not many of their old gang survived now: Arthur, the toothless, greasy haired lad from Bichill; Piers, a fine swordsman who had joined them not that long before their pardons; Peter Ordevill, a sailor who they knew was living in Selby; and James, the bowman who had never actually been a member of their gang but who'd saved all their lives when he warned them of an imminent attack by the Raven, Sir Guy of Gisbourne.

Robin, Little John, Will and Stephen started in Selby, where they found Peter Ordevill attempting to run a boatyard with little success. He was glad to leave the struggling business in the care of a neighbour and rejoin his old friends who he'd missed very much in the three years since they'd parted ways.

Next they moved on to Horbury and discovered James down on his luck and near-destitute. Robin had rewarded him with a fair sum of money for his part in their survival when Gisbourne had come hunting them but the bowman had struggled to find employment since then and, as a result, spent almost all his money. Like Piers, he was more than happy to join Hood's band of bounty hunters.

Finally it was Bichill, where they were reunited with the short but powerfully built Arthur. In his mid-twenties now, he'd been a quiet but dependable member of their old gang and, since their pardon he'd went back to his home village and used his wealth to open an alehouse.

Unlike Ordevill and James, however, he'd married and

had two children and refused to rejoin Robin and the others.

"You're putting your family in danger if you *don't* come with us," Will told him. "This outlaw, Philip, is coming after all of us. He knows who we are and, if he doesn't already, he'll eventually find out where we all live. Including you."

"So I should leave my wife unprotected?"

Arthur had matured in the years since Robin had last met him. He'd grown into an impressive man, with a proud bearing and a canny look about him, despite missing most of his teeth.

"She must have other family in the village," Will pointed out. "Send her to stay with them until we get this sorted."

"How long is that going to take?" Arthur grumbled. "I have a business to run here."

"We'll have a better chance of hunting the bastards down if we have as many of our old gang back together again as possible," Robin said reasonably. "We could do with your help and, as Will says, if you stay here you're just going to bring Philip and his men down on the place."

Still Arthur refused, and Robin could understand why. Bichill was a smaller place than Wakefield, with fewer able men and no seasoned warrior like Tuck to marshal the defences in the event of an assault.

"I'll tell you what," Robin said, after some thought. "We have to go to Nottingham to find Piers – you join us again, and your family can come to the city with us. I'll have the sheriff find somewhere for them to stay until this blows over."

Arthur mulled the suggestion over, knowing his wife, Mariam wouldn't like it, but also knowing Nottingham's walls would keep his loved ones safe.

"What choice do I have?" he sighed at last. "Can't just carry on hoping these bastard outlaws forget about me. Mariam will want her mother to come too though – she

lives with us since her own husband died two years ago."
As he glanced at each of his old friends in turn his face
brightened and he grinned. "Ah, but I suppose it'll be good
to be back in the greenwood, and free for a while again!"

As he'd done in Wakefield, Selby, Horbury and the other
places they'd visited in the recent weeks, Robin had
Bichill's headman, Johannes – an old, old man with flaking
skin and tired, red eyes – call a meeting, where they told
the locals of the possible threat and what they should do to
protect themselves against Philip's cut-throats.

Unsurprisingly, the people were frightened and
demanded aid from Robin as the sheriff's representative,
but he promised them nothing and advised them to set up
defences, even simple ones, to put their minds at ease.

Then, paying for a cart and two horses to pull it – the
whole party, including Mariam, her mother, and the two
infants – made their way as fast as they could to
Nottingham.

It was a surprisingly pleasant journey for Robin, as he
entertained Arthur's children – a boy and a girl – and put
their troubles to the back of his mind for a while.

The roads were in good condition thanks to the late
summer weather so the cart made good time and the
travellers made it to Nottingham without incident, rolling
in through the Chapel Bar gate and through the busy
streets towards the castle.

"Will – you and Stephen go and see if you can find
Piers. He was a clerk of some sort before he came to us,
and his family were wealthy so it shouldn't be too hard to
find someone who knows him."

"Easy for you to say," Will retorted. "It'll be like looking
for a needle in a box of fucking needles."

"Aye," Stephen agreed, and Robin couldn't help
laughing at the pair of them, with their sour faces.

"Piers de Toothill. There's not going to be very many
people with a name like that in Nottingham. Start at the tax

collector's place up the road there. We'll meet up in there later on, all right?" He gestured to a tavern, *The Blue Boar*, that was only fifty paces away, down a side street.

With a disgruntled wave Will wandered off towards the heart of the city, Stephen at his back looking as if he was about to go into battle.

"Moaning bastards," Peter Ordevill laughed.

"Aye, but they'll find Piers in no time," Robin nodded, confident in his friends' resourcefulness. "As for you two," he brought out his purse and handed over a substantial weight of coins. "Go and get provisions for the hunt, along with whatever weapons you might be needing."

James still had his faithful longbow but Peter needed both a sword and a bow since he'd kept neither when he bought his boatyard. The pair wandered off, soon becoming lost in the noisy, bustling traffic of the city, and Robin turned back to John.

"Right, let's go and see Sir Henry and find out what's to be done with Arthur's family."

As it turned out, the sheriff wasn't in the city that day – he'd been called to London by the king who was apparently trying to reassure himself of as much support as possible with the recent threats from France of invasion by his own wife, Isabella, and her – alleged – lover, Mortimer of Wigmore.

The sheriff's steward, William-atte-Burn, knew Robin well enough though, and he promised to see personally to the lodgings of Mariam and the little ones somewhere not too far from the castle, where the city watch would be able to keep an eye on them.

Before heading back down to the courtyard Robin and John made their way to the barracks to find Thomas, the sheriff's messenger. The young lawman still wanted to keep their group's numbers quite low for now, but he knew Thomas would be a good addition to their small band. The man had been a forester for years before the sheriff had promoted him – his skills would be useful, without a doubt.

Like the sheriff, though, Thomas wasn't around.

"He's on guard duty at the Hun gate," the quartermaster dismissed them with a bored expression. "The regular guard came down with a severe case of the shits so messenger boy got drafted in to take his place. Won't be off duty until this evening."

It was only early afternoon.

"We need to wait on Will and Stephen anyway," John shrugged, a small smile tugging at his mouth. "Might as well head for that tavern."

"Aye, good idea. Ask Thomas to come to *The Blue Boar* as soon as he comes back with his unit then, will you, friend?"

The quartermaster looked irritated and remained silent, until Robin realised the man was expecting a coin in return for passing on the message.

Rather than arguing with him – Robin was one of Sir Henry's personal staff after all, so far outranked this fat sergeant – he fished in his purse for the smallest coin he could find and tossed it at the man. "Don't forget to pass on the message or it won't be a coin you get next time, it'll be my boot up your fucking arse."

"Is that right?"

To both Robin and Little John's surprise the quartermaster got to his feet and glared at them, his hand on his sword hilt. "Jumped up young prick, coming into my barracks telling me what to do? You fucking arsehole, I'll –"

He never had the chance to say what it was he planned on doing, as Robin vaulted the counter that separated them in a heartbeat and, using both his hands, grabbed the sergeant by the neck and threw him backwards, against the wall. Teeth bared, his enormous shoulders bulged as he lifted the portly man off the floor.

"You'll what?" Robin growled, the quartermaster's face turning a deep shade of purple.

The man tried to hammer his fists into Robin's muscular arms but it did no good – his elevated position gave him no leverage and his face contorted as he began to lose consciousness.

"Enough, Robin."

Little John's amused yet insistent voice broke through the young bailiff's rage and, slowly, he released the pressure on the sergeant's neck, lowering the man gently to the floor although he didn't let go completely.

"You fucking tell Thomas we were here, and where he can find us, you fat bastard, or I'll take your face off next time."

He finally let go of the man, who fell, gasping and coughing loudly onto the floor of the chamber, too winded to reply.

Robin glared at the fallen quartermaster for a while, until John told him it was time to move and the fury that had built up inside him dissipated, like a smoke in the wind, and he wondered what had come over him. Aye, he was hot tempered at times – that's what had seen him become an outlaw in the first place after all – but he was normally able to control it nowadays. Throttling the sergeant was out of character for him.

At the back of his mind he knew it was the fear and stress of his disintegrating relationship with Matilda that had caused it, but he wouldn't admit it, not for a heartbeat.

He jumped back over the counter to stand by John. "Come on," he grunted, only slightly out of breath. "Let's find that tavern."

He never looked back at the quartermaster as they left the castle and walked back into the bright sunshine, but the man's eyes watched them go, burning with a murderous rage.

"That wasn't the best idea," John told him, shaking his

big bearded head in – mostly – mock indignation. "You never know when you'll need a quartermaster."

Robin ignored him and, by the time they made it back out to the courtyard the cart – along with Mariam, her mother and children and all their belongings – was gone, leaving a somewhat forlorn Arthur lounging against a wall, squinting against the bright noon sunshine.

"Everything sorted already? That was quick."

"Aye," Arthur nodded to Robin's query. "A couple of servants came out not long after you'd gone in and took them to the house. It's not far – I followed to make sure they were all right and to say goodbye. There's a weaver's shop next to it. Mariam and her ma will work there until this is finished."

"Perfect," John boomed. "And no doubt the little ones will find their own amusements in a big city like this."

"Speaking of amusements," Robin grinned, eyes sparkling. "We'd better head for *The Blue Boar* and wait on Will and the Hospitaller returning with Piers."

* * *

Philip and Eoin had woken the men that morning with kicks and shouts, exhorting them to get up and arm themselves.

They were going hunting.

It was a damp day, with a mist of rain in the air that might clear up or might turn into a thunderstorm but the men rose excitedly, glad to have a purpose at last, after their days sitting around doing nothing but drink, eat and brag about their exploits.

Mark felt a nervous knot in the pit of his stomach – surely they were finally going to head for Horbury and that bastard turncoat James. At last he'd get his revenge. He grinned at Ivo who returned the look, but on his face it was much less appealing, since Friar Tuck had smashed most of his front teeth out years earlier when they'd tried to rob and kill the hardy clergyman.

"James is mine, when we find him," Mark growled, his eyes flaring, but Ivo simply shrugged.

"As long as I get to sink a few ales and empty my bollocks in some pretty lass, you're welcome to him."

The gang had moved camp more than once in the past few weeks, covering dozens of miles in every direction, as Philip knew the law – particularly Robin Hood and his men – would be searching for them. For the past couple of days they'd hidden in a clearing not far from the village of Mirfield. The spot was well hidden by trees and a little stream passed close by, providing them with fresh water for drinking and cooking, while they had plenty of meat, eggs and bread, purloined from a village on their way past.

But Mark knew the men would get bored just hanging around the forest – they needed something to stimulate them or else they'd bicker amongst themselves and, once the ale barrels were broached, bickering could soon turn to violence. He knew Philip understood it too and was undoubtedly the reason for their little outing today.

Buckling on his gambeson, which he'd spent the previous night patching up since it was tatty after long years of wear and abuse, Mark nodded to Philip when the outlaw captain passed nearby.

"We heading for Horbury then?"

Philip stopped and looked at him, the infuriating, ubiquitous smile tugging at the corners of his mouth.

"No. Brighouse."

Mark's face fell. The village of Brighouse was just as distant from their camp-site as Horbury was, but, as far as he knew, none of the men Philip wanted to hunt down lived there.

"What? Why the fuck are we going there?" he demanded. "You said we'd be going after that bastard James. I've been waiting years to pay him back for what he

150

did!"

Eoin suddenly appeared at Philip's back, as if from nowhere, his great bulk filling Mark's vision.

"Do I have to explain every decision I make to you?" Philip asked, his voice low but his eyes hooded and dangerous.

"Well –" Mark began but he trailed off as Philip spoke over him,

"The foresters, the sheriff's men, Robin Hood...they all know by now that we're hunting for Hood's old gang members. They expect us to attack the villages where those men are living."

The rest of the outlaw band – their numbers swelled again to seventeen by now, even with the losses they'd suffered at the hands of Will Scaflock in Wakefield – gathered around to hear what their leader was saying.

"Do you really want me to lead the men to Horbury, Mark? When the villagers – and your friend James who, by your own admission is a crack shot with a longbow – will be watching for us? Are you really as stupid as you look?"

The men sniggered at that. Mark wasn't particularly unpopular or disliked, but the ever-growing group were not close and never would be. Philip was gathering to him men who were, by their nature, aloof, unfriendly and solitary. Men who didn't form friendships easily but would follow orders even when those orders would seem repugnant or downright wicked to most people.

More than one man had tried to join them recently only to disappear a few days later, when it had become clear he wasn't as brutal or unhinged as the rest of them. The last was a thirteen year-old from Grange Moor. He'd been full of bravado, despite his obvious nervousness upon meeting the gang of wolf's heads. Chased from his small village for stealing food from a baker's shop, the boy cried himself to sleep for two nights, even calling out for his mother as he slept. And then, on the third morning, he'd been gone.

No one asked, but Mark knew Philip had killed him. Their leader had no room in his gang for deadwood,

Ivo still stood beside him now, and Mark was grateful for his old companion's presence but, if it came to it, he suspected even Ivo wouldn't stand up to Philip or Eoin on his behalf.

"You see," Philip said, spreading his hands wide. "This is why I'm the leader and you're not. You'd have the men throw themselves into danger just to settle an old, meaningless score with a man you've not seen in years. Madness."

He scowled at Mark and shook his head dismissively, turning to address the others instead.

"Eventually I will hunt down and kill every last one of Hood's friends. On that I swore to God. But that task can wait! There's no point in us walking into danger when there's so many other, softer targets dotted all around the country for us to visit."

The wolf's head jerked his head at a young man who'd joined them only a fortnight earlier, yet had managed to get into fist fights with three of the other men thanks to his hot temper and inability to hold his ale. "Joseph – what say you? Would you like to travel to Horbury to hunt down Mark's old acquaintance? Knowing the law will probably be patrolling the area? Or would you rather we head for Brighouse – a small village with only a few dozen inhabitants that will present an easy target?"

The youngster smiled, inordinately proud to have been singled out by their captain, and Mark's heart sank. These idiots had fallen completely under Philip's sway.

"Brighouse!" Joseph shouted, jerking his fists and grinning like an excited hound. "I don't want to die on some lawman's sword – I want to stick *my* sword in some girl in Brighouse. That sword, there, I mean, not my real blade..." He trailed off, pointing between his legs sheepishly.

Instead of shaking his head in disgust at the irritating youngster, as Mark would have done, Philip stretched his mouth wide open, stuck out his tongue and waggled it suggestively, grabbing his own crotch and squeezing it at the same time.

The men roared in appreciation, even Ivo, much to Mark's chagrin.

"Come on then," Philip shouted, leading the way through the undergrowth towards the westward road. "Let's get to Brighouse and find some wenches to sheath our swords in! Mark can head for Horbury to meet his boyfriend if he likes."

Mark watched, stony-faced and forgotten, while the men moved off, laughing and joking and sharing tales of their previous sexual exploits. The sun, at last, poked out from between the clouds and bathed the land in a pleasant orange glow, as if blessing the gang's mission.

As they moved off, though, Mark was surprised to see Eoin looking back at him, a worried expression on his young face, and a tiny sliver of hope touched his heart.

The big man was protective of Philip and clearly felt a great deal of loyalty to his older friend who'd saved his life, but Mark knew Eoin wasn't the wicked, immoral bastard the rest of them were. The giant followed orders but, when they were looting and raping he never joined in with the worst of the violence; he hid his face behind a stony mask of indifference then made himself scarce while the others were enjoying themselves.

And here they were, off to attack a village, and Eoin's backward, worried glance, spoke volumes about the way things were going.

CHAPTER SEVENTEEN

"Oh, shit. Fuck me, they're coming. They're really coming!"

Luke-atte-Water glanced across at his companion, Blase, and, seeing the fear as plain as day on the younger man's face, jumped to his feet to have a look along the road.

Blase Cottar, a forester of just eighteen years, was right – Robin Hood's warning when he'd passed through a few days earlier seemed to be a timely one, as at least a dozen hard-looking men were striding purposefully along the heavily rutted path towards their village.

"Run," Luke commanded, clambering down from the tree they'd employed as a look-out post, his throat constricting, breath almost gone from him before he'd even reached the ground as fear filled his veins like a cask of strong ale. "Run!" he repeated needlessly, breaking into a breathless sprint as his wide-eyed companion thumped down on the hard earth and followed him away from the main road and into the safety of the trees.

He prayed to God that the approaching outlaws – for what else could they be, but the scum the lawmen had warned them about? – hadn't seen them. They weren't that far from the village but Luke wasn't that fast a runner, with his short stumpy legs and pot belly and he dreaded the thought of some nimble wolf's head overtaking them and...well, he carried a long knife but it would be much better to face these invaders from behind his warbow at a distance of a hundred paces or so.

There was a cry from behind him.

Blase.

For a heartbeat – just a heartbeat! – Luke continued running, his fear spurring him on, but the thought of leaving his fellow villager behind stopped him and he turned, drawing the blade from his belt and steadying himself for the attacker that had taken Blase down.

The assailant turned out to be a large divot in the grass, which had tripped the panicked young man as he fled.

Almost laughing in hysterical relief, Luke stamped back the few paces and grasped his downed companion by the arm, hauling with all his fear-given strength to help the forester back up.

They were almost at Brighouse and there were no signs of pursuit. They were safe.

Until the outlaws arrived in the village at any rate…

"To arms, to arms!"

The cry tore from Blase's throat as they raced into the village and Luke joined in when he was able to draw enough breath to do so.

Some of the people simply gaped at them like surprised fish but Robin Hood's warning had taken root in the majority of the locals' minds, and women ran to gather up their children as men hurried to gather the longbows and piles of arrows that lay stacked against the buildings in preparation for this day.

The headman, Gregor – a bear of a man with a bald, freckled head and flame-red beard – stormed out of his house and, in a deafening voice, repeated the lookouts' call to arms.

Luke watched in fascination as the people ran here and there, almost as if the whole thing had been practised and perfected. Children were escorted hurriedly to the church, the only stone building in the entire village, by their mothers, some of whom carried weapons and looked as if they could use them well enough if called upon.

The men, even youngsters and greybeards, took up positions hidden inside their houses or behind hedges and walls. The vast majority held longbows, which they were obliged to practise with every Sunday by law, but some, like Gregor, who strode into the centre of the road to meet the approaching outlaws, carried axes, swords and even spears.

Luke glanced around, noting the fear and nervousness that filled almost every face, and his heart sank.

These men that were walking calmly towards their little village were killers. He'd heard the stories of their brutal, callous exploits and it made his blood run cold to know he'd be facing such a force within the space of just a few more heartbeats and with only his fellow villagers to stand against them.

It was hopeless.

He would make a run for it, he decided. He had no children and his wife was forever nagging at him, why should he lay down his life? He was only twenty-six years old!

Christ help me, he prayed, but a look at Blase filled him with shame.

The younger man was plainly even more terrified than Luke. The outlaws had finally appeared on the horizon and their loud voices – they made no attempt to hide their approach, so filled were they with bravado – carried along the silent, deserted main road. A small wet patch appeared on Blase's breeches and Luke, surprising even himself, felt a rage welling up inside him.

Who were these outlaws, to come to Brighouse, frightening good people like Blase who had never hurt anyone in their lives?

His own momentary thrill of fear forgotten, Luke reached down and pulled an arrow from the earth at his feet, nocking it to his bowstring and raising the weapon in grim, icy determination.

The wolf's heads wouldn't find this village the easy target they expected, Luke vowed, and he hoped that all the other good men of Brighouse would be feeling the same way right now, their fear replaced with outrage.

"Halt, travellers," Gregor shouted, as the oncoming men

came close enough to address, and Luke spotted a couple of villagers pushing into the trees flanking the road, to take up positions behind the outlaws.

The defensive strategy was devised by Robin Hood and his companions, Luke knew. Gregor had fought in battles before but he had no real experience as a war leader.

Now they would find out if the plans were sound.

The outlaws stopped at the headman's challenge, sharing amused glances with one another, although Luke noted the man at the front of their line. That one had a smile on his face, but his eyes were hard and remained fixed on Gregor, boring into the bald man.

"What kind of welcome is this for weary travellers looking to spend a few coins in your village?" The hard-eyed outlaw shouted, spreading his hands out wide before jerking his head backwards to the enormous man that stood directly behind him, almost like a bodyguard.

"My friend here's hungry and it takes a lot to fill his belly. Your baker will be a wealthy man by the time we leave, as will the rest of your merchants and ale-sellers."

"Especially your ale-seller," one of the newcomers shouted happily, to a chorus of "aye"s from the rest of the motley crowd who were, it seemed, dying of thirst.

"There's no welcome here for the likes of you," Gregor returned, evenly, the axe held in his hands almost reverently and Luke suddenly knew his headman could use the vicious weapon; indeed, *had* used it not so many years before. The way he carried it spoke of past brutality that Luke had never guessed at and it gave the bowman an added jolt of courage.

He sighted along his arrow, aiming the anchor-shaped point directly at the outlaw captain but not yet drawing the hemp string taut.

"Now, turn around and take yourselves back the way you came," Gregor continued. "We were warned you bastards might turn up and we're ready for you."

The outlaw leader's smile faltered momentarily and, again, Luke felt his confidence grow. That had surely been a flicker of self-doubt and surprise – the wolf's head wasn't the unflappable, immortal monster everyone had pictured in their rampant imaginations when they'd heard Hood recounting the devil's exploits. He was simply a man, albeit a man with a giant at his back…

The outlaws had fanned out by now, spreading themselves wide to make themselves less of a target, but even Luke, with no previous battle experience, could tell that they were a disjointed, uncoordinated group. He wondered how they'd managed to evade capture for so long and shuddered when he surmised it must be because their skill at killing outweighed their lack of cohesion.

And yet, here they stood, with their infamous leader – a wanted rapist, murderer and enemy of God – presenting a perfect target for Luke's broadhead arrow.

He had to take the shot. He had to!

This was his chance to *be* someone – for his name to go down in history.

The wolf's head would die.

Gregor was repeating his demand that the outlaws leave the village as Luke slowly drew back his bowstring. Time seemed to stop completely for him and the outlaw captain's face grew to fill his vision until he fancied he could even see the crow's feet by the man's eyes.

He drew the string taut and inhaled a long, steady breath, utterly calm, all trace of his earlier terror gone.

The sharp, violent snap of an arrow being released filled the village.

And then all hell broke loose.

CHAPTER EIGHTEEN

Philip watched in surprise as the arrow tore past his face by quite some distance and, from the sound of it, buried itself deep in a tree trunk.

"The bastards are shooting at us," he muttered, turning, one eyebrow raised, to look up at Eoin.

The giant's eyes narrowed as another arrow sailed past them at an almost leisurely pace – clearly these villagers were no crack shots – then he lumbered forward, placing himself in front of Philip and using his bulk to shepherd his friend backwards, into the safety of the trees, like some great mother hen.

"The bastards," Philip repeated, shocked at the organised resistance they'd met. This had never happened before when they'd visited a village and he cursed Robin Hood once again. The man was a thorn in his side that he'd need to remove sooner rather than later. "Attack them," he ordered, waving his hand forward distractedly. "Show these peasants what happens when people stand up to us."

His men needed no further encouragement.

The bald headman had retreated behind a building when the shooting started. His furious voice could be heard castigating the man that had loosed the first, wayward arrow – both for starting a fight that might have been avoided and, more importantly, missing the target.

The arrows continued to slam into the trees though, and the outlaws waited, judging the best moment to charge, before, at last, half a dozen of them sprinted towards the village screaming unintelligible war cries.

Philip watched as an arrow – probably more by luck rather than any skill – hammered into one of his men, spinning the unfortunate backwards, howling in rage and pain and effectively out of the battle.

The other five of his followers made it to the village and were met by a similar number of locals, led by the headman with his war axe.

Fascinated now by the melee, Philip stared, rapt, as the big bald man brought his weapon down on the head of an attacker, then used his foot to brace himself as he tried to free the blade which had become trapped in the dead outlaw's skull.

He wasn't fast enough though, and an attacker whacked the blade of his sword against the headman's torso. The blow was a powerful one and it sent the headman reeling backwards although the ill-fitting mail shirt he wore absorbed most of the force so no blood was drawn.

Philip's eyes flickered on to the next of his men and he cursed inwardly as a villager, face scarlet and terrified, landed a lucky blow with his crude hammer, smashing the wolf's head's eye socket into a bloody mess.

His gaze moved on again and this time the view was more pleasing.

Mark's toothless mate, Ivo, was competent – skilled even – with his sword, and he skewered one of the villagers before drawing the crimson blade free and moving to hack at the next in the defensive line.

Mark himself was at the far left side of the attackers' formation and he was a little ball of fury, hacking and slashing with silent venom, although his blows were being batted aside competently enough by his opponent, a similarly sized man with enormous, hairy forearms and a blade so rusty Philip was shocked it hadn't shattered upon the first parry.

There was no way the outlaws could win this battle though – there were still at least two dozen archers hiding in the buildings, too frightened to come out and join in with the hand-to-hand combat, but they'd be able to fill the invaders with arrows eventually.

"Fuck it."

Philip spat in disgust and turned to walk away, back along the road to their camp a few miles away.

"Where are you going?" Eoin asked, his eyes flicking between the fight and his departing friend.

"We're getting nowhere here. Tell the men to follow."

Eoin stood for a few heartbeats, mouth open, confusion plain on his face. Then he roared for the men to retreat.

"Cover them!" he shouted at the archers next to him. "Make sure they get away."

The remaining outlaws – Mark, Ivo and one other – finished their opponents, although they had a hard time of it, with Mark needing to come to Ivo's aid before, at last, the three of them moved backwards, dead villagers at their feet and bloody blades held up, defensively, before them.

The villagers let them go, although there were a few more arrows loosed at their retreating backs. None of the missiles struck an outlaw and, as the beaten men drew out of range of the longbowmen the sounds of laughing and cheering could be heard.

The people of Brighouse had won, and their joy – pride too – filled the ears of the disgusted, retreating wolf's heads.

"Beaten by a bunch of farmers and peasants," one surly youngster spat as the outlaws turned the corner and the trees hid the site of their capitulation. He wiped the sweat from his filthy forehead before stopping to quickly remove the string from his bow. The other archers followed his lead, packing their own strings away into little pouches before they all hurried to catch up with Eoin and the others.

Philip could be seen some way in the distance, striding along purposefully, and Mark wondered what was going through their unhinged leader's mind.

Eoin was shouting along the road. "Wait on us!" but

Philip ignored them.

Mark knew how the man's mind worked and he suspected their defeat would be avenged in some brutal fashion. They would need to send a warning to the whole of Yorkshire – if they allowed the people of Brighouse to attack and even kill some of their number then there'd be nothing to stop everyone else in the north of England trying the same.

Philip was only walking and now Eoin broke into a jog, covering the distance between them in a few heartbeats. Mark wanted to hear what they said so he slapped Ivo on the arm and increased his own pace. "Come on, let's catch them up. I want to know what mad scheme that bastard will come up with for us next."

Ivo grunted but matched Mark's fast walk, rubbing his side where one of the villagers had managed to land a blow with some blunt weapon. The wrong end of a hatchet or maybe a hammer – it had probably cracked a rib or two.

Most of the outlaws hadn't bothered trying to catch their leader. In the black mood Philip was in, they knew it would be safer to remain a healthy distance away. So Mark and Ivo were able to hear the conversation as Eoin finally drew up beside his friend and, almost endearingly, try to comfort him.

"It's fine," the giant shrugged, a rueful smile on his face as he turned to look at Philip. "So they beat us – they had lookouts posted to warn them when we appeared. We'll learn from this and it won't happen again."

Philip remained silent as they walked, the only sounds the outlaws' many booted feet tramping along on the old road and the warning screeches of a pair of magpies hidden somewhere in the foliage overhead which clearly identified their approach as a threat.

At last Philip laid a hand on Eoin's wrist and squeezed. It was a fatherly gesture and surprised Mark, who wondered if their mad leader did actually have a more pleasant, caring side to him.

"You're right," Groves agreed. "We will learn from this. Next time we visit a village for supplies we'll go in smaller numbers, rather than as an invading force. We need things like arrows and eggs and salt and ale and so on so we'll just need to behave like every other traveller for a while."

Eoin grinned, so obviously happy that Philip's mood had lifted that Mark envied their friendship. Aye, he and Ivo had been companions for years but, if it came to it, he'd have no hesitation in leaving the toothless man behind if it meant saving his own hide. And he expected Ivo would feel the same way about him.

Loyalty was a rare and precious commodity in these dark times.

"What will we do now then?" Eoin asked, his gait relaxing as the tension and excitement of the battle left him and the relative safety of the forest swallowed them up again. "Shouldn't we get off the road? In case there's foresters or Robin Hood's men about. Don't want to make an easy target for them, do we?"

Philip waved a hand dismissively.

"Fuck Robin Hood, his mischief has already seen our numbers cut today. No, we stay on the road until we find some travellers."

Mark felt his stomach tighten into a knot and Eoin looked confused.

"To rob them?" the big man wondered.

"To send a message," Philip growled, and the smile that never seemed to leave his seamed face was gone.

"Christ help whoever we run into next on this road," Mark muttered.

"It'll take more than Christ to help them," Ivo said, nodding his head to draw his companion's eyes along the road.

Heading straight for them was a young woman, an elderly couple riding a rickety ox-drawn wagon, and, running along beside them, two small boys squealing playfully as they whacked at one another with sticks.

"You'd best head off back to the camp," Philip said without bothering to look at Eoin. "Start a fire and heat up the big pot of pottage we left there, eh? The rest of us will be along in a while."

* * *

Robin felt sick to his stomach. Never in all his life had he felt like this before. Even when he'd been captured by Sir Guy of Gisbourne, beaten mercilessly and thrown in Nottingham Castle's dungeon he'd not felt as upset as he did now.

Will Scarlet looked ashen faced, his lips a tight, bloodless, line, and he was a man who'd seen all manner of brutality as a mercenary fighting overseas alongside the Templars and Hospitallers.

"Who found them?" the coroner, Edwin of Mansfield, asked. He was the only man that appeared unmoved by the scene before them and Robin didn't envy him his job if it made him desensitised to such cruelty.

"Forester from Brighouse," Robin replied. "Came out hunting and chanced upon them. Poor lad will never be the same again, I'm sure."

The coroner grunted and moved on to look at the next body.

"The forester raised the alarm and messengers took word to the other towns and villages close-by until, eventually, we heard about it. Presumably news reached you and the bailiff there via the same route." Robin nodded towards a surly, fat man, Dunstan de Boer, the bailiff of nearby Halifax, which was also where the coroner hailed from. Brighouse was part of their jurisdiction.

"Aye, no doubt," Edwin agreed distractedly, examining the wounds in the corpse he was bent over.

Robin and his men had been in Barnsley when the news of the terrible crime reached them but, despite riding to the scene as fast as possible, the coroner and bailiff had been the first officials to arrive and begin the investigation.

"There's nothing to investigate here," de Boer spat in disgust as he came over, eyeing the bloody scene before them and handed a piece of parchment to Robin. "Here. It's all your fault apparently."

"My fault?" Robin demanded in disbelief, snatching the parchment from the sour-faced bailiff.

"Aye," the man agreed. "Read it."

Friar Tuck had taught Robin how to read a little when they'd been wolf's heads together in the forest and, since Robin's elevation to polite society, he'd grown more confident in his skills so it wasn't a difficult task for him to understand the neat letters that had been scratched into the parchment in – disturbingly – what appeared to be blood. No doubt from one of these poor victims.

"What does it say?" Little John demanded, crowding in to peer over his captain's shoulder even though he himself couldn't read more than a word or two.

Robin scanned the writing, forming the words with his mouth silently. Then he re-read it, before he met his giant friend's eyes and shrugged.

"It's from that bastard Groves, but we knew this was his work anyway. He says this is what happens when people attack his men."

"Attack his men?" Will Scarlet demanded, gesturing at the lifeless bodies in the grass around them. "These people wouldn't have attacked a gang of outlaws, what the fuck is he on about?"

"You haven't heard?" de Boer asked then carried on when he was met with blank looks. "The outlaws tried to get into Brighouse." He glared at Robin. "Your little motivational speech – just like the one you gave in Halifax – bolstered the men of the village into setting up lookouts and a local militia just in case they were attacked."

"Good on them," Will growled, to agreement from the rest of Robin's listening men.

"Aye, perhaps," the bailiff nodded. "But it seems this fellow Groves was a little upset at the fact a bunch of peasants attacked his men. And this–" he nodded towards the body the coroner was currently kneeling beside "– is the result. Carnage."

"How the fuck is that Robin's fault?" Scarlet demanded, pushing forward and pressing his finger into the fat bailiff's chest. "Would you suggest the people of Yorkshire just lie down and let these lunatics wash over them like a tide of blood and steel?"

De Boer stumbled backwards, fear written all over his flushed face and held up his hands. "No, well, that's not what I meant, really..."

"Peace, Will," Robin said sadly. "Maybe he's right."

"Oh, you have a word with him John, he's in one of those moods of his." Scarlet shook his head in exasperation and stalked away, along the road towards Brighouse. "I'm going to get a drink. Any of you lads fancy joining me?" He threw Dunstan de Boer a final, venomous glance. "I've got a bad taste I need to wash from my mouth."

"Aye, on you go," Robin waved at the others. "No need for you to all hang around here. John, Stephen and I will catch up with you shortly. Don't finish all the ale! Will – have a word with the headman before you start drinking. See what he can tell you."

"What the hell are we going to do about these bastards," John muttered, to no-one in particular and the coroner looked up, momentarily stopping his prodding at the wound in the old man's side.

"My advice would be to catch them and hand them over to sheriff as soon as possible," the man said, bluntly.

"Easier said than done," Stephen retorted, annoyed.

166

The coroner returned to his examination and the three friends stood, Dunstan de Boer beside them, staring down at the death that lay before them.

Robin's heart ached for the two little boys, not very much older than his own beautiful son, who had been stabbed repeatedly by, the coroner had told them, daggers rather than a longer bladed weapon. The young lawman's imagination worked of its own accord, and he saw Philip Groves, pretending to be friendly, calling over the children. Befriending them, then, when they were smiling and relaxed, his dagger had done its work.

Robin had no idea if that's what had really happened but the vision wouldn't leave him and he felt dizzy for a moment. Horror and disgust that a man could do such a thing to little children.

Still, at least the brothers – which they surely were, red-haired and green-eyed as they were, in matching little outfits – had died quickly.

The old man too had seemingly died from just a single sword thrust through the heart, probably trying to protect the others.

It was a different story for the women though.

The younger one – no doubt the boys' mother – had been stripped and raped.

He glanced across at the older woman. Even she had been raped, despite the fact she was at least in her sixties. Her toothless mouth hung open in death and again Robin's imagination, unbidden and unwanted, supplied possible explanations for what had been done to her before she too was silenced forever by a slash across the neck.

"We have to find these monsters," he whispered, eyes drawn back, inexorably, to look at the murdered children. He saw Arthur lying there and forced himself to turn away before he went mad from the horror.

"How?" John demanded. "You know as well as any of us how hard it is to find men in a forest the size of

Barnsdale. We evaded the law for years, even when there were huge parties of soldiers and foresters out looking for us after the rebellion."

Stephen concurred. "We'd need a thousand men to cover the land closely enough to flush them out and capture them. It's hopeless."

Robin stood in thought for a time, silent and grim. Eventually he shouted to the bailiff, de Boer, who had moved off to direct his foresters in covering and transporting the corpses to Brighouse for a Christian burial.

"You said a forester discovered the bodies?"

De Boer nodded. "Aye. Young man of about eighteen years, I don't think he'd ever seen anything like it."

"Take me to him. Maybe there's a way we can locate these murdering bastards after all."

CHAPTER NINETEEN

Sir Henry de Faucumberg read the letter from the king and felt a cold shiver run down his back as the words sank in.

This was what he'd feared for so long although he never truly thought the day would come: Edward was removing him from his post.

Well, not completely – he would still be the Sheriff of Yorkshire, but he was to lose Nottinghamshire. He had overseen both counties for a number of years now and, he believed, managed to do a fine job in the face of such trials as the Marcher rebellion in 1321 and the resulting lawlessness that followed. Robin Hood's outlaws hadn't been the only landless men infesting the forests during that time, yet he, de Faucumberg had managed to, mostly, bring things under control.

Until recently.

The king had been informed of the new band of wolf's heads spreading terror in Barnsdale and, if reports were true, in Sherwood as well now. It seemed Edward wanted Sir Henry to relocate north, to Yorkshire, while someone else – he had no idea who, the letter didn't say – would be assuming his duties, and his castle, in Nottingham.

The messenger who delivered the sealed scroll to him stood silently, head bowed, on the other side of dark oak desk, awaiting further orders.

"You may leave me," de Faucumberg said, nodding his thanks for the fellow's successful mission.

"I've to take your reply to the king –"

"Yes, I'm aware of that," the sheriff snapped, then his voice softened. It wasn't this man's fault he was being replaced after all. "Go and get yourself some refreshment. Ale, meat, whatever...I'll have my reply ready for you when you return."

The messenger couldn't help grinning as he bowed and hastily made his way from the room. De Faucumberg knew many barons and noblemen treated such men as if they were no better than animals and the poor lad was probably expecting he'd have to return to the king in London without a chance to do much more than take a piss and change his horse.

As the messenger disappeared though the doorway, the sheriff's steward, William-atte-Burn, peered into the room.

"Would you like anything, my lord?" he asked.

"Aye, bring me a jug of wine. The good stuff."

When the door closed again the sheriff sighed, rubbed a hand across his face, and sat in his high-backed chair, staring up at the ceiling, trying to marshal his thoughts. It was a fine day outside, and the sunlight spilled into his room catching myriad motes of dust in its bright glow, although the stone walls never warmed much, even at this time of year, so he felt pleasantly cool. The sounds of the bustling city not so far off, beneath Castle Rock, seemed to fade away as he contemplated his new orders.

Why would King Edward remove him from the prestigious position as Sheriff of Nottingham, with its attendant castle and welcome salary? Sir Henry had been loyal to the king, even when so many in these parts spoke openly of sedition and he knew the monarch appreciated that loyalty. Or at least he always believed so.

He felt anger build inside him: anger at the king for rewarding his years of service with this kick in the teeth; anger at those damned rebels, led by Thomas, Earl of Lancaster, whom the peasants seemed to revere now as if he'd been a saint; and anger at Robin Hood.

Hood, as an outlaw, had been a thorn in his side for a long time, de Faucumberg fumed, leading his merry band of bastards about the countryside, robbing powerful clergymen and even joining the ill-fated rebellion. Yet, when he'd been pardoned, the sheriff had rewarded the young man with a place on his staff and given him the job of rooting out this new robber-king of Barnsdale, a task Hood simply hadn't been up to so far.

The latch was lifted with a dull click and his steward came in carrying a tray laden with a jug of wine, one brass goblet and a selection of sweetmeats.

The sheriff felt his mouth begin to water at the little delicacies and he sighed, forcing a smile onto his lips. "Thank you, William. You've been a good servant to me."

The steward had been in de Faucumberg's service for the better part of five years, working his way up from his first position as bottler. He knew the sheriff quite well by this time and met his lord's eyes now.

"You look...flustered, Sir Henry," the man said tactfully. "Did the messenger bring bad news?"

"Of a sort, yes."

"May I help?"

The anger had gone from the sheriff by now. He was being hard on Robin – when a gang of criminals chose to hide out in the great forests of northern England there was precious little the law could do to find them and bring them to justice. He understood that better than anyone. He also knew that, if anyone could track down this Philip Groves and his men, it would be Hood.

His anger at the king had also begun to dissipate as he tried to make sense of his apparent demotion.

"Pull up a chair," he said to William, lifting the jug and filling the goblet with the precious red liquid and passing it to the surprised steward who had shared a drink with the sheriff before, but never the good stuff!

"My lord –"

De Faucumberg waved away the protestation before it could leave the man's mouth and leaned back in his chair, strawberry tart in hand and a thoughtful look on his bearded face.

"The king has removed me from my position as sheriff

here in Nottingham." He held up a hand to, again, silence the steward before he could speak and continued. "I'm to move to Yorkshire, using Pontefract Castle as my base. Presumably the seneschal there – Sir John de Burton – has already been informed of all this and it won't be a shock to him when I turn up with my entourage."

"Why?" William seemed to have forgotten the expensive wine in his goblet, so surprised was he at the news.

"That's what I'm trying to figure out. When first I read Edward's letter I assumed it was punishment for something. These new outlaws plaguing the countryside perhaps. God knows – as does the king – we've had more than our fair share of murdering, landless men in the forests around here over the years."

"That can hardly be blamed on you, though." William remembered his drink and tipped it back, letting not a single drop spill down his chin or around his lips.

De Faucumberg nodded agreement. "The king is beset with problems," he said, almost to himself, as he worked through the ideas that were presenting themselves to them. "Queen Isabella – damn her – has spent her time in France trying to raise an army. It won't be long before she arrives back on these shores with that idiot Mortimer of Wigmore and tries to usurp the throne. The king is doing his best to repair the coastal defences and fortifications in London but...why punish me? Does Edward not think me loyal enough? Does he fear I might join Isabella when she finally invades?"

De Faucumberg leaned forward to pour himself some wine, remembered he'd given the only goblet to William and sat back again with another strawberry tart.

"Perhaps the king isn't punishing you? Perhaps this is a reward for your loyalty to him over the years."

The sheriff gazed at his steward thoughtfully, finally catching William's meaning. "He's sending me north to be further away from whatever trouble might be coming..."

The idea made sense. Isabella and her supporters would not look favourably on those – like the Despensers and Sir Henry – who had been loyal to King Edward. By sending him further up north, to Pontefract, perhaps the sheriff would avoid the invaders' scrutiny when they seized power. Their attention would mostly be focused on London and the lands of the Despensers in the south.

And Isabella would take the crown for her son, de Faucumberg expected, eventually. This was one uprising too far – the king was too unpopular to remain in power thanks to those despised Despensers. The queen hated Hugh Despenser even more than most people; rumours suggested the man had actually raped her which would certainly explain her hatred of him, but Sir Henry had no idea about any of that.

"What do we do now then?" the steward asked, refilling his goblet, making the most of his master's generous mood.

"Make ready to move my household to Yorkshire. Have my possessions stowed on carts, tell my wife and children to prepare and make damn sure we take enough soldiers to deter those cursed outlaws from robbing us on the road!"

He stood up, a smile on his face and reached for the half-drained wine jug in salute. "Cheers William," he said, raising the whole jug to his lips, and spilling much of it into his grey beard as he tipped it into his mouth. "And God save the King."

He'd always liked Pontefract.

* * *

"You're the forester that discovered the murdered travellers on the road to the village, is that right? Blase Cottar?"

The Bailiff of Halifax had brought them to the church hall in Brighouse, a single storey timber building, with a couple of rickety tables on the floor and benches running along the walls, although the men had all chosen to remain standing. Somehow it didn't seem right to sit down for this discussion. He'd then commanded the headman, Gregor, to summon Blase to the hall.

The young man nodded, his glance flicking from the local bailiff to the larger figure of Robin Hood and the even more massive Little John. "Aye, it was me," he agreed in a husky voice. "Never seen anything like it and I hope never to again. I'll have nightmares about the lady's...well, you know what I mean." His nostrils flared and he went on, angrily. "What are you going to do about it, bailiff? We need more men to hunt down these bastards. Outlaws like that...they're worse than animals. I thought we'd chased them off but..."

De Boer looked annoyed at the forester's impertinent questioning but Robin interposed himself between the two men.

"We're doing all we can, Blase," Robin said, his voice low. Placating. He understood how the local felt – those murdered people hailed from the forester's own village. He'd probably grown up with the woman and seen the children playing innocently around the place every day. The sight of their bodies would have been a terrible shock. "But, as a forester yourself, you must know how hard it is to track even a large group of men in the greenwood, if they know how to use the terrain and foliage to their advantage."

The young man's shoulders slumped, but only for a moment, before his spirit returned. Robin liked this lad, and he liked him even more when he spoke again.

"I'd like to join you in the search for them. I'll not be able to sleep at night until the whoresons are brought to justice and the people around here are safe again."

"Good man," Little John rumbled from behind Robin's shoulder. "You're exactly the type we need if we're going to catch Groves's gang."

"Surely one more man isn't going to make a difference?" de Boer broke in, an irritated expression on his round face. "Especially one as young and inexperienced as this fellow."

Robin expected the forester would be much more useful in a fight than the haughty bailiff but he held his peace, knowing he might need de Boer's co-operation in the future.

"You're right," he said, raising a hand to stave off Blase's angry retort. "One man wouldn't make much difference, *if* we just wanted him to join us as we look for the wolf's head. But I have another idea," he looked directly into the young forester's eyes. "How would you feel about joining the outlaws? I mean," he clarified, seeing the confusion on Blase's face, "infiltrate their group. Become one of them."

De Boer said nothing to that. He knew very well such a mission could well turn out to be suicidal. If Groves or any of his men recognised the forester, or somehow found out his real identity...what had been done to the poor lady on the road would probably look like a pleasant experience in comparison to Blase's fate...

The lad ran a hand through his unkempt brown hair and said nothing for a time, lost in thought.

"I know we're asking a lot of you. You will be paid a salary from the sheriff's own purse, though," Robin said, but Blase waved him to silence.

"I'll do it." He set his jaw and dropped a hand to the dagger that was tucked inside his belt. "If this is the only way we're going to catch those animals, I'll do it."

"Good man," Robin repeated John's earlier sentiment, grinning at the forester who managed a tight, nervous smile in return.

Even Dunstan de Boer echoed Robin's words and clapped Blase on the back awkwardly.

"It would be better if there was someone else to go with

him," Little John said. "It'll look more believable if two men turn up looking to join Groves's gang. One wouldn't last that long on his own in the forest before the law caught him or other, less friendly outlaws. Two on the other hand – two could survive forever, taking turns as lookouts and watching one another's backs when they visited villages for necessary supplies."

It was a good point, Robin conceded, but finding another man to take on this deadly task would surely be impossible. He knew his own men – John, Will, Stephen, or any of the others – would do it, but they'd be recognised too easily. Robin Hood's gang had been known by almost everyone in the towns and villages around here.

"My friend Antony might do it."

The three lawmen looked at Blase hopefully.

"He's a good fighter, bit bigger than me too. And he could talk himself out of any trouble as you know bailiff." He gave a boyish, lop-sided grin which only grew bigger at de Boer's irritable grunt. "He'd be perfect, if I can get him to agree." He turned back to Robin. "How much will we be getting paid? That might make things easier."

"Ha, go and find him, Blase, we'll discuss your wages once he's here." The smile left his face and he grasped the forester's arms, just hard enough to get his point across. "Don't mention any of this to him though. Leave that to us. And do not tell another soul about it either. Your own safety depends on it, you understand?"

The slim young man returned Robin's grim look, nodded once then, released from the lawman's grip, turned and hurried out into the street to look for his friend.

"Tell us frankly, bailiff: what's this mate of his, Antony, like? You clearly have some knowledge of him."

"Aye," de Boer growled. "Cocky bastard. Troublemaker. He's got a smart mouth on him, as the lad said. He'll fit right in with a band of outlaws." His face softened just a little then. "To be fair, both he and Blase aren't wicked men. They like a drink, as do most young lads in Brighouse, and sometimes it gets them into trouble. But there's no evil in them. I hope we're not sending them into the wolf's lair simply to be torn to pieces."

Robin and John exchanged uncomfortable glances at the bailiff's maudlin words, but what other choice did they have? They could waste months – years even! – trying to stop Groves, while he and his followers robbed and raped their way around the entire county.

If, on the other hand, they had men of their own inside the wolf's head's camp...a trap could be laid and the hunt brought to an end much, much quicker.

No, Robin mused, Blase Cottar had stumbled upon the bloody remains of that family for a reason. God had lit the fires of vengeance in the forester's belly and now they would harness that flame.

A servant left a jug of wine and another of ale on one of the tables by the wall and, as they waited, John walked over and poured drinks for the three of them: wine for de Boer, ale for Robin and himself.

They stood in silence, lounging against the wooden walls of the hall, sipping from their cups and thinking about the terrible crime that had been committed just outside sleepy Brighouse.

It wasn't long before the door opened again and Blase came in, followed by a gangly youth with a straggly brown beard and a gap-toothed grin. He was very similar to Blase, although a little taller. The two could easily pass for brothers.

Antony was friendly and confident, although his enthusiasm as he greeted the two famous lawmen seemed somewhat forced, and Robin guessed the lad probably tried too hard to ingratiate himself with people.

It wasn't to his own, personal liking, but perhaps such fawning reverence would suit Philip Groves's egotistical mindset. Robin prayed that would be the case, and the outlaw leader wouldn't question the two young men too closely when they tried to join his gang.

"What do we do if the bastards want to rob and murder more people?" Antony asked when the situation had been explained to him, voicing the biggest concern Robin himself had.

"Hopefully you won't be with them long enough for that to be a problem," Little John said, placing his empty ale-mug back on the table with a hollow thump. "They're sure to lay low for a time – they'll be well aware of the manhunt that's going on for them after what they did here in Brighouse. So..."

"Once you're in with them," Robin continued, taking up where his giant friend trailed off, "all you have to do is tell them you're going fishing, or hunting, one day, then head for the nearest village and have someone carry news of their camp's location to us."

"You'll have to be vigilant," John cautioned, arching his back to stretch muscles that were beginning to ache from standing indoors for so long, oblivious to how intimidating he looked. "When word comes to us we won't waste time heading for the wolf's heads' camp and mounting an attack. Be ready for it when it comes, so you don't get in the way and take a friend's sword in the guts."

"Get in the way?" Antony spat. He'd heard all about what the outlaws had done to the Brighouse family and he, like Blase, had been friendly with the young mother. He was as ready as his friend to bring justice to the perpetrators. "We won't get in your way. We'll be hiding in the shadows, ready to plunge our blades into those murdering dog's backs."

Blase licked his lips but nodded. "Aye, we'll support you from inside the camp. What d'you want us to do if we can take their leader out ourselves? Should we take the chance? Or does the king need him alive to be made an example of on the gallows?"

Dunstan de Boer answered before Robin could come to a decision, telling them it was imperative to capture Groves alive.

"He must be made to pay, publicly, for his crimes," the bailiff said flatly. "After what he's done the people will demand their place at his execution. The king has more to worry about than this right now, but the law requires a hanging for Groves's actions. Now..." He walked across to place his own, drained, cup onto the table and nodded to Robin. "I must be on my way or it'll be too dark to travel back to Halifax. God give you good day. And please – catch these criminals. There's no place for such filth in my jurisdiction."

John pursed his lips and gave a little, disgusted snort once the bailiff left and closed the door behind him. "That was a dig at us you know," he said to Robin. "Arsehole of a man."

"He is that," Antony laughed, and Blase joined in, nodding.

"He's also stupid if he thinks I'll ask you men to put yourselves – or this mission – in jeopardy by trying to arrest Groves in his own camp, surrounded by his own followers. No," Robin chopped a hand across in the air, as if slicing an outlaw's head off. "If you get the chance to kill Groves, take it. If we could get him out of the way I'm convinced the rest of his gang will splinter and disband. He's the glue holding them all together."

"But the king –"

"The king's not here, lads," John butted in. "And he won't give a shit if we hang these outlaws or gut them in a fight. All he wants is the forest cleared of outlaws. So don't try to be heroes."

"Any more than you already are," Robin said, smiling grimly. "You know how dangerous this is going to be? And the probable outcome."

Neither of the Brighouse men replied to that, they simply

stood, stony-faced, possibly imagining their fate should they be outed as spies.

"How much are we getting paid?" Antony said at last, his smile returning, and Robin wondered if the young man was able to eat anything other than broth, so many of his teeth were missing. "I've got a few gambling debts to be cleared off."

Robin made them an offer and wasn't surprised when, with gasps of disbelief, they said they'd leave that very day to try and find their way into the outlaws' gang. To be honest, the money wasn't all that much, but it was a whole year's wages to the two young foresters who'd have taken on this job for much less, in the outraged mood they were in at the murders on their own doorstep.

"Please," Robin pleaded with them. "Be careful. You know better than anyone, Blase, what these people are capable of. Stick to your cover story and do *not* allow each other to become drunk. Ale will loosen your tongues and leave you vulnerable. You can drink as much as you like when we've destroyed the bastards."

"What *is* our cover story?" Blase wondered. "You have any ideas?"

Robin had been planning that since they'd made their way towards the village after examining the murder scene.

"Aye," he replied. "We keep it simple. The pair of you are foresters from Brighouse. I don't see any point changing that, because you know it and the fewer lies you have to tell the less chance there is you'll be caught out. So...you're from Brighouse, but you're shit foresters because you take bribes to let people go when you catch them up to no good and you hate the bailiff, de Boer, always undermining his authority. You were caught yourselves, by a farmer, two weeks ago, when you tried to steal one of his sheep, and chased out of the village by an angry mob. The people hereabouts didn't like you anyway, because you were always drinking and starting fights, right?" They nodded, rapt, and the big lawman continued. "You've been sleeping rough in the greenwood ever since, and robbed a few travellers, spending the money you've managed to steal from them on bread, eggs, cheese and so on in Brackenhall, where no-one recognises you. And you've been using your bows –" again he stopped and looked at them hopefully "–you can both shoot a longbow can't you? As foresters I'd hope so. Yes? Good. Well, you've been using your bows to hunt deer and so on. Your crime was a small one so no-one's been putting much effort into the search or you. Until today, when the massacred family was discovered – although you don't know about that – and the forest's been crawling with foresters, the sheriff's soldiers, and Robin Hood's men ever since. Are you taking all this in?"

Blase nodded silently and his friend shrugged non-committally. It was a lot to remember Robin admitted to himself, hoping the tall youngster would make the effort to get all of the cover story clear with Blase before they met Groves and his gang. If he didn't they'd both be dead.

"So you ran away from Brighouse, and, since you'd heard rumours about the big group of wolf's heads near Mirfield that were looking for new recruits you headed there to try and join them. You knew you wouldn't survive long on your own, with all the lawmen scouring the greenwood. How does that all sound? Does it make sense? Aye? Good." He emptied the last dregs of ale in his cup into his mouth and belched. "I suppose that's all then."

"How do we find them though?" Antony asked after a time. "We could spend months wandering blindly around Barnsdale and never stumble across their camp."

"As I said, we've had reports from friends of ours and we believe they're based somewhere near Mirfield. I'm sure the outlaws will find you once you get anywhere near their camp-site. They'll have lookouts posted all around their perimeter – as much to detect the law as to find new

181

recruits. Remember, Groves *wants* new men – he wants to lead an army. So it shouldn't be too hard to get inside their camp."

"Staying there very long will be another matter," John warned. "Like Robin says: be careful, and look for the first opportunity to carry word of your location to the headman in Mirfield. We'll hide outside the village and tell him to pass your message to us when he has it, then you go back to Groves so they don't notice you're missing."

"Good luck." Robin clasped Blase's arm before moving on to Antony. "Go and gather some food and your weapons. Then say your farewells to your families, but *do not tell them where you're going*. And go over your cover story as you prepare to leave – your lives depend on it so you'll need to get it right. I'll send word to the sheriff to send us the soldiers he promised, so we're ready to make our attack as soon as we hear from you."

"What about our money?" Antony said, waving away John's confused look. "I know we can't take it with us just now but I'd like to know my family won't go short if we don't come back..." His voice trailed off a little, as the realisation of their situation finally sunk in.

"Rest easy, friend," Robin nodded reassuringly. "I'll leave your money with the headman. Gregor isn't it? I'll leave it with him. If anything happens to you, he'll make sure your families receive it. Otherwise, you can collect it once we wipe out Groves and his men for good, and then have the best drinking session of your lives."

"You can buy us one too," John grinned and the mood in the room seemed to lift again before the young foresters opened the door and left the church hall.

Behind them, Robin and Little John stood in silent contemplation for a time, praying to Almighty God and the Magdalene for Blase and Antony's safe return, and the success of the mission.

But both lawmen knew they'd probably just sent the

Brighouse foresters to a violent death.

CHAPTER TWENTY

Henry of Elmstow, dean of Lewes Priory, was an elderly man with a deeply lined face and wild grey eyebrows. Like many older people, he was cranky and had little patience for the stupidity of youngsters.

It didn't help that Prior John de Monte Martini was also an irritable old man with a temper and both of them seemed to take pleasure in being vicious and nasty towards the young novices who'd been chosen to accompany them on their visit to Wakefield this summer.

"You boy," the dean shouted at Conrad, a young red-haired, freckle-faced lad of only thirteen, "bring more wine for the prior, and hurry up."

The boy sprinted over to the rumbling, covered wagon, which carried not only the dean and the prior, but also, in a compartment in the back, the stores of wine and food which were for the high-ranking clergymens' own personal use. The dean tossed the empty skin at him and he fumbled it, earning an exasperated sigh from his superior, before he scooped it up and refilled it from a stoppered jug.

Without a word, the boy handed it over to the prior deferentially. The elderly man never said a word of thanks and the dean waved him away with a sour expression on his seamed face.

Conrad stood, head bowed, for a few moments as the wagon was carried along the road by two big horses, and then he fell back into line behind it, along with the other novices and the mercenaries who'd been hired to guard the party on their journey north.

The red-haired youngster came from a wealthy family – his father owned a successful fishing business in Hastings – but, being the third son, his parents had sent him off to Lewes to become one of the Black Monks. A Benedictine.

Fate was cruel, Conrad thought – his eldest brother was a partner in their father's business, while the other joined the Hospitallers and was away somewhere learning to become a sergeant-at-arms or a knight or some other noble – exciting! – thing. And here he was...

"How many more days do we have to journey?" A voice broke in, shattering his thoughts and he turned to look irritably at the speaker who finished his query without noticing Conrad's angry glance. "My feet are killing me."

"We've only just left Oxford, there's still days of walking to go yet," the freckled young man replied. "So your feet better get used to it. Unless you want to ask those two for a lift on their wagon."

He nodded towards the groaning cart that they were following like rats after a piper he'd heard about from his widely-travelled father.

The other novice's eyes widened and he shook his head at Conrad's suggestion. "I'll just try and keep up."

"Ach, you'll soon get used to it. My feet hurt too at first but the blisters went away. Now it's my thighs that burn at the end of the day but I'm sure that'll pass too."

"It's my back that aches," another, older novice asserted, overhearing the conversation, and Conrad smiled sympathetically, turning away and focusing on the road ahead.

"Do you think there'll be any trouble when we get to Wakefield," the boy next to him asked.

"What do you mean, Gervase? Why would there be trouble?"

"You must have heard about the prior's run-in a few years ago when he made this same journey to check up on the running of Wakefield. When Robin Hood attacked him?"

Conrad's head snapped around at the mention of the infamous wolf's head. Here was a tale that needed to be heard.

"I don't know what you're talking about," he said. "Tell me!"

Gervase grinned and nudged the older boy on his other side. "Reynard told me about it. He went last year and heard the villagers talking about it. It's a famous tale in Wakefield – the people there hate Prior de Monte Martini."

Conrad grunted, understanding their feelings. The old man was arrogant and mean and if he'd done something to annoy Robin Hood...

"Tell me what happened then," he demanded, keeping his voice low for fear of their superiors in the wagon overhearing their conversation. He knew such a conversation would be rewarded with the prior's harsh version of penance which often meant self-flagellation rather than simply reciting a few *Pater Noster*s.

Reynard was an excitable lad, which made him a good companion, but even he knew to speak in hushed tones, so Conrad moved to walk closer beside him, leaning his head in to listen as the other boy told him all about de Monte Martini's visit to Wakefield five-or-so years earlier. How the prior had allegedly said something horrible to a local girl and been rewarded for it by having his nose broken by Robin Hood. That event was what had made the fabled Hood into an outlaw, for he'd been forced to run away and hide in the forest or the prior would have seen him hanged.

To the novices who weren't particularly fond of their scowling prior, the story was exciting and amusing. There'd been lots of times when they'd have loved to smack the old bastard in the face and this tale was almost as good.

"Is that why we've got so many mercenaries with us?" Conrad wondered, eyes casting about at the hard-looking armoured men who surrounded them, both on horseback and on foot. There were around a dozen of them and the flame-haired novice simply assumed the prior's wagon carried money or some other valuables which would account for such a large armed escort. But now... "If he fears the wolf's head no wonder he wanted so many guards!"

Reynard broke in, shaking his head with a superior air, as if, at fourteen, his extra year made him so much more knowledgeable and experienced than Conrad or Gervase. "Nah, the mercenaries are just a precaution because there's always outlaws ready to rob travellers. Robin Hood isn't a wolf's head any more. He was pardoned, didn't you know that?"

The younger novices were too interested to feel irritated by Reynard's patronising tone and, as the morning and the miles passed, sore feet and adventures in far-off lands were forgotten, replaced with tales of Robin Hood and his loyal men.

Conrad was looking forward to reaching Wakefield now. He hoped the pardoned wolf's head would be there. Meeting a famous outlaw would be a dream come true!

* * *

"What d'you mean, you've never heard of me? I'm a famous outlaw."

Philip grinned but his expression wasn't mirrored on the face of Prior John de Monte Martini, who scowled, clenching and unclenching his fists although Blase couldn't tell whether that was from fear or rage. Probably both.

"Philip Groves? My brother Matt was one of that bastard Robin Hood's men. No doubt you've heard of *him*..." The wolf's head spat onto a clump of bracken, the thick saliva dripping down unpleasantly from one blooming yellow branch to another. "But you can't be from around these parts if you haven't heard of me. Everyone knows me in Yorkshire. Me and my lads here."

187

He gestured to those of his men who were visible, ringing the Prior's party and there was a gleeful cheer from many throats as the robbers hailed their leader's salute. Blase and Antony joined in with the shouting, not wanting to appear out of place.

It had been simpler than they'd feared to join Groves's band. The outlaw captain was trying to attract as many people as possible to his metaphorical banner, so almost anyone that looked like they could wield a sword was welcomed into their group after only some cursory questioning.

The Brighouse pair spent four hours travelling to Mirfield then, from there wandered for three days around the forest close to where some of the locals in the alehouse told them the outlaws had been heard, singing drunkenly or screaming, as if fights amongst them were common. Blase hadn't asked them why no-one had sent word to the sheriff about the gang's whereabouts – it was clear to him. If the law turned up and were unsuccessful in hunting down Groves's men – which was probable – the people of Mirfield would suffer; their informing would be suspected and acted upon by the ruthless wolf's head and the village would end up a smoking ruin.

They'd wandered the greenwood, hunting as they went, even lighting a camp-fire on the first two nights, and made no attempt to conceal themselves or be silent. They were stopped in their tracks on the third day by the giant, Eoin, and four other dirty, scowling men.

Antony had done most of the talking. His boyish smile contrasted with the steel evident behind his gaze and the outlaws seemed to take to the tall young man immediately. Blase was accepted as Antony's companion and, once they'd told Eoin their story about being hounded out of Brighouse by lawmen searching for someone else they were in.

Especially since they carried a brace of hares and even a

small deer which was unfortunate enough to cross Blase's path just as he'd been about to unstring his longbow.

Meat was always welcome in Groves's camp.

"It's just a shame you don't have a barrel of ale with you as well," Eoin smiled, clapping them both on the back as they'd headed towards the wolf's heads' base a short distance away in a location that had clearly been well-chosen for its defensive properties.

That had been two days earlier, and Blase had spent the time well, making a mental map of the whole, squalid camp and its surrounding area, while Antony drank and bantered with their new 'friends', drawing attention away from his friend's surreptitious reconnoitring.

He noted the small but steep rock face that backed onto the location from the north, meaning a sneak attack from that direction was improbable; he measured the distance along the thick, near-impenetrable trees that fringed the southern and south-eastern edges of the area that would impede any attacks either on foot or from longbows; he scouted along the river which ran to the east, finding no fords nearby; and he memorised the location of the gap in the foliage which was, essentially, the only way to gain easy access into the camp.

The place was well chosen, Blase thought, although he wasn't a military tactician and he didn't have the experience Robin and his men did when it came to reading terrain. So he stored his observations in his head, praying he'd have a chance – soon – to pass them onto the bailiff. Hood, or one of his friends, would doubtless be able to find some holes in the seemingly impenetrable defences.

Before they had a chance to slip off that morning without it being too obvious a lookout turned up and told Groves there was a party of men approaching with a large covered wagon drawn by horses.

"Looks like clergymen," the lookout reported. "Some high-up fucker will be in the cart drinking wine and eating

189

sweetmeats. There's a few young novices trailing along at the back looking miserable and a handful of mercenaries but they won't be a problem if we surprise them."

A group of travellers like that meant two things to Groves and his men: money and sport.

Blase's heart had sunk like a stone when the seemingly ever-smiling wolf's head ordered everyone to gather their weapons and make ready to ambush the clergyman's cart. The young Brighouse man had just been glad that no women were reported to be in the travelling party – he had no desire to see another raped and bloodied corpse adorning the Yorkshire grass.

But now that the outlaws had waylaid the travellers Blase wasn't so sure the lack of females in their company would mean less unpleasantness. The novices, fresh-faced and cleanly scrubbed in comparison to the hairy-arsed wolf's heads, seemed to be just as attractive to some of the men as any pretty girl, judging by the comments Blase could hear his new companions making.

He glanced at Antony who shared his pensive frown as one of the clergymen in the cart – the eldest of the two within – shouted at Groves.

"Yes, the prior knows very well who Robin Hood is – and God will judge that sinner at the Gates of Heaven one day. But it is you, sir, who don't know who you're dealing with." The skinny old man lifted a foot out of the cart, almost entangling the limb in silk curtains, and placed it on the road before returning to his diatribe. "This is Prior John de Monte Martini – one of the most powerful and influential men in all of England."

The prior must have realised that news wouldn't help their situation at all and he slapped the back of his companion's head, hard, the noise of the blow ringing throughout the clearing in which the outlaws had sprung their trap.

"Shut up, Henry," the churchman muttered, dragging his

dean back, fully, into the wagon. Blase saw the novices at the back smirking and he guessed the dean – and no doubt the prior too – weren't much loved by the youngsters. He hoped they'd still be smirking by the time this was all finished.

De Monte Martini was also an elderly man, as became apparent when he struggled out of the cart and stood as straight-backed and haughty as he could manage in front of the watching outlaws, breath rasping in his throat even after such a small exertion.

"What's the meaning of this?" the prior demanded, not addressing Philip Groves but rather his own mercenaries who stood, weapons drawn but unused as they sized up the situation. "I paid you to defend us, not to allow scum like this to try and rob us. What are you waiting for?"

The mercenary leader, a man almost as tall as Eoin and even harder looking, with a scar right across his jawline, shrugged his broad shoulders. "There's more of them than there is us," he said, reasonably. "And they have their bows trained on us."

Groves threw back his head and laughed at that. "I like you," the wolf's head told the guard. "Why don't you and your men join us? We're making a lot of money robbing arseholes like your prior there. We can always use more men, isn't that right, Antony?" He beckoned to the Brighouse man, who somewhat sheepishly walked across the damp grass to stand beside Groves.

"This young man and his friend only came to use a couple of days ago, because they'd heard how well I reward my followers. Here." He pulled out a purse that positively bulged with coins, reached inside and used his thumb to flick one first to Antony, then another to the mercenary. Both were snatched from the air as their targets spotted their colour: silver.

"In God's name," Prior de Monte Martini shouted, striding forward to slap his mercenary on the head as he'd done with the dean. He had to reach up though, and the guard simply sidestepped the blow before it landed. "Defend us, or face Christ's wrath!"

Groves laughed again and shouted some blasphemy which Blase couldn't quite make out, but the prior's shocked face told him all he needed to know.

The outlaw turned his attention back to the mercenary, whose men had slowly been edging their way closer to him, preparing for the worst.

"Last chance, friend. Join us, or join them," he nodded at the dean and the prior, "in their God's arms."

Antony had followed the mercenaries lead and shuffled his way back to his friend's side, knowing this stand-off wasn't going to last much longer.

"What the fuck do we do?"

Blase didn't reply to his companion's whisper. How could he? If they joined the prior's forces they'd give themselves away and, more worryingly, would be dead, since the outlaws outnumbered their opponents. But they couldn't attack the mercenaries could they?

They were innocent men, just trying to earn enough money to put a crust on their tables.

In the end, the choice was taken out of their hands.

"Ah, fuck 'em, they had their chance," Groves roared, to his men as a whole. "Kill the guards and do what you will with the novices, but I want the prior alive."

The mercenaries had been hired by the dean and he'd chosen cleverly. This particular group had a well-earned reputation for their loyalty and professionalism, which was reflected in their fee, at almost double what most other sell-swords demanded.

As Groves shouted his orders the guard captain lunged forward, plunging his sword into the stomach of the nearest target.

Antony.

The Brighouse youngster didn't even try to defend

himself, so swift was his attacker's move, and Blase, shocked, stumbled backwards, away from the bloody blade that had taken his friend's life and now wavered in the air, ready for more victims.

He tried to regain his equilibrium, bodies surging past him as the outlaws, howling with joy at the prospect of a fight, loosed their longbows and threw themselves at the surviving mercenaries who clumped together in a tight formation.

The first wolf's head to reach the defensive formation fell as he, seemingly with no regard for his own life, tried to run right through the sword points that faced him. Blase watched in morbid fascination as another outlaw, howling some weird battle-cry, did the same, ending his life on the tip of a mercenary's blade.

What insanity was this?

Not all of the outlaws were crazed though. The rest engaged the defenders, falling into a steady, almost rhythmic battle, with cries of pain, or anger, seeming to engulf the entire world as Blase looked on, too frightened to move.

He stared in surprise as some of the outlaws ignored the fighting and ran straight past towards the novices. Surely they posed no threat?

He turned back towards the battle which was almost over already. Only the mercenary captain still stood, and he was beset on all sides. He'd managed to kill at least three of his opponents but it was futile, as a myriad small slashes and cuts pierced his torso and legs before, at last, the proud man dropped onto the grass where he was hacked to bloody pieces by whooping outlaws.

Still, Blase stood rooted to the spot. Sickened, terrified and bewildered, with no idea what to do. He'd thought finding the murdered family on the road outside Brighouse had been bad, but actually witnessing the brave mercenary captain chopped apart like a piece of beef turned his brain to pottage. Nothing could be worse, he thought, until a pitiful cry came from the ground behind the battle and his eyes were drawn there, almost against his will.

"No," he breathed, his voice nothing more than a sob.

At last, his legs decided to work again and he ran, into the trees, tears streaming down his face, hands pressed against his ears as he tried to block out the screams of the novices.

CHAPTER TWENTY-ONE

"Calm down, lad, for fuck sake, it can't have been that bad."

Will Scarlet glared at the sobbing Blase as the young man tried, haltingly, to relate his tale and provide Robin's men with the information they needed to find Groves's gang.

"Easy, Will," Little John growled. "He's not much more than a boy and this is the second atrocity he's seen in a short space of time. Let him gather himself."

Robin nodded agreement and Scarlet raised his hands, in apology or exasperation the lawman couldn't tell.

"Here," he said, handing Blase a mug of strong ale. "Get this down you, it'll help with the shock."

The Brighouse man took the drink from Robin with shaking hands, spilling much of it over the sides and into the rushes on the alehouse floor, but he managed to upend it and drained the contents almost in one go. He spluttered and coughed, head down but raised his arm aloft, gesturing the mug for a refill and Robin called on the landlord to bring more ale.

Robin's party had been camping not far outside Mirfield for the past two days, and they'd made the headman, Jacques, well aware of their presence. When Blase ran into town he'd been spotted straight away and Jacques himself had run to the bailiff's camp-site to apprise him of the situation and lead the men back to the hysterical forester.

Eventually, the drink took effect and the young man's shaking subsided although he still looked like someone had walked across his grave. He finished describing what he'd seen happen to the clergymen's party, confirming that it was, certainly, Prior John de Monte Martini who'd been in the wagon. Robin knew it wasn't Christian, but he felt a secret glee at the idea of that bastard finally meeting his end. The old man had caused him so much trouble, it was only natural to feel some satisfaction at his demise. Still, he mused, it wasn't the rest of the prior's party's fault – Groves and his men had to be stopped and the defiled novices avenged, it was as simple as that.

"All right, first of all: are you able to take us to the outlaws' camp?"

Blase looked terrified at the idea but he knew it would be impossible to direct the lawmen there just by describing the way. He nodded, taking another pull from his mug, which Robin pushed away, not wanting the lad to be too inebriated to help them.

"Let's go then. If Groves noted your absence he might guess where you've gone and move their camp."

The bailiff patted his sword hilt unconsciously and nodded towards the doorway which Will and John moved through and began issuing orders to Arthur, James, Peter, Piers and the rest of the men.

Robin had sent a messenger from Brighouse to Nottingham days ago, when Blase and Antony first headed off to try and join the outlaws. Sir Henry de Faucumberg hadn't left Nottingham to take up residence in Pontefract yet, thankfully, so, when he received the message from Robin he despatched the bailiff's hand-picked soldiers to Mirfield; all except Thomas, who remained with the sheriff.

Nineteen men should be enough, along with Hood's friends.

Blase sighed heavily and glanced forlornly at the ale mug but Robin gently helped the younger man up by grasping his arm then guided him outside. He tossed a few coins onto their table and waved to the landlord who grunted his thanks as the big lawman made his way out, into the sunshine. A squall had hit the countryside a short while ago so Robin was happy at the dispersal of the clouds and the warm air that now made the puddles steam gently.

"Ready, lad? Good. Take us to Groves's camp then."

They left the horses behind knowing they'd be of little use in the dense greenwood, and, as they walked, the young spy told the lawmen about his observations of the outlaws' base: its location and surrounding terrain; defences; number and quality of defenders; and his own thoughts on how best to assault the place.

"How high is that cliff you mentioned?" Will asked after Blase had finished. "The height of three men?" He grunted. "I'd say we can send a few men to climb down there then. We've got ropes and the scum won't be expecting an attack from there, even when they see us coming from the other directions."

"And the river can be crossed," John mused. "Not by me though, I'm a shit swimmer."

"You swim fine," Stephen growled. "You just don't want to get wet."

"That too," the giant grinned. "I had a bath in the spring."

"Aye, we know," Will spat in mock disgust. "Smelly big bastard."

Robin laughed along with the others, happy that the mood hadn't grown maudlin or fearful amongst the men. "Peter, you find two or three volunteers from the sheriff's men who're strong swimmers and show them what they've to do."

Peter Ordevill lowered his eyebrows at the idea. "How come I always have to be the one getting fucking soaked?"

"Because you were a sailor," Robin grinned. "Stands to reason you must love being in the water."

"I don't think you understand how ships work," Peter grumbled but he fell back in the formation to find the men he'd need as Robin looked at Blase again.

"You said the outlaws are in awe of Groves but they're

197

not disciplined, from what you saw at least?"

"That's right," Blase confirmed. "They do what he tells them, but they didn't act like a military unit. I mean, like the way I'd expect an army to act," he mumbled, face flushing, knowing his lack of experience in these matters must be obvious to everyone there. "When we practise with our longbows on a Sunday, Gregor makes us act like soldiers. We have a job, and a place, and we stick to them. But the outlaws just seemed to mill about doing whatever they wanted. Complacent. I suppose they think their camp won't be discovered and, if it is, the lookouts they've got posted will warn them in time." He shrugged. "If we manage to get there without being spotted your men will have the advantage, thanks to your discipline and experience."

Blase was fairly sure Groves only posted two, possibly, three lookouts, all to the south west, which was where the path led to their camp-site. He'd taken his own turn there on one of the nights but had not seen or heard of anyone travelling in other directions to be lookouts.

Their plans were well set long before they arrived on the outskirts of the outlaw camp and Robin was quietly confident today would mean the end for Groves. At last. He wasn't counting his chickens before they hatched though; he knew from bitter experience things like this didn't always work smoothly.

"Blase, you lead Will close to the position you know there should be a lookout. He'll deal with it. Then run back and get us when the road is clear."

As the pair headed off like phantoms into the undergrowth Robin gestured Peter and the two volunteer swimmers forward and told them to be on their way. They were to swim the river and conceal themselves in the trees that Blase said fringed the outlaw base on the eastern side, attacking with their longbows as soon as they heard Robin blow his hunting horn. That was a new tool for the lawman, who'd never used it when he'd been a wolf's head himself since their best defence had been not giving away their location.

Now, though, it would come in handy.

He sent Stephen and Arthur off with another two men – and ropes – to head west then come round on the northern side of the camp's location. They'd climb down and, like the swimmers, await the signal before attacking with bow and sword.

This felt good to Robin. He'd missed the days of leading his men as a fighting force and now, despite the possibility of death in the coming battle, his spirits were higher than they'd been for a long time. He re-checked the straps on his gambeson were snug, his chain mail vest had no obvious holes, and he unfurled his bowstring from its pouch on his sword-belt, stringing his warbow with it. His men – those who were archers – followed his lead.

He was ready and, from the grim expressions on the rest of the mens' faces, they were too.

Blase appeared, breathing heavily but Robin was impressed by how close the forester got to them before his presence was noted.

"The lookout's dead," he reported. "I shouted up to him, saying it was my turn, and when he came down Will..."

Robin didn't need a picture painted, he knew how efficient Will was as an assassin.

"This is it then, lads," he called, not shouting but making his voice loud enough to address the remaining men that were with him. "They must still be in their camp or there wouldn't have been a lookout. We're probably going to be outnumbered, unless some of the wolf's heads have gone off to a nearby village for supplies. But it'll make no difference. They won't be expecting us, and their resolve will crumble when we attack them from all sides." He grinned. "This is where we finally put an end to Philip Groves's reign of terror."

And I end that cursed family for good, he thought.

They began to walk, following Blase, who looked terrified, along the overgrown path, until they met up with Will. He'd disposed of the dead lookout's body somewhere out of sight and he fell into step on Robin's left side – Little John was on their captain's right, as usual – as the party headed for the outlaw camp.

"We're almost there," the forester whispered, and Robin gave a nod of acknowledgement before waving him the back of their party, alongside James and Piers who were bringing up the rear. Blase was no soldier and would only get in the way once the fighting started at the front.

Robin felt the blood begin to pump faster in his veins and he slid an arrow from his belt, nocking it to his bowstring as he walked.

This was it.

Killing time.

There was a fire burning in the camp ahead as Robin and his men approached. The trees were thick all around and the smoke was dissipated by their leaves but it could still be glimpsed and the smell was unmistakable. As was the smell of food cooking.

Little John's stomach rumbled and Robin cocked an eyebrow at the giant, receiving a sheepish frown in return.

Not a word was spoken as they walked stealthily through the gap in the foliage that Blase assured them led directly into the outlaws' camp. Every one of them looked warily about, ready for the attack which would surely come once they were spotted.

Being watchful wasn't always enough, though.

Just ahead of them the forest gave way to a clearing, just as Blase had described. Half-a-dozen men sat around the fire, mending torn clothes, eating roast meat from wooden trenchers and conversing quietly but in a relaxed manner. One man stood a little off to the side, apparently cleaning his longbow.

There was a sudden snap as that wolf's head spotted them and, incredibly quickly, grabbed an arrow from a pile on the ground next to him, nocked it to his bow and released the deadly missile at them. As he shouted the alarm, his arrow hit one of the sheriff's blue-liveried soldiers just behind and to the left of Robin.

"Fuck. Take cover!" the lawman spat, crouching behind a worryingly slim young beech, while raising the hunting horn to his lips and blowing. He was rewarded with the sound of a war-cry from the east, followed a few heartbeats later by the easily-recognisable sound of Stephen, roaring some prayer to Almighty God as he led his men into the attack from the north.

The sheriff's man wasn't dead, only injured, as the arrow had caught him in the shoulder, but time wasn't on their side. The soldier would have to suffer unaided or they'd lose the momentum. He wondered where the rest of Groves's men were, but they'd have to wait until his men defeated those in the clearing. He filled his lungs and roared.

"Attack!"

The outlaws were thrown into disarray, disoriented completely as they were beset on three sides by armed men.

The one with the longbow managed to aim a second arrow at them and, again, his aim was true but not deadly as it slammed into another of the sheriff's soldiers, taking the screaming man in the arm this time and throwing him onto the ground which was muddy and churned from many footprints.

Stephen came up behind the archer before the man could loose again, hacking downwards into the outlaw's shoulder, sending a great gout of blood into the air and almost severing the arm completely.

The remaining outlaws weren't as brave as their now-dead comrade. Two more died where they stood, shocked by the lawmens' appearance, not even defending themselves, before Robin shouted at his men to stand down. Clearly the battle was over, for now, and he wanted to question the survivors.

He praised Stephen's group, and the sodden trio who'd swam the river for their fine work, then turned back to the rest of the men.

"John, James, Arthur – disarm them and bind their hands behind their backs. The rest of you, remain alert! We don't know where Groves and the rest of his vermin are so be ready for them."

"They're gone," an outlaw blurted, eyes fearful, clearly hoping to ingratiate himself with Robin by providing information. "Philip took the rest of the men to find a new camp to the north. He was worried our –" he looked nervous as he realised what he was saying and corrected himself as he continued, "*their* raid on the old prior's travelling party would bring the law down on us."

"Shut your mouth, Alf," another of the outlaws shouted. "You fucking turncoat bastard!"

Little John rammed his fist into the man's solar plexus, dropping him onto his knees, breath blasted from him, before he pitched forward flat onto his face.

"Carry on," Robin growled at the talkative wolf's head. "Why are you lot still here?"

"Philip wants to set up as many friendly camps as possible, all over England, so his gang has a safe haven to go to whenever they need it. We were supposed to lie low here and take care of the camp-site until they needed to come back and use it again."

Little John met Robin's gaze and shook his head. "You have to admire Groves's ambition."

"Fucking arsehole's stretching his forces too thin,

though," Will noted. "We can pick little groups like this apart no problem, like we just did here. He'd be better keeping all his men together."

"How many are left in Groves's main party?"

The outlaw shrugged. "Probably about twenty-five or thirty. I don't know, I'm not good at counting."

"There's about fifty, at least," the man John had punched gasped from the ground, defiantly. "That's why we can afford to break up into smaller groups – we still have enough men to take you bastards on when the time's right."

"There's nowhere near fifty," Blase said, coming forward to stand beside Robin. "Sure, some of them weren't in the camp when Antony and I were here, so there's no way to be certain of their numbers but it can't be as many as fifty."

"He's right," Stephen agreed, gesturing around the clearing. "This place isn't big enough to hold that many men."

"Shouldn't we find the rest of their lookouts?" Piers asked, brushing his hair back from his handsome face somewhat nervously.

Robin waved dismissively. "We'd never find them and they've probably heard the fight. They'll be long gone, either to catch up with Groves or just to try and find somewhere to become anonymous. I think we're safe from an attack by a couple of lookouts. That being said," he nodded at John to lift the winded wolf's head. "It would be folly to tarry here longer than necessary. That one could be lying about Groves heading north. We'll go back to Pontefract with these whoresons – the sheriff can decide what's to be done with 'em."

"We were new recruits, we didn't have anything to do with any robberies or that," the outlaw called Alf opined. "Isn't that right, lads?"

"You're a lying sack of shit," Blase shouted, rushing

forward to press his face against the older man's face, his patience and restraint finally worn through. "I saw you using your knife to tear the clothes off one of those novices." He spun to address Robin. "We should just string the bastards up right here and now. They were all part of it."

Will laughed humourlessly. "It'd save us guarding the three of them all the way back to Pontefract," he said. "I like the lad's idea."

Robin shook his head. "We're representatives of the law now, we have to uphold it. As much as I agree these men deserve a long, painful death – assuming they *were* party to what Blase told us about – it's not our place to decide that. Come on. We'll go and see where de Monte Martini's party was attacked, just in case there's any survivors."

Again, the belligerent wolf's head broke in, grinning. "I doubt it. If any *were* left alive, they'll be wishing they hadn't been."

Little John swept the man's legs away and, as he collapsed onto his face again, the giant pressed his hand into the back of the outlaw's head, forcing his face into the mud so he couldn't breathe.

"One more word from you, sunshine, and I don't care what Robin says, I'll fucking suffocate you in the dirt. All right?"

He held the man for a while longer before dragging him back to his feet. His face was completely brown, apart from his eyes and the pink of his tongue as he tried to drag gusts of air into his lungs. On another, less bleak day, it would have been a hilarious sight.

The outlaw never opened his mouth again as they searched for the remains of the prior's wagon and its attendants, which Alf guided them to.

There was silence all around when they finally found the site. A silence full of sorrow, pity, horror and rage that Groves's gang were continuing to carry out such brutal crimes.

As expected, there were no survivors. The novices had all been murdered, while the guards were hacked apart with such savagery that even Stephen narrowed his eyes at the sight of the mutilated corpses.

The money and valuables had, obviously, all been stripped from the wagon. The horses that had drawn it were perhaps spared, as there was no sign of them. No doubt they were carrying some of the wolf's heads northwards at that very moment.

An elderly man, spindle-legged and pot-bellied, had also been killed. Run through by a sword by the looks of the single wound in his belly.

"That's not de Monte Martini," Robin muttered, somewhat disappointed. "Probably his dean or something. Search the area – see if you can find the prior."

His men moved to obey the order, fanning out for quite some distance into the trees in case the prior's body had been carried away from the main site, or perhaps he'd run off and been hacked down.

But there was no sign of the elderly clergyman and Robin's heart sank. Groves had escaped again, and another atrocity committed, but for some reason de Monte Martini's disappearance worried him more than anything else.

"What happened to the prior?"

Alf shook his head and the puzzled look on his face told its own story. "I don't know. I wasn't paying attention to..."

"You mean you were too busy brutalising one of those young boys," Robin spat, "to notice anything else?"

The outlaw remained silent, eyes downcast.

"What about you two? Where's the prior's body?"

The man that John had assaulted looked as though the belligerence was beaten out of him by now so he didn't reply and neither did the final surviving wolf's head who just shrugged when the lawman glared at him.

"Come on, there's nothing else to be found here," Robin sighed, at last. "We'll get our horses from Mirfield and tell them to send a party to bury the dead. Make haste, it'll start to get dark soon."

He walked quickly along the path, back to the main road, despite the tiredness that was beginning to spread through his limbs.

"Groves will have to wait for another day. Again!"

* * *

The journey back to Pontefract was a slow one, much to Robin's irritation.

His men had their horses, but they now had Blase and the three prisoners in their party. Blase refused to ride behind anyone, saying the rocking motion made him ill, and the captured outlaws seemed too volatile to force into the saddle with anyone else.

So the four men were forced to walk.

The wolf's heads were tethered to Robin and Little John's mounts, with Blase jogging along at the rear of the long procession, puffing and blowing. He couldn't go home to Brighouse yet, as Robin knew Sheriff de Faucumberg would want to question him – wring every bit of information he could get about Groves from him.

So they made poor time and, to make matters worse, the weather turned. It had been sunny and hot for weeks but now the rain pelted them as they plodded along the westward road, their cloaks sodden and the water dripping in rivulets from the horses' long faces.

"Fuck this," Robin huffed when they were still hours away from their destination and the road had become mostly mud. The sun was beginning to set and thunder seemed to rumble far off to the south. "We'll stop here for the night. Make camp!"

His experienced eyes had noted the thick trees which

206

would shelter them and provide support for the treated animal skins his men all carried in their packs to use as roofs for make-shift shelters when needed. As he dismounted, a sudden memory came to him of this place, or perhaps just one very much like it. A memory of his friend Much, smiling as they shared a joke together and it brought a lump to his throat.

He stood for a moment, wondering again what the point of his life – *anyone's life* – was, but the men's bustle eventually brought him back to reality and he started moving again.

It didn't take too long for them to tie the water-proof hides to the trunks and branches of the alder and beech trees beside the road, forming a rudimentary little circular village around the camp-fire which had its own roof to stop the downpour from extinguishing it.

The rain dripped down from the lush green leaves above, drumming on the animal skins rhythmically, as Peter Ordevill and Arthur set up the spit and began to cook some of the meat they'd found at the outlaws' camp. The smell of wood smoke and roast pork filled the damp air and the atmosphere was fine, especially when Little John broached a cask of ale, also taken from the wolf's heads' camp-site.

As darkness descended the fire crackled and spat, casting a homely orange glow around the place, and the incessant rain only served to make their dry shelters seem even cosier.

The three outlaws were made to lie on their sides, bound hand and foot under one of the poorer quality animal skins. They were mostly dry, and Robin made sure they were given enough to drink and small portions of food: tough dried meat from their own supplies, not the succulent roast pork that Peter was turning on the spit over the fire.

As usual, they set a watch, with either Robin, Will, John or Stephen being awake for each turn, accompanied by a couple of the other men. Before they retired for the night, though, they drank ale, ate their fill, told stories and sang songs.

The thunder they'd heard earlier had come closer, bringing even heavier rain with it, along with lightning which sheeted above them gloriously. The men, drunk and glorying in the freedom they felt out there in the greenwood, roared their songs ever louder, grinning and dancing with one another as if it was Mayday.

Some of the sheriff's soldiers, younger men, started arm-wrestling with one another, which led onto wrestling matches in the rain. Robin and his old, experienced, friends watched the entertainment with knowing smiles, laughing at the mud-coated, drink-fuelled younger men.

Of course, it didn't take much ale before Will decided to show de Faucumberg's men how a real man wrestled and he waded in, throwing bodies this way and that, roaring with laughter until a fist caught him, accidentally, in the eye, and he dropped like a stone.

Some of the others continued to sing raucously as Scarlet rubbed at his face, checking his fingertips to see if there was any blood from his injury but, even if there was, the mud that coated his face and hands would have hidden it anyway. That didn't stop him roaring with outrage and launching himself at the poor lad that had dealt the stinging blow.

Little John, alert as ever despite the massive quantity of ale he'd supped from the cask, jumped between Will and his victim and the whole thing turned into a sprawling, wet mess of limbs and anger.

Robin, Stephen and everyone else too sensible to get involved watched in the firelight as the filthy combatants rolled about the forest floor, storm raging overhead, filling the air with cracks, booms and unfettered, joyful laughter.

No, they hadn't killed or even captured Philip Groves that day, and the vast majority of his gang had escaped them. But out here, far from the villages and towns they called home, Robin's men revelled for a time in the unsullied freedom of the greenwood, enjoying the camaraderie only the aftermath of a battle could bring.

"What are we going to do about Groves?"

Robin, seated on an old moss and lichen encrusted log, spread his hands at Stephen's question. "We'll ask the sheriff for more men when we finally reach Pontefract." He upended his mug and downed its contents before wiping his mouth and sighing happily. "Groves can't hold his gang together forever – they're bound to get sick of us constantly after them, with no reward other than the spoils of the occasional robbery."

Stephen grunted, his mouth almost breaking into a smile as Will tripped Little John, sending the giant face-first into the mud again, the sheriff's young soldiers crowding around, trying to make the most of John's temporary defeat to pile onto Scarlet.

Robin looked on, the red flickering firelight making his unshaven features appear grim and almost hellish to Stephen's devout Christian eye. "We'll stop them, don't worry about that. But for now..."

The lawman stood, only a little unsteadily, and gazed down at the Hospitaller sergeant. "I'm going to sleep. Wake me when it's time for my watch. And don't let them kill one another, eh?"

CHAPTER TWENTY-TWO

Blase slept not at all, even when the men had all finished drinking and settled down for the night. He'd taken first watch, at sundown, along with one of the sheriff's guards, and Gareth. When they were relieved, both of those had then grabbed ale skins and joined in with the other men's revelry but Blase wasn't in the mood for drink

For a long time he simply lay in the darkness with his eyes shut, but the atrocities he'd witnessed during the ambush of the clergymen seemed to play out again, over and over, in his mind's eye. He wondered if he'd ever be able to forget those scenes; it didn't feel like it.

The sounds of camp – men snoring softly, cooling logs and embers in the almost-extinguished fire cracking, and the breeze whispering softly through the leaves all around them – should have made him drowsy but it was no good. From his position he could see the sleeping form of the wolf's head, Alf, who, although bound hand and foot, lay on his side, eyes closed, mouth open, breathing rhythmically.

The bastard had no conscience! How could a man sleep so contentedly, knowing the terror, agony and humiliation he'd brought on innocent young novices just a short time before? It beggared belief.

Truly, some men in the world were simply evil, Blase thought, clenching his fists as the outlaw let out a little snuffle before rolling over onto his other side, as if turning his back on the watching Brighouse man.

Disgustedly, Blase screwed his eyes shut and tried to concentrate on the sounds of the forest in an attempt to quiet his bleak thoughts. A long time passed and he grew ever more awake and frustrated, as he knew it would be dawn soon and he'd need to travel the next day, exhausted.

Robin and his men wouldn't allow him to lag either.

He stared at the sleeping outlaw who'd turned in his sleep again so his face was visible. The man must have been enjoying a dream, as a little smile twitched at the corners of his mouth, just visible in the slight orange glow from the low camp-fire.

Blase watched, anger mounting, as Alf chuckled.

Furiously, but as stealthily as he could manage, Blase crawled across the ground like a great spider. He glanced around to make sure no-one was watching – Will Scarlet was on watch along with two of Sheriff de Faucumberg's men, but they were all looking outwards, away from the camp-site.

He reached Alf and drew his dagger soundlessly from its leather sheath, bringing it up to the outlaw's windpipe. It would be so easy to just draw it, hard, across the skin.

Too easy for the sodomite.

Blase wanted the man to know how he was dying, and why.

He clasped his free hand around Alf's mouth and squeezed. The wolf's head's eyes opened instantly, the whites seeming almost as if they were glowing, contrasting as they did with the gloom all around and Blase pressed his mouth to the groggy man's ear, warning him against making a sound. He pressed the blade against Alf's throat to emphasise the seriousness of his threat.

"Having a nice dream were you?" Blase growled. "Reliving what you did to that poor boy before you and your mates killed him?"

The outlaw stared at him fearfully, knowing he was utterly defenceless.

"Robin Hood might want you to face the king's justice, as the law says. But we both know justice can be bought, and men who should be hanged sometimes are allowed to go free because they have wealthy friends or because they offer to perform some other service to those sitting in judgement."

He was breathing heavily and his palms were slick with sweat. He'd come across here with the intention of executing the wolf's head but now, he wasn't sure he could do it. To take an unarmed, bound man's life was much harder than he'd expected, especially since Blase had never killed anyone before.

If Alf simply lay there quietly, Blase knew he'd lose his nerve – the righteous anger he'd felt while watching the sleeping outlaw was dissipating already and the fear of being caught by one of the lawmen was growing with every heartbeat.

Alf misread his young attacker's expression though, and, assuming he was about to be murdered, jerked his head back and tried to cry out for help.

Blase's reactions were fast though and he was able to clamp his hand back over the outlaw's mouth just as the cry came out. At the same time nervous, terrified excitement coursed through his veins and, without thinking, he slashed his dagger brutally across Alf's neck, opening a great, gaping wound which spurted blood up and across his arms and chest.

Releasing his captive, Blase looked around desperately, knowing the three watchmen must have heard the wolf's head's frightened cry before he'd been able to silence the bastard.

Incredibly, the sheriff's two men were nowhere to be seen – presumably they were patrolling somewhere to make sure they didn't fall asleep – while Will Scarlet remained seated on a log with his back to the bloodstained Blase.

He turned back and sighed with relief and horror, seeing the outlaw was already dead.

Hurriedly, he crawled back to his bedroll where he found his travelling cloak and drew it around himself. There was no way he'd be able slip away and wash the blood from himself until morning; the best he could do was cover it up.

He pulled his blanket up and, shaking badly as shock began to set in, spent some time weeping silently before, mercifully, sleep somehow stole over him.

* * *

Of course, Will Scarlet *had* heard Blase attacking the outlaw. The experienced mercenary had been fully aware of every movement the Brighouse man made as he crept clumsily around the camp-fire in the direction of Alf and his bound, dozing companions.

Rather than raising the alarm, or calling out to the young man, Will had quietly ordered the oblivious sheriff's men who were sharing the watch with him to take a walk around the camp's perimeter, ostensibly to make sure all was well.

Scarlet was curious to see what Blase planned to do. He was sure the young forester didn't have the balls or the brutal nature needed to kill the defenceless outlaw, but there was no harm in letting the lad land a few punches to try and make himself feel better about what he'd witnessed.

It was, then, something of a shock to Will when he heard Alf's cry cut-off before it was fully formed. There'd been no obvious sound of violence – no thump as a fist hit flesh; no crack as bone met bone. Just a shout of fear which ended in silence before Blase, panting heavily, crept back to his blanket and sobbed like a child.

Despite the darkness, Will had witnessed the whole thing, and what he hadn't seen with his eyes, his mind had filled in the blanks.

As the sun started to light up the sky that morning the men came awake and the crime was discovered, sending a ripple of shock around the entire group, uncomfortable at the idea of a man being murdered beside them as they slept.

The two remaining prisoners shouted for justice, demanding the killer be found and made to pay. It was one thing to be tied up and taken to jail, but quite another to see your partner-in-crime brutally murdered on the grass next to you. They made so much noise that Piers eventually punched one of them in the mouth and feinted at the other. Both fell into a sullen silence after that, but they weren't the only ones outraged at the crime.

"Did you see nothing?" Robin demanded, his arms spread wide as he glared into Scarlet's eyes. "How could you miss a man being murdered just yards away from you? Were you sleeping? Or drunk?"

Will's eyebrows lowered dangerously at the suggestion he'd been derelict in his duty. Sleeping while on watch was a heinous crime.

"You know me better than that," he growled. "Me and the sheriff's lads were awake and alert the whole time. Whoever killed the wolf's head must have been as silent as one of those Assassins the Crusaders feared so much." He shrugged. "Fuck him. He deserved to die anyway."

Robin clenched his fists and gritted his teeth at his old friend's flippancy. The truth was, he *did* know Scarlet well enough to know the man would never fall asleep on watch. He also doubted the outlaw had died as silently as suggested, and that could only mean one of two things: either Will had seen who carried out the brutal murder; or Will had been the killer himself.

The bailiff discarded the latter idea almost instantly. There was no sign of blood on Scarlet, and the terrible, gaping laceration that ended Alf's life must have sent a shower of crimson onto his killer's hands and arms at least.

Robin was relieved that his friend hadn't murdered a defenceless man, but disappointed that he'd lie to protect the murderer.

Sadly, he swung away from Will and raised his voice to address the camp in general.

"Everybody up. I'm going to check you all myself. The killer will have bloodstains on him so you shouldn't be hard to find."

Without needing to be asked Little John fell into step beside his captain as they moved around the men, and Robin was glad of the giant's presence, as always. He felt stupid inspecting his own men, especially those he'd known for years like Arthur, and it helped to have John beside him to share the burden.

The inspection didn't take long.

Blase, pale and fidgeting, turned away when Robin met his eyes and, when the bailiff looked down the dried blood was obvious on the Brighouse man's hands, since he'd not had time to rinse it off in the stream that ran beside their camp.

Robin turned his head towards Will, but Scarlet just shrugged and returned his gaze with a stony expression.

"Did you do it yourself, Blase? Or did you have helpers?"

To his surprise, the young man replied in a strong voice, full of conviction.

"I did it myself. Only wanted to teach him a lesson – give him a little taste of the pain he'd inflicted on those novices. But he tried to shout for help and..." He shook his head defiantly. "The bastard deserved to die."

There were murmurs of agreement from many of the others and Robin could tell from Little John's expression the big man felt the same way.

What could he do? The other prisoners cried out again, demanding the killer's arrest.

Before Robin was able to make up his mind Will stormed across to stand next to Blase protectively.

"What are you going to do then? Arrest the lad?"

"I'm a lawman now," Robin muttered. "I can't just let

this go. He slit a defenceless man's throat for fuck sake!"

Scarlet waved his leader's words away, mouth twisted derisively. "So we've one less prisoner to guard on the road to Pontefract. Good."

The rest of the men, taking confidence from Will's defiant words, were louder in their agreement now.

Again, before Robin had a chance to speak, his volatile old friend continued.

"Are you forgetting the time you chopped the fingers off Lord John de Bray when we robbed him?"

"That was for what he did to your daughter, Scarlet," Robin retorted, growing angry himself now.

"Aye, and what Blase did to that wolf's head was for the boy the whoreson raped. Four years ago you'd never have batted an eye at justice being served like this. Let it go."

The bailiff looked around at the men, knowing this was a crucial decision he had to make. Yes, Alf was an outlaw so, in theory, outside the law. But the man had been in their custody, and tied up. He was sure that made Blase a murderer. Whether it did or not wasn't his decision to make though – that was up to the sheriff, surely.

Yet it was obvious he would lose the support of the men – apart from John perhaps – if he arrested Blase and took him to Pontefract as a prisoner.

Ever since Friar Tuck had taken him to task for the way he treated debtors, Robin had tried to uphold the law as fairly as possible; to do things by the book. And that meant treating everyone as equals – even a rapist and a terrified young forester who'd seen too much death and depravity in recent days.

But they still had to catch Philip Groves, and to do that, Robin needed the support of these men.

Shaking his head in anger, Robin jerked his head in the direction of Brighouse.

"Go. Back to your home, out of my sight."

There were cheers at that, and Blase sagged visibly from

relief. Only Will didn't join in with the celebrations. He stared at Robin for a moment then turned his back on the bailiff.

Scarlet hadn't changed much in the years since they'd been free men, but Robin had.

Not for the first time he wondered if things were better when they'd all lived in the greenwood together, outcast and outlawed, but brothers in arms. Then an image of his son playing in the garden outside their home came to him, and he felt terribly homesick, wishing he could just take his family and leave all this behind forever.

"Mount up," he shouted hoarsely, pushing the feeling away. "I want to get to Pontefract today, if we can. And if anyone ever asks, Alf attacked us when we first arrested him and was killed in self-defence."

Will Scarlet glowered at the surviving prisoners and pointed at them. "Understand, you two? Keep your mouths shut about it, or you'll meet the same fate as your friend."

It had begun to rain again but only a drizzle that tailed off after a short time, and the road to their destination was in decent repair so the high towers of Pontefract Castle soon came into view.

Robin nodded in satisfaction, looking forward to a decent meal, some cool ale and discussing their next move with the sheriff. He wondered absent-mindedly if Sir Henry had settled into his new stronghold which had once belonged to Thomas, Earl of Lancaster. The sheriff, as a staunch royalist, had been an enemy to the earl, who was beheaded outside the castle after the ill-fated rebellion. Again, it struck Robin how much things had changed for him: he'd been on the Earl of Lancaster's side during the rebellion, fighting against the sheriff and the king, yet here he was a few years later, heading to a meeting with Sir Henry, a man he called friend as well as employer.

Was his life better now? It was certainly different…

"Someone approaches," Little John said, eyeing the road

ahead and the small dust cloud that marked a lone rider moving at some speed towards them.

"Looks like a comrade of mine," noted one of the sheriff's men. "Whoever he is, he's wearing a blue surcoat like the ones we usually wear."

Force of long habit made some of Robin's friends grasp the hilts of their swords or draw bowstrings from their storage pouches but the bailiff had already recognised the rapidly closing horse with its distinctive white flash on its chest.

"It's Thomas, he's spotted us," he said loudly. "And by the way he's pushing his mount I'd say he's on some urgent mission to a nearby village."

The blue-liveried rider drew closer, his steed's hooves a blur and Robin felt the first prickle of unease.

"He's pushing the horse too hard to be heading to one of the surrounding villages," Will growled, drawing his sword which prompted some of the others to follow suit. "Either he's being chased –"

"Or he's coming for us," Stephen finished, pulling his own blade free from its sheath and spinning it in his hand expertly, face set, ready for whatever Thomas's hasty approach might herald.

The rider shouted something, but his voice was blown away by the wind until, at last, he came close enough to be heard.

"Hold, Robin! Go no further if you value your life!"

"What's going on, Thomas?" the bailiff demanded, eyes flashing at the unexpected threat from a man he'd come to know well in recent times. "Has something happened to Sir Henry? Is Pontefract under siege?"

The sheriff's messenger pulled hard on his horse's reins, bringing the sweating beast to an expert stop just before them, its great sides heaving, eyes wide.

"Worse," he broke in. "You've been declared an outlaw!"

CHAPTER TWENTY-THREE

It wasn't all violence and robbing – most of the time Philip's outlaw band enjoyed relaxing in their forest camp, just as Robin Hood's men had done not so many years earlier. Unlike Robin's men, Philip's followers didn't train with sword or bow very often, but they did share a love of drink and song and, if it ended up in a disagreement, so much the better.

Mark sat with Ivo on one such evening of revelry, drinks in hand, watching as some of the other recent recruits arm-wrestled for silver coins. The atmosphere was light and good-natured so far and Ivo nudged his friend with a leer.

"You should have a go. Those idiots will look at your size and underestimate you. I'll put some bets on and we'll win a nice little haul."

Mark watched as the giant, Eoin, dispatched another young contender with ease, his great tree trunk arm bulging with muscle, and Ivo's suggestion seemed a good one. Mark knew there was more to the contest than simple brute strength – technique and a little mind-games could bring a smaller man victory over a much larger opponent.

Still, Eoin, cheered on the whole time by a tipsy Philip, was a formidable foe. Only one of the outlaws ever came close to beating the giant but even that lad had folded eventually. The betting would be good for anyone willing to go against Eoin.

"All right," Mark smiled, showing his fine white teeth in the gloom. "I'll have a go. Don't bet all our money though – I probably won't be able to beat that big bastard and we don't want to be left with nothing to show for the past few weeks."

Ivo cackled and even slapped a hand on his thigh like an exuberant child as he stood and made his way over to talk to the rest of the onlookers who were watching Eoin attempt to beat two men at once. This bout was purely for amusement but the cheers were louder than ever as it seemed like the massive wolf's head might actually win. Slowly, though, one of the men began to shift Eoin's left arm, and, unbalanced by the unusual position, beads of sweat stood out on his forehead and a vein near his temple looked like it might pop, it bulged so obscenely.

Mark saw Ivo begin his haggling with the spectators, their eyes turning to look over at the challenger with the fine teeth and slightly manic stare. More than a few of them feared the little man, but apparently none believed he had any chance of defeating Eoin who, at last, succumbed to his two opponents and sat now, grinning and rubbing his arms as Philip filled a mug from a cask of ale and handed it to his old companion.

"You ready for another one?" Ivo asked, walking across and clapping Eoin on the shoulder with a wide smile. "Think you can beat my mate Mark?"

The big wolf's head looked across in surprise, fixing Mark with what seemed to be a surprisingly astute gaze before he shrugged and drained his ale.

"Aye, why not," he smiled, wiping his mouth with a grubby sleeve. "But this is the last. I want to sit and listen to some singing and drink myself senseless after this."

He stood up as Mark approached the log that was being used as a table and stretched his arms up above his head and around in a wide circle, groaning loudly as the muscles expanded. It made him appear even more enormous than usual and the outlaws who'd taken Ivo's bet on Mark smiled at the show of power. Surely their money was safe – Mark might seem something of a lunatic but he was much too small to defeat Eoin, the popular champion.

The pair seated themselves on smaller logs and eyed one another across the 'table', attempting to gain some psychological advantage before the competition had even begun.

"You sure about this?" Groves called, the ever-present smile wider than ever. "Eoin's double your size and already proven his strength. We don't want you getting hurt."

Mark took off his tunic which he'd been wearing since sundown as the air had cooled, despite the season. Now the flickering firelight cast shadows over his bare arms, revealing the hollows and swells of hard muscles in his biceps. For a small man, he was quite powerfully-built, but Eoin flexed an arm, the great bicep bulging to almost the size of Mark's head.

The men murmured in appreciation and anticipation of winning Ivo's foolishly wagered money and Mark shrugged as if he knew he'd no chance of winning.

"Let's do it, then," he smiled, placing his elbow on the fallen tree trunk and offering his hand to the giant.

Eoin nodded and set down his own arm, grasping Mark's hand gently and staring hard into the smaller outlaw's eyes.

The burly wolf's head, for all his bulk, wasn't as menacing as Philip Groves or Mark himself – both of whom wouldn't hesitate to stab a man in the back if it meant a few silver coins – but Eoin's gaze held a steely determination that somewhat surprised Mark. He'd expected the jovial giant to be too tired and ale-content to take this final bout of the night very seriously, but the man's stare suggested otherwise.

Perhaps this wasn't such a good idea after all...

"Ready?" Groves demanded, coming closer to look in turn at each competitor who nodded assent without taking their eyes from one another. "Go!"

There were calls of "Come on, Eoin," and other encouragement from the onlookers. None of them bore Mark any malice as far as he knew, but Philip's lieutenant was popular thanks to his easy smile and affable nature – the fact the men all had money riding on his victory helped cement their loyalty.

Neither man gave way for a time, eyes, and arms, locked in position until, at last, Eoin's greater weight began to tell and his hand very slowly shifted Mark's round, towards the smooth bark.

"You've got him!" someone cried to roars of agreement but, somehow, Mark locked his arm in place, halting the downwards movement. He didn't say a word, but a small smile tugged at the corners of his mouth as Eoin, flagging after so many earlier bouts, saw his own arm begin to twitch under the stress.

"Is that it?" Mark asked, allowing himself to smile fully now as he saw the sweat again forming on his foe's face, one bead even rolling down into Eoin's eye. The salty perspiration irritated the big man, and he blinked, but couldn't afford to lift a hand to wipe it properly for fear of disturbing the equilibrium.

More shouts of encouragement were raised, less cheerfully this time, but Mark noticed Groves didn't join in. His brooding presence could be felt though, even if Mark didn't take his eyes away from the giant's.

At last, to ever more desperate cries, Eoin's stamina waned and the smaller man began to gain the upper hand. Sensing victory, Mark pressed home his advantage, not wanting to allow his opponent a chance to rally. With a grunt, he put all his strength into one more push and steadily, inexorably, Eoin's arm fell sideways, downwards, until the back of his hand was pressed into the bark and Mark let go, standing up with a whoop of triumph, his perfect teeth shining in the darkness.

Only Ivo joined in with the victor's cheer, although, to their credit, the rest of the men, even the vanquished Eoin, congratulated the little wolf's head on his shock win.

"Any more of that ale?" the giant asked Philip, grinning despite his defeat and again rubbing his exhausted limbs.

Groves handed over another mug, threw Mark an

unreadable expression, then stalked away to sit with the rest of the men who'd decided to follow Eoin's earlier suggestion and start a song or two, as Ivo moved amongst them collecting his winnings with a hideous smile.

The two combatants were left pretty much on their own, for the first time since they'd met on the road outside Flockton.

They sat, sipping their drinks, recovering after what had been, after all, an extremely draining contest. The men's song started and, although it wasn't the most musical effort, it was boisterous and loud and soon had all in the camp tapping their feet, singing along or even capering drunkenly like courtly minstrels.

Slightly apart from the main body of revellers, Mark decided to take the opportunity to find out a bit more about the giant who was Groves's right-hand man; the information might come in useful one day but if not, it would while away the evening since Ivo had joined in with the dancers, celebrating his new-found wealth.

"That was a hard match. Reckon I only beat you because you were exhausted."

Eoin looked sideways at the smaller wolf's head and shrugged non-committally. "Probably, but you seemed to have a way of stopping me just as I thought I had you. You'll have to teach me that trick sometime."

Mark laughed but shook his head. "Oh no, I can't give away my secrets – don't have your size so I have to make the most of any advantage I can get, eh?"

Eoin smiled and stood up, slowly, groaning as he did so. "You need a refill?"

"Aye, that'd be good."

The big outlaw returned moments later with two brimming mugs, handed one to Mark and lowered himself back down onto his log. They sipped at their ales, slower now, knowing their limits and wanting to retain some semblance of control. They were wanted after all, and, although there was little chance of any force of lawmen coming to attack them at this time of night, it wasn't prudent to become too inebriated.

Of course, not all of their fellows agreed.

"Look at the state of that arsehole," Mark said, shaking his head in disgust as he watched a man throwing up all over himself then rolling onto his back and mewling pitifully, complaining that the forest was spinning. "If Hood and the sheriff's men were to find us now he'd die in the dirt, covered in his own puke without even knowing he'd been skewered."

Eoin grunted agreement but didn't reply, his foot tapping in time to the men's song. It was a different one now, faster than the first tune they'd belted out and all the more raucous for it.

A few heartbeats passed then Mark said, "So how did you end up here, a wolf's head hiding out in the greenwood? A man of your size would have been a great mercenary. Ever try it?"

Eoin didn't seem to hear at first, lost in the song as he was, but at last he realised he'd been asked something and turned, startled and wide-eyed to look at Mark.

"What? No...I was never a mercenary. I've never been trained how to fight like a proper soldier, with a sword and shield and stuff. Never even learned to use a longbow."

Mark had already guessed the giant was no archer – he was a bear of a man but didn't have the freakishly large shoulders or left arm that bowmen always developed.

"But I know how to handle myself, so I did work sometimes as a bodyguard for merchants or the like. Don't have any desire to go killing people that don't deserve it though, so heading off on a crusade or that never interested me."

The smaller outlaw wasn't entirely sure but he didn't think anyone from England had gone off crusading for decades. He held his peace however and watched Eoin, waiting for him to continue his tale.

The song finished, the big man sipped his drink, and then he turned a bleary eye on Mark.

"You want to hear my story then?"

"I'm an Irishman, really," Eoin said, and Mark thought the man looked proud of his place of birth, although he couldn't think why; one place was as bad as another as far as he was concerned. "I lived in a village called Clondalkin until I was ten," the giant continued, oblivious to his audience's indifference. "With my ma, da and three sisters."

"Four women in one house?" Mark smirked. "That must have been a pain in the arse eh? One's bad enough."

Eoin didn't return the smile; if anything he looked downcast at the memory of his family. "No, I loved them all – they were good sisters; looked out for me when I was too small to do it myself. But there was no work in Clondalkin for my da – he'd trained as a stonemason but no-one was looking for churches or the like to be built. So he decided to take a ship to England because he'd heard they were always building palaces and monasteries and shit like that over here. He took me with him so I could learn his trade, although once he found a job we were to send word to my ma and the others and they'd come and live with us here."

He sipped his ale, staring into the middle-distance thoughtfully and Mark waited, not wanting to disturb him.

"I've never seen them since," the big wolf's head eventually continued and again lapsed into a maudlin silence. This time, Mark had to prompt him to continue or they'd have sat all night without ever reaching the conclusion of the tale.

"What happened?"

Another sip of ale. "My da fell overboard on the journey

here."

"Fell overboard? Was he drunk?"

"No, my da could handle more ale than anyone I've ever known. I never once saw him drunk although he liked his ale as well as any man." He spat into the grass. "But that's what the captain of the ship told me when I woke up the next morning and found my da's sleeping pallet empty."

"How can a man just fall over the side of a ship?" Mark wondered. He'd only sailed a couple of times and been ill on both occasions. "Maybe he was seasick and lost his balance when he was puking. Or a big wave caught him."

"The sea was calm that night, and my da'd been on enough boats that he wasn't bothered by seasickness. No," he clenched his great fists. "I always believed one of the sailors pushed him over the side. Why, I don't know – maybe they got into a fight over a game of dice or something. I never did find out, but the captain was a good man and promised to take me back to Ireland on their return trip, even though we'd only paid for the journey over. Must have felt sorry for me when I started crying."

Mark blew a long breath. "Just as well; England's no place for a little lad all on his own. You'd have been fucked. Literally, probably."

Eoin threw him a stern glare and Mark shut his mouth, trying to hide behind his ale mug as he took another pull.

"Anyway, I helped them unload the ship when they got here. Liverpool I think we docked. We must have stayed a night or two so the men could visit the taverns and whorehouses but we sailed back home soon enough and the captain – a small, older man called McGinty – found a merchant that was heading for my village and I hitched a lift on his cart. When we got there though..." His face was bleak in the wan firelight and Mark fancied he could see tears glistening in the big outlaw's eyes. "My ma and sisters were gone, along with the rest of the people."

"Gone? Where to?"

"Who knows?" Eoin mumbled. "Someone had attacked the place. Chased or killed the people and burnt down most of the houses."

"What did you do?" Mark asked, finding himself more interested than he'd expected when the story first began.

"What could I do? The merchant went onto the next village along the road to sell his wares then he took me back to the docks. The only person that had shown me any kindness was the captain of the ship. I went back and asked him to give me a job on board. Cleaning, labouring, lookout – anything at all. I had no home, no family that I knew of and was still just a boy."

His voice trailed off and Mark knew self-pity was almost overwhelming the giant – the bitter memories and the ale combining to make the world seem an even more unfair shithole than it was normally.

Without speaking, the little wolf's head moved to take Eoin's cup from his unresisting fingers and refilled it, along with his own, from another cask someone had just broached, handing it back with a sympathetic smile before returning to his seat on the log.

"Did the captain agree to it? Take you on I mean."

"Aye. He'd seen my da, who was almost as big as me from what I can remember, so McGinty must have known I'd be a useful hand eventually. And there was plenty of work for a boy to do on board a ship – jobs the men hated." He shrugged. "But it was better than begging in the streets somewhere."

"How the hell did you end up here then? Surely life as a sailor was better than this?"

Eoin's face turned wistful, which was vast improvement over the man's previous sour expression Mark thought.

"Aye, life on the ocean was fine, for a time. It got old eventually, but for the first two years or so I enjoyed it well enough. At least, as well as any youngster who'd just lost his entire family in the space of only a few weeks. I

228

scrubbed the decks, helped prepare meals for the men, darned and waterproofed their clothes, pitched in when it was time for repairs after any storms had damaged the mast or hull...All sorts of jobs. And we didn't just go between Liverpool and Dublin either – I saw places like Bristol and, a few times, France – although only for a short time before we had to cast off again. No, you're right: it wasn't a bad life."

"Why'd you leave then?"

The giant's bleak expression returned, and this time something else blazed in his eyes. Anger, Mark thought. Murderous anger.

"I'd grown in my time aboard the ship. I wasn't as big as I am now, but I was about the size of most men. Bigger than you." His mouth twitched in an attempt at a smile before he went on grimly. "I think the sailors sometimes forgot who I was – how I'd come to be on board their ship I mean – when they were drinking. I wasn't the little boy any more. One night I was below decks with some of them, sitting out a squall. They were bantering as men do," he looked across at the outlaws around the camp-fire who were still telling tales and singing, if not quite as boisterously as before. "I didn't drink very much then – I'd learned my limits even at that age – but I'd had a few swigs of wine or whatever foul tasting shit they were tossing back, I forget now. It's not important." He halted, as if he knew he'd been rambling and wanted to catch his breath. "There was a man – tall, with a black beard he kept trimmed in some stupid style. He didn't seem to realise I was there, started going on about how he'd got into an argument with a traveller from Ireland once, and 'accidentally' shoved the man overboard."

"Your da!" Mark burst out, rather drunk by now, and fully engrossed in the story.

Eoin shrugged and shook his head. "Someone must have nudged him, for he glanced over at me and, when he'd realised who I was, he changed the subject, and so did the rest of the men."

"It must have been your da," Mark repeated his assertion. "Is that why you left? Because you couldn't bring yourself to share a ship with the bastard?"

Again, Eoin shook his head, and his eyes came up to meet Mark's.

"I left because the captain made me. The man that had been boasting about killing the traveller was the captain's brother."

Mark sat for a moment then, not following, asked, "So?"

"He wasn't happy when the bastard disappeared overboard during the night. The men told him I'd overheard their conversation and he thought I'd pushed him over to avenge my da."

"Did you?"

"You're fucking right I did," Eoin growled through gritted teeth. "I waited until the deck was empty and he went out for a piss, then I sneaked up behind him, lifted him by the feet and shoved him right across into the sea. His scream of fear was swept away in the wind – not a soul noticed he was missing until the next day."

He raised his head to look up at the starless, cloudy sky and thought back to that night. "We were on our way back from Sweden at the time. He died in the Norwegian Sea. It was fucking freezing. I hope he lasted a long time before the water, or cold, finally took him."

"Good for you," Mark said, but the giant ignored the hollow words.

"The captain couldn't be sure if I'd killed his brother or not or I'm sure he'd have shoved me into the ocean too. But he didn't. He never spoke to me again, then, when we made it back to Liverpool again with our cargo his mate threw me off the ship."

Some of the outlaws were beginning to fall asleep and Mark rubbed at his eyes tiredly. He wanted to hear the rest of Eoin's tale though.

"What did you do in Liverpool? You were still just a boy weren't you?"

"I found some other orphans and fell in with them. Stole food, robbed people, just lived on my wits for a while but I'd started to really grow by then, so I was almost the size I am now. One of the local gang leaders noticed me and took me in with him. He thought I'd be a good man to do his dirty work but to be honest I was never very good at hurting people just because some bastard told me to." His voice trailed off and he glanced across at Groves who seemed to have nodded off while sitting upright. "I'm much better at it now though."

He stood up, grunting with the effort, and disappeared into the trees where the sound of splashing on dried leaves carried to Mark and he decided he needed to relieve himself too.

"How did you meet up with Philip then?"

Eoin turned and looked blearily at him, shaking his manhood with a small slapping sound that Mark did his best not to hear. "Eh? Oh...I was in a tavern one night. Someone must have recognised me or maybe they just didn't like my face – attacked me with fists and chairs. Philip was there and he saw it all. Jumped into help me and it's well he did for one of the bastards was about to stick me with his dagger."

Mark did his breeches back up and the pair of unlikely companions returned to the log that had played host to their arm-wrestling match hours earlier.

"Philip saved you?"

"Aye. And I've been indebted to him ever since. I'm not much of a leader, or a thinker."

Mark held his peace at that.

"So I was happy to follow Philip wherever he led. And we've done alright over the years. Look at us now." He grinned but there was a tinge of sadness in his eyes, Mark fancied. "Anyway, I'm done. Time I was asleep." He waved a hand and moved away to his bedroll which was beside his old friend and leader.

As he watched him go, Mark glanced up at Groves and noticed the man wasn't asleep at all – he was wide awake and staring at him with an unreadable expression. A shiver ran down his spine and he turned away hurriedly to find his own blanket.

* * *

Sir Henry de Faucumberg rubbed at his eyes with his fingertips and blew out a long sigh. The past couple of days hadn't been good ones.

Pontefract Castle was a fine new residence. Once described by King Edward I as "the key to the north", it boasted a number of towers – the King's and Queen's Towers being particularly impressive – all connected by sturdy walls with a huge keep crowning the whole pile.

Sir Henry's wife liked the place, although he himself found it strange when pilgrims would come to visit Thomas, Earl of Lancaster's tomb, which was just outside the castle walls. The executed rebel had become almost a saint to some of the people in Yorkshire which seemed absurd to the sheriff who'd known the earl and hadn't thought him very saintly at all.

He was glad enough to still be in a job, and a position of power though. Sheriff of Yorkshire, with temporary stewardship of Pontefract Castle, was far better than nothing and, judging by the news that came from the south, it was probably better to be as far from the capital as possible. Queen Isabella and her followers were gathering strength in France, and sure to mount their invasion within months.

The only really pressing problem Sir Henry had to deal with was the blasted outlaw, Philip Groves, and his murderous gang. But the sheriff had confidence in Robin Hood – the bailiff would use his skills to bring the outlaw down soon enough and then, hopefully, life would be nice and simple.

And then, two days ago, Prior John de Monte Martini had appeared out of nowhere in the great hall, shrieking like a madman, face black and blue.

Sir Henry bore no love for the greedy prior. He well remembered the proud Hospitaller Knight Sir Richard-at-Lee throwing a bag of money at the clergyman and humiliating him rather amusingly, which was no worse than the arrogant peacock deserved. He also knew the unscrupulous man owned a number of brothels which didn't seem at all right for a man of the cloth, so the sight of his battered face brought the sheriff a measure of satisfaction.

Until the prior began to speak.

The sheriff stared ahead, into the empty hall, as the scene played itself out again in his memory.

"De Faucumberg," de Monte Martini shouted, catching sight of the sheriff as he was helped into the great, high ceilinged room by two of the guards. "What do you here? Why aren't you in Nottingham?" The prior waved a hand feebly, dismissing any reply. "Never mind, it hardly matters. Will someone bring me a chair? And some wine, in God's name? Is this how you receive a guest of my standing?"

The sheriff waved a hand and William hurried away through one of the alcoves, returning a moment later with a high-backed chair which he helped the prior collapse into. Another servant followed a short time later with a goblet of wine and a platter of sweetmeats. De Monte Martini drained the wine and gestured irritably at the servant to refill it while he stuffed the savoury food into his mouth as if he hadn't eaten for days.

Sir Henry sat in silence, patiently waiting for the man to

finish his meal, wondering as he watched what might have befallen the wealthy clergyman.

"Outlaws." The prior glanced up from the platter momentarily to spit the word out, as if it were a pip from one of the grapes he'd just devoured, then he looked down again to search for his next mouthful.

"Outlaws," the sheriff repeated. "They did that to your face? Where's the rest of your party?"

"Dead!" De Monte Martini cried out again with an outraged look. He tried to stand up but didn't have the strength and slumped back heavily in his chair, sipping wine with a faraway look. "The wolf's head and his friends killed them all and," he looked up to glare at the sheriff again, "it wasn't an easy death he gave them. Some – the younger novices – were even raped. It was...like I'd descended into Hell. Why is it when I visit my estates in this part of the country the lawless scum are allowed to brutalise me?"

De Faucumberg was too shocked to reply for a time. Groves's men were worse than a plague.

"My condolences, father," he finally managed to say. "We've been troubled by these outlaws for a while but I swear to you, on my honour, I'll see them brought to justice for their crimes against you and your retinue. Could you describe the men? Their leader?"

"I know very well who their leader was," the prior grunted, sneering at the sheriff's words. "And I can describe his men too, they held me captive, beating and torturing me, before letting me go; I assume they thought I'd be too weak to make it to safety, but God gave me wings. One was an angry, vicious man, while another was a lumbering giant."

Sir Henry nodded at the description. The 'angry, vicious' man could be anyone, but the giant was clearly Groves's right-hand man, Eoin. It was De Monte Martini's next words that shocked him to his core though.

234

"And the man leading them? Aye I knew him well... it was Robin Hood!"

The hall was fairly busy that afternoon as the sheriff had been dealing with a number of petty criminals and petitioners looking to gain his aid for one reason or another. Now, the people gathered there – who'd remained in the hall when the bruised prior had been shown in, sensing the intrigue that was sure to follow – began to gossip loudly.

"Robin Hood?"

"The bailiff's men did that to a clergyman?"

The vast majority of the voices were disbelieving but Sir Henry heard one woman muttering to her daughter, "Once a wolf's head, always a wolf's head." He knew there would be plenty of other people, especially those who didn't know Robin personally, who'd believe him capable of these heinous crimes.

It wouldn't be the first time a lawman had abused his position after all...

For his part, the sheriff didn't trust de Monte Martini's tale. Yes, the man appeared earnest, and clearly *someone* had assaulted him, but Sir Henry had grown to know Robin fairly well over the past few months and years. Something like this wasn't in his character. Even if it was, Little John wouldn't stand by and watch youngsters being molested. The whole idea was ridiculous.

He stared down from his own, raised, seat and met the prior's gaze. Their eyes locked for a heartbeat before de Monte Martini raised his voice, loud enough so everyone in the hall could hear him.

"Well? What say you, Sheriff de Faucumberg? Are you just going to sit there, or are you going to do something about the wolf's head and his murderous companions?"

What could he do? Everyone in the county knew the tale of Robin Hood punching Prior de Monte Martini in the face during the Mayday games – it was legendary. If Sir

Henry denied the prior's charge he'd be calling the powerful nobleman a liar to his face, in front of dozens of witnesses. And, knowing the wily old bastard as he did, the sheriff suspected de Monte Martini would already have made a sizeable donation to Queen Isabella's supporters. If she was successful in deposing the king and placing her son on the throne, as seemed inevitable, Sir Henry didn't want her to have any reason to doubt his loyalty.

Crossing Prior de Monte Martini would ensure the usurper wouldn't see Sir Henry very favourably – the man's influence truly was that far-reaching.

There was nothing else to do.

"I hereby declare Robin Hood, and all those currently in his party, to be outlaws. Sir Roger?"

There were gasps from the onlookers as the sheriff beckoned the captain of his guards.

"Sir Roger, I task you with arresting Hood and his men. Take a dozen men. Start by heading to Hood's last known position, in Mirfield."

The sheriff hoped Robin was long gone from there and wanted to buy the bailiff a little more time to hear about this farce and make himself scarce.

He shared a knowing look with his captain as the powerfully-built man left the room. Sir Roger knew, and liked, Hood; he'd not shirk from his duty if he and his men came across the newly-outlawed bailiff, but the sheriff knew his captain would do all he could to avoid any such confrontation.

Prior de Monte Martini shouted his own advice though. "Wolf's Heads are fair game for any man or woman. No need to arrest them, Sir Roger. Just kill them and save everyone any more trouble. Hood has a strange way of escaping imprisonment, as Sir Henry knows full well..."

The captain nodded non-committally and strode from the room but the hall had become a mass of voices and even a few angry shouts from those who knew Robin and his friends. The sheriff ignored the hubbub and gestured to his steward, William, again.

"See the prior is given comfortable lodgings for the night, suitable to his station, and have someone tend to any wounds he may have. New clothing and so on..."

The steward hurried to carry out his orders and de Faucumberg stood up, shouting to the nearest guardsman to clear the hall. Business was over for now.

As the great room emptied he noticed the slim figure of Thomas who was apparently on guard duty himself that day. He caught the eye of the man – taking care to make sure de Monte Martini, who was slowly shuffling out of the hall by the eastern door aided by the steward – didn't notice.

"My lord?"

Sir Henry took in the sight of the messenger and was satisfied at what he saw. Thomas was always clean shaven, his hair trimmed neatly, and his blue surcoat free of stains or rips. The man was reliable and trustworthy, a good soldier, and his appearance was testament to the fact.

It was just as well, for Sir Henry needed a loyal man right now.

"You know as well as I do that Robin didn't attack that little shit's entourage."

Thomas nodded, a sour look on his face, but held his tongue.

"Sir Roger will head west to Mirfield, but we both know the bailiff's most likely already completed his mission there and will be heading back here to report, unless he's went off somewhere else chasing Groves's gang. I want you to watch the roads approaching the city to the north east. They should return any day, unless bad luck sees them run straight into Sir Roger; I'm sure he'll try to keep out of their way but he's had his orders to arrest Robin so… God knows how that might work out." He ran a hand across his face irritably. "Assuming that doesn't happen, when you see Robin's party returning ride out and warn them off, all right?"

"Where should they go?"

The sheriff shook his head. "I don't know, but if they come here the prior will demand their heads. I'd rather avoid that scenario if possible since I simply don't have the political clout to stand against him. It would turn into a bloodbath." He grasped Thomas by the arms and looked at him. "De Monte Martini won't be around for long, I'm sure. He'll head back down to Lewes and this will all blow over. Until then, Robin and his friends will simply have to stay out of the way."

The messenger had hurried off to complete his mission and now Sir Henry came back to the present with a start.

It had been two days since Sir Roger rode to Mirfield, ostensibly to arrest or kill Hood and his men. Two days that the prior had spent haunting the castle like a spiteful wraith, drinking the sheriff's best wines and eating his own weight in meat while continually asking him if he'd managed to find the wolf's head.

Sir Henry felt a sense of anger building inside him but he repressed it, knowing it would do no good to get into an argument with the man.

Damn de Monte Martini and his wicked lies. Why protect Groves by blaming his crimes on someone else? What possible motive could he have for this?

238

CHAPTER TWENTY-FOUR

"Revenge," Robin muttered in disgust. "Pure and simple. That's why de Monte Martini's accused us of robbing him when he knows fine well it was Groves's gang. Christ above, the two of them must have planned this."

Will Scarlet nodded agreement. "The prick hasn't been able to forgive us for stealing all his money, or you for giving him a sore face. Not very Christian of him is it?"

No-one laughed at the joke. Instead they looked warily back towards the road, although it was barely visible from where they'd decided to hide themselves. An old grove of beautifully lush beech trees would provide good cover, surrounded as it was on the ground by juniper and bracken should anyone come hunting them from Pontefract.

When Thomas brought them the news that they were outlaws once again it had been an awkward few moments, as the sheriff's soldiers who were in the party looked warily at Robin and his friends, wondering what the hell might happen next. Would the companions turn on them, fearing the sheriff's men might do the same now that their legal status was, at best, ambiguous?

Before nerves could get the better of anyone Robin had told the blue-liveried guardsmen to head back to Pontefract on their own. It was highly unlikely they'd have been implicated in any crime by the Prior, so they were told to filter slowly back into the castle – with their give-away surcoats removed and concealed inside their packs until they were safely inside the stronghold again.

"Sir Henry's been forced into this," Robin told them. "You all know he's an honourable man. He won't see any of you punished just for being a part of this, but let's make sure his hand isn't forced again, eh? If you head back to the castle one by one it'll attract a lot less attention than if you all turn up at once in full uniform. You go back with them Thomas, with my thanks for your warning."

The messenger nodded grimly.

"What about you lads?" one of the soldiers asked. "Seems unfair that you've been falsely accused. Maybe we can speak with the sheriff, tell him what the real story is?"

Will snorted. "Unfair? Unfair he calls it. Fuck me, that's an understatement if ever there was one."

Robin waved him to silence irritably. He knew Scarlet was merely trying to lighten the mood but this wasn't the time for it.

"I'm sure he knows exactly what's happened, but thank you for your offer." He smiled and thrust out a hand to the guardsman. "You're all good men. Once the Prior's gone off back down south and this passes I'll look forward to your company again."

The soldier shook his hand grimly, obviously angry at the injustice of the situation but accepting the reality: he was merely an insignificant piece on a political gaming board. The truth didn't count when it came to an accusation by someone as influential as a rich, corrupt prior.

When the sheriff's men headed along the road back to Pontefract with Thomas that morning they left behind a small, and rather downcast, group of friends.

"You think the prior will head back to Lewes soon then?" Peter Ordevill wondered, idly picking dirt from under his fingernails with a dagger.

Robin laughed mirthlessly. "I have no idea. I wouldn't put it past the bastard to hang around up here just so he can make sure Sir Henry puts plenty of resources into our capture."

James shook his head. "I don't know this prior personally but..." he trailed off in confusion. "It seems a bit far fetched to me. Groves murdered his acolytes. Surely he'd want to see the outlaws pay for that crime? Not to mention the fact Groves could have demanded a hefty ransom for the prior. It doesn't make any sense to me."

"If you knew de Monte Martini, you'd understand," John replied sadly. "He might be a churchman but he's the devil incarnate. Ask Friar Tuck the next time you see him."

Robin agreed with his old friend. "Aye, it might seem strange but it's clear that's what's happened. Groves must have offered to spare de Monte Martini's life – and given up any ransom – on condition the clergyman accused us of his crimes. They both win from it – the prior kept his life while the law comes after the one man they both desperately want to see dead: me!"

"And us," Stephen muttered ruefully.

"Don't forget Groves must have stolen a hefty amount of money from the prior's wagon so might have been less inclined to look for a ransom when he had a chance to take us down instead."

"You're such good friends with the sheriff now," Will broke in. "Will he really tell his men to bring us in and hang us if they do?"

Robin didn't reply. He didn't know the answer to that question himself. Yes, he believed Sir Henry was a good man, who wanted to do the right thing. But he also knew their so-called friendship would count for little if the sheriff was ordered to hang them by whoever was running the country at the time. And he couldn't blame him – why should de Faucumberg throw everything away by refusing to dispense 'justice'? It would do no good anyway – if Robin's friends were captured and the sheriff refused to execute them, someone else would take his place and see the job done.

The outlawed bailiff had no intention of putting his unlikely friend in that position; they'd have to deal with this problem themselves…

The eight of them – Robin, John, Will, Stephen, Arthur, Peter, James and Piers – sat in gloomy silence for a time, each wondering what would become of their families and the new lives they'd managed to carve out for themselves since they'd been pardoned three years ago. A gentle breeze played through the big leaves in the beech trees, bringing welcome relief from the heat which was quite intense, even here in the shade.

At any other time the men would have thought this a glorious summer's day and cracked open a cask of ale but today...Robin looked around at his friends' faces and felt as though he was at a funeral.

He still hadn't decided what their next move should be. In the short term they had to get away from Pontefract in case any patrols stumbled upon them. But where should they go? He desperately wanted to head for Wakefield. Home. He could explain what had happened to Matilda and the two of them could gather their money and take Arthur north, to Scotland. They had enough money to live well, without any of this hassle.

His eyes strayed to his friends again, though, and he knew the idea of a retreat to Scotland was nothing more than a fantasy. He couldn't leave these men to their fate, even assuming Matilda would agree to take their son and go with him, and that seemed highly unlikely. No, he was their leader – he'd simply have to find a way out of this ludicrous situation.

* * *

Sir Henry de Faucumberg had spent the morning working on the monthly accounts in his chambers, trying to avoid the prior. The sheriff had a horrible suspicion the old clergyman would hang around in Pontefract for weeks, just to make sure the hunt for Robin Hood didn't let up.

The one time he'd ventured outside to enjoy the sunshine for a few moments he noticed one of his guards – out of uniform for some reason – heading along the passage that led to the prior's quarters, where the elderly man was supposed to be recuperating in bed. De Faucumberg felt sure the guard was one of the party Robin had taken to try and arrest Philip Groves and he'd been glad to see his men returning in secret. Clever, and doubtless Hood's idea.

Why the man had been walking towards de Monte Martini's chamber he had no idea but he'd hoped it was to throttle the troublemaking old bastard.

With a sigh, he made the sign of the cross and silently begged God's forgiveness for his vindictive thoughts before turning weary eyes back to the pile of ledgers before him. He hated being cooped up in this little room on such a fine day – he should have been out hunting or even just riding to one of the nearby villages to check on things – but it was better than being accosted by the prior who seemed in surprisingly good health considering his supposed ordeal at the hands of the outlaws. Of course, they'd sent men to recover the corpses of de Monte Martini's murdered entourage but the search party hadn't returned yet. If they came back with a dozen brutalised bodies things would be very bad for Robin and his men.

There was a gentle rap on the door which the sheriff recognised as his steward, William's and he called for the retainer to enter, hoping it wasn't bad news.

"My lord." William made a shallow bow as he stepped into the room. "Your presence is...*requested*, in the great hall. Prior de Monte Martini has some news, apparently."

De Faucumberg muttered an oath and dropped the documents he'd been working from. No doubt the prior had demanded rather than requested his presence and what choice did he have but to obey the summons? He could make the old pain in the arse wait of course but what would be the point? He'd have to make his way to the hall and find out what this was about eventually.

"Alright," he groused, getting slowly to his feet, limbs tight from sitting too long. "But don't be giving him any more of our good wine. He's had enough of it already – give him the cheap stuff. If the bastard wants better he can visit a tavern and buy it himself. Come on."

Pontefract Castle was just as grand as the one he'd left back in Nottingham and it took a while for them to traverse the stone staircases and draughty, high ceilinged corridors that led to the great hall. Time for the sheriff's mind to whirl through possible reasons for this summons.

Most likely the meeting was simply for the prior to reiterate his desire that the wolf's head – Hood – be brought to justice, but maybe there was some new development in the ridiculous saga.

William threw open the heavy oak door that led into a corner of the great hall and Sir Henry strode in without announcement or fanfare, heading directly for his chair which sat on the raised dais at the head of the room, ignoring de Monte Martini's greeting until he'd taken his seat.

"What's this all about?" he demanded without preamble. He might need to pander to the clergyman but he wasn't going to pretend he liked the tonsured old tit. "I'm a very busy man you know, I don't have time for frivolities."

"Frivolity? My entire party raped and slaughtered and you call it a 'frivolity', Sir Henry?"

The sheriff tried to protest but de Monte Martini carried on without pause.

"It seems one of your own men knows exactly where Robin Hood is hiding but, instead of informing us, actually rode to meet the wolf's head and *warned him he was to be arrested.* That is why their party hasn't returned here as expected."

The sheriff had to stop himself from glancing over instinctively at Thomas, who he'd seen in his usual place to the side of the dais. How the hell had the prior found out about this? And did he know it was the sheriff that sent the messenger to Robin with the warning?

"I know you couldn't possibly have known about, or been involved in this," de Monte Martini went on smoothly, his expression saying the exact opposite to his words, "but that's not important. What you have to do is, first, arrest that traitor there," he nodded in Thomas's direction, "and then send soldiers to the location I've marked on this map. Your men know how to read a map I trust? If not, I'll lead them myself, should someone be kind enough to help me mount a horse."

De Faucumberg raged inside but he was experienced enough in statecraft not to let it show on his face.

"I trust you have some evidence to back up your accusation of my guardsman, Father? The man has been a loyal servant to me for years and –"

"I have enough proof to satisfy me, Sir Henry," the prior nodded. "Another of your men – someone who was in Hood's own party until this morning, in fact – passed this information onto me. I can't tell you the man's name, of course, I agreed to keep his identity confidential in case he should suffer reprisals from friends of the outlaw. Trust me," he said, almost leering at the sheriff, "my accusation is sound. Your man there – Thomas is it? – is guilty of aiding and abetting a wanted criminal. I suggest you arrest him now, before he does any more damage to this investigation."

De Faucumberg sat there for a time, not sure what he should do. He'd told Thomas to ride out and warn Robin after all – the man had only been following orders. That whoreson he'd seen earlier, the guard who'd been out of uniform, it must have been him that had informed on Thomas. Why? It wasn't important right now, although the sheriff vowed to find out sooner rather than later.

He gestured to a pair of his soldiers who flanked the huge main double doorway into the hall. "Arrest him," he said, motioning towards Thomas. He looked directly at the messenger as the guards converged on him, trying somehow to silently tell the man not to worry, they'd sort this, one way or another.

Wordlessly, Thomas allowed himself to be grasped by the guards who disarmed him with apologetic looks then led him out of the room, towards the dungeon. Sir Henry turned his gaze back to the prior, nodding his head.

"That's the first of your suggestions done then. But your demand that I send men to that location on your map, well...You're asking me to send my men into a probable ambush. You know better than any how deadly Hood and his men are. They'll cut my soldiers to shreds as soon as they get close to his hiding place, assuming your information is accurate." He shrugged and made an exaggerated sad face. "On top of that, most of my garrison know the wolf's head and respect him. I doubt we'll be able to find anyone willing to lead this hunt with any enthusiasm, since my captain, Sir Roger, is already off on a similar errand."

The sheriff spread his hands and stretched out in the high-backed chair, pleased with himself, knowing his words were true.

"I'll do it."

Every eye in the great hall turned to the speaker – a slightly overweight, balding man of advancing years, wearing the livery of a sergeant.

De Faucumberg cursed inwardly, feeling as if the entire situation had run away from him and was no longer within his control.

The speaker was his own quartermaster, one of a handful of men he'd brought with him from Nottingham thanks to his efficiency as a storeman. What the hell was he doing here, in the great hall, instead of at the barracks?

"What was that?" De Monte Martini asked, a small smile playing on his lips as he turned to look at the volunteer. It was obvious the prior had expected this, although the sheriff couldn't explain how. Did the quartermaster have an issue with Robin or one of the other men in his group? If so, it was the first time de Faucumberg had heard about it.

The prior was a weasel, that much was certain. Somehow he'd managed to gather information on the sheriff's own men, and all while he was apparently recuperating from a near fatal encounter with a gang of brutal outlaws.

"I said, 'I'll do it,'" the quartermaster repeated. "Sam Longfellow, sergeant of the sheriff's garrison." He introduced himself, as if it was the first time he'd ever met de Monte Martini but de Faucumberg knew that must be a sham.

"There you go, Sir Henry," the prior beamed, clearly delighted to have won this battle of wits. "It seems we have someone to lead your men in the hunt for the depraved wolf's head."

De Faucumberg glared down at the quartermaster, gesturing the man to stand before him so he could see him better. He knew him of course, but not particularly well and, as he eyed him now it was plain the man spent most of his time in a storeroom rather than in combat or even training for combat. Longfellow was of average height and carried a roll of fat around his midriff. His eyes were hard and determined however, as if he'd waited all his life to be given a chance like this and meant to make the most of it.

The sheriff waved a hand, partially in agreement, partially in irritation. Fine – let the portly oaf lead a few men to find Hood. He was absolutely certain the legendary wolf's head would have no trouble evading the quartermaster, who was from Nottingham after all, or sticking an arrow through his eye if necessary.

"So be it," he growled, looking again to the prior. "The sergeant can take a dozen men –"

"Come now, sheriff. He'll need a larger force than that."

"Well it's all I can spare," de Faucumberg retorted. "In

case you didn't know there's another gang of outlaws running wild in the county – I need men to look for them too, not to mention the captain of my guard has already gone off with many of my soldiers on your errand. So think yourself lucky I'm even giving you a dozen."

"No matter," the prior said, bowing his head apparently deferentially but that small, superior smile was still on his red face. "I'm sure it will be enough. They have no idea we know exactly where they are so it should be a simple enough matter, shouldn't it?"

De Faucumberg didn't answer the question. He got to his feet and, with a final contemptuous nod to the prior, left the hall, William-atte-Burn following faithfully at his heels.

As he strode back to his study the sheriff contemplated the recent turn of events. It was as bad as having Sir Guy of Gisbourne around, watching his every move. Well, Robin had dealt with Gisbourne, and no doubt he would deal with Prior John de Monte Martini as well.

Christ, if he doesn't, de Faucumberg vowed, *I'll shove the old bastard down a long flight of stairs myself.*

CHAPTER TWENTY-FIVE

Thomas allowed himself to be led away by the two guards – men he knew and had even shared a few drinks with on occasion if they happened to meet in the barracks or town when off-duty.

In truth, he was too stunned to do anything except walk numbly, meekly, from the room, flanked on either side by the other soldiers. Thankfully, they respected him enough not to try and restrain his arms or any other rough treatment that was routinely doled out to prisoners.

In fact, none of the trio said a word as they headed along the echoing corridor that led towards the prison beneath the castle. The guards were clearly embarrassed at having to detain their erstwhile colleague, and Thomas's mind was still whirling, as he wondered what would happen now.

Would he be left to rot in the prison, forgotten like so many others before him? Would the sheriff set him free and restore him to his duties once the prior left to go home to Lewes? Yes, he felt quite sure Sir Henry, honourable and fair as he always appeared, would let him go eventually, and the thought helped him relax, the knot in his stomach slowly dissipating as they walked.

And then he thought of Robin and his friends, hiding not far from there, oblivious to the fact that crawler Longfellow was going to attack them with a much larger force. If someone didn't warn Robin – again! – he would surely be cut down by the quartermaster's men. He glanced surreptitiously at his escorts, wondering which of them might carry the message in his stead but realised that would be a mistake.

He didn't know how either man felt about Hood and besides, could he ask the young men to put themselves in that position, with Prior de Monte Martini desperate to weed out what he saw as informers?

No, it was no use, there was only way to warn Robin.

Without giving himself time to think, he turned slightly to the side and threw a vicious punch that connected with the guard on the left's temple. It was a tremendous blow and sent the man clattering, dazed to the floor, his halberd falling on top of him as he went.

The second guard reacted quickly, but the halberd was a clumsy weapon, wholly unsuited for combat in such close quarters. He tried to bring the butt up, into Thomas's guts, but the sharp end of the long pole-arm smashed into the wall, spraying sparks, long before it came close to the messenger's body.

"I'm sorry," Thomas grunted through teeth gritted so tightly he wondered they didn't shatter under the pressure, and grabbed the unfortunate guard by the head, pulling him down while bringing his own leg up.

The man's cry broke off as he took the full force of Thomas's knee in the mouth. He wasn't unconscious though, so, despite his natural aversion to it, Thomas landed a punch on the side of the downed man's head, then another, before he rose up, panting, staring wide-eyed at the two incapacitated soldiers.

I hope I haven't injured them badly, he thought, but there was no time to waste worrying too much about their fate. If he didn't get the hell out of the castle right now his chance would be gone; and any other guards seeing what he'd done to their colleagues wouldn't look too kindly on him, even if he was one of the better liked of de Faucumberg's garrison.

He quickly sized up the situation, realising there wasn't time to find rope to bind the guards. Still panting from the fight, he began to run, heading back, the way they'd came, desperately praying no-one else would come out of the entrance to the great hall as he charged past, heading for the nearest way to the stables.

250

As he burst through the door into the courtyard it became apparent news hadn't yet filtered out from the hall of his own arrest and incarceration. A few workers – labourers mostly, tidying up the worst of the day's refuse after a number of food and drink deliveries had been made – glanced his way but, seeing his blue livery, turned back to their tasks. It didn't do to stare at soldiers; perfect recipe for a sore face or even a night in the gaol.

Still, Thomas knew running as if all the demons of hell were after him would attract attention from someone who might try to find out what was wrong, so, when he spotted another guard outside the stables he slowed his pace to a fast walk, which felt to him more like a crawl.

"Well met," the soldier smiled at him as he approached, and Thomas's heart sank again. It was young Andrew, a lad with Scottish parents and someone he really didn't want to have to assault if the sounds of pursuit reached the courtyard. And that was sure to happen within the next few heartbeats, as soon as one of the beaten guards regained their senses.

"Afternoon," Thomas grinned, doing his best to appear calm as he strode right past the guard, into the stables where he grabbed his saddle and tack and pulled the bolt that held his mount's stall shut. "What you up to today? I've just been given an urgent message to take to Nottingham. The sheriff's not a happy man – think that prior's causing him all sorts of trouble." He grinned, feeling like it must have looked more like a terrified grimace and, without stopping to putting the saddle properly on Ajax he jumped nimbly up, onto the palfrey's back and kicked his heels in, urging the beast into a walk towards the main gates.

Andrew's eyes narrowed in surprise as he took in the sight of the sheriff's messenger riding bareback, while holding the redundant saddle grasped between his legs and the horse's neck, and he ignored Thomas's question, dismissing it, no doubt, as meaningless small-talk.

"Are you not going to saddle that animal before you ride out?" he asked, his unlined face showing confusion although not hostility. Yet.

"Ah shit," Thomas muttered as, finally, cries of alarm filtered out from the doorway he'd just come through moments earlier.

Andrew's hand fell to his sword and he began to draw it, still hesitant, yet apparently beginning to realise he should do something, even if he didn't have a clue what.

"Wait," he shouted, just as Thomas's mount broke into a canter.

"Stop him!" It was the guard that had taken a knee to the face. Blood caked his nose and upper lip, but he seemed otherwise unhurt and Thomas sighed inwardly, as he glanced back and saw him, thankful he hadn't hurt the man badly.

"Stop him!" The cry was repeated, louder, more forcefully and the two guards manning the gate looked across, wondering what the noise was about. Thomas was well known to both of them and the sight of him riding towards the gates was a familiar one, so it took a few heartbeats before they understood what was happening.

"Close the fucking gates, close them now! Stop him escaping!"

The gate-men, at last, ran down the steps from their positions atop the ramparts and threw themselves at the big gates, shoving them slowly yet inexorably shut, as Thomas bore down upon them, his steed's hooves thundering on the hard earth like hammers.

Andrew had joined the chase by now too, sword fully drawn and Thomas knew he'd be lucky to survive this. The guard he'd assaulted would probably lay about him in sheer rage and Andrew and the gate-men would join in as the battle-fever and confusion overtook them.

The courtyard was filled with excited and angry voices

now, as soldiers ran to cut off his escape and workers stopped what they were doing to watch the entertainment, some cheering Thomas's escape while others hoped the gates would shut. None of them had ever seen a horse running head-first into a gate before.

But Ajax was the fastest horse Thomas had ever ridden, and the most fearless too. Despite the danger, it allowed itself to be urged on at full tilt and, somehow, impossibly, they were through and out onto the main road!

The gates clattered shut behind them just a moment later, muffling the outraged, despairing cries and Thomas couldn't help laughing out loud, punching the air with his fist at their great escape.

He chanced a look back and saw the gates were already being dragged back open. Inside, for sure, soldiers were mounting the other horses in the stables and would soon be after him. He prayed they wouldn't follow until Longfellow and his whole force were ready. At least then Robin and his mates would have time to get their own horses and ride off with something of a head-start.

Another laugh tore from his throat as he pushed Ajax along the road towards the greenwood. He might be an outlaw himself now, but he'd never felt so alive!

* * *

"What's that?"

"What's what?" Stephen replied to Little John's rumbling question, eyeing the dry skin on the tip of his index finger before pulling a small dry piece off flicking it onto the grass.

"That. Listen."

They did, and Piers nodded. "I hear it now. Hooves. Someone's coming this way."

"Not again," Arthur muttered, getting to his feet reluctantly.

"Let's move," Robin ordered, his voice low but the command carrying easily over the sounds of sighing foliage.

The men flowed towards the road almost as one single body, their old training and previous time together lending them an intimate understanding of one another's movements and anticipation of Robin's desires in regards to their positioning.

Will, along with Stephen, Piers and Arthur, hid in the trees on the far side of the road, while Robin, John, Peter and James found places on the near side, stringing longbows or drawing swords, ready for who – or what – ever was charging towards them.

They didn't have to wait long for the rider to reveal himself – Thomas's voice filled the air as he approached, the alarmed tone reaching them long before the words resolved themselves into a meaningful message and Robin held his great warbow ready to loose should any threat appear at the back of the sheriff's messenger.

"Robin! John! If you're still here, show yourselves! You've been betrayed!"

Before he could thunder past on his impressive warhorse Robin and John raised their own voices and stood out in the road, waving at the oncoming rider.

Thomas spotted them and even at that distance the relief was plain on his face, but he barely slowed as he came on, his eyes almost as wide as his mount's.

"Get your horses," he shouted. "We have to move. One of the guards from your party came back to Pontefract a short time ago and told the prior you were here. They arrested me but I escaped. The entire garrison will be on their way; we have to flee, now!"

"Do as he says," Robin shouted, sprinting back in the direction of the clearing where they'd tethered their mounts, the men following close on his heels.

"What about the two prisoners?" James shouted,

glancing back at Groves's men.

"Leave them," John ordered. "The sheriff's men will find them and know who they are. Justice will be served. Now, move it!"

Before long, all of the friends were leading the horses through the undergrowth, back to the main road, where they hastily mounted and looked to Thomas for guidance since he seemed to be the man that knew the most about their situation.

"Where to?" Stephen asked, simply.

"For now, anywhere," Thomas replied grimly, kicking his heels in and leading them at a canter towards the west.

"Ride for Wakefield," Robin commanded, to looks of surprise. "I know it's probably the first place they'll look for us, but trust me – we'll be safe."

They pushed the horses hard for a time, until they skirted Featherstone and at the fork Robin led them off the main road, onto the less used, less well maintained track to the north-west. It would take a little longer to reach Wakefield that way, but would keep them hidden from any pursuers. Robin knew it was too late in the day to reach his home village so, as soon as possible, they led their horses off the path and into the trees.

Exhausted, both from the ride and the fact night was beginning to fall, Robin and the others dismounted and began to set up camp with hardly a word passing between them. Despite their tiredness they went about their business efficiently and, before long bedrolls were sited under animal skin shelters, water had been collected from the nearby beck, and lots drawn for watches.

As the sun finally passed beneath the horizon and only a dim glow lit the camp, the men wondered what had happened in Pontefract Castle earlier that day.

"So why did one of the sheriff's soldiers betray our position to de Monte Martini?" Little John wondered, when Thomas had filled them in on what he knew of the day's events. "Not to mention Thomas's part in it, and de Faucumberg's too."

"Who knows," Robin shrugged. "Maybe the man owed money for gambling debts, or rent or something, and he hoped the prior would pay him for the information. It's not important now."

"Not important?" Will demanded, brow furrowed in consternation. "It's important to me when someone tries to have me killed! We should be finding out who the informant is and hang the scum from the nearest tree. Like we'd have done in the past."

"Maybe you're right," Robin conceded the point, not looking for another argument over morals and honour. "But we've got more to worry about right now than some faceless guardsman."

"What *are* we going to do?" Arthur wondered. "And, more to the point, what about my family down in Nottingham?"

Robin raised a hand reassuringly. "Have no fears for them, the sheriff wouldn't do anything to them, even if he thought we genuinely had turned feral and carried out the attack on de Monte Martini's party. No, they're safe and better off out of the way, trust me." He shook his head though, sipping at a cup of stream water – none of the men really felt like supping ale that night, not with the knowledge pursuers were after them. "As for what we're going to do? I have no idea. For now, we escape that fat quartermaster and let things settle down a bit. Then..."

"Then we need to do what we were supposed to be doing all along," John growled. "Find Groves's gang and put an end to them. If we can capture any of them alive, they can tell of their part in the crimes against the prior and we'll be free and clear."

Piers, James and Arthur all liked that plan and murmured their appreciation, but Will wasn't so keen.

"This is all down to that fucking churchman," he spat.

"If what you say is true, the sheriff knows the charges against us are horse-shit – he's just declared us outlaws to appease the prior, right? So why don't we just ride to Pontefract and kill the bastard?"

"Kill de Monte Martini?" Peter Ordevill demanded. "Are you serious? We can't just walk into Pontefract Castle. Have you ever seen it? The place is a fortress!"

"So we camp outside on the road until he heads back to Lewes," Will retorted. "He won't stay up here for long, he's an old man and if the sheriff's not making him too welcome..."

Robin looked at Stephen. The Hospitaller didn't say much but he was shrewd and his time as sergeant-at-arms for their old friend Sir Richard-at-Lee had given him valuable experience.

"What d'you think, Stephen?"

The bluff Yorkshireman was picking idly at his fingertips but he glanced up and nodded towards Will.

"I like Scarlet's idea. God knows I've had enough of corrupt, self-serving churchmen. But –" he continued before Will's smile could grow too wide. "We don't have the luxury of time. We're not the fabled band of outlaws everyone knew and feared any more. Those days have passed and now we're just another group of men fallen foul of the law. Aye, our reputations might see us safe for a while, but there'll be plenty of hard men in the villages hereabouts that might want to try and collect any bounty they think's on our heads."

Robin blew out a long breath thoughtfully, glad he'd asked Stephen's advice; the man was more perceptive than people realised.

"So, although killing the prior might very well solve our problem," the Hospitaller went on, "I don't believe we have time to wait – we have to act fast. And that means finding the remnants of Groves's gang and destroying them, as John suggested."

There were a few, "aye"s and Robin smiled. "That's settled then? Will, are you happy to go along with that?"

Scarlet looked angry at losing the chance to hunt down their accuser but he brightened at last. "Aye, fair enough. I want revenge on those Groves almost as much as I want to choke the life from the prior."

"All right," their young leader stood up, unlacing his breeches and making his way behind a tree to empty his bladder, his voice carrying easily through the still evening air. "We'll head for Wakefield at first light then, and see about finding where Groves has gone to ground."

"Why Wakefield?" Arthur wondered. "Wouldn't we be better heading for somewhere less obvious? Somewhere none of us have ties to?"

Robin reappeared from the gloom, shaking his head. "As Stephen just said – there's going to be people all over the country who'll want to make a name for themselves by taking us down." He smiled and tapped the side of his nose with a wink. "Besides, the sheriff's men will never find us in Wakefield. You'll see what I mean on the morrow..."

* * *

Sergeant Samuel Longfellow, lately quartermaster of Pontefract Castle's barracks, now leader of a dozen men with no ties or loyalty to Robin Hood, sat atop his cantering horse as if he was the king himself. He'd waited all his life for an opportunity like this, and now it had fallen into his lap he meant to make the most of it.

Of course, he was no regular foot soldier – he was a sergeant, and he enjoyed the prestige that position brought. But he'd always felt he deserved something more; something that would allow him to make his mark on the world, not to mention earn a decent wage at the same time.

He'd been an only child whose father died when he was fourteen, but his uncle managed to secure him a place as a raw new recruit in Nottingham's garrison, where he'd served loyally for a few years. His mother had been inordinately proud of him when he won a promotion to sergeant and the position of quartermaster, but that had been fifteen years ago, when he'd just turned twenty. She was long in her grave now, and Sam had never managed to progress out of the stores he occupied almost every day, ordering boots or shields or docking soldiers' wages for not taking care of their kit.

When Sheriff de Faucumberg had moved north from Nottingham to Pontefract his captain told Sam he'd been hand-picked to make the move with them. At first he was cheered, and wondered if it would mean a new role but... although he'd never admit it to himself, he was far too comfortable as quartermaster to seek advancement. It could be a dangerous job, guardsman, and he liked a cosy storeroom when the days grew cold and winter winds howled about the castle, be it Nottingham or, more recently, Pontefract.

Still, that jumped up yeoman Robin Hood came from nothing – a wolf's head, for Christ's sake! – to the position of *de facto* bailiff. When the younger man had come swanning into Sam's barracks back in Nottingham, making demands and then actually assaulting him...it was too much. Sam had never been hit in all his adult life and it was indescribably humiliating to cower before the huge former outlaw, especially with that giant oaf John Little smirking down at him the whole time.

Now, Hood and his men rode ahead of them, judging by the tracks in the mud, surely aiming for Wakefield, and Sam Longfellow meant to kill the wolf's head, or at least see one of the soldiers the sheriff had granted him do it.

One way or another Hood would die – not be arrested, that was too dangerous –and Sam's name would be remembered for generations to come the man that finally stopped the legendary outlaw who'd run riot over northern England for so many years.

It was early morning, not long after sunrise, and Longfellow had woken bright and eager, rousing his men with shouts and kicks any drill sergeant would have been proud of. He may not have boasted the experience, or physique, of a battle-hardened knight, but he had plenty of self-belief and arrogance.

It didn't take long for the party to splash some water on their faces from the skins in their horses' saddlebags, down a little ale with some bread or cheese then hastily mount up and resume the ride towards the little market town Robin Hood hailed from. They hadn't seen any sign of the fugitives since last night, when their trail had led off along a smaller track that was almost overgrown with lush summer foliage.

Longfellow and his scout – a grizzled old veteran of almost fifty years named Harry who knew the area well – both felt sure Wakefield was Hood's ultimate destination and decided to ignore the narrow trail that their quarry had taken, with its encroaching vegetation and treacherous footing. They guessed it would be quicker for them to take the left fork in the path, past Sharlston Common and head for the well-maintained main road that led straight to Wakefield over good ground.

Now, as the rising sun cast long shadows over the land it seemed a prudent choice. Wakefield was almost in sight, according to old Harry but, even better than that, they could see Hood and his men on the clear road ahead. The outlaws must have rejoined the main road to cross the River Calder and now the chase was truly on.

"Sam," one of the men near the front of the party shouted back over his shoulder. "We might catch them before they reach the village if –"

"You address me as 'sergeant'," the quartermaster retorted haughtily, although his voice carried away in the wind and he wasn't sure the impudent soldier heard him.

He went on anyway. "Charge men, let's catch the bastards before they can lose themselves amongst the hovels in Wakefield! Remember, Hood and some of the other men in his gang are from around here so we may face some resistance."

The formation turned into a loose arrowhead shape, as the faster and more enthusiastic of the soldiers kicked their heels in and urged their mounts into an almost uncontrolled gallop. Sam found himself not quite at the back of the group and that suited him fine. He could direct his men better from there, he thought.

He was no coward – he still had brawny arms despite the paunch, and knew a bit about how to wield the sword at his waist – but the best leaders kept themselves back so they could direct their forces, didn't they? It was only sensible.

As they approached the village Longfellow tried to count the men they were pursuing. Eight, as far as he could tell, although the speed of his mount made it hard to be sure. He wasn't used to riding as fast as this, but he knew his force outnumbered the outlaws and that was all that really mattered. He could see Thomas, the sheriff's erstwhile messenger, riding in the ranks of the wolf's head's gang and he wondered what insanity had caused the man – a career soldier with years of dedicated service – to throw everything away, simply to help that arsehole Hood.

His thoughts were brought up short as it became clear his party would never catch up with the fleeing outlaws before they reached Wakefield.

What should he do? His lack of experience made him hesitate and the men he led, without a direct command from their leader, held back, allowing the outlaws to disappear into the village, behind low houses and winding, random streets.

"The church!" Longfellow cried out, staring ahead at the direction the fugitives had taken through the buildings with sudden understanding. "They must be heading there to seek Sanctuary. Aim for the steeple, and..." he drew his sword from its scabbard and brandished it in the air as heroically as possible, "grant them no quarter! These men are outlaws and –"

His noble speech went unheeded by the men he led, who, ignoring the villagers that milled about narrow streets, shouting angrily at them for riding like lunatics, spurred their horses through the streets towards St Mary's, eager for glory and renown.

Cursing at the fact his orders weren't being listened to, even if the outcome was ultimately the same, the quartermaster kicked his heels in and gripped his mount with thighs he knew would ache in the morning, unaccustomed as he was to riding like this.

"There, they've gone inside!" Harry shouted excitedly, as the lawmens' party bore down on the small church with its recent extension to the rear. The face of a giant, bearded man glaring out at them was momentarily visible, before he slammed the heavy door into place and Longfellow expected to hear the sound of a lock or bar being thrown into place.

Only the door hadn't shut properly – it had become lodged on something – a small stone or other piece of debris perhaps – and now whoever stood behind it slammed it again with a similar lack of success.

Longfellow saw his chance and spurred his horse towards the jammed doorway, throwing himself clumsily off the beast as he arrived, somehow managing to land on his feet.

A voice could be heard from inside.

"Move, John, get into the room there with the others, I'll get this."

Longfellow recognised Hood's voice and, sensing an opportunity, ran up to the door which opened wide.

The famous archer stretched down and brushed aside the

little stone that lay there and then rose to slam the door shut at last.

With a grunt, Longfellow threw himself forward, the tip of his sword snaking inside. There was a cry of pain and dismay and then the door bounced off the steel blade, which the quartermaster drew back for another thrust, but he was too slow this time.

The heavy door was, at last, slammed shut with a great boom that shook its frame then there was the unmistakeable thud of a locking bar being thrown into position.

"Surround the place, lads," the sergeant shouted, inspecting his bloody sword with a grin on his face. "There's bound to be other ways out of the building and I don't want to lose them; not when we've got them cooped up nicely like this."

The soldiers did as they were told, dismounting and spacing themselves evenly around the building, weapons drawn, as Harry also climbed down from the saddle and warily approached his sergeant standing by the barred doorway.

"I got him," Longfellow grunted to the scout, a satisfied smile on his round face. "I don't know how badly, but I injured Hood. Look."

He showed the crimson on his sword to Harry, who mumbled, "Nicely done, Sam," then the quartermaster stepped back and took in the small church, admiring its pleasant lines and general state of good repair. The newer part to this side of the building was somewhat jarring to the eye – the stone being less worn and less discoloured than the original structure which, Longfellow surmised, must date from at least a century earlier, but, overall, it was a pleasant looking old edifice.

As they stood there, shouting could be heard from around the corner of the far wall. Angry shouting that was coming their way.

"Ready men," the sergeant warned, his voice wavering only slightly. "That could be them attacking from another direction."

It wasn't. The voices owners' came striding around the side of the church towards them and Longfellow allowed himself a tiny inward sigh of relief. It wasn't the outlaws, it was just a couple of clergymen, although the fury in their eyes shone like an oil lamp at midnight and even old Harry took a hasty step backwards as the churchmen came close.

"What's the meaning of this?" the biggest of the two demanded. "Armed soldiers seeking to enter our church by force? Have you no honour gentlemen?"

Longfellow squared his shoulders and glared indignantly at the speaker – a friar judging by his somewhat tatty grey cassock and tonsured head.

At that moment a group of hard-looking men turned up, led, shockingly, by a young woman with strawberry-blonde hair. They glared at the newcomers but the blue surcoats each of Longfellow's soldiers wore marked them clearly as the sheriff's men and the villagers held back without drawing their weapons.

"What's all this, Tuck?" the woman demanded, eyes never leaving Longfellow, hand resting threateningly on the pommel of the sword at her waist.

"We're pursuing a gang of vicious outlaws, girl," the quartermaster broke in angrily, feeling somewhat nervous under the woman's hard stare. "They've locked themselves inside this building and I mean to see them evicted and taken to Pontefract to face justice. So stand aside, the lot of you, before we start breaking heads!"

"Have you never heard of Sanctuary?" the second clergyman – a simple priest and far less intimidating than the friar – demanded from behind his friend.

"Aye, of course" Sam replied. "But I fear these men are so wicked even God wouldn't see them protected. They attacked one of your own – Prior John de Monte Martini of

264

Lewes – killing and despoiling his entire party in mean and blasphemous ways!"

"Did they now?" the friar asked softly. "Well, be that as it may. It's not up to you, or I, to decide who deserves Sanctuary. Those men inside are under God Almighty's protection and there they shall remain, so I suggest you ride off back to the sheriff and report your failure."

"I'll do no such thing," Longfellow cried, his face turning scarlet at the friar's lack of respect. "I didn't come all this way to be turned back by a single door. If you won't show us another way into the building, I'll have the damn thing broken down. I have the sheriff's authority in this." He turned to one of the soldiers and pointed at him imperiously. "You – find the village blacksmith and requisition a sledgehammer. We'll take the door right off its bloody hinges if needs be."

It seemed fairly obvious where the smithy was and the guardsman, with a nod of assent towards his sergeant, hurried off towards the southern outskirts of the village where the sound of a hammer striking an anvil could be clearly heard.

The priest appeared to gain courage at this threat to his beloved church and he pushed round the friar to face up to the quartermaster.

"You'll regret this," he muttered. "Damaging the house of God? Defying the protection that He's granted to those inside?"

"Aye," the big friar agreed, his voice taking on a powerful tone that spoke of fire and brimstone and divine wrath. "May the Lord strike you down should you seek to enter this church without His blessing!"

The heavy portent in the friar's words made Longfellow nervous but he had no intention of giving up now, when Robin Hood himself was only a couple of inches out of his grasp. Surely God wouldn't protect such a notorious wolf's head, would he?

As they stood, at an impasse and glaring silently at one another, the soldier sent to fetch a sledgehammer reappeared and he wasn't alone, the blacksmith following at his back demanding to know what was going on. It seemed word had spread about the trouble at St Mary's, as everyone in the village began to congregate in the road. The sheriff's men fidgeted and fingered their swords nervously, not liking the angry atmosphere that seemed to pervade the entire crowd.

"Got it." The soldier held out the hammer to Longfellow, adding, as an afterthought, "Sergeant."

The quartermaster looked at the tool but didn't reach out a hand to take it. He was in charge after all; this wasn't a job for a leader.

"Break the door down then, man," he ordered, waving a hand towards the thick slab of oak and black-painted iron that separated them from the outlaws.

"Here, what's going on?"

The friar replied before Longfellow could even see the speaker.

"The sheriff's sent these men to hunt down Robin Hood who has, apparently murdered some people and sought refuge in our church, Patrick. The sergeant here wants to force his way inside and arrest them."

The man addressed as Patrick pushed his way through the ever growing crowd and stood beside the clergymen, his face every bit as indignant as the friar's, but the quartermaster had suffered enough now. He was the sheriff's representative and, as such, had the authority to do what he had to do to apprehend or kill the dangerous criminals inside St Mary's stone walls.

"Enough of this!" he shouted, grabbing the hammer from the guardsman. "Everyone step aside or you'll all be arrested for obstructing the king's justice." He glared around at the villagers who didn't seem to take his threat too seriously which only angered him further, and he swung the heavy hammer up onto his shoulder as he stepped towards the church door.

The locals muttered amongst themselves, but they enjoyed a decent relationship with Sir Henry de Faucumberg, particularly in recent years, and no-one wanted to ruin it by impeding his soldiers.

"This is ridiculous," Patrick scowled. "Robin is a lawman like you."

"*Was*, a lawman like me," the sergeant replied. "Now, he's nothing more than an outlaw. Now stand back. Men!" he shouted. "Prepare to move inside and take these bastards – dead or alive. I've already bloodied Hood, and the rest will face the same fate."

The locals reacted in various ways to that statement: some cried out in fear for Robin, while others laughed at the idea of this portly quartermaster besting Hood in battle. The young woman leading the armed men seemed to shrink though, which surprised Sam and lent him courage as he watched her turn to the burly friar with a stricken look on her lovely face.

With a great cry, Longfellow hefted the great hammer aloft and brought it down to batter against the door which shuddered and splintered but only a little.

"We have to stop them," the girl shouted, making to draw her sword, eyes blazing, but Tuck restrained her, whispering something into her ear which seemed to calm her, as he did so.

"I'm warning you," the friar shouted at Longfellow, still holding the furious young woman's arm and raising his head skyward as if invoking God's righteous wrath. "Enter this building by force and you'll pay the price."

As if in answer to the man's pronouncement, it began to rain. There was nothing as dramatic as the boom of thunder or a sheet of lightning, but the sky did grow gloomy and Longfellow felt the first droplets of drizzle land on his cheeks and forehead.

Falling to his knees, the friar began to recite some prayer in Latin, his voice a low, unnerving monotone. When the sound of the crowd faded and the voice of the priest joined in with the prayer Longfellow felt the hairs on the back of his neck rise. Even the young woman that had been ready to stab him mere moments ago stood placidly, watching the sky.

Sam smashed the hammer into the door again though, his forehead creased in determination.

The rain fell and the churchmen's prayer grew even more disturbing as the priest's voice rose slightly in pitch, away from the friar's, and the originally harmonious chant became dissonant and jarring.

It seemed to Longfellow that the only sounds in the entire world now were the rain, which had grown heavier, the hellish prayer, and his own laboured breathing as he battered the hammer's iron head against the door for a third time.

This time, though, he was rewarded with a splintering and the wood gave way around the lock.

Dropping the tool from his tired hands the sergeant stepped back a pace, wiped the rain from his eyes and sucked in lungfuls of air. The door had swung open of its own accord but the interior of the church was dark, and the opening gaped like a hideous mouth.

He shook his head at the absurd thought, realising the clergymens' sinister prayer and the gloomy atmosphere were combining to make him nervous.

"This is your final warning," the friar muttered as Longfellow stepped towards the door, sword back in his hand and the scout, Harry, at his side.

"Enter this place at your peril."

The door suddenly slammed shut against its frame with a bang and the quartermaster jumped involuntarily, but it must have only been the wind. The lock was useless now anyway and the door simply fell open again, but now the dingy interior looked even more intimidating.

Even if God wasn't about to strike him down for violating his Sanctuary, Hood and his men were inside and armed to the teeth.

The young woman who'd led the small war-band glowered at the sheriff's men, white faced and clearly on the brink of drawing her sword and unleashing the killing fury that blazed in her eyes. Longfellow knew she'd be more than a match for him if it came to that, but the friar held his palm up to her, smiled reassuringly, and it seemed enough to hold her in check.

Thank God.

"Come on you men," he shouted at his soldiers. "Do what you're paid for. Get in there and arrest the wolf's heads. Move it!" He gave old Harry a shove but the scout stumbled to a halt and simply stood, gazing wide-eyed in through the shattered doorway. The rest of the soldiers also refused to move at first but Longfellow screamed at them to obey his orders or face charges of insubordination and, eventually, they did as they were told and headed for the entrance.

"You'll pay for this," the friar told him softly, but he simply snarled in return and followed the soldiers.

As they funnelled slowly inside there was an enormous crash that seemed to reverberate throughout the entire structure. As one, the sheriff's men stopped in their tracks and turned to gape, wide-eyed at Longfellow.

"What the hell was that?" he shouted, spinning to gaze outside at the two watching clergymen, soaked in the rain.

"What was what?" the priest replied, brow furrowed in confusion.

"That banging sound," the sergeant shouted, turning to stare nervously back into the gloomy church.

Thunder rumbled overhead, culminating in a massive crack of lightning and at least one of the soldiers actually whimpered in fear. Longfellow glanced back again at the impassive churchmen then, squaring his shoulders and mumbling a prayer of his own to God, pushed past his soldiers, deep into the new section of the building.

It comprised a single, large room that, from the look of it, served as a private area of worship. In essence, it was a smaller version of the main church, with a few pews facing towards a small, sparsely furnished altar. In the left corner was a statue of the Virgin Mary cradling the infant Christ, while the right housed another female statue which Sam assumed must be the Magdalene.

But the room was empty. Hood and his men were nowhere to be seen.

"Where are they?" the quartermaster whispered, eyes drawn to the statue of Mary Magdalene which seemed to be glaring back at him judgementally.

"Where are they?" he repeated, almost hysterically. The room had only one other exit, through a door that led into the main, old building. But it was bolted from *this* side – the outlaws couldn't have possibly gone through that way.

"God has granted them Sanctuary," a voice said, close to his ear, and he jumped in fright, spinning to see the portly friar standing there. The man had somehow managed to sneak up on him without making a sound, like a wraith.

"And now," the friar continued, voice rising to a crescendo as his gaze moved from one soldier to the next, finally coming to rest on Longfellow himself. "I suggest you leave, before you feel the force of His righteous wrath!"

There was another almighty crack of lightning outside and that was it. The soldiers panicked and ran for the exit, not wanting to spend another moment in a church that had somehow swallowed up half-a-dozen outlaws without a trace.

Longfellow, feeling the hard stare of the friar on him, was loathe to scurry out like a frightened child; not without a parting word.

"I'll find Hood," he growled, pressing his face close to the tonsured clergyman's. "Sanctuary or no, I *will* bring him to justice. And if I find out you had anything to do with this..."

The friar stared back at him, totally unafraid, which angered the sergeant further, and he jerked his forehead forward, aiming for the man's nose.

Somehow, despite the dim interior of the church, the friar evaded the attempted head butt and before he knew what was happening, Sam found himself sprawling face-first on the hard stone floor, a horrendous pain in his right kidney.

The storm growled outside, blending in with the groan of agony that slipped from his mouth and he wondered what the hell had just happened. The fat friar couldn't possibly have moved that fast without some divine intervention.

"If you ever return here seeking to defile His hospitality again God will not be so merciful." The churchman hissed, glaring down at him with the murderous strawberry-blonde woman at his back, a terrible expression on her face. "Now – begone!"

Sam knew he was beaten. His men had fled and he'd been knocked to the ground by some invisible angelic force. How could he fight against God Himself?

Without another word, the lawman scrambled back to his feet and staggered out of the church. Whatever had happened here, his quarry was gone. He should have known the legendary wolf's head Robin Hood would have help from Above.

As he ran to catch up with the rest of the sheriff's men he failed to notice the short cudgel in the friar's hand, or the enormous grin that spread across the man's round face.

Another huge crack as lightning sheeted across the sky made him run even faster, oblivious to the incredulous stares of the villagers.

CHAPTER TWENTY-SIX

When Robin slammed the door on the pursuing soldier there had been a brief, welcome moment of respite as he and his men caught their breath in the cool church interior.

It didn't last long.

"Why the fuck are we running from those arseholes?" Will Scarlet demanded, puffing hard, and, in a moment of clarity, Robin was hit by the fact his friend was already well into middle-age. It made him feel old himself, despite his mere twenty-two years on God's Earth.

"What else can we do?" he replied. "We can't fight them."

"Why not?" Scarlet spread his arms wide and glared at his leader. "They might outnumber us but we'd still take them down easy enough."

"That's not what I mean. Me and John have probably played dice and drank and even been on jobs with some of those men. They're only following the sheriff's orders. I won't cut them down like deer, not if I can avoid it."

"Aye," John rumbled agreement, his beard and hair rendering him almost invisible in the gloom. "Besides, the sheriff's men aren't all unskilled, clumsy oafs. If we get into a pitched battle with them there's a good chance at least some of us will die."

Will snorted in disgust, then noticed Robin clutching his side and he squinted, trying to see what was wrong.

"What's up with you?" he demanded, coming across to stand next to his captain, a look of concern replacing the anger that had been displayed there for most of that day. "You been cut?"

"Aye," Robin admitted, glancing down himself at his side. He took his hand away and the sparse light made the fresh blood there glisten. "It's just a scratch but I'll need it dressed before long."

"And yet you won't let us just go outside and kill those bastards?" Will shook his head in disbelief. "Even though they tried to kill you. So what the hell *are* we going to do then? They won't just give up now that we're in here – they'll be hunting for some way to smash the door in as we speak. We'll have no choice but to fight them then."

"Aye, he's right," Stephen said, the white cross on his red Hospitaller surcoat plainly visible despite the paucity of light. "It's noble of you to avoid engaging them and all, but...when they come through that door I won't be hanging around." There was a soft hiss as he pulled his sword from its leather sheath. "The whoresons mean to put an end to us and I'll not stand here praying to God when I've got cold steel in my hand that can do its own bloody work."

The rest of the men murmured agreement but they couldn't see the small smile on Robin's face.

"All being well, none of us will need to strike a blow this day," he said, moving past them, further into the newly constructed section of the church which wasn't as dark, as the meagre daylight filtered through the narrow stained glass windows that depicted the Magdalene, Christ and some rapturous angels. He lifted a medium-sized candle from the altar and lit it from the sanctuary lamp that burned constantly to symbolize the presence of Christ.

The men followed him silently, and Tuck's irate voice carried through the thick door at their backs. The words weren't clear enough to make out but he was obviously haranguing some poor unfortunate.

"I think I'd rather be in here," Arthur said lightly, "than out there on the end of the old friar's tongue."

Robin handed his glowing candle to Piers, who was the closest to him, then headed past the small altar into the corner of the room, before he turned round and looked at the rest of the men, his right hand reaching up to grasp an iron candelabra set into the wall. The candles it held were dormant, but a flash of lightning lit up his face in a myriad of colours as it came through the multi-coloured panes of glass, revealing his gleeful smile which was like that of an expectant child at Yuletide.

"Look, Robin," Will muttered, turning to eye the door as if it might be broken down any moment, "I don't know why you brought us here but we need to either get out through one of the other doors or make ready to fight." He glanced about the room, as if assessing its defensive qualities.

Robin pulled down hard on the candelabra he was holding.

"Like I said: no fighting."

Almost instantly there was a click from the centre of the chamber and the men nearest the source of the sound jumped back in surprise.

"What the fuck was that?" Peter Ordevill demanded, his voice low and tight.

"Watch your language," Robin chided, walking over confidently, bending down and...disappearing into thin air.

"Robin!" Scarlet shouted, charging forward, sword drawn, loyalty to his friend overcoming his fright. "What the hell?"

Beneath his feet, Robin smiled up at him.

"A secret chamber!" Piers burst out, his cultured voice brimming with excitement as he pushed past Will, almost extinguishing the candle in his hand as he hurried to look down into the floor at his grinning captain. "I've read stories about them, but never thought I'd see one for myself. This is great!"

"Did you know about this all along?" Scarlet demanded, glaring at Little John, who shrugged and smiled enigmatically but didn't reply as he jumped down into the hole beside Robin and reached up to take the candle from Piers.

"Come on, the lot of you," John commanded, as the

sound of something striking the door reverberated around the room, mirroring the thunder that had started outside. "Get down here, before they break in and see us standing like cows ready for slaughter."

There was another booming thud and this time the head of a hammer was just visible as it tore through the thick wood of the door, and the men did as they were told, jumping down through the trapdoor into the newly revealed basement which they soon realised was much bigger than the small opening that Robin had disappeared into.

The guttering candle cast eerie shadows on the walls of the underground chamber, but every one of the men managed to fit inside before Robin leaned up, grasped a handle on the underside of the hinged flagstone and pulled it down over his head.

There was another click and, in the wan light, they could see there was no gap above.

"It's in," Robin muttered in relief, as if he'd been worried his clever device might not work properly. "Extinguish that candle, just in case the light can be seen from above."

Despite the fact they were underground the sounds of the storm outside and the thudding of the hammer on the door still reached them clearly as they huddled in their stygian hideaway.

"How did you know about this place?" Stephen's voice, bursting with curiosity, sounded harshly in the dead air of the secret chamber.

"Know about it?" Robin whispered in reply. "I paid to have this new section of the church built. Seemed a good idea to have the stonemasons put in this sanctuary, just in case I ever needed somewhere to hide. The floor is all heavy flagstones, apart from the trapdoor, which is the same stone but a much thinner, lighter piece, supported by a timber frame and held shut by a lock. The candlestick has a wire running from it to the lock."

"So who's going to pull the candlestick back?" Will wondered. "We're all down here."

"No need. The lock has a spring mechanism so it slips back into place on its own, and we can open it from down here just by pressing on the wire."

The doorway above crashed in under the force of the hammer and the unmistakable sound of many booted feet filled the room directly over head. Confused – and clearly frightened – voices could be heard as the sheriff's guardsmen wondered where in God's name the outlaws had gone.

Another peal of thunder seemed to shake the very stones of the building and then...silence.

Robin nodded to himself in satisfaction. Tuck must have played his part perfectly, terrifying the soldiers so much that they believed God himself had literally spirited their quarry away.

And, given the fact a thunderstorm had blown up from nowhere, in the middle of a glorious summer's day, perhaps He had.

* * *

When the sheriff's men had gone – to where, Tuck wasn't sure, although he didn't expect them to return to Pontefract in disgrace just yet – those villagers curious enough to brave the storm crowded around St Mary's demanding to know what was happening. Where were the outlaws? Had they really been spirited away by God?

"I know no more than you," Father Myrc shouted in reply to the babble of questions. "But Robin himself paid for the extension to our church, from his own pocket. If God would grant Sanctuary to anyone here, it would be Robin Hood."

"Let us in," someone shouted, to a chorus of agreement.

276

Even the headman was caught up in the excitement. Had a miracle truly happened here in Wakefield today?

"Can we go inside?" he asked, his eyes moving between Father Myrc and Tuck with the expression of a dog begging for table scraps.

Tuck grinned. "Aye, Patrick. We should all go inside and witness God's work for ourselves. Follow me!"

The big friar led the way in through the recently smashed doorway, a smile of satisfaction playing around his lips. Robin's plan had worked perfectly – no-one, so far at least, suspected it was all an elaborate trick, the foundations of which had been laid, literally, when the church's new section was erected just months earlier. Only Tuck and Patrick knew about the hidden chamber beneath the great flagstones that the people all stood on.

Robin had kept the hideaway a secret, knowing it was safer for everyone. The fewer people that knew about it, the less chance there was of someone giving it away under duress. He'd told Tuck and the headman about it when the building work was completed and, although none of them expected there'd ever be any need to use it, they'd conspired to come up with the scenario that had just played out, almost exactly as planned.

The storm had been a quite incredible coincidence, coming at exactly the right time, Tuck mused, but it didn't surprise him that much. God had marked Robin Hood for great things, as as the Friar had already seen many times in recent years.

"Good God," Patrick Prudhomme muttered, wide eyes scanning the chamber's interior and Tuck nodded at the performance – the headman would have made a good mummer. "It's true. They've gone." He knelt, hands clasped before his breast, eyes raised aloft to the crucifix that hung from the wall high above.

The majority of the villagers that had followed them in – a good two dozen or more – dropped to their knees, mimicking the well-respected headman, sighs and even little laughs escaping their lips at the idea of Wakefield's legendary son and his friends being saved from death by God Himself. Truly, that young man had made life very interesting in the village since he'd come of age.

One or two, less credulous than the rest, peered around for signs of hidden exits, rapping the stone with the hilts of eating daggers in hopes of finding a false, hollow wall or stooping to inspect the floor for evidence of a trapdoor.

They didn't find anything and after a while left, shaking their heads and wondering what the hell had happened.

Tuck knew the hinged flagstone that swung up to allow access to the low basement was cunningly disguised but he also knew the gloomy interior of the church made it much harder to spot. If one knew where to look though, they might notice the lack of grout around that particular stone and perhaps realise the earthly nature of the outlaws' disappearance, so the friar sighed with relief when the less pious, more inquisitive members of the congregation filtered away, back into the still torrential rain outside.

The rest of the people inside the church were happy to accept the miracle though, and seemed like they might spend the rest of the day on their knees, offering prayers of thanks to God for delivering Robin and the rest from the wicked sheriff's guardsmen.

The plan had worked perfectly but there was still danger; that portly fellow who'd led the soldiers didn't look the type to give up easily. Tuck expected the sergeant would be back just as soon as he regained his courage and was able to cajole or threaten the rest of his troop into following him.

"What the hell happened here today?" Matilda whispered out of the corner of her mouth. "Where did Robin and the others go?"

Tuck winked at her but didn't reply.

"All right, everyone," the friar shouted, clapping his

meaty hands loudly over the sound of muttered prayers. "There's nothing else to see and it's time you all returned to your work. You can come to Father Myrc's Mass tomorrow and give thanks properly then. Offerings too, will be gratefully received."

For once, no-one groaned at the transparent attempt to take money from them, so great was their astonishment at the miracle they'd witnessed that day. In reverential silence they walked, heads downcast, out of the church and back to their daily lives.

Tuck watched them leave then faced Matilda and lowered his voice. "You have to go too – we need to make this look as believable as possible. Trust me: Robin is safe. Come back when night falls and you can see for yourself."

"But –"

"Trust me," he hissed and it was enough, despite the questions burning within her. She knew Friar Tuck could be taken at his word

A small number of folk tarried, wanting to spend as much time as possible in the blessed room, and the friar – aided by Patrick Prudhomme – politely but firmly shooed them out into the rain, the headman following to make sure everyone left. When they'd all gone, Matilda included, Patrick stood beside Tuck and they shared a small smile.

Only Father Myrc remained inside the new wing of St Mary's, still kneeling, head bowed, facing the altar, and Tuck felt guilty at the sight of tears streaking the man's face. He truly believed God had blessed his parish that afternoon and the friar couldn't bring himself to tell the priest the truth of the situation.

"Come on," Tuck said softly, moving back inside and clasping Father Myrc's shoulder. "We need a drink after all that. Some of the good communion wine will help calm our nerves and we can work on a sermon together for tomorrow's Mass."

The priest looked up at him with an expression of such

joy that he knew he could never let him find out about the hidden room. They left the chamber in silence together, through the bolted door that led to the main building.

Outside, the headman watched them go and slipped back inside, pulling the remains of the broken door over, shutting off most of the view to any prying eyes outside. Then he wedged a piece of smashed wood beneath it to stop any nosy villagers returning and wandering in.

The storm had slowly moved on into the east taking the worst of the rain with it, the thunder only a low occasional rumble and the sheeting lightning just a memory. Inside the church Patrick hissed, "You can come out, now," and there was a clicking sound.

Robin's face appeared in the trapdoor and Prudhomme grinned down at him.

"They believed it," the headman said to a nod of satisfaction from the wolf's head.

"Thank you, Patrick," Robin hissed sincerely. "You can get off now, if you like. Might be a good idea to get the carpenter to come and fit a new door as soon as possible, just in case anyone comes back and looks too closely at the floor. Oh, and can you ask Matilda to come and visit me here in a little while? Tuck told me she was worried but handled herself well. Best ask Will's girl, Beth, to come too."

He shook Patrick's hand gratefully, then unbolted the double doors that led into the main church building and stepped in, followed by his friends, who all grinned conspiratorially at the headman.

They'd escaped! Robin knew it had been worth asking the stonemasons not to fill in the new basement with rubble as they'd planned, and the money he'd paid them to fit the cleverly designed trapdoor had repaid itself in unspilled blood.

Well, perhaps not quite unspilled, he corrected himself, glancing down again at the crimson stain soaking his gambeson. He knew he should get that seen to as soon as possible.

* * *

"This is bollocks. I honestly thought you'd bring us riches and glory, even if we were outlaws." Mark shook his head in bemusement at Philip's leadership. His statement was accurate but he said it in front of all the men, knowing it would plant ever more seeds of doubt in their minds and, possibly, leave an opening for him to step into. If Groves wasn't going to make them rich, there wasn't much point in remaining part of his gang, not when the man was such an arsehole to him.

He looked at his old mate Ivo, hoping for some support, but the toothless bastard had looked disgusted with everything and everyone lately, and that expression remained on his seamed face as he picked dirt from his fingernails with a knife that was far too big for such a delicate job.

"What do you suggest?" Groves asked, voice low, almost earnest, as if he genuinely wanted Mark's opinion.

Mark knew better of course but he shrugged anyway, playing his part for the rest of the men's benefit rather than their leader.

"I don't know. Where are we?" He licked his finger and held it up theatrically, to feel which direction the slight breeze was coming from now that the storm which had utterly drenched them had moved away. An old, wise acquaintance had once told him you could tell where you were by the direction of the wind and, while he hadn't a clue what the man meant, he thought it would look impressive to pretend he did.

"About a four miles west of Mirfield," Groves replied with a hard stare, before Mark could go through his little routine any further.

"All right, we have a few choices then. Either we pick on one of the smaller villages – like Slaithwaite – knowing they'll not be able to fight us off, despite our depleted numbers." He returned Philip's stare, letting the horse's arse know he blamed him for their reduced force. "But Slaithwaite and those places are poor. Are we looking to steal a few loaves and a cask of ale? Or are we trying to make a bit more coin?"

"Get to the point," Eoin rumbled from his usual place at Groves's side.

"We're not all that far from Kirklees," Mark said, and left it at that.

He could see the men who'd gone to Kirklees just a few weeks earlier to kill the tanner thinking back, remembering what the place was like.

A few years ago the village was part of some Hospitaller's commandery, and the knight had overseen the place well, making it a prosperous settlement, with more wealth than most villages of its size. The Hospitaller was hanged for some reason though, and the king had replaced him with a faceless clerk, which meant the outlaws wouldn't have to face some grim crusader and his well-armed retinue if they chose to rob the place.

It would have been a fine target even without the priory situated not far from the main village.

"Kirklees Priory," one of the men, a fat middle-aged fellow with a shocking ginger beard, mused, "has nuns in it."

There were a few, excited shouts of "nuns!" at the fat man's pronouncement and he grinned, black teeth showing unpleasantly through the matted beard.

"Aye, nuns. I've seen 'em. The place is run by some tall bitch but there's a few tidy young girls cooped up like little birds in a cage."

The outlaws babbled amongst themselves, the ones who'd been to Kirklees before telling those who hadn't what it was like, enthusing about the prospect of defiling a pretty girl in a habit before stealing all the golden crucifixes and candelabras the priory certainly housed.

"Very well," Groves shouted, grinning and waving a hand with a flourish. "Kirklees it is. Sharpen your blades lads, and give your cocks a good clean. Nuns are a step above the usual whores you lot share a bed with."

There was a great deal of laughter and Mark felt a sense of satisfaction at his manipulation of the situation, knowing he'd have been ignored a mere week ago. The warm feeling left him though, and an icy chill ran down his spine as he caught Groves's eye, and saw the murderous gleam there.

He was playing with fire and he knew it couldn't go on for ever. The time when Mark would have to either sneak off in the night or kill Philip grew nearer with every passing day.

And Mark had no intention of running away.

CHAPTER TWENTY-SEVEN

"Bugger this!" Will Scarlet cursed, face the colour of his nickname, once the outlaws were safely gathered in the nave of St Mary's. The storm had cleared and it was dry outside but the interior of the old building remained gloomy and even somewhat chilly despite the season.

After the initial excitement of the day had passed and the village returned to its business, Friar Tuck, after spending some time in the manse chatting about the miraculous events with Father Myrc, left the awestruck priest with a skin of wine and returned to the church to find out what his friends planned next.

"Mind my language Tuck," Scarlet went on, "but I've served my time as a wolf's head and I'm done with this arsehole brother of Matt Groves. We've tried your hiding thing," he pointed at Robin, eyes almost glowing with anger in the gloom. "Now it's time we find Groves and his men and deal with their shit for good."

"Aye," Stephen said, and the rest of the men, Little John included, nodded and murmured their own agreement.

"You're right," Robin admitted. "The hard part will be finding the bastards and engaging them on ground of our own choosing."

"Well you can't hang around here," Tuck stated. "You'll be fine for tonight but the sheriff's men will be back tomorrow. I could see it in their captain's eyes. He's got it in for you Robin; you should be careful."

"Sergeant," Robin muttered in reply, to a confused look on the friar's round face. "Longfellow's no captain," he clarified. "Just a sergeant; and nothing more than a quartermaster at that. If he comes back, next time he might not escape without a broken face or worse."

They all gathered around Tuck and he smiled at them.

"I'm so glad you managed to escape without bloodshed."

He stopped as he noticed Robin's grimace, then peered down at the big longbowman's side.

"You're wounded," he burst out, hurrying across to pull his young friend's hand away then, seeing the blood caking Robin's gambeson, his old battlefield instincts took over.

"One of you go to the vestry – it's over there – and bring me a piece of linen. Anything! There's plenty in there. Who's got a needle and thread?"

There was a moment where nothing happened as the men looked at one another in surprise, then Stephen headed towards the vestry, telling them he knew what to look for since he'd used it all himself many times over the years to help his injured comrades in arms.

Little John fished in his pockets and found his needle and some twine which he handed to the friar.

"Get that off," Tuck ordered, unbuckling Robin's light armour so, when Stephen returned the outlaw leader was naked from the waist up. His body was hard and lean, with toned muscles that rippled in the candlelight, but even his physique was no match for the sharpened steel that had pierced his side.

The injury wasn't life threatening, having missed all the major organs, but Tuck didn't want it becoming infected or opening even wider so he cleaned the wound with some communion wine, then he used the needle and thread to stitch it neatly shut and bound the whole thing with a long strip of linen which the Hospitaller had torn from an altar cloth.

"Your secret room came in handy, eh, Robin?" he said as he used his teeth to bite off the twine. "But now what? Where will you go? Do you think the sheriff will send more men after you? He has to know the charges against you are false." He brandished a fist vengefully. "Maybe I should have given Prior de Monte Martini more than just a bloody nose the last time we met. Ah," he sighed and bowed his tonsured head before looking up, skywards. "Forgive me Father, that is an uncharitable thought."

"This is all your fault right enough, you old sot," Will said, but his eyes sparkled playfully. He and Tuck had been through a lot together and formed a bond of friendship most men never experience. "If you'd killed him when you had the chance we wouldn't be in this position now."

"We'll spend the night here in the church," Robin said with a small smile as he watched his companions banter. "Then find somewhere to camp by the main road in the morning. Perhaps we can get some news about what's happening from travellers coming from Pontefract." He shrugged, clearly not holding out much hope of that but unable to formulate any better plan after such a long day. "If you could bring us a few supplies before we leave that would be good. Eggs, smoked meat, bread, that sort of thing."

"Ale," Arthur shouted. "Don't forget the ale."

"You want me to carry a cask of ale here?" Tuck demanded, one eyebrow raised in mock disgust. "Think again, lad. I might manage a sack of food, but you can find your own drink. Any ale I find will be going down here." He patted his paunch almost affectionately and Arthur laughed in defeat.

"Thank you, my friend." Robin came across and clasped the friar by the shoulders. "You played the part of the outraged, vengeful clergyman to perfection today. Without you, I'm sure Longfellow would have had his men tear this church apart stone by stone until they found us."

"You take care," Tuck replied, ignoring the complimentary words. "Be sure and set guards, even tonight with the stone walls to protect you. It's not just de Faucumberg's men that are after you, and we have no idea where Groves and his gang are hiding out."

"Have no fears for us. We know how to play this game

better than any in England. You get back to Father Myrc and your communion wine and rest easy."

They clasped arms and then, waving cheerfully to them all, Tuck made his way out the front to return to the manse, James bolting the massive doors at his back, then the companions sat in thoughtful silence, exhaustion bearing heavily on all of them.

"He's a good man," Will said, after a time.

"Aye," Robin agreed, then his hand fell to his sword hilt instinctively as a sound from outside the rear door came to them.

The others grasped their own weapons and gathered around, ready to face whatever danger might appear from the darkening evening outside.

"It's just me."

The men sighed in relief as they recognised Patrick Prudhomme's voice.

"I've brought visitors."

* * *

There was a scream as the lad chosen to stand guard on the northern road into Kirklees spotted the outlaws, too late, and his cry was cut short by the blade that tore through his guts and out the other side.

Philip pulled it free, but plunged it in again, to end the boy's life and any chance he might alert the villagers with his sounds of dying.

"Nicely done," Ivo nodded approvingly and, again, Mark felt a little stab of dismay – jealousy even – that his long-time companion was so taken by Groves, despite the man's brutality leading them nowhere so far. Nowhere they couldn't have gone themselves at least.

What was it about the smiling lunatic that attracted hard men to him? Hard men who'd never needed or wanted a leader to tell them what to do before, yet even now, despite their lack of riches and ever-present threat of arrest or death, Groves seemed to have some sort of charisma that bewitched them all.

All except Mark, of course.

"Thank you," the outlaw captain smiled, acknowledging Ivo's praise. "You can do the next one if you like."

"Not if I get there first," one of the others hooted and Mark looked away in disgust. Unlike him, these men, even Ivo it seemed, weren't that bothered about making their fortune and heading off to somewhere they could live as free, wealthy men.

All they wanted to do was kill, and drink ale, and empty their balls into women, willing or otherwise. The thought brought him up short. Mark realised he was different to the others as he watched Philip, Eoin by his side like a faithful hound, striding along the main road as if they owned the place.

He enjoyed violence, it was true, but not in the way the likes of Groves did. A good fight was always the best way to work up an appetite, and if you could steal your target's purse and buy yourself a meal and a few mugs of ale, well, that was one of life's simple pleasures surely. Any man enjoyed that – it was just the way things were.

He began to move, hurrying to catch up, again feeling an irritation as Ivo didn't even notice he'd fallen behind.

Eoin was the exception, of course, he didn't enjoy hurting people so much, and surely had some aversion to seeing women raped, since Philip always sent him away when the wolf's heads were planning on enjoying some lass. It was a truly strange partnership between the smaller, vicious leader and the almost gentle giant.

Mark decided he'd see what the day brought them here in Kirklees before making up his mind what to do next. Perhaps he'd be better off just leaving and heading back to his old haunts outside Horbury. His plans, or hopes, to supplant Groves were plainly ludicrous – he wasn't popular enough with the others to carry it off. Even if their revered leader was killed by some frightened villager that day, their group would either select the docile Eoin as their new captain or, more likely, simply disband, returning to whatever holes they'd crawled from in the greenwood before Groves's brutality had rallied them to his cause.

There were cries of alarm now as more people saw them and, suddenly, from his left, Mark spotted movement in his peripheral vision. Instinctively, he pulled his sword free of its sheath and swung upwards, parrying a length of wood that had been destined to stave in the top of his skull.

It was one of those frightened villagers – a thin, middle-aged man, with brown hair flecked by grey. He stumbled as his blow was turned aside, gasping in fright, and Mark, blood really pumping now, forgot all about his earlier thoughts. With a vengeful grin he brought his blade around in a shallow arc, into the villager's neck, sending him stumbling sideways, a gaping red wound suggesting he'd be dead within moments as his his lifeblood pumped out onto the eager, dry ground.

"That was silly," he chided the dying man, stepping over him and wandering into the house he'd appeared from.

There was no-one inside and Mark moved slowly around the single-storey dwelling stuffing whatever valuables he could find into the sack he'd brought. A silver fork and spoon set and an engraved pewter mug were the best pieces there, so he went back out into the sun and, seeing the villager was now dead he rifled the corpse's pockets, happy to find a couple of coins.

Maybe their work today would be worthwhile after all – it had been a good idea of his to come to Kirklees. Perhaps they'd even try to break into the castle that once belonged to the Hospitaller knight; there was sure to be money and quality items for the taking there, assuming its current occupant didn't employ many guards, of course.

And then...the priory, and its pretty nuns.

He grinned wolfishly and, with a howl to match the expression, hurried along the road to catch up with the rest of the gang, never noticing the boy that watched him through a gap in a hedgerow.

* * *

For the third time that day, Robin heard almost the same worried cry.

"You're hurt!"

Matilda had come into the new wing of the church with a stony expression, wanting to make things hard for her estranged husband. The sight of him though – topless, with a bloody bandage around his torso – made her forget their recent squabbles and a hand flew to her mouth while her eyes met his fearfully.

Little Arthur, however, ran to his father with a huge smile and, oblivious to the bandage, buried his blonde head in Robin's side.

"Ow!"

The burly archer pulled back instinctively but a grin creased his face and he leaned down to lift the boy high in the air, spinning him around while his men scattered out of the way to avoid being hit by a tiny flying foot.

The squeal of delight made everyone there smile and Robin finally stopped whirling around and hugged Arthur in close, eyes shut, great arms squeezing gently yet so firmly it was as if he never wanted to let go.

Matilda came across and gazed at her husband. Her earlier concern had almost evaporated as Robin seemed to prove his wound was only a slight one after all with the wild spinning of their son.

He smiled at her though and the expression was infectious. She couldn't help returning it, despite herself.

"Da!"

Another diminutive figure appeared in the doorway

beside Patrick and Scarlet's face lit up as his thirteen year-old daughter Beth charged into the room and mirrored Arthur's previous cuddle, hanging onto Will for dear life.

"Are you alright?" the girl demanded imperiously. "I heard you were an outlaw again. What were you thinking? We have a farm to look after."

Will looked down at her with an enormous smile on his face and a wistful look in his eye.

"You sound just like your ma," he said at last, before he led her to a corner of the nave where there was a low wooden bench. They sat beside one another and he tried to explain himself as if she were the parent and he a naughty child.

Will once had a wife and three children but hired thugs had murdered them all and Beth was the only survivor. For a long time Scarlet had believed she was dead too, and bitterness had threatened to consume him completely, until Robin had found her and reunited them five years ago.

Beth was the stars and moon to Will Scaflock. She was everything.

As the two families came together again the rest of the men made half-hearted excuses and went through the broken door into the night to allow them a little privacy. Some, like Little John and Arthur, had gloomy expressions as they went, wishing they too could see their wives and children, but they couldn't begrudge their friends this small measure of happiness in such an uncertain time.

"What's happening?" Matilda demanded when, at last, the men had gone and Robin ushered her and Arthur to another bench on the opposite side of the room from Will and Beth. She kept her voice low but her tone carried to every inch of the nave.

Robin replied in a low, dejected voice, almost as if he was about to burst into tears and Matilda's attitude softened noticeably as she grasped his hand and they

291

began to speak. Much of their conversation could be overheard though and Will stood, gesturing to Beth, not liking what he was hearing.

"Come on, lass," he said loudly. "Let's go out for a walk and I can tell you what's been going on."

Beth threw him a pretty grin and they went out through the door, leaving Robin's family alone in the church.

When they'd gone, the big longbowman hugged his son again, loving the feel of the child in his arms as he and Matilda stared at one another.

"Well?" She finally broke the silence. "What are we going to do now?"

CHAPTER TWENTY-EIGHT

Once the village had settled down for the evening Robin and the men slipped away into the greenwood and found a suitable spot not far from the main road where they set up camp.

The place would have been useless in winter but the lush summer foliage meant they wouldn't be easily spotted by travellers and there was a small stream nearby where they could water their mounts, refill their own skins and rinse their faces when they awoke in the mornings. The vibrant green leaves of the beech and ash trees all around kept them sheltered from the bright summer sun too.

Of course, Robin hoped they wouldn't be there very long before some solution to the current mess presented itself. Still, it didn't hurt to prepare for the worst and the site they'd selected would be adequate for a week or so before they'd have to find somewhere more permanent.

Experience told him the men would soon grow bored of their life out in the greenwood. Hunting and fishing were fine pursuits, providing both entertainment and food, but they'd need more than that or tempers would fray and fights would break out over petty matters. Especially if some of them took to the ale as a way of offsetting the tedium.

So, seeing some of them had developed paunches, he and John set up archery targets and organised wrestling matches.

It was clear they'd all moved on in the years since Robin had led them previously. Little John, of course, was still used to being told what to do by his younger friend, but the likes of Will Scarlet and Peter Ordevill, both middle-aged men by now, didn't seem inclined to accept directions the way they used to. Which was perfectly understandable –

they'd spent the past three years as free men, doing their own thing and answering to no-one. It was a lot to expect them simply to fall back into their roles as foot-soldiers as they'd once done.

The one that surprised him the most, though, was Arthur.

When they'd lived as outlaws before, Arthur had been barely out of his teenage years, with greasy brown hair and an easy, if toothless, grin. Now, he was a man nearing his mid-twenties, married, and a father to two children. He'd changed a lot in the past few years and now, although he wasn't disruptive, clearly resented where they'd ended up and wasn't as open to following orders or training with the others.

When Robin pointed all this out to John, the big man simply shrugged.

"It's only going to get worse the longer we're stuck out here. The lads have had their time out here and thought it was all done with when we were pardoned. They don't see themselves as wolf's heads any more, even if that's essentially what we all are for now. Our old hierarchy has dissolved. Arthur may be the most openly pissed off at present but the others will end up the same if we can't find a way out of this before much longer."

There didn't seem to be any way out of their situation for now, though, so Robin was pleased when most of the others joined in with the archery and wrestling fairly enthusiastically. They were forced to use muscles that hadn't been properly exercised in a long while but seemed to enjoy the opportunity to regain some of their old martial prowess.

Cleverly, Robin had kept Scarlet on side by drawing him aside the first day at the new camp and asking him, earnestly and truthfully, for his help leading the men. Specifically, he'd asked Will to reprise his former role as swordmaster, training the men in regimented exercises and organizing sparring matches.

Will, a farmer nowadays, raised a sceptical eyebrow at the idea but he'd agreed.

"I could do with brushing up on some of my old skills I suppose," he said, then smiled ruefully and squeezed one of his biceps. "Won't hurt to harden some of these ageing muscles either."

And so the sounds of swords – real, steel ones rather than the old wooden practise ones since they didn't have any with them – clashing together and the snap of bowstrings filled the air around their camp much as it once had years earlier.

"How come you don't have to do any of this shit?" Arthur groused, as he was paired off with Piers for another wrestling match.

Sweat dripped from his hair which didn't seem as greasy these days. Robin supposed his wife had made him wash it more often or maybe he'd just outgrown the condition.

In truth Robin *had* planned on joining in with the sparring – he simply hadn't got around to it that day as he and John had been setting up the archery targets and seeing to other things around camp. Still, he didn't need exercise half as much as the rest of the men, since he and his enormous right-hand man had continued to train with sword and bow and staff in the years since they'd been declared free. As bailiffs they'd not seen as much violence as they had as wolf's heads, but it made sense to remain fit and sharp since people didn't take too kindly to being put out of their homes over unpaid debts.

He didn't say any of that to Arthur though, as the man had presented him with the perfect opportunity to re-establish his claim to leadership of their group.

Robin wasn't their captain simply because he was a quick thinker, or charismatic, or skilled with words, although he was all of those things.

One reason he was the leader was because he was a better fighter than any of them.

Maybe it was time to remind them all of that fact.

"You think you can take me, Arthur?" he replied, eyes hard but a small smile playing on his lips to offset the tone of his words.

The other man looked a little taken aback at the challenge. That wasn't what he'd meant at all, he'd simply been irritated at having to sweat on such a hot day while Robin apparently took it easy. Still, he couldn't back down now, could he? Not in front of everyone. A steely expression came over his face as he remembered he wasn't a boy any more – he was a father, and could hold his own with any man in England.

"Aye," he nodded, trying to return Robin's smile but only managing a grimace. "Why not?" He spread his arms wide and made the age-old, universal gesture for, "come on then, if you think you're hard enough."

Excited looks passed between the rest of the men as they realised what was happening and caught the tense undercurrent in the air. They crowded round, forgetting their own training as they came to watch what was about to happen.

Arthur was a short man, more than a head smaller than Robin, but he was stocky, with strong limbs and an iron determination that had been such an asset to their gang in days gone by.

Could he beat their captain?

No-one offered odds and, without preamble, Robin squared up to his opponent and the match began.

Despite the size difference, they seemed evenly matched at first but it didn't last long.

Robin knew he needed to make a statement here, so, when they locked arms, straining against one another, he wasted no time in the usual staring-out contest that started such a fight. With lightning speed, he brought his hands inside Arthur's grip and broke it, knocking the other man's arms away, then he simply stepped past Arthur, set his foot, and used his shoulder to trip the smaller man.

"Wahey!" someone cheered and there were a few laughs but Arthur rolled and jumped back to his feet instantly. He was breathing harder than he should have been though and Robin could see his opponent really *did* need practise. He'd never have been winded at this stage of a wrestling match four years ago.

Without waiting for that "come on, then" gesture, Robin came forward again and, again, they grabbed hold of one another. This time Arthur was more careful, and also even more irritated, and he tried to spin around Robin so he could lock his arms around him and haul him down but, as he moved, Robin grabbed his hand and twisted. The move ended with Arthur's arm locked agonizingly behind his back.

Normally, Robin would have left it at that and let his opponent tap to concede but not this time.

Pulling up even further on his arm, he forced Arthur onto his knees on the grass and held him there for longer than was really needed.

He was sending a message though, wasn't he?

"Enough," Arthur shouted through gritted teeth, trying to offset his humiliation by laughing through the pain. "I yield. You win!"

Still Robin held him and turned to stare at the onlooking men. They looked back at him and he was sure they understood what was happening.

They remembered now why he was their leader. And they remembered not to fuck with him.

Allowing a grin to crease his handsome features, he released Arthur's arm and bent down to congratulate him on a hard-fought bout, even though everyone could see it had been anything but.

Arthur had the good grace to accept the comment though and, with that, it was over.

Robin knew the man wasn't the type to hold a grudge

over the public defeat and he glanced back around at the rest, who were still watching the day's excitement.

"What are you lot gaping at?" he demanded, playfully now. "You've all gone soft. Get back to your training or Groves and the sheriff's men will squash you underfoot like a turd in Shitbrook Street."

They all moved off, chatting about Arthur's beating and John nodded in appreciation.

Before any more could be said the sound of running came to them.

"The road," Robin hissed, head tilted slightly as he tried to glean as much information as possible from what they were hearing. "Two runners I think, coming from west. Let's move."

Without so much as a mumble of discontent, the men followed his order, even Arthur who picked himself up from the ground and hobbled along at the back of the party, rubbing his bruised shoulder.

* * *

John Bushel was a hard worker. Everyone in Kirklees knew that, and they also knew how skilled he was as a carpenter so he was never short of work. As a result, he had a nice house with two storeys and the finest chicken coop in the whole village.

Life had been perfect, especially when his son, Ecbert, was born four years ago. But then, just last winter, his wife, Emily, was struck down by a fever from which she'd never recovered.

When she died their son became even more important than he already was to John. Little Ecbert was the thing that kept him going in the hard times, when Emily's face would appear in his mind's eye and grief would threaten to overwhelm him.

A man breaking down and crying in front of his fellow

villagers? That wouldn't do at all – he'd be the talk of the place. So, unless he was in the privacy of his own home where he could let out his pain without fear, the carpenter would picture his son, smiling and playing, shouting "daddy!" whenever he felt that familiar hard lump in his throat.

As a result of all this, when Ecbert came running into their house that day, wide-eyed and breathless, John instantly rushed to him, dropping his hammer and forgetting the repair he was making to the wall.

"What is it my pet lamb?" he cooed, scooping the boy up and hugging him tightly. "Was someone mean to you?"

The child pressed his face into his father's shoulder and hugged him fiercely.

"Bad men. Bad men hurt David."

The words were muffled but John heard them well enough, and the boy's fear couldn't be clearer. It transmitted itself to him like a disease as he remembered the warnings Robin Hood had given them about the dangerous outlaws stalking the area.

Still holding his son close, he hurried back to the rotten wall joist he'd been replacing and leaned down to lift his hammer. All he cared about at that moment was defending Ecbert, no matter who had come to their village.

"What did you see?" he asked, voice soft and as reassuring as he could make it given his own anxiety. He knew the boy wasn't a liar; knew something terrible had happened in Kirklees.

Maybe still was happening.

"Scary man, daddy. Lots of them came along the road but one was behind the rest. David ran out of his house and tried to hit him with a stick but the bad man had a sword. There was a lot of blood, and David wasn't moving." He stopped and looked at his father with innocent curiosity. "Is David dead?"

John's heart was pounding by now and he tried

desperately to clear his head. What should he do?

He should go and help the rest of the villagers fight off whoever was attacking Kirklees, of course. That was what he *should* do.

But his son – who appeared to have forgotten all earlier fears as he looked curiously at the blackened, mouldy wall stanchion his father had been removing – was the only thing that truly mattered to John Bushel.

They would have to look after themselves.

The sounds of fighting came to them then – men shouting, thuds as weapons connected, a scream of sheer horror – and Bushel made up his mind.

Still holding on for dear life to his four-year-old son, he put down his hammer, grabbed a sack and filled it with cheese and bread from the larder dug into a hole in the corner of the room.

"Can you hold this for me?"

Ecbert responded with an earnest smile, apparently recognising the seriousness of the situation, and pushed out a small hand to grasp the food.

John ran for the door, retrieving the hammer as he went, and peered cautiously outside along the road.

The sounds of fighting were done already. Now there was simply an eerie silence.

"Hold onto me tightly."

He was a fit, lean man of twenty-five and, moving from house to house so as not to be seen out in the open by their invaders, soon made it to the eastern edge of the village, away from where the sounds of fighting had emanated from, heaving a huge sigh of relief as they reached apparent safety.

"Wait, daddy!"

His son gripped him tightly and he stopped reluctantly to look at the child, a chill running down his back, sweat making the hammer he held feel like it would slip from his grasp if he was forced to use it to defend them.

300

"What is it?"

"If we're running away," Ecbert said, matter-of-factly, "we need to take Herny."

Another relieved gasp escaped Bushel's lips and he resumed his flight.

Herny was Ecbert's favourite toy – a wooden soldier John had carved for him. He had, in fact, carved a full set of the little military figurines for the boy but, for some reason, one stood out from the others. The child couldn't say "Henry" and so the soldier had been christened "Herny".

Another Herny could be carved, if need be. Another Ecbert couldn't.

"We'll be back for him, don't worry."

Knowing he couldn't carry the lad, who was large for his age, all the way to Dewsbury, he set him down and grasped his hand.

"Come on, son. We need to get away from those bad men and bring help." He started walking and his son dutifully followed, face earnest, as if they were going hunting elves or fairies.

Part of John Bushel felt shame at leaving his fellow villagers behind, to die at the hands of the animals that had come to their quiet village.

But another part – the greater part – didn't give a damn about the villagers as long as his little boy was safe. On foot, as they were, they'd get to Dewsbury in a couple of hours and aid would be sent.

What else could he do?

So they walked, or ran when John could manage it, and, for much of the time, he carried the boy who began to complain of sore legs and hunger just a mile into their journey.

"Shut up," Bushel groused, his fear making him irritable, and he cuddled the lad in close, cupping the back of his head in a calloused hand and stroking his hair to offset his harsh tone.

Before he could mumble an apology to Ecbert though, he drew up short and hefted his hammer. Or he tried to heft it, but his hand was slick with sweat and the heavy implement slipped from his grasp to land on the dusty road with a dull thud.

"Jesus and all his saints," the man breathed in disbelief, not even stooping to retrieve the hammer. "Is that you Stephen?"

A group of dangerous looking men stood on the road before them and the child turned to look at them, before his arms tightened convulsively around his father's neck and a sob of fear filled the air.

It was the one dressed in chain-mail that Bushel's eyes alighted on, though. The one with the white cross and red surcoat; the livery of a Hospitaller.

"Aye," the soldier replied, although nothing more was forthcoming and John realised the man had forgotten who he was; it had been a few years since Stephen had lived in Kirklees after all, and Bushel must look quite different to how he'd been back then.

"Praise be to God," the carpenter mumbled, grasping little Ecbert tightly and leaning down on the floor before his legs gave way at the sheer relief he felt at that moment. Of all the people to meet, surely the Hospitaller sergeant-at-arms was exactly who was needed right then.

"What's wrong with you, man?"

Bushel glanced up at the tall speaker and now recognised him, and some of the other hard men flanking him, too.

"Praise be to God," he repeated. "Robin Hood. You boys have to get to Kirklees, now, before those bastards kill everyone!"

CHAPTER TWENTY-NINE

It didn't take long for Robin to extract the carpenter's story from him and Stephen, who still didn't remember the man, swelled with righteous fury. He'd been told of the tanner Edmond's murder and this – another attack on the usually sleep little village – was too much for him to stand.

"They would never have dared strike at Kirklees if Sir Richard-at-Lee was still the preceptor there. We'd have ridden out and smashed the scum to bloody pieces." His voice shook as it often did when he spoke of his former master, only this time there was an added edge to it as he imagined the horrors Philip Groves and his men would be doling out to the innocent folk he once lived beside.

The men hastily mounted their horses which were tethered to trees and bushes just beside the road, and Robin pointed down at John Bushel.

"You head for Dewsbury with your boy. You'll find a small track if you look to the right of the road, just about half a mile along the way. It'll lead you there quicker, and out of sight of any more marauding outlaws. When you reach it, raise the alarm and tell them to send word to Pontefract."

Will Scarlet cried out in disbelief.

"You want to bring the sheriff along at our backs? When the man wants us arrested?"

"Go!" Robin nodded grimly to the carpenter from Kirklees and the man didn't need to be told again, as he led the boy by the hand along the road at a trot.

They kicked their horses into a gallop and, shouting to be heard over the wind whipping past, Robin addressed Scarlet.

"We can't afford to let Groves escape again; the sheriff will bring men enough that we'll be able to track the outlaws before they have a chance to get very far."

There was a reply from behind but it was unintelligible, and that was probably just as well. The important thing was all the men were with him and Kirklees was only a short ride away. This time, he prayed, let us catch this evil monster and we can all go back to our own lives…

He'd only just begun to brood on that life of his back in Wakefield with Matilda when they saw the smoke and, from the amount, knew it wasn't a normal cooking fire.

Kirklees was ablaze again, and this time it wasn't just the tannery on the outskirts of the village.

They thundered into the village like avenging knights but there was no-one to be seen. Only a couple of dogs mooched around, ears flattened against their skulls, watching the newcomers fearfully as they slunk between buildings looking for food.

"No…" Stephen moaned, and it was the first time Robin could ever remember hearing such an anguished sound come from the taciturn Hospitaller. "We're too late."

Will waved a hand dismissively and jumped down from his horse, running to grab a bucket from beside the well in the middle of the road.

"I don't see any corpses, do you?" he demanded, rhetorically, lowering the vessel into the water and dragging it back up, brimming over. "Most of the villagers will have run away and hidden in the forest. Groves and his men have probably moved on already."

He ran over to the flaming building – a weaver's shop from the looks of it – and threw the water onto it. The flames died momentarily in that one spot, but the rest of the conflagration soon had it burning again.

"Come on, give me a hand for fuck sake, before the whole place goes up!"

Some of the men moved to obey Scarlet but Robin shook his head. "No, leave it. We're not here to put out a fire. Groves is getting further away the longer we stay here; if we don't catch him he'll be free to pillage and burn more towns and villages. Come on, Will, get back on your horse and let's find the outlaws tracks before it's too late. And be careful – they may still be here."

So they moved on, deeper into the village, eyes searching for signs of violence and death. It didn't take long to find it.

"There," Little John cried, his great voice startling almost everyone and they looked at where he pointed.

A man lay on the street, face-down, the back of his head a bloody mess.

As they continued along the road there were more dead bodies and Robin hoped fervently that Will's earlier assertion was right, and the majority of the villagers had indeed escaped.

"Bastards. Bastards."

Robin glanced across at Stephen and, when he saw what the Hospitaller was looking at, he shared in the sergeant's outrage.

An elderly woman lay in the shadow of a low house, her face bruised and her skirts thrown up.

Robin looked away, not wanting to violate the dead woman any more than she'd already suffered, but Stephen suddenly let out a little choked cry and threw himself from his saddle.

"She moved," he said over his shoulder to the unspoken question. "She's alive!"

"Stay alert," Robin growled, wary of an attack. Caught in the open like this, they'd be an easy target if Groves and his men were still around.

Stephen gently pulled the defiled woman's skirts down to cover her modesty and did his best to speak softly, reassuringly. His gruff voice and grim demeanour weren't usually viewed as reassuring but Robin could see the lady's body relax as the Hospitaller spoke.

"Find me some water," Stephen demanded and Ordevill

305

dismounted, heading into the house the woman lay outside. He returned moments later with a small wooden cup which he handed gingerly to the sergeant-at-arms so as not to spill any of the liquid.

"Here."

The woman opened her blood caked lips and sipped at the cup the Hospitaller proffered. A small sigh escaped her as the cool water caressed her throat, although most of it dribbled down her chin and inside her torn tunic.

"The men who did this to you," Stephen asked, keeping his voice low. "Where did they go?"

For a time she said nothing, just stared up at the sky as if her spirit may already have fled, and Robin, growing impatient at their delay was about to order the advance, but then she looked at the Hospitaller and croaked something none of the men could quite make out.

"Where?" Stephen asked again, the patient tone of his voice surprising Robin who'd never seen this side of his old friend before.

Again, her voice came out as little more than a gasp but this time the single word she uttered was unmistakable: "Priory."

Stephen's head whipped around to look at Robin and they shared the dreadful thought. Groves and his gang had done their bloody work in the village and now moved onto the nuns just a short way along the road in Kirklees Priory.

The women there didn't stand a chance, unless Robin's men could get there soon.

The order didn't need to be given – Stephen sat, left hand fidgeting for a few heartbeats, wondering what to do with the dishonoured woman, but she waved a hand feebly and blood leaked from the side of her mouth as she mumbled, "Go. Stop them before they..."

Her voice trailed off and the Hospitaller reluctantly got to his feet, his eyes never leaving the woman as he stepped to his horse and expertly pulled himself into the saddle.

"You men: hold!"

Every head turned at the voice which came to them from the road they'd just come along, and Will cursed as they saw who it belonged to: the quartermaster, Longfellow.

"Fuck!" Robin muttered, echoing Scarlet. "We don't have time for this bollocks."

"That carpenter must have run into them on his way to Dewsbury," Arthur surmised.

"What do we do?" John asked, pulling his longbow from its place in his saddle and hurriedly, yet nimbly, stringing it by pressing it down on the ground to provide enough slack for him to loop the hemp noose around the upper horn, his massive arms making the task look easy.

Robin sat for a few heartbeats, weighing their few options. Either they killed the sheriff's men or they tried to enlist them in the hunt for the *real* killers of Prior de Monte Martini's party.

Whatever he decided, it was imperative they were quick, or every nun in Kirklees would be dead by the time they reached the place.

He took in the men approaching their position and cursed inwardly. He didn't know a single one of them so there was little chance any of them might feel any sense of friendship towards him. No, they were here to do a job and, spurred on by the vindictive quartermaster, they would do their best to arrest or kill Robin's men.

Thomas edged his horse forward, to face the newcomers, and the sight of his own blue tabard which matched their own, made the oncoming riders slow. They might not know Robin as a friend, but most of them knew Thomas and liked the man.

"Sam," he shouted, raising a hand to further try and halt the riders advance. "We can deal with this later; right now Philip Groves and his gang are on their way to the priory." He paused, to let the full meaning of this words sink in, then, as he opened his mouth to continue, Hood rode past him at a canter to meet Longfellow at the apex of the oncoming formation.

"You can arrest me once this is finished," Robin shouted. "I won't even put up a fight. But we have to stop the outlaws and, with our forces combined, we have a much better chance."

Longfellow's soldiers had taken in the scenes of death and devastation as they'd rode through the village and, although they didn't know Hood personally, they all knew of his reputation as an honourable man.

His suggestion made sense to them.

All, except their sergeant.

Longfellow wasn't interested in the nuns of Kirklees Priory, or in teaming up with the man he'd been sent to bring to justice.

The quartermaster's sword was already in his hand as he and his men rode along the road. The rest of his party fell back, warily, at the sight of Hood's men with their own weapons at the ready, understanding they'd already be dead if the likes of Little John with his huge loaded longbow had desired it.

Only Robin held no weapon. He faced the charge of Sam Longfellow, making no attempt to draw his blade or move to the side; he simply stared at the portly quartermaster whose red face was set in a determined grimace as he brought his arm back for a killing blow and the glory of fulfilling his mission.

Will and John shared a look, wondering if they should shoot the charging sheriff's man, but their young leader's calm demeanour suggested he knew what he was doing.

Or did he? Had his recent troubles with Matilda ruined his appetite for life? He'd already been injured by Longfellow not long ago, an injury which would preclude his movement somewhat if he *was* going to make some inspired acrobatic leap out of the way...

To be honest, Robin wasn't really sure what he would do

when Longfellow's attack came but he knew from bitter experience how hard it was to ride a horse and swing a sword with any accuracy at the same time. He was praying that the quartermaster, who spent almost his entire life stuck on a chair in Pontefract Castle, wasn't a skilled horseman.

It didn't seem like much of a gamble but there was always the chance Longfellow liked to ride as a hobby.

If he did, well... Robin would be dead within the next few moments.

The sheriff's men watched in fascination as their leader's mount pounded along the hard road, wondering what the hell would happen to them when the wolf's head was decapitated, as he surely would be. And yet, Hood's men, who sat astride their mounts, apparently as calm as if they were watching a sunset, lent the scene a weird, otherworldly quality.

Screaming a monosyllabic battle-cry that contained all the frustration and anger at his life's unfulfilled potential, sergeant Sam Longfellow reached the immobile Robin Hood and brought his longsword around hard enough to cleave a man's body right through.

* * *

Robin wasn't riding a trained, battle-hardened warhorse, but the beast knew enough to jink, unbidden, to the side as Longfellow swung his blade.

The man's cry of rage ended embarrassingly as his blow met fresh air and, unbalanced, he fell right off the side of his own horse and landed head-first with a dull thud on the ground, sword flying into a bush. His mount continued to run for a short distance and then stopped, glanced back it its downed rider, then began cropping the grass at its hooves.

Robin heaved a sigh of relief as his men – and some of

the sheriff's too – burst into mocking laughter, relieved at their friend's escape and finding the sight of the ruddy-cheeked quartermaster rolling on the ground like a stranded turtle utterly hilarious. Some of the men actually had tears rolling down their cheeks and clutched at their sides as if they'd split.

At last, the man got back to his feet, rubbing his knee where he'd landed hard on it, a mask of sheer rage twisting his red face.

"What the fuck are you pricks laughing at?" he demanded, glaring at his men. "Attack them!"

He looked once more at Robin then stepped towards the bush that had claimed his sword, but the wolf's head was finished giving the sergeant chances.

Kicking his heels in, he spurred his horse into a canter, closing the distance between himself and Longfellow in an instant, and, as the man spun to see what was happening, Robin kicked him hard in the face.

Again, the quartermaster fell to the ground unceremoniously but this time Robin threw himself from the saddle and landed on top of him, ready to deliver another blow or two to end the fight and move on – at last – to the Priory.

The injury he'd suffered at Longfellow's hands the previous day suddenly sent a burning pain lancing through his side though, before he could land a single punch and the quartermaster, outraged and now frightened for his own life, began throwing his arms around, jerking like a landed fish.

It was an unorthodox fighting style, but it worked, as a couple of times his arms clattered into some part of Robin and, buoyed by the fact he was still alive, he rammed his fist up and was rewarded with a sharp pain as it hit something.

"Christ above," Will muttered as they watched the combatants go at it. "I think we've seen enough of this. If

310

Robin won't at least injure that bastard he's going to end up dead, and we've got a building full of nuns to save."

John nodded, his bearded face tight with concern. Seeing his friend struggling with the sheriff's sergeant was unpleasant to watch. Why didn't Robin just break his arm or something?

Before anyone could move, though, it became clear that the outlaw had, at last, finally decided enough was enough. The wound in his side had re-opened and fresh red blood could be seen staining the already brown, pierced gambeson.

"Enough of this!" he roared, pressing a forearm onto his opponent's neck and pushing down with the whole weight of his body. The quartermaster continued to throw his arms and body around but the combatants were locked too closely together now and it did him no good.

The men looked on in silence as Sam's eyes bulged horribly, his face turned purple, and the fight went out of him along with the spark in his eyes.

"Enough. You'll kill him," Harry shouted half-heartedly, dutifully, knowing his sergeant had brought it on himself. "He's one of the sheriff's men, just like you."

The words penetrated Robin's murderous haze at last and he released the pressure on Longfellow's throat, flopping back onto the grass with a heavy gasp.

For a few breaths the victorious wolf's head lay there, staring up at the near-cloudless sky, the quartermaster's riderless horse chewing a long patch of grass the only sound, then he sat up without so much as a glance down at his opponent and walked slightly unsteadily back to his own mount, staring at Longfellow's soldiers.

"You men can either join us as we seek to stop the real outlaw gang, or you can fuck off back to Pontefract to tell Sir Henry what's been happening out here." He pressed a hand to his bloody side with a wince then grasped his horse's bridle. "Or you can fight us and die here and now.

311

I'm done playing games with you."

As he hauled himself back into the saddle the sheriff's soldiers looked warily at the men facing them. Will, Little John, Arthur and James had dismounted and all held their longbows ready to shoot at the first sign of an attack. Still mounted were the rest of Hood's party, the Hospitaller sergeant at the forefront, sword in hand, looking like something from a heroic fireside tale.

Harry nodded and turned to face the others in the sheriff's group. "Go with Hood and help him stop whatever's happening at the priory." He jumped nimbly down onto the grass and walked across to the prone Longfellow. "I'll stay here and try to bring Sam around, if it's not too late."

He met Robin's eyes but there was no accusatory note in his look – the quartermaster had started the fight and been beaten fair and square. He was lucky the fabled longbowman hadn't just shot him down as soon as the chase had begun, especially after Sam had stuck him with his blade the other day.

"Good luck," the grizzled scout said, grudging respect in his voice as he leaned down to loosen Longfellow's light armour. "You'd best get moving or it'll be too late."

"You should have that wound re-stitched," Stephen said as John and the rest clambered back atop their mounts, but Robin shook his head.

"No time, come on."

The party, swelled to more than double its previous size now, moved off at a canter along the track towards Kirklees Priory and Stephen shook his head in frustration.

"Fine, but when we get there you better stay back, out of the way, or the next fight you get in might be your last."

CHAPTER THIRTY

The guards in the blue surcoats looked unimpressed and the one facing Patrick Prudhomme shook his head.

"I don't care what's happened – the sheriff is busy. You'll need to come back in the morning and try again."

"In the morning?" Wakefield's headman's voice rose to a shout but he, somehow, managed to hold himself in check despite his instinct being to grab the obtuse soldier by the throat and throttle some sense into him. He was used to people doing as he told them back at home, but here, in the big castle, he wielded no power at all.

"It'll be too bloody late by morning you arsehole; it's probably too late already. Kirklees was under attack this morning. Philip Groves and his gang will have moved onto the priory by now. Even if de Faucumberg sends men they'll probably be too late to save the nuns but you have to at least tell him."

The guards looked at one another and shrugged. They had their orders: Sir Henry wasn't to be disturbed for the rest of the day and he'd been in a foul mood ever since Prior de Monte Martini had arrived there days earlier so no-one wanted to brave his wrath.

Patrick couldn't believe he was being fobbed off and refused to accept the rejection. The messenger from Dewsbury had come to Wakefield with the news of the assault on Kirklees earlier in the day and Patrick told the man he'd deliver the news to Pontefract himself. After riding here so hard, he *would* be heard!

"Listen, Robin Hood is in Kirklees right now. Or at least he was when I left Wakefield to come here."

That got their attention. By now everyone in Pontefract knew about Hood's new status as an outlaw and both these guards were friends with Thomas who'd escaped from custody only to ride off to join the wolf's head company.

The sheriff would want to know about this. Wouldn't he?

"All right," the smaller, yet apparently senior, guard nodded. "Follow me." He threw a glance back at his companion as they entered the keep. "If this goes tits up, I'm blaming you."

"I gave orders not to be disturbed."

The sheriff looked fed-up rather than angry which the guard, Joseph, took as a good sign.

"I know, my lord, forgive me, but..." He gestured at the messenger from Wakefield who, irritated by the long delay in delivering his news, pushed past and hurried to stand in front of de Faucumberg's stained oak desk.

"Groves's men have attacked Kirklees. Robin's gone after them but you'll have to hurry and send men *now*. I've been on the road for hours and your guards," he glared at Joseph who returned the look stoically, "have held me up even longer."

Patrick was glad to see his words had the hoped-for effect, as the sheriff jumped to his feet instantly and focused his own angry look on Joseph.

"Send word to the stables, I want my horse saddled and ready to ride. And have the duty sergeant muster a dozen men if he can find them. We must go to Kirklees."

When Joseph hurried from the room to see to de Faucumberg's orders, the sheriff moved into the adjoining chamber and returned moments later, strapping his sword-belt around his waist, an old yet pristine suit of chain-mail over his shoulder.

"How do you know about Groves attacking Kirklees?" he asked, glancing at Patrick as he threw the light armour over his head and hurriedly buckled it on. "Is Robin alright? I didn't seriously expect any of my men to injure him or try to arrest him, I was just trying to placate that

314

bastard prior..."

He broke off as one of the gambeson's buckles got caught in the outer layer of brown fabric and Patrick moved to help the sheriff undo it.

"A carpenter from Kirklees reached Dewsbury around midday with his little boy and told them of the attack." He tugged at the thread around the sheriff's buckle and was rewarded with a small snap. Then he pulled the straps tight and locked them in place with a satisfied nod before looking at Sir Henry's face again. "He said Robin and the boys rode straight to the village to help but he had no idea what might have happened after that. He also met your men on the road. That sergeant – Longfellow is it? – headed for Kirklees too. The messenger from Dewsbury came through Wakefield on his way here and I offered to bring his news to you since his horse was old and hardly up to that ride."

The sheriff cursed, loudly and imaginatively.

"According to barrack gossips, Longfellow is more interested in killing Hood to gain de Monte Martini's favour than capturing the *real* outlaws. Damn that prior and his ridiculous accusations. Come on. God knows what we'll find when we get to Kirklees."

De Faucumberg walked through the doorway and along the deserted corridor that led towards the stables on the southern side of the castle.

Patrick, hurrying to keep up with the grim-faced sheriff, shook his head in bewilderment.

"If you know Robin's innocent of the crimes he's accused of –"

"Politics," de Faucumberg snapped, with a glare over his shoulder at Wakefield's headman as their footsteps echoed along the stone passageway. "Surely you know how things work, Prudhomme?"

Patrick didn't, but he held his peace, not wanting to show his ignorance.

They emerged into a bustling courtyard and Sir Henry nodded in satisfaction. The guard, Joseph, had managed to get things moving as around a dozen of the garrison were preparing to ride out. The balding stable master strode across leading a great warhorse and nodded his head respectfully to de Faucumberg.

"Kirklees, sheriff?"

"Aye," de Faucumberg confirmed, placing his foot into his mount's stirrup and, with a grunt, climbed into the saddle. "Kirklees. We're probably going to be too late – God help them – but we'll ride hard and pray."

He looked at Patrick. "Are you coming with us?"

Prudhomme shook his head.

"My horse isn't up to another fast ride like that, my lord."

"Spend the night here then," de Faucumberg nodded graciously. "I'll have word –"

"No. Thank you, Sir Henry but I'll head back home. I want to be with my family and friends this night. Just in case Groves and his men, well...escape..."

De Faucumberg pursed his lips but clearly saw the sense in Prudhomme's words.

"Fair enough. You head for home, but I promise you, Patrick, I'll do all I can to make sure Groves is hunted down and Robin is safe."

Wakefield's headman smiled and gave a small wave in salute as the sheriff's party headed at a trot for the gatehouse and the road west.

"De Faucumberg! Wait. Wait I say!"

The sheriff turned in the saddle, his whispered curse somehow reverberating around the stone walls over the hollow clop of hooves, and he didn't even attempt to force a smile onto his face as Prior John de Monte Martini ran out of the castle towards them.

"Where..." The prior laid a hand on Sir Henry's horse's rump and bent double, gasping for air after his short run.

"Where are you going?"

The sheriff kept his horse moving so the accursed prior would have to keep up and become even more breathless. *Maybe the vindictive old bastard will keel over and die if I tire him out enough*, he thought hopefully, but replied in an even voice.

"You seem to have recovered well from your injuries, Prior. I've just had word that your attackers are at work again in Kirklees, so we ride there now to stop them. We may be too late already though, so..." he leaned back, raising himself high in the saddle so he towered over de Monte Martini, "we must be off!"

"You'll damn well wait on me," the prior spat, lowering his eyebrows imperiously and turning to raise one of the stable boys' attention.

"No time!" de Faucumberg shouted, but de Monte Martini shot his hand up in the air then brought it down to point imperiously at the sheriff.

"Enough. You *shall* wait on me." He glared at the boy who'd run to him. "Saddle a horse for me, lad. And nothing too big," he added, as the stable-hand ran off to do as he was told.

De Faucumberg nudged his mount closer to the prior and the sheriff leaned down to address the clergyman in a low voice.

"This is no joke. The outlaws – the *real* outlaws, I mean – have attacked the nearby town of Kirklees. And by now they've probably already torn the place a new arsehole. Forgive my language," he muttered, insincerely as the prior glared up at him. "I don't have time to wait on you, or to look after you once we get there. Apparently Groves was planning to attack the priory and, if he does, the nuns there can pray all they like but it won't save them."

"And neither shall you save Robin Hood," the clergyman replied. "I know what you're doing; you hope to kill this other gang of criminals then blame all the crimes of

England on them so Hood and his lot get another pardon."

The stable-boy appeared leading a pony which was smaller than the others the sheriff's men were mounted upon, but it was young and strong and would have no trouble keeping pace with them.

"Not this time," de Monte Martini finished, as the lad helped him climb into the saddle. "I'll be there to see you either arrest or execute Hood for his many crimes. The king wields little power in England now – his queen, Prince Edward, and their supporters will come from France soon enough, and you can trust me when I tell you they are friends of mine."

He left the sentence hanging in the air between them as he nudged his pony over to stand next to the sheriff's warhorse.

De Faucumberg curled his lip and glared at the prior but he didn't rise to the bait.

From the front of the party the sergeant looked back, confirmed everyone was ready to move, and shouted the advance.

As they walked their horses through the gates then kicked them into a canter along the main road to Kirklees, Sir Henry wondered if he could just skewer the damned prior when no-one was looking, but immediately offered a silent prayer of contrition for such a wicked thought about one of God's chosen.

He couldn't just kill the man, but *something* would have to be done if Robin and his friends were to be saved the hangman's noose.

* * *

"Mother Elizabeth! There's men at the door, and I don't think they're here to pray."

The young nun – no more than sixteen years old – had come barging right into the prioress's chamber with barely a knock on the door and stood in front of her now, chest heaving from her mad dash. The alarm was evident on her sweet, unlined face and it transmitted itself to Elizabeth de Stainton.

"Get a hold of yourself, Sister Jane," the prioress ordered, keeping her voice level so as not to add to the girl's consternation which could easily lead to an outbreak of mass hysteria.

It wouldn't be the first such occurrence and it was never pleasant dealing with the aftermath.

"Are the men inside?"

"No, Mother," the small nun replied, shaking her head vigorously. "I wouldn't open the door to them – one of them looked right in the viewing hole and his breath stank of ale or wine or something – so they've started hammering on it. They're laughing and joking as if it's all a big game, but I don't know how long the door will stand up to them." She looked at the floor sorrowfully, as if the whole situation was her fault. "They're very big men. Hairy," she finished in a whisper.

The prioress stood, her tall frame seeming to fill the small chamber, and looked down at her young charge.

"Don't be silly, girl," she admonished. "That door has stood against marauding Vikings. It's almost as old – and as strong – as the stones the priory's built from. Come – let us see what these frightening men want with us. I'm sure they only seek meat or ale or a bed for the night."

"That's what I'm afraid of," the young nun mumbled to herself but the prioress pretended not to hear.

It didn't take long for the pair to reach the front door which, thankfully, still stood intact although an unshaven, rough-looking face peered through at them.

Leered through at them.

Some of the other nuns had begun to congregate around the door, talking in excited, nervous voices, but they hushed as they saw the prioress appear. Her commanding

319

presence seemed to calm them but the man peering in the open viewing port whistled softly in appreciation and made an extremely crude comment to his unseen friends. Their laughter made Elizabeth de Stainton's blood run cold but she kept the fear from her face and strode confidently across to the locked door.

"What do you want?" she asked, as cordially as she could manage although nervousness made her voice harsher than she intended.

It hardly mattered to the men outside who laughed and hooted suggestively at her question.

"What do we want? What do we want?" the face at the door shouted gleefully.

"A good fucking!" another voice cried and was met with uproarious laughter..

The prioress turned to Sister Jane and fixed her with a stern glare.

"Run to the bell tower and ring it has hard as you can. Don't stop until your arms can't take it any more." She glanced around at the rest of the gathered nuns and selected one at random. "You go with her and help. We must try and raise the alarm so the men in Kirklees come to our aid."

She'd tried to pitch her voice low enough that the would-be invaders couldn't hear her but there was another raucous, sinister laugh from the other side of the door and the man pressed his face against the iron grille to glare in at the prioress.

"The men of Kirklees won't come to help you, Mother. They're all dead."

The prioress shuddered as the insane, sadistic laughter filled the air outside again and was soon joined by a rhythmic hammering as someone sought to kick the door down.

Some of the younger nuns began to sob in terror and even the older ones who'd seen things like this before looked nervous.

The priory had been besieged by drunk men in the past but this was different. These men were truly frightening.

Evil.

"Get a hold of yourselves," Mother Elizabeth growled. "Follow me."

The front door was sturdy – constructed from oak with massive iron hinges and a heavy ash locking bar which she made sure was firmly in place – but it wouldn't last forever, not once the outlaws started hacking at it with axes or found a fallen tree to use as a battering ram. So the prioress led them through the chapter house to the infirmary, sending them all up the stairs to the tower which adjoined it.

There was only one person – an elderly man from the nearby village of Slaithwaite – in a sick-bed, and the prioress ordered two of her larger nuns to help him hobble out into the stairwell where they would be safe behind another sturdy door.

For a time at least.

"Sisters Pauline and Marjorie – gather blankets from the beds. Sisters Elaine, Sarah and Letitia – collect food from the larder next to the infirmary. As much as you can carry, hurry now. Sisters Bernadette and Erin – bring that barrel of water. There's a cart to help you in the corner there. Come on now, move! We have little time before those heathens break the door down."

She watched in satisfaction as the women followed her orders without question, their tasks seeming to offset the terror that threatened to overwhelm them all.

"The rest of you – what are you staring at?" she barked. "Why are you standing on the stairs, watching us? Get up there, now! Into the tower with you all. Take the food and blankets with you as you go. The water barrel can stay at the bottom; it's much too heavy to lift up there."

As the ladies worked the sound of thumping came to

them. The outlaws must have found a log to use as a battering ram much quicker than the prioress expected. Clearly some of them had been off finding the thing while the man at the door distracted the nuns.

"Get in, quick!"

The women followed their superior's order, wide-eyed and fretful, but then angry as the prioress closed the door from the outside and locked them in.

"What are you doing, Mother?" An old matron she recognised as Sister Joanne, her voice muffled by the sturdy door, demanded. "Get in here with us or the heathen invaders will defile you!"

The prioress wanted to get in there with them, more than anything.

It would have been the sensible thing to do. The easy thing.

But she had to remain out here and at least *try* to stop these men from rampaging through the entire priory, doing whatever they would to the nuns in her care.

"Push as much stuff as you can against the door!" she shouted through to the women in the tower. "Hold them off as long as possible; someone will come to our aid when they hear the bells. God will make sure of it, have no fear sisters!"

She ran to the infirmary door and pushed it shut just as one of the marauding outlaws appeared in the adjoining brede house, a maniacal smile on his face and, more worryingly, a bloody knife in his hand.

"Come out you bitch," he cried but the prioress threw the bolt just as his body hammered into the wood. It held, but the metal was thin and bent slightly under his weight. Gasping a prayer she grabbed a wooden linen cabinet that stood beside the entrance and, gritting her teeth, managed to upend it so its heavy body blocked the door.

Exhausted now, mentally and physically, she sank down, her back against the fallen cabinet and barely registered the thuds from the outlaws' hammering as they tried to get in.

"Try as much as you like," she thought with a grim satisfaction. "But by the time you get past me and this door, then into that tower where the rest of my girls are hiding out, help will be here."

And then she realised she'd forgotten Sister Jane and her companion in the bell tower.

CHAPTER THIRTY-ONE

"The bell!" Robin shouted as they neared the priory and heard the doleful tolling roll out across the countryside. "If someone's trying to raise the alarm that means they're still alive. Come on, we're not too late!"

He kicked his heels in and the palfrey surged forward. Behind him, he could hear the pounding hooves of the rest of the men's horses and he gritted his teeth, praying to God that they'd be in time to stop Groves's men from abusing the innocent nuns of Kirklees.

The bell never ceased its urgent clang as they thundered through the old, ruined gateway and into the main courtyard, but it was apparent the marauding outlaws had gained entry, as the main door was smashed to firewood and a makeshift battering ram – an upended young beech tree with most of its branches still intact – lay discarded in the opening.

Robin thought about splitting his men – sending some to circle the perimeter and prevent any of Groves's men from escaping – but he discarded the idea. The outlaws probably had more men than they did and, truth be told, if they wanted to escape it would be better than allowing them to rape the nuns.

That bell, though...It continued to toll, sending its peal of alarm throughout the land, and it was obvious the outlaws would seek to silence it as soon as possible.

"John!" he shouted. "With me. We'll try and get into the bell tower before Groves's men smash their way in and deal with whoever's trying to raise the alarm. Will," he turned and placed a hand on Scarlet's arm.

"You're in charge. Lead the rest into the main building and do what you can to take down Groves's men."

He nodded to Stephen, who returned the gesture grimly,

as he finished his orders.

A big carrion crow watched them from the top of a wall, cawing irritably every time the bell rang and the bird reminded Robin of the last maniac he'd faced – Gisbourne. The Raven. A shiver ran down his back and he turned away from the black crow, hoping it wasn't an ill omen.

"Don't take any chances, lads. They outnumber us. Just drive them off if you can, but take care of yourselves first. Remember what these men have done; they're not to be taken lightly."

"Where are you going?" Arthur demanded.

"The belfry. Whoever's ringing that bell will need our help," Robin shouted in reply as he led John away, to the back of the building, hoping they'd find an entrance to the tower there.

"Now – go!"

* * *

"What are we going to do, Sister Mary? That door won't last for much longer."

The young nun was terrified and it was plain in her voice, which was shrill and bordering on hysterical, as she looked, wide-eyed, at her companion.

"Eh? What will we do? In God's name, why won't you ever talk?"

Sister Jane ran across and grabbed her silent companion by the arms.

"What are we going to do, Mary? They'll be in here soon and they'll ravish us, and kill us! Speak, damn you! Please, speak!"

The girl let go of her stoic, silent companion and slumped down, her back against the far wall, tears filling her eyes.

Of all the women in Kirklees Priory only one – the Prioress – knew why Sister Mary hadn't spoken a word since she'd joined them ten years ago after some terrible incident in her home village of Holderness.

And yet, the tall woman was popular thanks to her patient, forgiving nature. The rare smile she would bestow on one of them was like the sun breaking through heavy grey storm clouds.

That smile was completely absent today though, replaced – to Sister Jane's surprise – by a stony determination. It was the look, the younger girl imagined, of a knight about to lead his men into battle.

Only they weren't knights. They were simply two nuns trapped in the bell tower of the priory; separated from their hideous doom by nothing more than an oak door and its rusty old lock which would surely give way any moment under the protracted kicking and hammering from the men outside.

There was a splintering sound as the wood at the bottom of the door suddenly cracked under the assault from outside, and Jane shrank back, whimpering.

Where were the other nuns? Why had they forsaken her and Mary?

Tears streamed down her face at the incomprehensible thought of some filthy, brutal wolf's head forcing himself inside her, then she watched in amazement as her mute compatriot lifted an old broom from a corner of the room, smashed the bristled head off, and then stood facing the doorway with the pole as if she was St George about to battle the dragon.

The door buckled under another kick from outside and gave way just beneath the lock.

They were doomed.

"In nomine Patris," Jane muttered, staring at the ruined door, dreading her fate. "Et filii et Spiritus Sancti..."

The door came crashing in, smashed to pieces, and there was a cheer of satisfaction from outside.

Please, Holy Father, the girl thought, *let me die*

quickly...

CHAPTER THIRTY-TWO

The jowly outlaw walked slowly into the belfry. Warily, like a stalking cat, his eyes swept the room, passing over the two nuns who had, by now, ceased pulling on the bell ropes. A look of surprise registered on his face as he saw the taller one holding a broom handle, but he looked past her dismissively, searching for, presumably, someone who might pose a real danger to him and the grinning companion that followed him inside.

"Oh, yes," the first wolf's head nodded, satisfied that only the two girls were there. He undid the lace on his breeches slowly, licking his lips and staring at Sister Mary. "One each, eh? God...is... good!"

He strode forward, breeches flapping open around his fat, hairy belly, but the silent nun jabbed her broken pole at him and he had to dodge backwards to avoid being stabbed.

"That's enough you bitch," the man spat, his smile fading. "Give me that."

He stepped forward, faster than his girth suggested, and snatched the makeshift weapon from Sister Mary's hand, throwing it back towards the broken down door. "That's better. Now, come here my beauty, and show me what a nun's tits look like."

His companion laughed and stepped past him towards the cowering girl on the floor who tried to back away; as if she could somehow disappear *inside* the stone wall.

"They're both young and pretty," the portly one noted, as if he was weighing up a pair of fresh loaves on a baker's table. "It's a shame we're in a hurry – I'd have liked a go on yours as well as this big one."

Sister Mary launched herself through the air at him, a

furious scream tearing from her throat – the first sound Sister Jane had ever heard the older nun make – but the man brought his fist up and hammered it against her cheek, sending her crashing to the ground, dazed. The second sound she'd made in ten years or more escaped her lips then, and it was a groan of despair.

"That's better. Now, this won't take long, or hurt all that much."

The wolf's head leaned down and ripped the nun's habit open, exposing her breasts. He eyed them hungrily and glanced at his comrade who was similarly poised over his own conquest. The second outlaw had gone even further, stripping the younger nun completely naked and now grasped his engorged member in his hand as he tried to press it inside the sobbing girl beneath him.

The fat outlaw felt himself become even more inflamed with lust at the sight and turned back to Sister Mary who stared up at him from dead, cold eyes, all the fight apparently gone from her.

He was more experienced at this than his friend and managed to thrust himself inside her at the first attempt and he groaned loudly with pleasure.

It didn't last long.

Sister Mary's eyes fixed on a point behind her rapist and she mouthed a single, shocked, word.

"You."

A chill ran down the outlaw's back and the climax he was so close to completely disappeared as he realised someone the girl found even more frightening than him was in the room with them.

Pain exploded in the side of his head as a massive boot slammed into him and he fell to the side, cursing, his ear ringing horrendously.

Before he could move to defend himself the boot cannoned into his head again. And again. Then he felt a fist punching repeatedly into his kidneys and, dimly,

329

despairingly, understood that fist contained a knife.

"Bastard. Won't be raping any more women you bastard."

Little John straightened up, panting from the climb up the stairs and the effort of killing the outlaw.

Robin had dealt with the other man in a similar fashion and his blood now covered the nude Sister Jane who was crying hysterically, curled into a ball in the corner, her eyes locked on the dead face of her rapist.

John looked around for something to cover the girl's shivering body but there was nothing in the belfry.

Robin tried to calm her with soothing words but she'd gone into shock and didn't even seem to register his presence as he gently placed her torn clothing across her in what was, ultimately, a futile gesture.

Little John shook his head sadly and looked down at the nun he'd saved, if a little too late.

"Are you alright, lass?" he asked, softly, but something in her eyes made him pause.

She was much more lucid than her crying companion as she stared at him, fear and something else in her eyes. Disbelief?

"It *is* you," she mumbled, her voice a barely audible croak.

"Do I know you, girl?" John said, feeling a strange sense of deja vu settling over him.

"You killed my da."

Again, the words were nothing more than a raspy croak and John had to stand for a moment, replaying them in his mind before he finally understood her.

Little John had killed lots of people in the years when he was a wolf's head. He had no idea who her father might have been.

He looked at her with a growing sensation of dread, taking in her luminous eyes, and his mind was suddenly thrown back to a night ten years ago, when something just like this scene had played out back in his home village of Holderness.

"The baker," he whispered, and a sensation – as if someone had thrown a cask of ice-water on him from above – swept across his body.

His legs seemed to turn to mush and he slowly lowered himself to the floor as images filled his head and a lump rose in his throat threatening to make him almost as hysterical as the brutalised young girl in the corner.

"John!"

Robin, terrified by his friend's behaviour, assuming the giant had been mortally wounded, ran to his side and grasped him by the shoulder.

Tears sprang to the big man's eyes as he continued to gaze at Sister Mary, her own eyes glistening in a similar fashion.

"What is it?" Robin demanded, completely lost by this turn of events.

"You're the baker's lass," John mumbled. "That night...that night is the reason why I had to become a wolf's head. The reason why I missed so much of my son's growing up..."

The sounds of fighting seemed to have stopped in the priory beneath them and Robin strained to listen, wondering what the hell was happening, yet he knew whatever was going on in his friend's head right now couldn't be disturbed.

He hoped Will and the lads could take care of themselves for a while longer.

"I didn't mean to kill your da," John said to the girl, a hard edge appearing in his voice as self-pity vied with his naturally soft, generous nature. "I just wanted to help you and your sisters before he burned your house down."

Robin suddenly realised who the nun was.

Her father – the baker in Holderness, and a violent drunk – had killed his wife one night, threatened to burn down

331

the house with his three daughters inside and then been in the act of raping one of them when John had broken down the door and stopped him. In the fight, John accidentally killed the man and, thanks to the corrupt local magistrate who demanded a huge bribe to let him off with the crime, the giant had been forced into the greenwood where he'd joined Adam Bell's gang and become a wolf's head.

The nun was that child John had saved from her rapist father.

The big man had told Robin the story a few years ago and he recalled it now. The poor girl had apparently gone mad with that night's horror, become completely mute, and been sent off to live in a priory.

Kirklees Priory, evidently.

Now, more than a decade later, the two of them stood here, reunited, in almost exactly the same horrifying situation.

"I just wanted to help," John repeated, his voice filled with the pain of his ruined life and wasted years apart from his family.

For a time no-one said anything and Sister Jane's heart-rending cries had dropped to become a low sobbing, but Robin finally became impatient. His friends might be dead or dying in the building beneath – they had to go to them.

"Come on, John," he said, not unkindly but firmly. "We can deal with this later. For now we need to get back to Will and the others and somehow find a way into the main priory buildings, past Groves and his men."

Sister Mary tore her eyes away from her two-time saviour and looked at Robin. She got to her feet, pulling her habit back around herself almost as an afterthought and reached inside one of its folds, pulling out a large iron key.

"To the undercroft. Door at bottom of this tower," she told him, pressing it into his calloused hand. "Leads underneath the chapter house to the gyle house." She stopped and rubbed at her throat as if the effort of speaking after such a long time had worn it out.

"Thank you," Robin nodded, assuming the chapter house or gyle house was where they needed to go. "Will you and your friend be all right?" He gestured to Sister Jane who, so shocked was she to hear Mary speak, had ceased sobbing and now watched them from unblinking eyes.

The tall nun nodded and he turned away to head back to the stairwell.

Little John remained standing, looking at Sister Mary, emotions vying within him: Satisfaction that he'd twice saved this young woman from rapists; anger that his own pleasant life had been ruined because of her father's wickedness; sorrow that her life had similarly been irrevocably changed from its previous course; and fear. Fear that had stayed with him for the past eleven years, that Mary and her sisters hated and despised him for killing their father.

Some men wouldn't have given that a second thought but John had carried their supposed hatred of him for years, like a child who couldn't understand why a previously friendly dog suddenly turned on him. He might have been the hardest man Robin Hood had ever known, but in some ways Little John was also the softest.

"I only wanted to help you," he repeated, voice breaking, and angry tears spilled down his cheeks to be lost in his great beard.

He flinched in surprise when soft arms encircled him and the nun stretched up to speak into his ear.

"I know that now. Thank you."

The full horror of that fateful night, and all its terrible repercussions, seemed to wash over John with her forgiveness and a huge sob racked his body. The two of them embraced as if millstones had been, at long last, removed from around their necks.

For a long moment they stayed like that, then John, embarrassed, stood back, nodded to Sister Mary while

333

wiping his nose and eyes on his sleeve, then he gritted his teeth and lifted his quarterstaff from the floor where he'd dropped it when attacking her rapist. A dagger had been much more useful than the unwieldy length of oak in such close quarters.

"Right," he growled, the fire of retribution blazing almost joyfully in his eyes as he spun to follow his captain. "Let's get into that chapter house and deal with the rest of these bastards!"

* * *

Will and the rest of the men were pinned down with no way to get inside the chapter house. The door was smashed in from the outlaws forced entrance, but any time Scarlet's men tried to storm the room they were forced back by arrows and crossbow bolts.

Making a charge would be suicide but even so, Will was tempted when he heard their despised quarry, Philip Groves, shouting out at them.

"You boys out there better get comfy," the voice sneered. "It seems the prioress was too brave and noble to follow the rest of the nuns inside the stairwell. She's stayed right out here to entertain us! Very thoughtful of her wouldn't you agree, Hood?"

"He doesn't realise Robin's gone to help whoever was ringing the bells," Arthur whispered.

"Nah, he doesn't," Will agreed. "But it hardly makes a difference to us."

Arthur's slightly smug smile dropped away when he recognised the truth in Scarlet's words. It didn't matter where Robin was – the simple fact was, they were stuck out there while the scum inside were free to violate the prioress in whatever way they liked.

And, knowing what those 'men' had done to Prior de Monte Martini's party, Arthur feared the nun would not have a pleasant time of it before she was put to the sword.

"What are we going to do?" Stephen demanded, as there was a strangled shriek from inside the great chamber. "We can't just stand here like statues while they take turns to defile her!"

The Hospitaller – a soldier of God after all – was outraged at the way Groves and his men treated members of the clergy. It seemed, somehow, worse than anything they'd done to common laypeople. The prioress was the Lord's representative on Earth, by Christ! Raping such a woman was surely the worst of sins.

Will didn't like it much more than Stephen but he shook his head, eyebrows lowered in consternation.

"Not much else we can do," he said.

Thomas looked thoughtfully at the scowling sergeant-at-arms.

"Unless we can find another way into that room," the sheriff's messenger mused."You any idea how they usually lay out a priory like this, Stephen? Is there a standard plan the builders follow? I mean, can you think of a side entrance we might look for?"

The Hospitaller shook his head.

"I have no idea about that. Every building the Church owns is different. Besides, we'd need a key to get through any other doors leading in there; the prioress will have made sure they were all locked and tossed the keys out the window or something so the outlaws couldn't find them."

It was hopeless.

"So what are we going to do," Arthur repeated Stephen's original question.

Every one of the men gathered outside the chapter house gritted their teeth and grasped their sword hilts grimly – impotently – as a scream reverberated around the stone walls, only to be cut-off by the sound of an open hand meeting flesh as, presumably, Groves or one of his followers slapped her into silence.

The quiet didn't last for very long though, as mere moments later the high-pitched sound of pained gasping could be heard, mingled with grunts and sniggering.

"I don't fucking know," Will shouted, partially from rage and partially to drown out the distressing sounds from within the chapter house. "Robin's the one that always comes up with some clever plan."

Arthur nodded; that was true.

So where the hell *was* their young leader?

* * *

Right at that moment, Robin and Little John were traversing the undercroft, but the going was slower than they expected.

The key Sister Mary had given them worked perfectly, granting them access through the thick door that stood at the very bottom of the belfry stairwell. But, once inside, they realised getting from one end of the building to the other wouldn't be as easy as they'd hoped.

For the undercroft was, naturally, pitch black.

Of course, both men had flint and steel in their packs but they were in a hurry. The scream from the prioress came through the wooden floorboards from above just as they entered the black room, and they didn't want to waste time attempting to make a small flame to light the torch that sat in a sconce right next to the door.

So they blustered into the undercroft like blind men, stumbling into barrels and crates, tripping over many of the unseen obstacles with hissed curses or whimpers of pain, gripping one another's sleeves, one or the other taking the lead as they groped their way towards the opposite end of the room.

"Where the fuck are Will and the rest of the boys?" John murmured, as more laughter and another outraged scream filtered through the floor to them. "Why haven't they finished those bastards? Gah!"

His questions were cut off as he smashed his shin against some low, angular box and Robin, who'd somehow avoided the obstacle, pulled his giant companion towards him – and the safe path – with an exasperated sigh.

"They must be pinned down or something, I don't know. Wait!"

They came to a stop as the sound of many booted feet clattered above them, leading in the same direction they themselves were moving.

For a few heartbeats they simply stood there, in the impenetrable darkness, listening and trying to understand what was happening in the chapter house above.

All seemed quiet, but then voices could be heard – happy voices, no doubt belonging to friends sharing some joke.

What in the name of God was happening in the chapter house?

Robin and John strained their senses, feeling like newborn babes trying to make sense of a new, unfamiliar world, and then an all too familiar sound returned.

A woman crying in despair and rage.

But now, at last, Robin, hand stretched out before him to feel for obstructions, found his fingers pressing against solid wood.

They'd finally reached the door on the opposite side of the undercroft.

Urgently, he used his left hand to feel around for the lock then, finding its smooth iron easily enough, pushed the key in and, as slowly as possible to avoid a loud click, turned it.

He pulled back on the door and squinted as daylight flooded his eyes from a window high above.

With a nod to John, Robin led them up the stairwell, nervously grasping the hilt of his long knife while John followed.

The giant sheathed his own bloodstained knife as they

climbed though – he knew the chapter house would be a large room with high ceilings. Plenty of space to crack skulls with his beloved quarterstaff…

They reached the landing and Robin held up a hand, pressing his eye up to the keyhole on the door that separated them from their goal.

The prioress's sobs were barely audible now but at least one of the outlaws was still using her, probably with the rest standing around either watching, or satisfied and therefore bored with the show.

"Ready?" His voice was almost silent.

John nodded. By now, after so many years together, he hardly needed to hear Robin to understand what he was saying.

"Let's go then. Hopefully Will and the others will see us coming in and attack from the opposite side. Make as much noise as you can."

He used Sister Mary's master key to open the door and, with one last look at each other, the two friends charged inside.

Little John could make a *lot* of noise.

CHAPTER THIRTY-THREE

For the second time in under an hour, Robin found himself killing a rapist.

When the door to the chapter house opened he ran into the centre of the room without slowing and slammed his knife, point first, directly into the outlaw's temple with such force that the man's head flew sideways in a burst of crimson while his thrusting body remained where it was, entwined with Mother de Stainton. Their bodies shuddered sideways and the prioress screamed, long and loud at the new horror, her mind unable to properly take in what was happening.

Robin stared down in disgust and sorrow, mind reeling as he recognised the man he'd just executed. Martin Black, former landlord of the Boar's Head in Dewsbury.

Time seemed to stand still as he tried to take in everything that had happened since he and John evicted Martin what seemed like a lifetime ago. Had Robin been the catalyst for it all? Was everything his fault? What if he'd never thrown the little man out of his alehouse?

Little John's enormous staff had, by now, taken out the only other man in the room.

That second outlaw had spun at their approach, hand reaching for his sword, but before he could pull it halfway free from its sheath John's staff had almost torn through his belly, sending him flying backwards onto the floor. As he lay there, gasping in agony, eyes wide with terror, that same quarterstaff had slammed mercilessly down into his face again and again.

"All right, John. I think he's dead."

Will Scarlet strode across the room, grabbed hold of the giant's arm and they locked eyes for a long moment, until John relaxed and nodded.

The outlaw – his face a smashed, red mess – was most certainly dead.

"Where the fuck's the rest of them?" Robin demanded at last, kicking Martin's corpse off the prioress, too angry and confused to care about his language on consecrated ground.

"Don't know," Stephen replied as the rest of the men funnelled into the chapter house, warily looking around for threats which, apparently, weren't there any more. "Things went fairly quiet a little while ago."

"Aye," Arthur agreed. "Must have known they couldn't hold out here forever so they escaped." He nodded at a door in the eastern wall which lay slightly ajar. "The two you just killed must have been desperate to empty their balls. Unlucky for them."

"Ask her what's been happening," John suggested, quietly, nodding towards the red-faced prioress who had thankfully managed to pull her habit around herself and now sat back against the stone wall just like Sister Jane in the bell tower, watching them silently.

Her face was pale and Robin's killing fury went right out of him at the sight of her.

So much misery Groves and his men had inflicted on these innocent nuns today, not to mention the dead and violated back in Kirklees. It almost made him question his own faith.

Shaking his head to clear the blasphemous thoughts he knelt beside the prioress and spoke to her softly.

"Where are the rest of your nuns?" he asked.

For a moment she simply stared at him, lost in her own private hell and surprised by the question. Was this man more interested in bringing her aid than killing the outlaws?

"In the infirmary."

Her voice was like the wind on a barren, invader-salted field and it was truly horrible to hear.

Will strode across, boots thumping on the flagstones, and glanced at the blood-stain on his leader's gambeson.

"Look, we need to move *now* if we're to catch those bastards. They've already got a head start, presumably through that open door. Are you going to just stand here talking to the nun while they make good their escape?"

Robin's eyes flashed but before he could make a retort John's low voice broke in.

"He's got a point. We have enough men to finally make an end of them, if we move now. One of us can stay behind and take care of the prioress and the rest of the women."

"All right. Arthur, you wait –"

"Arthur?" Will demanded. "Arthur's not got a scratch on him."

"But there might still be some of Groves's men here," Robin replied reasonably. "I want to leave someone behind that I know I can trust to take care of the situation."

"So stay here yourself," Scarlet growled. "You're badly wounded, Robin. That needs stitched up before it splits wide open and you bleed out; you're in no state to go on with us."

His young captain peered at the red on his gambeson and seemed surprised by the size of the fresh stain. The battle fury had hidden the extent of his injury until now. Still, he shook his head and made to push past the men.

"No, Robin," Will grabbed him and glared into his eyes, but his voice became surprisingly earnest. Almost pleading. He leaned in close so the others wouldn't hear.

"Listen, I saw you talking with Matilda back in the church at Wakefield. I didn't hear what you were saying but I can guess. I know you've had enough of this life but...you're my friend. I won't let your death wish lead you to an early grave."

He grasped Robin by the arms and squeezed, hard. "You have a wife and a little boy that need you. You're not throwing your life away."

The room became as silent as a tomb and Robin gave Will a strange look.

"I don't have any wish to die," he said.

"So stay here and look after the women. John can wait with you and stitch that wound; the two of you will be enough to secure the place. Me and the lads will go after Groves and his men and bring the bastards to justice. Then, when all this is over – take your family and make a new life for yourselves in Scotland, away from all the bad memories of Much's death, and Allan, and everything else."

There was silence, as everyone waited to hear what would happen next.

Unexpectedly, the prioress's voice chimed in.

"You're injured, Robin – you should stay here as your friends say. I'll have my girls take care of your wounds."

Robin thought about it, then, with a groan, dipped his head and grasped it in bloodied hands as if he would collapse.

"See?" Will chided, grabbing him and supporting him until the dizziness passed. "She's right."

Truly, Robin had lost more blood than he realised and, now that the battle-lust had worn off he felt almost as weak as a baby.

"All right. Go, Will. Hunt Groves and his rapist mates down."

He clasped Scarlet's hand and they shared a smile. "Give them no quarter. Wipe every last one of them from God's Earth."

"We will," Stephen grunted, clapping Robin on the arm and heading for the open door on the opposite side of the room. "Come on, boys, let's get moving. Eyes open, stay alert!"

As the experienced Hospitaller took control of the situation, marshalling the men behind him and passing through the doorway with weapons ready for a possible attack, Will grinned and turned back to Little John.

"You take care of Robin. Make sure the nuns get that wound cleaned and bound up. I've lost enough friends over recent years. Besides, all the stories say Robin Hood's immortal and I don't want to put that particular legend to the test."

"Get on with you," John nodded. "I'll see he's patched up."

When the men had gone it was as if a hurricane had just swept through the place and left only debris, dead bodies, and a sorrowful atmosphere.

"How do we get into the infirmary then?" Robin finally asked the prioress, forcing a smile. "Let's get those women out of there."

The nun looked at him for a moment, a strange look on her tear-streaked face before, at last, she nodded to another doorway and replied in a dead, hollow voice.

"Through there. The key to the stairwell is on top of the door frame within."

Robin nodded, wondering at the woman's state of mind, then, with a glance towards John, walked across and opened the door as directed.

As he passed into the room some sixth sense – some tiny sound perhaps, or a change in the air around him – made him flinch and check his forward stride.

It wasn't enough to stop the tip of Philip Groves's sword tearing through his gambeson and deep into his body.

* * *

"That was Robin!"

Will Scarlet reined in his horse, oblivious to the rest of the men he commanded. The others continued riding along the obvious trail left by the outlaws which led to a path through the trees a short distance away.

Stephen noticed Scarlet falling back in the formation and, slowing his own mount, turned in the saddle to raise his palms, and an eyebrow, upwards in surprise.

But Will was already riding back, hard, towards the priory.

The Hospitaller hadn't heard the scream of anguish from the old builing behind them so he'd no idea why Scarlet had just left their party to ride back the way they'd just come.

Stephen had his orders from Robin though, so, as always, he followed them, kicking his heels in and urging his horse into a gallop along the outlaws' path again.

Scarlet would always be a law unto himself.

* * *

Little John's reflexes were honed to a razor's edge and he'd started moving almost before Groves launched his attack on Robin. With an anguished cry the giant lunged into the room the nun had pointed them towards and thrust his staff towards the wolf's head, catching the man – the bastard! – flush on the back of the skull.

John knew better than to think that was the fight done though, and he whipped the long length of oak back, close into his body, and it was just as well he did as a man nearly as big as he was tried to slide the tip of a short sword into his guts.

He spun the staff round and caught the blade, knocking it sideways before it could do him any harm. If it had been held by most other men it would have gone flying onto the floor, but the huge outlaw that faced him – the one called Eoin surely, from the descriptions John had heard – held onto the hilt with gritted teeth.

The strike must have hurt though, as the outlaw stepped back and switched the sword to his left hand, shaking the right vigorously as if that would deaden the pain from

Little John's powerful parry.

On the stone flagstones Robin held the wound in his back, the gambeson there torn completely away to reveal a wide crimson stain that had begun to spread down his breeches.

John's eyes moved on to take in Groves who was still stunned but attempting to get back to his feet.

Two against one would be bad odds.

Roaring like a caged bear, Little John thrust out at Eoin again, pushing the man back, then, without thinking, he jumped onto Groves's back.

The outlaw crumpled under John's terrific weight and, before he could even cry out, John stamped down viciously on the back of his head, smashing his face into the floor.

"No! You'll kill him!"

Eoin's anguished voice rang around the cramped chamber and John glared at him.

"Just like you've killed *my* friend Robin you bastards."

The huge outlaw might have been unskilled, but he made up for it in fury now as he came for John, swinging his short sword in cut after cut and thrust after wild thrust and the vastly more experienced lawman had to employ every skill and technique he'd learned over the years to block or dodge everything Eoin threw at him until, at last, an opening presented itself.

There was a crack of bones snapping as an upward parry saw John's staff strike brutally against his attacker's wrist, shattering it, and the sword fell to the ground with a ringing clank that seemed to echo forever around the stone walls.

Ignoring the roar of pain, Little John stepped back, transferring his weight to the rear foot, then, mindful of the close quarters, he swung his quarterstaff and exploded forward, putting all of his considerable power into the tip of the wood.

It met Eoin flush on the forehead and threw the big outlaw flying like a rag doll.

Again, using only half the length of the staff because of the cramped dimensions of the room, John brought it back and then slammed it around, sideways, in a low arc into the side of the fallen Eoin's head.

When blood appeared from the outlaw's ear a short time later John knew his opponent was dead, and he dropped to his knees next to Robin who was gasping and clutching at his new injury.

"Are you all right?" John demanded, battle fury making his voice more brittle than he intended but he was too frightened by his young friend's wounds to disguise it. "Don't move! I'll need to see to that before you spill your blood all over the place. Why the fuck did that nun –" he broke off as he began gently easing Robin's gambeson buckles apart.

"Why the fuck did you send us in here to an ambush, woman?" John finished with a roar once he'd finally prised open the last of the ruined light armour's fastenings. "We came here to help you!"

"I'm sorry!" the prioress shrieked from the adjoining room, tears streaking her face. "They said they'd hide outside until you were gone then smash the door down and rape all my girls. They..." Her voice dropped and she continued in an anguished whisper. "The things they said they would do. I couldn't bear it. And two of them had already taken their turn on me by then – I knew they would fulfil their wicked promises. God forgive me..."

"God might, but I damn well won't," John cried. "You've sentenced Robin to death."

He'd finally managed to peel back his friend's gambeson and the blood-soaked tunic beneath, and what he saw terrified him. The wound was wide and deep.

It had to be fatal.

Tears sprang to his eyes and he could feel his mouth

filling with saliva but he tried to hide it from Robin; he didn't want the injured lawman to see him sobbing like a child.

On the floor behind them Philip Groves turned his head slowly and looked up at the kneeling giant.

The outlaw's face was blood-stained and his nose so badly broken that he was forced to breathe through bruised lips. He was dazed and close to unconsciousness, but still held his short sword tightly in his right hand.

Taking a deep breath, he softly lifted the blade from the floor and swept it back, eyes fixed on Little John's hamstring. He may not be strong enough to slice right through the enormous lawman's leg, but he'd at least maim the big whoreson for life.

He gritted his teeth and a fierce, insane grin twisted his face as he swung the razor-sharp sword as hard as he could.

* * *

The scream reverberated around the priory and Little John turned, shocked, to see what the hell had happened.

Behind him, Will Scarlet had parried Groves's sword with his own, stopping the weapon just before it reached John's tree-trunk leg and now Scarlet stared at the scene before him.

His young leader lay blood-drenched and apparently mortally wounded beside a tear-streaked John, while another massive outlaw was dead on the floor and Philip Groves wept in fury and frustration at Will's feet. Outside, the prioress's crazed wailing provided a hellish backdrop to the whole thing.

John and Will both moved at the same time to finish the outlaw captain but before they could do it another man burst into the room, puffing and breathless.

"Hold! Hold, I say!"

It was Prior John de Monte Martini with Sir Henry de Faucumberg and more soldiers at his back.

"That man deserves a trial," the clergyman gasped, his voice tired but still filled with the natural authority men born into great wealth always have. "Leave him."

The sheriff looked anguished, especially when he saw Robin terribly wounded on the ground, but he seemed incapable of over-riding the prior's orders.

Will hesitated, glaring at the newcomers, then down at Robin's pale grey features, then at Groves's horrifically bruised yet smiling face. He turned back to Little John and it was as if they shared the same thought without a word passing between them out loud.

De Monte Martini wanted Groves alive so he could use the outlaw to testify against Robin and the rest of them. To blame them for his party's massacre. Groves would walk free again.

Not this time.

Scarlet roared and thrust his sword into Groves's back as John repeated his stamp from earlier. There was a dull thud as the outlaw's skull hit the floor, then a heartbeat later another, and another, as both John and Will gave free reign to their fury and everyone else shrank back through the doorway into the chapter house at the terrifying display of unrestrained, explosive violence.

When it was over Philip Groves was unrecognisable. His head was nothing but pulp and his torso a wet, red mess.

John and Will stood breathlessly, staring down at their handiwork with blank expressions on their faces as if they didn't know what had just happened.

Prior de Monte Martini was ashen faced but somehow pulled himself together. He stepped back into the small chamber and pointed at Robin's two friends, looking sideways at the sheriff who'd reluctantly followed him in again.

"Arrest those men. What are you waiting for de

Faucumberg? We just watched them murder a man before our eyes!"

The sheriff stood, mute and stunned, glancing back out at his guards. Some looked as if they might vomit while others were almost as pale as Robin who still lay unmoving on the floor between Little John and Will Scarlet.

Even those of the sheriff's guards who'd seen many battles before were shocked by Groves's brutal death.

"Are you listening to me?" de Monte Martini demanded, voice seeming to regain its usual strength and power to irritate. "I told you to arrest those murderers, De Faucumberg. Arrest them! And know something else." His voice dropped to a satisfied whisper and he locked eyes with the sheriff, a smug little smile tugging at one side of his mouth. "I sent letters to Archbishop Melton in York and Henry of Leicester, one of the queen's closest friends, apprising them of Hood's crimes. There will be no pardon for the wolf's head this time, no matter what happens. The man *will* hang."

The prior grinned at Sir Henry's stricken look then turned and shouted out through the doorway to the blue-liveried soldiers who were pretending not to listen to their superiors' argument.

"Enough of this talk. Get in here you fools and take these murderers into custody. If the sheriff won't do his job, I'll do it for him."

The guardsmen hesitated.

"When the Queen supplants that fool Edward I'll see you stripped of your office, de Faucumberg," the prior growled in satisfaction. "Stripped of your office, penniless, with your family destitute –"

"Oh shut up, you old windbag."

The sheriff slipped his hand into a pocket on the side of his right thigh and the dull gleam of a blade glinted before he plunged it into the prior's stomach, dragged it upwards brutally, and then shoved the stricken man onto the floor next to Eoin's great body. He quickly knelt and placed the bloody dagger by the dead outlaw.

There was another shocked silence then as the guardsmen came back into the room and tried to make sense of the scene before them.

"At last," de Faucumberg cried, throwing his hands in the air. "The giant wasn't dead – he sat up and stabbed Prior de Monte Martini in the guts. Help him!"

His soldiers rushed forward but the prior was already dead. One or two of the smarter ones glanced up at the sheriff but no one questioned his version of events.

"He's dead, my lord sheriff," one reported in the clipped, spare tones of a drill sergeant.

"Oh no, best take him away then and see his body is returned to Lewes where it belongs."

The men hesitated and de Faucumberg gestured at them to hurry up. When they – and the prior's corpse – had gone he turned back to look at Robin and his friends.

"Good on you. I've wanted to do that for years," Will Scarlet grinned, and de Faucumberg returned the expression although with a little less enthusiasm and a lot more nausea.

"How's Robin?" the sheriff said to John, retrieving his blade and wiping it on Eoin's sleeve before returning it to its sheath. "Why haven't you cleaned and stitched his wound yet?"

"Give me a fucking chance," Little John shouted. "Every time I try to deal with it someone else comes into the damn room and distracts me."

"What the hell happened here anyway?" Will asked. "I thought the prioress said the outlaws had all left?"

"She lied," John growled.

"So where are they?" The sheriff was confused himself.

"The ones that aren't dead are heading north," Will replied. "Stephen and the rest of the lads will catch up to

350

them soon enough. I just hope they're not outnumbered."

"I have reinforcements right here. Lead them after your friends, man! Let's end this for good when we have the chance."

Will shook his head at the sheriff's order.

"No. I have to wait here with Robin. It was only a few years ago I was laid up here at death's door myself and Robin never gave up on me."

De Faucumberg grabbed Will by the arm, none too gently. "Listen to me man – there's nothing you can do here now. But your friends might end up cut to pieces by the remnants of Groves's little army. Only you know the route they've taken. I'll wait here with Robin and see he's taken care of. He's my friend too."

"He's right," John agreed. "You should lead the reinforcements after Stephen and the others. With that lot at your back the outlaws won't stand a chance."

Will looked down at Robin, an anguished look on his ruddy face, and it seemed like he'd refuse to leave his captain's side yet again. But, at last he breathed a heavy sigh and nodded.

"All right, but you make sure someone deals with that wound of his properly." He gestured to the sheriff's guardsmen and strode towards the door. "Follow me then you lot, and fucking hurry up!"

When they'd gone the place was almost eerily quiet. The prioress had finally stopped sobbing and Robin's breathing was shallow now, after its earlier harshness.

John left the room, leaving Sir Henry staring impotently at his fallen bailiff and the giant's low voice could be heard asking the prioress for medical supplies. The sounds of hurried searching – cupboard doors being torn open unceremoniously and their contents tossed aside – came through the open doorway until, at last, the big man returned with wine, a needle, some twine and a long bandage.

"Help me."

Sir Henry nodded and knelt on the other side of Robin's fallen body.

"What do you want me to do?"

"Couldn't find any water to clean it, so this stuff will have to do. I hope it doesn't make things worse."

John poured the wine onto both wounds liberally – the main, entry one at the front, and the one on Robin's back where the sword had come right through. Then he used an extra piece of balled-up bandage to wipe clean the areas on Robin's skin around the wounds. They still oozed fresh crimson though, which couldn't be a good sign. At least the one on the back wasn't as wide as the one on the front, which would require stitching if their friend was to have any chance of survival.

"Hold it shut for me," John said to the sheriff, nodding to Robin's injury as he tried, more than once, to thread the twine through the eye of the needle, his shaking fingers refusing to co-operate.

At last he managed it and slid the needle into his friend's skin. As he did so, Robin's eyes flickered and he looked up at them, silently. He never said a word as the wound was stitched shut but when John had finished and the sheriff wound a piece of clean linen around his torso the fallen bailiff opened his mouth and gestured weakly for John to lean down.

"Listen to me, my friend; my brother." The voice was dry and resigned and carried the heavy weight of a dozen deaths. "I'm done."

"No, you're not," John disagreed, forcing a smile, but his eyes were welling up again and his grimy, anguished face was a terrible sight. "We've sewn you back together."

Robin shook his head feebly. "I'm done. Tell Will and the others that I love them all."

Tears streamed down John's cheeks again to become lost in his great beard and he choked back a sob as the best friend he'd ever had grasped his arm and squeezed it reassuringly.

"Now, before it's too late, I'd ask you and Sir Henry to do me one last favour..."

* * *

Stephen had managed to follow the fleeing outlaws north, possibly towards Scholes, but their pursuit wasn't as fast as he'd have liked, as the trail was hard to follow. The hard summer ground meant footprints were few and far between while the thick foliage not only masked any passage through it but might also harbour an ambush.

Will Scarlet came riding up at the back of them, Strawberry's hooves pounding furiously and two dozen blue-liveried soldiers at his back. Clearly Will wasn't worrying about any ambush and, when Stephen turned to watch his approach the look on Scarlet's face made it clear an ambush would bring a welcome opportunity for him to deal out more violence.

"What's happening?" the Hospitaller demanded. Never before had he seen the former-mercenary with such a strange expression on his face.

"Groves and his right-hand man are dead."

The rest of the men cheered at the news, and the reinforcements, but Will's face remained grim as he reined his horse in beside Stephen and glanced around at the others.

"I think Robin's done for."

"What? No, he can't be!" James gaped in disbelief. "No one can best him."

Will nodded. "Maybe not, but Groves surprised him; ran his sword right through him from the looks of the wound. The second bad injury he's taken in a few days. But the worst thing was John's face." He broke off and looked at Arthur and Peter. "You've known Little John for years, as

I have. You ever seen him in tears?"

The two former outlaws thought about it for a second then shrugged. The very idea of the friendly giant weeping seemed somehow obscene.

"Don't think so," Arthur muttered. "I expect it would take a lot to make him cry."

"Exactly," Will agreed.

Stephen's voice cut through the melancholy.

"We can find out how Robin is once we've dealt with Groves's gang. Come on."

Will sighed sadly, nodded once, then his usual confident demeanour returned and he scowled at the Hospitaller.

"Lead on then, man. Let's fucking end this."

* * *

When Philip decided to remain behind in the priory so he and Eoin could lay their trap for Robin he'd wondered who to place in charge of the rest of his gang. None of them were really leaders, apart from one: the little devil from Horbury: Mark.

"I know this is what you've wanted all along," Groves had smiled at the smaller man as they stood by the open door that led outside. "And, in truth, I'm sure you'll make a decent captain. Just remember, Eoin and I will rejoin you soon enough so don't get any ideas. Even your mate Ivo will support me if it comes to it, and the rest of the men don't trust you."

"Where should we go?" Ivo asked, eyes shifting nervously as he looked at the priory grounds, fearing Hood's men might realise they were escaping and come for them.

Groves shrugged. "I don't know the area as well as some of you. Mark? You've been a wolf's head around here for years. Where do you suggest leading the boys?"

Mark thought about it, trying to picture the local area in

354

his head.

"Scholes," he said at last. "It's a small village about four miles north of here. There'll be no threat from the locals but we can get supplies and wait there until you and Eoin catch up to us. You know where it is?"

Philip shook his head and Eoin grunted which Mark took as another negative.

"Just head directly north from here. Pass right over the first main road you come to, then turn east at the next one. That will lead you straight to us."

"We'll be in the ale-house," Ivo said, flashing his toothless grin which contrasted so starkly with Mark's own stunning white teeth.

"I'm sure you will." Groves returned the smile and waved them off, like a mother shooing naughty children back out to play. "Go on then. We won't be long, assuming the prioress does as she's told."

Mark nodded and wished Philip luck although, inside, he was hoping Hood and his lawmen would kill the bastard.

The gang looked around warily, then, seeing no danger, sprinted off towards the trees, the small man from Horbury at their head.

Now, almost an hour later, Mark knew they'd almost reached Scholes but they could hear the sounds of pursuit and he wasn't sure what they should do.

Ivo glared at him and spread his arms wide.

"Well? You're our leader now," he spat. "What do we do? We can't hope to outrun the bastards, not when they're mounted and we're on foot. I'm exhausted already."

Mark continued to jog but he knew his old companion was right; they'd be caught soon enough.

He turned back and looked at the men he was leading. Not one of them would he call a friend – even Ivo had switched his allegiance to Groves now. What did he owe any of them?

Nothing.

He'd be as well making off on his own, into the trees. He knew the area better than any of them and he'd have a better chance of surviving if he was on his own, since Hood's men would chase the main body of outlaws rather than searching for one lone straggler.

"You're right," he replied to Ivo, pulling his sword free from its sheath. "Hold, lads. We need to make a stand and this is as good a place as any."

The men stopped, most of them breathing hard, tired from the day's exertions and their flight here. Another fight with a group of mounted lawmen was the last thing they wanted.

"You men with longbows," Mark shouted, pointing at the nearest archer. "String them up and hide in the brush there, either side of this clearing. As soon as Hood's men show themselves – skewer the bastards."

He swept up his sword and gestured with the point at the remaining outlaws. "Everyone else, take up position in those bushes there, directly facing the trail. When the riders appear our bowmen'll bring the foremost of them down and throw the rest into a panic. When that happens, we fucking wade into them, all right?"

There was a low, half-hearted murmur of agreement and Mark shook his head in disgust.

They stood little chance of surviving this. They might take some of the lawmen down but that didn't interest Mark; he wasn't in this simply to kill – he wanted wealth and status and freedom, just like Robin Hood had found.

He was very much like the fabled wolf's head-turned-lawman, he thought.

As his men faded back into the undergrowth he too pushed through a stand of blackthorn bushes and dropped to the ground, curling into a ball so only the most assiduous of searchers would find him. Of course, he wouldn't be able to join the rest of his men when they engaged Hood's soldiers but he'd decided to wait and see how the fight went before leaving his hiding place.

If the outlaws were winning he'd crawl out and take his place at Ivo's side, just like old times. If they were being butchered – as Mark expected – he'd simply remain where he was until it was all over and the lawmen fucked off back to Pontefract or Kirklees or wherever they were based.

He didn't feel guilty about leaving the others to deal with the fighting – he owed them nothing. Besides, the odds of them surviving against Hood's men were tiny and there was no reason for him to throw away his life for men loyal to Philip Groves.

Fuck them all.

Safe in his blackthorn cocoon he peered out as a knight – no, not a knight, a Hospitaller sergeant-at-arms – rode into the clearing, flanked by a stocky horseman with a murderous look on his ruddy face, and braced himself for the thud of arrows hammering into those grim outriders.

But there were no snapping bowstrings and the colour drained from Mark's face as he realised his longbowmen had deserted.

Ivo hadn't though. He didn't read the situation and, like a fool, blundered out, shouting a war cry, into the path of the horsemen who hadn't slowed their progress at all.

The Hospitaller's horse careered into the toothless wolf's head, almost a thousand pounds of muscle and steel smashing him onto the ground.

A few more of Mark's outlaws shuffled into view, swords and axes raised, but they were clearly nervous and disorganised.

The second rider had reined in his mount when he noticed Ivo attempting to engage them and he now turned and charged back, sword in hand, to help his companion.

More of Hood's men appeared. Only the most foolhardy or battle-fevered of the outlaws stood their ground but they were mercilessly dispatched within mere moments and

Mark tried to squeeze his body into an even smaller ball, knowing he'd be shown no quarter should the lawmen find him.

He looked on as the Hospitaller slid down from his saddle and grasped Ivo by the shoulders with gauntleted fists, dragging the wolf's head upright.

"Where's the rest of your gang?"

Ivo's face was twisted in pain and it was clear he'd be no use to anyone now. The collision with the horse must have damaged him internally, Mark thought, with a pang. They'd been through a lot together over the years, even if they had drifted apart over recent months.

The Hospitaller brought up his knee and hammered it into Ivo's guts, furious at the lack of a response. Then he punched the outlaw brutally in the face and let him drop onto the ground to die.

That was it.

Philip Groves's gang was finished.

Mark felt an almost hysterical laugh building up inside him at the terrible reality of his situation and he struggled to force it down. He'd planned on leaving his men to fight without him, but almost all of them had run off into the greenwood, and now he was alone and surrounded by those merciless lawmen.

At least he had a good hiding place – the bastard's would never find him and night would fall soon. He'd slip off and make for Horbury. If there was a bright enough moon that night, and he could stay awake, he'd be there by morning. There were friends in Horbury that'd help him, for the right price.

"Come out, Mark."

The voice was startling close behind him and he jerked around, hand flailing for his sword, but a boot hit him on the nose.

It wasn't a very powerful kick, as the blackthorn bush made it hard for his attacker to get a clean shot, but it still hurt.

"Over here lads, I've found one of them!"

Again, the face looked in at him and Mark almost sobbed with rage.

It was Hood's man and Mark's one-time gang-member, James. Another man who'd followed him only to betray him! It was too much to bear.

Knowing he'd be hanged as soon as these bastards took him in, the prone wolf's head exploded forward, the tip of his sword aiming for James's face but his target, knowing how violent Mark could be, was prepared and dodged easily out of the way.

This time the boot made a clean contact with the side of his head and he dropped like a stone onto the forest floor, dazed.

"Good work," the Hospitaller said, striding over to join James and clapping the big longbowman on the back. "Tie the whoreson up and we'll take him back to the sheriff. Looks like his mates have all gone off and left him."

The lawmen's mocking laughter stung – it sounded like they all joined in – and Mark tried to spit on the sergeant-at-arms.

"You'll be sorry, arsehole. Philip and Eoin will be along to help me any moment now. You'd be as well letting me go."

Even as he blurted it out, he felt disgusted with himself, but the fear of being hanged terrified him and, if threatening these men with retribution at the hands of Barnsdale's most notorious outlaw would save him, Mark would try it.

But the mocking laughter sounded even louder as he was punched full in the face by James then unceremoniously thrown over the back of a horse and tied there for the return trip to the dungeon at Pontefract Castle.

* * *

Will took a deep breath and, followed closely by Stephen, pushed the door open and stepped back into Kirklees Priory, dreading what they might find there.

The nuns had been freed from their incarceration in the infirmary tower and now they moved about the place – busy but silent, like wraiths, shocked at the nightmare that had visited their quiet little corner of England that day.

Most kept their eyes lowered as they went about the business of putting the place back in some sort of order, but one, a thin woman with a kindly face, led them into the chapter house. The bodies of the men killed there earlier had been removed, presumably for burial or, perhaps, for public display somewhere to deter other would-be outlaws. Will guessed Philip Groves's body would suffer such a humiliating fate but his lip curled in an unsympathetic sneer at the idea.

Serve the bastard right.

"Where is he?" Stephen demanded, his rough local dialect sounding harshly in the quiet chamber.

The sheriff appeared from the side room where Robin had been so terribly wounded by the wolf's heads and strode across to them, his face drawn.

Grim.

"Where is he?" Will repeated the Hospitaller's question. "Is he..." His voice trailed off before he changed tack. "Is he all right?"

"I'll be honest with you," Sir Henry said, looking Scarlet in the eyes. "You saw his injuries. He lives yet, as far as I know, but he asked to be taken back to Wakefield to see his family one last time."

"Why didn't you get him into one of the beds here and have the nuns patch him up?" Stephen asked. "Surely that would have been more helpful than carting him along the road. The women here helped Will recover when he'd suffered a terrible injury. I'm sure they'd have aided

Robin."

De Faucumberg sighed heavily. "There's no doubt of that, but it was his wish to go home and it seemed the right thing to do. John went with him, taking a couple of my men as an escort."

The three men stood in silence for a time, none of them wanting to put their fears into words in case they came true.

"What now then?" the Hospitaller finally growled. "We managed to capture one of the outlaws alive. The rest we killed."

Sir Henry smiled at the sergeant's directness.

"One alive, eh? That's good. The people will enjoy seeing him receive justice – we'll make an example of him. I expect you and your friends will want to go after Robin and John?"

"Aye," Will nodded.

"Off you go then. I'll see you are all paid handsomely for your work in tracking down Groves's gang. For now, though, I'll take the prisoner back to Pontefract with my guards along with Prior de Monte Martini's body."

"He's dead?" Stephen demanded, eyes growing wide. He hated the churchman almost as much as Robin did, since de Monte Martini had tried to ruin his master, the Hospitaller knight Sir Richard-at-Lee.

"Aye, he's dead," Will confirmed, raising an eyebrow in the sheriff's direction but remaining silent on the true manner of the prior's death. "Come on, we can celebrate that later. For now, we need to get to Wakefield. I want to see my daughter and check on Robin."

They made to leave the high-ceilinged room but, as they began to move, de Faucumberg grasped Scarlet by the arm firmly and they looked at each other again.

"Prepare yourselves for the worst. It may be the time has come for Robin to leave us."

Will stared back at him for a heartbeat then nodded.

361

"We'll pray for him on the road."

Just then the prioress walked in, spine straight, head held up as proudly as ever. Outwardly, she appeared to be no worse off for her terrible ordeal that day.

"Where are you going?" she demanded. "You can't ride – it will be dark soon."

Will scowled at her, angry at her part in his leader's condition, even if her actions were understandable.

"Go – bring the rest of your men inside," she ordered. "You can all spend the night here in the chapter house. I'll have meat and bread brought in for you from the stores."

"Ale too?" Stephen asked, like a small boy hoping for a strawberry tart.

"We don't have much ale," the prioress replied. "But I'm sure there's plenty to be had back in Kirklees if you want to send someone to fetch it."

"I'll go myself," the sergeant-at-arms declared, already heading out the door. "I'll take Arthur and Piers with me and send the rest of the men in."

"If any of the villagers are in need of succour, bring them back with you," the tall nun commanded. "No doubt the wolf's heads left a trail of violence before they reached here."

"Thank you," Sheriff de Faucumberg bowed his head to Mother de Stainton when Stephen had gone. "I am grateful for your hospitality. I'll have my men do their best to repair the damage the outlaws did to your doors since we'll be here for the rest of the day now."

The nun dipped her own head to the sheriff and made her way out of the room.

Will held his tongue. Berating the prioress wouldn't help Robin and she'd suffered enough for now anyway.

"You should rest," de Faucumberg said, clapping Scarlet on the shoulder. "Before you collapse from exhaustion."

"Nah, I'd only make myself insane thinking about how fucking horrible the world is. I'll go out and help your men

362

find timber to repair those doors."

It was going to be a long night.

* * *

The journey to Wakefield took longer than usual. The horses were well rested after the previous day's exertions, but none of them – Will, Stephen, James, Arthur, Peter or Piers – really wanted to reach their leader's home village.

What awaited them there?

The weather didn't help matters either. The day had started dull and grey, with a heavy, funereal fog covering the land all around the priory. As the sun made its inexorable way higher into the sky it burned the mist away but heavy grey clouds took its place and, when they were still five miles from their destination the rain came. Just a mist at first, it soon turned to a torrential downpour that even the best quality cloak couldn't keep out.

Even that couldn't spur the party into a gallop, but, eventually, inexorably, the miles were eaten up by their mounts' hooves and Wakefield came into sight.

"Where will he be?" Arthur asked no-one in particular.

"At home, idiot," Will retorted. "Where else would he be?"

Arthur took the rebuke with a sheepish grimace.

"In the ale-house?" Peter suggested, but his attempt at levity fell flat and the grim silence settled back over the small group as they rode towards Robin and Matilda's modest home.

"We'll wait here," Stephen said, gesturing to Will. "You go in and find out how things stand."

Will nodded and slid from his saddle, handing Strawberry's reins to Arthur who looked more frightened than Scarlet could ever remember seeing him.

"Don't worry, lad. He'll be fine."

Arthur forced a smile onto his face and Will patted his

leg reassuringly before turning and walking up to the Hood's front door.

He knocked, but there was no answer from within. He tried again with similar results so he turned back to the others, gave a small wave, and pushed open the door.

The interior of the house was gloomy and it took a moment for his eyes to adjust but when they did he saw the great figure of Little John, sitting on a stool and staring straight ahead. On the other side of the room sat Matilda, who looked at him as he entered but didn't say a word.

And then Will's eyes were drawn to the centre of the room and settled on what John was staring at.

The Hood's table, where they ate their meals, contained something other than bread and cheese that day.

Will gasped and threw out a hand to steady himself against a wall as he felt the strength leave his legs at the sight of the shrouded body in the centre of the room.

"No! Matilda…?"

His voice became a pleading sob and he somehow forced himself to walk to the young woman's side.

She looked up at him and their eyes met, then she rose to her feet and embraced him as he began to weep uncontrollably.

* * *

St Mary's was busier than anyone in Wakefield could ever remember. It seemed like the entire village – along with folk from most of the settlements roundabout, including Sheriff de Faucumberg – had come to say farewell to their famous son.

Robin Hood.

The young man that had punched a lecherous prior in the face and fled into the greenwood five years earlier was now a legend, as were his friends Little John, Will Scaflock and Friar Tuck.

It was the latter who presided over the funeral mass that day and he'd never felt so sad before.

The rest of Robin's old gang stood near the front of the church, heads bowed, while the villagers looked at them, awestruck, as if they were heroes. Which they were, of course, since they'd stopped Groves's gang, but none of them felt like it. Their leader was dead after all. What was there to be proud of?

The mass began, hymns were sung, Tuck spoke and then Will, Stephen, John, Arthur, Piers, James and Peter Ordevill filed slowly outside. They came back a short while later carrying the shrouded corpse on a bier.

Some of them cried openly and Tuck wanted nothing more than to run to them and hug them all, to share in their unhappiness, to remember Robin in the greenwood, not here, in death.

He remained at the dais though, as was his duty, as Robin was brought forward.

Arthur had to step outside he was sobbing so hard. Others, like Little John, hid their sorrow behind stony masks until the bier was set down in the church and Tuck continued the mass.

Matilda stood at the front, her eyes downcast as if frightened to look at the shrouded body before them. Little Arthur wore a bored expression, as though he had no idea what was going on. Robin's parents, along with his sister Marjorie, stared straight ahead, perhaps unable to take in what was happening.

Tuck spoke of Robin's bravery, his skill in combat, his leadership, and his good deeds as an outlaw. Mostly, though, he talked about their friendship and how much he'd miss him. He had to stop at one point, as a great lump seemed to fill his throat and his composure deserted him. He simply stared out at the congregation, silently, as the tears streamed down his round face. At last he apologised and was finally able to continue the ceremony.

And then they all filed outside and the shrouded body –
now lifted into a plain casket – was lowered into the
ground and covered with dark, rich earth, while those that
knew him best wept and sought to comfort one another.

Robin Hood was dead.

* * *

"What will you do now then, Will?"

Scarlet sat for a time, holding his drink and staring at the
wall in the ale-house as if he hadn't heard Stephen's
question. Robin's funeral had been held the day before and
the men had remained in Wakefield, none of them wishing
to leave yet, knowing that once they did it meant the end
of their camaraderie for ever.

So here they sat, in the gloom of the local alehouse, fire
lit even in summertime since the trees grew so thickly
around the place that it was forever shrouded in shadow.

"Go back to my farm, I suppose," Scarlet finally
shrugged, his finger playing with a small dribble of ale on
the polished table before he finally looked up. "What
about you?"

The Hospitaller shrugged and looked down as if he
wanted some spilled ale of his own to play with.

"I hear the Grand Master of my Order has recommended
Thomas l'Archer be removed from his position as head of
the English chapter since he's an old doddering bastard
that's blown all the Order's money. When he's gone I'll
seek re-entry into the Order. It's all I ever wanted."

Will grinned and turned his eyes to the stocky young
man beside him.

"Arthur? What you got planned now?"

Arthur smiled and sipped his ale. "Bring my family
home from Nottingham and make a go of the tavern I
hope. The money the sheriff paid us for killing the outlaws
will help me do the old place up a bit and maybe bring in

some more business. What about you lads?"

Piers, Peter and James had all decided to take up the sheriff's generous offer of a place in his guard as sergeants, with good pay. Each of them hoped to gain promotions within a short span of time and Piers said as much.

"You going back to the priory in Lewes, Tuck?"

"No, Will," the friar shook his head. "I'm quite happy here. Wakefield is my home now and, with de Monte Martini dead, I'm a free man again."

They sipped their drinks for a while and the alehouse started to fill up as the local labourers finished their days toil and trooped in looking for bread and beer.

The men all knew King Edward was close to being deposed by his wife and her supporters and it gave them great hope for the future of England. Edward had been a decent man, as Little John and Robin had found when they met him what now seemed like a lifetime ago, but he'd been a poor king who'd let their country fall into turmoil.

Isabella's expected invasion would surely see her and Edward's son – also called Edward – on the throne, and a new, glorious era for all in England.

"John?" Arthur asked softly, peering up from his ale mug as the volume in the alehouse rose with the influx of cheery new patrons. "You staying on as a bailiff?"

"I've seen enough sadness and death," the giant replied, shaking his head firmly. "For now at least. I might go back to smithing. Or I might take my wife and son off to visit some foreign land since we have all this reward money from the sheriff!"

He drained his ale mug and hoisted it aloft to draw the landlord's attention, a great smile appearing on his bearded face as he turned back to the others.

"Let's just get drunk tonight, lads, and forget how shit the world is. It's been an honour to fight alongside you all."

Another round of drinks was placed before them by the pretty serving girl and the men lifted the foaming mugs solemnly.

"To Robin Hood," John cried with a twinkle in his eye. "He brought us together, made us wealthy, notorious and – most importantly – *free*. I'm proud to have known him as a friend."

The others cheered as one, long and loud, raising their mugs high in a heartfelt, hopeful salute that filled the small alehouse with its power.

"To Robin!"

EPILOGUE

Two weeks after Robin's funeral, Will Scarlet came into the village to buy some supplies. Already, even in such a short space of time, the stories around Hood's death had begun to circulate and grow; it wouldn't be long before the minstrels would make the death much more romantic than it had actually been. One conversation Will had overheard at the alehouse two nights earlier brought a rueful smile to his face – apparently, according to the old sot telling the tale, Robin, knowing he was dying in Kirklees Priory, had forced himself to his feet, grasped his longbow, and with one final incredible effort, loosed an arrow out of the window, ordering Little John to bury him wherever it landed.

When one of his audience challenged the story-teller, saying Robin had been buried in St Mary's just along the road, the man nodded and smiled. "Aye, that's how far Hood's arrow went. All the way here, from Kirklees!"

On his way home that night Will passed St Mary's and stopped for a moment to look in on Robin's grave. Someone had stuck an arrow in the fresh earth.

It seemed Robin Hood's legend was destined to grow and grow. No doubt people would still be telling tales about him twenty years from now.

Will had moved back into his farm with Beth since the funeral, using some of Sheriff de Faucumberg's reward money to hire the local carpenter who repaired that damned fence that kept falling down. He'd then settled into the same routine he and his daughter had kept before Groves's gang had shown up.

The rest of the men returned to their homes or, in Stephen's case, to London, where he hoped to find a Hospitaller knight sympathetic to his quest to be welcomed back into the Order.

Their going, in the wake of his young friend's death, left Scarlet feeling bereft and he'd found himself trying to spend as much time as possible with Beth to offset the loneliness. She wasn't a little girl any more though and he knew his constant hanging around was beginning to irritate her so that was why he'd rode the short distance to the centre of the village that morning.

Beth did her best but, in truth, their farm had been neglected in recent weeks. Still, the field of barley he'd planted was ripening nicely and he wanted to hire a few of the local labourers to help him harvest it and the alehouse was the best place to put the word out for that.

As he rode Strawberry along the main road Robin and Matilda's house came slowly into sight and he felt a pang of sorrow.

The door opened and he reined the palfrey in, not really sure if he wanted to meet the young widow. What would he say to her? It was embarrassing but such situations made him awkward and he just wanted to avoid a meeting like that, for a few more days at least when their shared pain wasn't quite as raw.

It was then he noticed the laden cart on the other side of the road, already hitched to a pair of horses. Henry Fletcher and his wife – Matilda's parents – stood there, solemn faced.

Matilda stepped out into the street leading little Arthur by the hand and walked to the cart, helping the boy up into the back, beside whatever was already loaded there under a canvas.

Will thought back to the day in St Mary's when they'd been forced to seek sanctuary there, and the half-overheard conversation between Matilda and Robin. They'd talked of family in Scotland and a desire to start a new life there.

He felt another twinge of sadness as he realised Robin's young family were leaving Wakefield and then his eyes narrowed. Had he imagined it? As Matilda walked towards her parents the robe she wore parted slightly and, for just a moment, Will had caught a glimpse of her belly.

Was she pregnant?

The robe fell back, covering the young woman again and Will's sorrow returned, stronger than ever.

Robin would have been a father again in a few short months, had he not been taken from them by Groves's blade.

The fletcher and his wife embraced their daughter quietly, then she climbed onto the cart and took a last, lingering look at her home. At last she cracked the reins and forced the horses into a walk.

Scarlet remained silent, feeling like he was somehow intruding on this sad scene, but his eyes followed the slow-moving cart as it rumbled along the road. There was no-one else around right now since everyone was at work so it didn't take long for Matilda and Arthur to pass the last house in the village and reach St Mary's.

Will bowed his head and sighed. It felt like this, more than anything else, marked the end of the fellowship Robin's friends had enjoyed. The last, final severing of all ties as everyone went their own separate way. He doubted he'd ever see some of them again.

Knowing it would do no good to let such gloomy thoughts take hold of him right then, he heaved a deep breath that brought his shoulders up and raised his head as Matilda's cart rolled past the recently-extended church.

Just then the sun broke through the clouds directly over the street, making him squint but...what was that?

A figure seemed to detach itself from the shadows cast by the great oak beside St Mary's and haul itself into the cart which never slowed and was soon swallowed up by the trees on the outskirts of the village.

Shocked, Will wondered if it had really happened. And then he wondered if he should kick his mount into a gallop and make sure Matilda was all right.

One thing stopped him though, and a wave of cold seemed to run up his arms and down the back of his neck as he pictured again little Arthur's expression when the shadowy figure had climbed into the cart next to him.

The boy's face had broken into a huge smile.

For a time Will sat there atop his palfrey, and then a grin slowly spread across his face too.

"Come on, Strawberry," he muttered, kicking his heels in, urging the beast into a walk. "Let's go and hire those labourers. It's going to be a good harvest this year."

THE END

Author's Note

This has been the hardest book I've written so far. I expected it to finish around the 90,000 word mark but it kept going, as if I didn't want it to end! The Forest Lord series has been more successful than I could ever have imagined so perhaps it's understandable that, as it neared a conclusion, it became harder to write.

But I got there at last and I hope you enjoyed it and found the ending satisfying. I originally planned to kill Robin outright but when it came to it I decided to leave it open-ended and let the reader decide for themselves how things might have gone.

I know there are probably quite a few historical inaccuracies in the novel but it was unavoidable at this stage of the series. I could do pretty much whatever I liked with guys like Sir Henry de Faucumberg and Prior de Monte Martini in the earlier books and it would still fit within the historical time-line, but now they're entrenched in the stories and I had to make things fit my own narrative. So de Monte Martini did NOT die violently at the sheriff's hands in real life but I felt it made the story more exciting. I'm also sure he was nothing like as horrible as I've portrayed him in the books, for which I apologise profusely. Artistic license and all that...

Thank you so much to everyone who has bought these books over the past three or four years. You have made a dream come true for me and not everyone gets the chance to say that in their life, do they? Yes, I still have a day job, but the Forest Lord books have sold enough copies that I'm about to reduce my hours at work and that will mean I have a full day extra every week just to write.

And I have lots to write yet! I've just finished a brand new short story starring Little John and Robin, and then

I'll do a Will Scarlet novella to fill out the time it'll take me to research my next series.

Does the idea of a warrior druid in post-Roman Britain sound interesting? It certainly excites me! Battles, magick, and adventuring, all against the backdrop of these wonderful windswept isles – what's not to like? I can't wait to get started on it. If you're a friend of mine on Facebook (add me!) you'll have seen the photos I take when I'm out working around Loch Lomond and Loch Long etc. and that's the sort of places that will make an appearance in my new books. Instead of being tied to Yorkshire and Nottingham I'll be exploring the whole of Britain, in all its glory.

Please join me for it – it'll be great!

With very best wishes to you all,

Steven A. McKay,
Old Kilpatrick,
September 23, 2016

If you enjoyed *Blood of the Wolf* please leave a review on Amazon or Goodreads or wherever you can. Good reviews are the lifeblood of self-published authors, so, if possible, take a few moments to let others know what you thought of the book.
Thank you!

If you'd like a FREE short story take a moment to sign up for my mailing list. VIP subscribers will get exclusive access to giveaways, competitions, info on new releases and other freebies.
Just visit the link below to sign up. As a thank you, you will be able to download my short story "The Escape", starring Little John.

https://stevenamckay.wordpress.com/mailing-list

Otherwise, to find out what's happening with the author and any forthcoming books, point your browser to:

www.facebook.com/RobinHoodNovel

http://stevenamckay.wordpress.com

And on Twitter, follow @SA_McKay

THANK YOU FOR READING!

Made in the USA
Monee, IL
01 July 2021